John Donnelly's Gold

by Brian J. Noggle

Jeracor Group LLC
5643 South Haseltine Road, Brookline MO 65619

ISBN-13: 978-0-9832123-0-0

The Beginning

Robert Davies tried to log onto FuckedCompany.com, and he could not, and he knew he was fucked.

The chair squeaked as he leaned back. He double-checked the URL in the browser's address bar; it was correct. He pursed his lips and typed the URL again. Again, Microsoft Internet Explorer showed him its regular, unhelpful, the-page-cannot-be-displayed screen. It suggested he might want to check his browser settings.

Robert typed in www.nTropics.com, the address of the Web servers sitting in the large, bomb-shelter safe room in the basement. His company's site popped up, with its neo-Aztec cursive logo and gold bar icon. He typed Instapundit.com, and the popular blog loaded. His Internet connection was indeed active. But when he tried to get to FuckedCompany.com again, the same.

The first time was happenstance, the second time coincidence, and the third time, Auric said, was enemy action. This was the other shoe, and the axe was going to fall, and he wanted to be sure, so he went looking for Daryl.

Daryl was the local guru. Whenever someone with less than three months' experience at nTropics.com needed some help with his or her workstation, that person went to the two network administrators in the unlit office that probably was a supply closet before nTropics took over the building. Those who had more than six months' experience, few as they seemed to be, would go to the same guy that the certs-from-a-book weenies did: Daryl Simon. So Robert made his way up a half flight of stairs into the Customer Support Room.

Daryl studied his computer screen. His visibility, and the high level of background noise imposed by fourteen other technical service reps all in open cubes, didn't bother him. When Robert got close enough, he saw Daryl was reading some system board review, dazzled and probably slightly intoxicated by the speed of the front side bus and the RAID capabilities.

"Ahem," Robert mentioned after standing for a moment at the edge of the half wall, just over Daryl's shoulder and conveniently noticeable for anyone, probably, but Daryl.

"What's up, Robert?" Daryl said.

Robert dropped his voice. "I can't get to F Company."

"What?"

Robert hated to say it, so he hissed, instead. "I can't get to FuckedCompany.com!"

"You kick your Cat5 out?"

"No, I haven't lost connectivity, I just can't get to the site. That means they're blocking us, and that means we're going out of business."

"What's up, guys?" Kevin Horton appeared and asked.

"Robert can't get to Fucked Company, so we're all fired." Daryl tapped on his keyword.

"What's Fucked Company?" Kevin said.

"The Dot-Com Deadpool," Robert said.

"It's a rumors site," Daryl said. "When a company's thinking about layoffs, someone drops Fucked Company an e-mail and the guy puts it up on the Web. A lot of times he's got actual e-mails and whatnot. Mildly amusing."

"As long as you're not on it," Robert said.

"If you can't get to the Web site, why don't you just can the net admins, Robert? Why do we all have to pay for their incompetence?" Kevin rubbed his cheek with the arm he was leaning on. Elbow up, he looked foolish instead of nonchalant, Robert thought, but Robert's idea of nonchalance tended to parade rest. Hands behind the back in a non-threatening way. Kevin liked to repose like that, in his Dockers and collared shirts, dressed in business casual to rank him somewhere above the casual information technology rabble. He probably stuffed a sock down his trousers, too.

"Yeah, I can't get it either. Their server's probably down." Daryl's machine displayed the non-helpful Internet Explorer screen, too.

"Pud's always saying that other companies block the site from their intranets right before they lay off forty percent."

"Who's Pud?" Kevin said.

"He runs Fucked Company," and Robert knew he wasn't getting anywhere.

"Robert gets laid off and fired more than Chicago Blackhawks coaches." Daryl said.

"I used to work in a grocery store," Robert offered as an explanation. He'd seen more mustached Mikes start out as assistant managers or store managers, only to be canned when the store failed to pull in its four percent in a declining economy and a declining urban environment.

"Can't you get around it?" Kevin said.

"Get around what?"

"If they are blocking it out. Go ahead, show him."

"All right." Daryl looked around.

"You going to spoof your own IP address to get around the firewall?" Kevin said.

"You been taking community college classes again? Spoof your own IP and the domain server won't talk to you." Daryl tapped at the keyboard, zooming through the menus and dialog boxes in his Internet browser without the mouse. He liked that. Seventies hackers didn't need a mouse back when the MIT and Bell Labs boys stayed up for days with machines with less power than a cell phone and loved it. He was born fifteen or twenty years too late, into a world where to be a computer guru, you had to be esoteric. But he was. He looked around to make sure no supervisors or collared shirts besides Kevin were around him. "This is a proxy server in Vancouver that doesn't keep logs. Forget this address." And before they could see it, he had typed it into the edit box and tabbed to the OK button and hit the space bar.

He hit the combination of keystrokes to refresh the screen, and it started downloading, and Robert felt the flash of triumph that trumped his dread.

NTROPY.COM
The going-nowhere travel company http://www.nTropics.com started the day with a lame-ass pun for a name and is going to end the day with 33% less staff as they begin the slow decay to nothingness. Rumor has it, they've also blocked us, too. Enjoy your vacations, suckers.

"Oh, shit," Kevin said.

"I knew it," Robert offered as consolation.

"That does suck," Daryl said.

"How would I make my car payment?" Kevin wondered aloud.

"You'd probably have to default on it," Daryl said.

"How many more payments you have on that Schwinn?"

"It's a Rand, and it cost seventy bucks at K-Mart. Maybe one of those chicks that you got that Eclipse for will help with the payment?"

"I didn't tell most of them my full name. Well, thirty-three percent isn't that many. Hey, I've been here a year and a half, and you guys have been here a while, too. They're going to let go some of the new people, maybe, and we'll be okay. We're going to turn a profit next quarter, so this is just a move to boost the stock price until then." Kevin sounded like he had convinced himself.

"Right. They're going to shed some of the new people, the ones with the H1Bs and no stock options, or the ones with the options with strike prices higher than ours. To what union do you belong, where seniority matters? They're going right after us, because we're the most expensive and the most expendable." Robert hissed again.

"Shit," Kevin said, and looked at the clock on the far wall. "It's 9:02, and I'm going to be at my desk so I'm recognized as a valuable employee." He spun off and was gone down the corridor.

"That's probably not a bad idea for you, either." Daryl slipped on his headset just as his first call for the day jittered on his phone. "nTropics.com, You can take us anywhere, this is Daryl, how may I help you?" he sang.

Almost nostalgically, Robert strolled back to his cube. He had come to this office building, walked this bright and nondescript corridor thousands of times, probably, on his way to Daryl's cube or on his way to the shiny coffeepot that was always full or to the grey tiled restroom. It was his job, and he belonged there, but he knew that could quickly change; if he gave his notice, as he had before at other workplaces, he would feel the workscape click somehow alien, as if the lighting had shifted a little blue, a little cold. He could feel it starting even now, when Matt Brier didn't look up as he passed, didn't say hello.

No, this time, he would be the one TOFTing it, taking one for the team. And he felt gloomier than the stairwell at the turn, where the light from the upper landing didn't shine and the lower landing couldn't reach. And the door clicking shut behind him was final, again.

*   *   *   *

Damn little punk might have been right about the Web site, whatever little piece of high tech rubbernecking that was, but he was not right about my losing my job, Kevin Horton thought as he strode into the lemon yellow warren of cubicles that comprised nTropics' marketing department. Or at least the small portion of the marketing underlings. Maybe warren really didn't describe it; Kevin didn't know what a warren was, but he'd heard the phrase somewhere before. But it was a warren if the cubicles in a warren huddled against the perimeter walls, leaving the center of the room open, with a table and a large Rubbermaid trash can that served as a basketball hoop for the marketeers' wads of paper.

Kevin nodded his hello to Angie, whose blonde hair was almost white and made her thin face more ghoulish than it had to be; he almost bought her a bottle of any Miss Clairol product to color that hair. He turned smartly into his cubicle in case Dobson, V.P. Marketing and former Marine, was watching. And then he fired up Little Aqua, the Macintosh they issued him. Everyone else got PCs, but the marketing department got Macs. Word was that a former Director of Marketing Strategy had wanted them, sometime in the swirling mists of ancient history, before Windows finally caught up with Mac. Word was the same DMS left to work to be a branding consultant to Fortune 500 companies and was now selling insurance in West County, but his legacy lingered on.

Michele, one el, thank you, Isbert, from the French, thank you, tapped at his door. "Good morning, Kevin."

"What's up, Michele?" Kevin continued typing in his password and watched the monitor blank out before displaying his desktop, wallpapered with the image of Jann Arden. Kevin thought the one-hit wonder was hot. Daryl said she probably reminded Kevin of his mother.

"You know the Tivoli's doing a retrospective of Humphrey Bogart movies all this month?"

Kevin squinted at her. Her silhouette stood in the entrance to his cubicle, backlit from the windows on the eastern wall. "What?"

"The Tivoli's showing several Humphrey Bogart films, one a night and in rotation. Tonight's *The Treasure of the Sierra Madre*. I was wondering if you were going to see it."

"No. Why would I?"

Because you said you had a picture of Humphrey Bogart on your room in your frat house in college, Michele thought. "You look like the Bogey type." She shifted her weight too nervously for her own taste.

Paul Minkel, the current Director of Marketing Strategy, poked his head into the cubicle. "Good morning," he addressed Kevin and Michele economically, saying two greetings of the day at once.

"Morning, Boss," Kevin said. "I have the best idea for the South Coast Travel Expo next month," he offered. Look at me, he thought, I am a valuable addition to the nTropics staff.

"Hey, great, can you write it up and send it to me ASAP?"

9

"You bet, I am going to do it right now," Kevin clicked his mouse to open a new message window to demonstrate his earnestness.

"Good morning, Paul," Michele offered.

"I'm glad I got to catch you two together. Listen, JD's got a special, cross-divisional project coming up, and I was hoping you'd both be interested in working on it."

"Hey, anything for JD," Kevin said. JD meant John R. Donnelly, the CEO of nTropics.com, the first person Kent and Thom hired when they realized that they were way over their heads with the Web site they built and ran on a Web server in Kent's basement. Of course, when they got VC money, the suits wanted them to hire an established name to run the corporate side of the company. John Donnelly, formerly of Aquatech, Inc., was that man. After the IPO, Kent and Thom had cashed out and left it all to JD. Kevin heard they were sailing somewhere on Kent's boat, but that's better than running nTropics, Kevin thought. The tech boys were the backend of the business and the rock upon which everything stood, but it took someone with people skills to provide a long-term vision for the company. JD did that well.

"How much time will that take?" Michele said. "I'm already working on the summer company-wide message updates and wouldn't want to shortchange the effort."

Just like her, Kevin thought. You want to give something your all, but to get ahead, you've got to give all something. Maybe he should write that down.

"Oh, it's not going to take too long at all. There's an organizational meeting this morning at nine-thirty. I want you to both go to it and if it seems like too much for you, just say so, and I'll make other arrangements." Paul looked at his watch. "That's about twenty minutes, so get settled in and get down to Conference Room B. I'll catch you later."

"Right-o, Boss," Kevin said. He'd have enough time to drum out the e-mail and grab a cup of coffee. He'd be on the joint thing, all right—hell, he'd try to run it. They wouldn't can him then.

"See you in twenty, then, Kevin? Save me a seat?" Michele said.

* * * *

Michele disappeared into her cubicle, across and down from Kevin's, so that if she tipped back and turned, she could see who came in the room or who went out. Which really only mattered when she saw Kevin come in or Minkel go out.

10

She wondered how serious he had been about liking Bogart at all, or if he even remembered mentioning the photograph, and she doubted it. He obviously was not interested in her, preferring blondes, probably, that complemented the red sports car well.

Michele logged her little Apple onto the network. She set Microsoft Word for Macintosh to open when she logged in to remind her what she was supposed to be doing. Developing content for the greater glory of nTropics. Banging the inane messages 'leveraged' by outside consultants for ludicrous sums of money into a cohesive set of sentences that somehow resembled a paragraph.

She had a list of the random thoughts tacked to her cubicle wall just to the right of her monitor. "nTropics. You can take us anywhere." "nTropics. You can get there from here." And for the analysts and whatever the hell else they called necktied nitwits with briefcases full of other people's money, literary gems like "nTropics delivers consumer travel value for Net travelers." and "nTropics leads the Internet consumer/business online ticketing marketing space."

The twits who wrote that work twenty hours a week for hundreds of thousands of dollars a year, she knew, and that's the best they could write. Maybe they were cynical, and maybe, she thought, I am bitter, but eight years and almost a hundred thousand dollars for an MFA, and they dictate what sort of crap I produce. She grabbed the page by the bottom and tugged it out of the wall, sending the tack skittering across her desktop.

All right, maybe she was having one of her turns this morning, she thought. She was turning thirty in thirty days, chasing younger men who rebuffed her at every turn, still could not get David Albernathy, the protagonist in her version of the Great American Novel, to meet Cynthia without forcing them, and she came to this place every day to squint in the fluorescent artificial sunlight and to peck out Web sites which people only skimmed, to cobble stone words into marketing materials, and doing so much nothing she had to carry it in two hands. If she lived a life which ended after forty years of this, she would die now and let the inertia carry her.

She took a deep breath and a shot of the stale coffee from the common urn. Easy, she thought. In ten minutes, I will go to this meeting, and I will take notes like a good girl, and I will maybe get to sit by Kevin. Not that that's worth anything, but she had worn her black short skirt, as short as she wore with her thighs, and she had planned to ask him out, since he wasn't bothering to ask her. But that had not gone so well.

She took another hit of the coffee, looked at her watch, and the blank page on her computer monitor.

* * * *

Robert opened the bottom drawer on his cubicle desk, the one sized for file folders. Instead of file folders, it contained a half-empty box. Robert took the thumbtacks from the wall, withdrawing the photograph of Monica and him. About six years old, but Robert hadn't changed, although he heard Monica had put on weight after their three month relationship ended. He also took down the St. Louis Zoo Friends calendar and the laminated Far Side panel. He put the thumbtacks neatly in the drawer organizer in the top drawer, where he had kept the company pens lined neatly.

His phone beeped, startling Robert from his precision. "nTropics, this is Robert," he said slowly, carefully.

"Robert, Dave. Listen, I was trying to get those changes to the airline selection screens. Have you checked those out recently?" His manager sat in a cubicle only twenty feet away, and Robert could hear him almost as clearly without the phone. Dave would not want to tell Robert face-to-face he was dot-kaput.

"Yesterday morning," Robert said.

"Yeah, you were working on those yesterday afternoon, right? Any chance you could check them in so I can have a look at them?"

"Sure," Robert said. He opened up the source code control tool and navigated to the proper directory. All the code and HTML files bore his stamp: rdavies. The tool kept track of who was working on each piece of the program. For a brief, shining moment, Robert thought about deleting the pieces of the Web site he had been working on so that they would not use them, but he realized that they could always roll back to yesterday morning, anyway, and it would not hurt nTropics one bit. An ineffective, futile gesture from a developer they thought was ineffective and futile. He'd not give them the pleasure of that. So he checked all of his work from last night in.

He wished he were smarter, that he could exact revenge with some sort of logic bomb or something, where an untraceable malevolent computer force would hurt them somehow. He didn't know enough sys admin stuff to pull it off, but Daryl would. Robert hoped Daryl had done something like that.

"Great," Dave said. Robert imagined him watching Visual SourceSafe in his own cubicle. "Listen, I'm sorry to spring this on you, but Donnelly's holding a high-level design review meeting this morning, and I had to send someone from our department, so I gave them your name. Can you hop on down to Conference Room B at 9:30?"

"Yes," Robert said.

"Great! Thanks. I'll catch you later, Robert."

"Goodbye, David," Robert returned the phone lightly to its cradle. It was 9:15. He looked over his bare desk, all of its personal content now in the box, and back onto his computer screen. The least he could do would be to clean up the computer to make it easier for the twins They'd probably just ghost it, anyway, but it gave him something to do. He began by deleting all of his e-mail and personal files on the machine and ended when he restored the desktop to its default. And then, at 9:22, he picked his box up and went to Conference Room B, leaving so that he would be a few minutes early, even now.

*   *   *   *

"Not a problem, Mrs. Johnson. We'll get that taken off of your credit card presently. Is there anything else I can do for you today?" Daryl said into his headset. "Then thank you for calling nTropics, and you have a nice day." He punched the button that broke the connection.

Cathy Benyon stood just inside his cubicle. "You're supposed to be going to the meeting?" she raised her voice at the end like it was a question.

"What meeting?" Daryl said.

"It's in your e-mail."

Daryl ALT+TABbed from his customer screen pop application, which displayed the customer information based on the Automated Number Identification service information passed from the phone company. The same data that makes Caller ID possible, when piped through the custom database application that nTropics paid too much for, delivered the name, address, and transaction history of the customer before the Customer Service Rep said hello. Well, about fifty percent of the time it did. The other half was random data or none at all, which meant the Customer Service Rep had to ferret this out of the customer.

Microsoft Outlook popped up, and sure enough, Cathy's message for a meeting request had arrived at 8:58. "There it is." He tabbed and pressed enter to open it. "A seminar on improving customer response times? Lesson one, stop helping them."

"I signed you up. You want to get down there?"

Daryl pressed a hot key to accept the meeting request, a purely

13

symbolic gesture. "You bet. How long do I have?"

Cathy's face twisted. "It's 9:35."

"Right!" Daryl clicked to set his rep status as Away. "Excuse me," he brushed past her. "Where was that?"

"CR-B," Cathy said. Daryl knew she wasn't happy with him or with his call time, but he was taking steps to make sure that the customers knew what they needed and that he could get it for them, and the old hack could just tap her foot all she wanted.

Conference Room B was on the main level of nTropics' sprawling office building, not yet a campus, really, but enough of a hike when you were five minutes late. The upper deck, the ground level floor, was definitely the next tax bracket up from the Customer Service Pit, because it had wainscoted walls, real plants every dozen feet, and helpful signs pointing one to the proper places. The signs were all in the same font, and none of them were 36 to 48 point Benyon Hand.

When Daryl passed the foyer and saw the two large gentlemen in Visitor tags standing by the receptionist's desk, he thought nothing of it. They didn't look like interviews, but who knows these days? Any monkey that can keyboard a line of Java or even HTML is in demand.

Something about a similar looking gentleman, about six foot four and two-twenty, standing outside Conference Room B with a clipboard, suddenly bothered Daryl. A lot.

"Who are you?" the gentleman said.

"Daryl Simon. Who are you?"

The guy checked the clipboard. "You're late."

"What the hell does it matter? Just think of it as cutting my call time," Daryl said, and only then did he connect Robert's delusion and the big man in the blue suit with yellow tie, and by that time, the man was opening the door and almost shoving Daryl in.

The entrance to Conference Room B faced the front, so Daryl could not see about forty faces, most of which would probably be grim. Instead, Daryl saw the faces of John Donnelly, CEO, Brad Williams, CFO, and Jeff Yes, short for Yesermitski or something like that, the HR Director. That triumvirate would grim any face. Jeff was standing, and the C*Os were sitting at the head table. The big man shut the door behind Daryl softly, and Jeff did not skip a beat.

"Your COBRA benefits can begin at the end of the month, if you need them. If you find something else by then, of course, you might have insurance as part of that package, but make sure it starts at your date of hire if you elect not to take advantage of COBRA; some employers have a six month waiting period before delivering benefits, in which case you might be uninsured...."

Daryl saw Robert Davies' cowlick sticking up from the top of his brown-haired head in the second to last row. Daryl saw the box beneath Robert's chair and was sort of happy that Robert finally got to use it. The seats on either side of Robert were empty, so Daryl took one.

"If you'll look on page fourteen of your packet, you'll find the application for COBRA benefits. Remember to send those in before the end of the month. Thanks." Jeff sat down.

John Donnelly stood up. "Thanks, Jeff.

"I know this separation comes as a shock, and it's hard on all of us. nTropics recognizes what you've all contributed to the company, and we appreciate it; but this is a time to look not to the present or past, but to the future, and we need to reorganize, to slim, to survive. If we had any other choice, we would pursue it; however, the current market conditions indicate we need to become leaner, hungrier, and not rest on our laurels and accomplishments. Thank you, all."

"Who the hell is he talking to?" Daryl said.

"He's practicing the speech for the news releases and to give to those who will carry on bravely without us," Robert said.

Brad stood up. Dark hair and sharp nose, he tried not to scowl. "Of course, all of you can guess what impact this news will have on other employees. With that in mind, we ask that you please clean your desks out quietly and leave the campus by 10:15. We've got some people here from a temp agency to help you in any way you need." He nodded to a couple more of the men in blue suits. Assorted other former employees took this as a sign to stand up and head for the exits.

"Shit, you guys, what do we do?" Kevin said as the meeting broke up.

Daryl put his hand to his temple and folded his fingers over his right eye. He deepened his voice. "We die."

"What are you talking about?" Kevin said.

"Haven't you ever seen *The Last Starfighter?*" Daryl asked. "At the end, the bad guys' ship is all but destroyed, and they're about to crash into an asteroid, and the lieutenant says to the general, 'What do we do now?' Never mind.

"I guess we meet at Conroy's at 10:30," Daryl said. "What do you think?"

"Conroy's?" Michele asked, appearing behind Kevin.

"It's a bar on the other side of the office court, on Olive," Daryl said.

"I'll get a table. I'm ready to go now." Robert headed for the door.

* * * *

Conroy's was a long, narrow establishment, with a bar running a quarter of the length of one wall, near the front and the door. Robert sat with his back to the wall in a high booth, swinging his feet freely above the floor. He hovered over a dark beer on the high, darkly stained oak table. He was almost hunched over the Guinness, but he kept his eyes moving towards the door. When Daryl showed up, he was glad, for he hated to drink alone in public.

Daryl sat on a stool and flagged down the waitress to order a Killian's Red. IT geeks always ordered by name, and it was never something on draft.

"Did you leave a logic bomb?" Robert said. The waitress was back quickly. She was probably the first one in for the lunch crowd, and Robert and Daryl were all that existed of the lay-off crowd. A couple of guys hovered at the bar near the plate glass up front, staring wistfully out and another guy hid in the dark and pumped quarters into a Golden Tee.

"Naah," Daryl said, finishing the drawn out A sound as he elevated his mouth for the first gulp of beer.

Kevin appeared at the table. "Naah, what?"

"No logic bomb."

"Huh?" Kevin said.

"Robert just asked me if I left a logic bomb at nTropics. I didn't."

"What's a logic bomb?" Kevin said, almost over his shoulder; his finger was in the air, and almost all of his non-conversational attention was directed toward the blonde waitress in the circulation-restricting top.

Daryl breathed heavily. "That's when someone writes a batch script or fires off a process that wipes the devices when that someone doesn't give it the proper cue to not do so. Usually, gruntled system administrators set it up like that in case they become disgruntled quickly."

"What do you mean, wipe devices? You mean format hard drives?"

"Yeah, Windows-boy," Daryl said.

"When someone sets up a logic bomb, they deploy a standard procedure or batch file that every day checks to see if the person who set it up logs in to defuse it. If that person doesn't log in or somehow defuse it every day, the logic bomb starts its countdown. And when it reaches zero, poof! It does something. And since it's after the person left, it's hard to determine it's sabotage, especially if it's only done by a customer service rep." Robert explained with exaggerated patience.

"Except it wasn't done by a customer service rep," Daryl said. The waitress came over and got the next round. Kevin ordered a Black and Tan.

Guinness over Bass, or Bass over Guinness, or something like that, Robert thought. He's on his way to nowhere fast, and it'd be a shame to get there alone, so Robert ordered another Guinness for when his ran out.

"Why not?" Kevin seemed intrigued by the idea, but he usually was by things over his head, Robert guessed.

"Why? It seems like a lot of effort for a little sick satisfaction." Daryl said.

"Hello, Kevin. And Daryl, right?" The marketing woman appeared, standing next to Kevin. "And...."

"Robert Davies, formerly a Web developer with nTropics.com, Incorporated, traded on the NASDAQ as NTRP. N-Twerp. Antwerp, site of the Battle of the Bulge. In this case, the battle of the slimming," Daryl said. Robert wondered if Daryl had any breakfast and doubted it.

"This is Michele is bare," Kevin said.

"Michele is what?" Robert said. She was wearing a reddish or mauve sweater, which fit rather nicely on her, and a short skirt. She had a broad set of shoulders and mortal-sized breasts, but the sweater emphasized her upper femininity. Robert remembered he only had a bagel for breakfast about five hours prior. Not a lot to slow the absorption of liquor by his body, so he probably ought to regulate it himself. If he could remember to.

"Isbert. My great-grandfather was from France." Michele extended a cool hand to Robert, who wiped the sweat and beer condensation from his and took it lightly for a moment.

"How long did it take you?" Daryl said to Kevin.

"Take me what?"

"Took me twenty minutes," Michele said. "I had a guy named Barry trying to help. Some temps. He was trying to empty drawers on one side of my cubicle at the same time I was working the other side. He wasn't careful at all."

"Pinkerton Temporary Services," Robert said, and then he realized nobody would know what he meant, so he took a quick drink and finished his beer. That was only one, with another in front of him.

"It took me seventeen minutes. When I got back to my computer, they'd locked my account out, so it was only a matter of boxing up everything. They even had a box waiting for me, and my own personal assistant named Roger. You think they were armed?" Kevin caressed his concoction. He was mostly done with the Tan.

"No," Robert said. "Some of them did not even fit in the blue suits they gave them, so it's obvious they were not used to them, and they were not tailor made to hide pistols."

"You sure?" Kevin said.

"Yeah," Robert said. "An oversight on their part, maybe. With the dot-com shakeout, they should be more cautious. Who knows what flaky developer might have a gun?"

"Well, they're lucky I didn't." Kevin took a pull.

"You don't mean that, Kevin," Michele said.

"I might. I cannot do a logic bomb, but I want to do something."

"Revenge?" Daryl said. "Isn't that cliché?"

"Well, they screwed me out of some stock options. Shit, I was going to retire at twenty-seven."

"You want to go slash his tires?" Daryl said.

Robert shifted uncomfortably. He looked to see where the waitress was, but she was looking out the front window, leaning over the bar and talking to the bartender. Well out of earshot, he hoped. If anything bad did happen to nTropics, he didn't want anyone to see him among conspirators, even if the conspirators didn't do anything.

Kevin thought it over for a moment. "No."

"How about egg his house? I hear he lives over off Litzsinger."

Michele shook her head. The waitress brought her a Guinness, too. She would be damned if she ordered a Coke when the men were drinking harder at 11:00 in the morning. The waitress put another glass in front of Kevin, too.

"No, nothing like that. Never mind." Kevin finished a beer.

"So what are you going to do now, Daryl?" Michele said.

"I don't know. Probably hang out for a while, maybe go out to Colorado. I've got some people I know out in Boulder who'd let me crash there for a while."

"I've talked to Brown Shoe and Fleishmann-Hillard. But with the economy slowing, I'm not sure they're hiring," Michele said. "What about you, Robert?"

Robert shifted. "Well, I've got an income yet, because I work part time some nights and weekends, so I am not hurting. I guess I'll look for something, or contract. Or contract till I find something."

"You're working nights?" Michele said.

"Um, yeah," Robert said. He concentrated on not flushing under the woman's attention.

"What are you doing?"

"A little video shop. By my house in Overland."

"No kidding?" Kevin said

"Yeah. It's enough to pay the bills, just in case.... Well, I guess this is the case."

"Shee-it, you're working what, forty-five or fifty at nTropics. Were. That's a lot of time." Kevin said.

"You've got a house?" Michele said.

Robert straightened. "Well, yes, but it's nothing special Just a little two bedroom in Overland."

"We should go back to your place, Robert," Daryl said. "We can get some beer cheaper at a liquor store and keep drinking if we care to get drunk."

"I'm not sure. I haven't cleaned for company." Robert looked at the remaining quarter of his beer and wondered if he could nurse it until they all had something better to do.

Kevin dropped the black Guinness half of his beer. "I want to steal John Donnelly's gold bar. That will be my revenge," he announced. He meant the tropical doubloon thing, that John Donnelly had bought and incorporated into the nTropics logo.

"Ar, captain!" Daryl said.

"I'm serious," Kevin said, his voice rising. "I'm going to steal the damn thing!"

The waitress and bartender broke off their conversation and looked over.

"I'd like to see your house," Michele said.

Robert threw the rest of his beer back, swallowing the smooth beer and rising steadily, he hoped, to his feet. "Let's go," he said.

Robert's House

Robert showed them his two bedroom bungalow on Tennyson Avenue. When he said the house wasn't ready for company, Robert was not exaggerating; he had not taken the normal extra steps he would have taken if he had known others were coming, such as running his duster over the hardwood floors or over his bookshelves and entertainment center. Wiping down his kitchen counters. Organizing the basement, which contained his computer, filing cabinets, magazines of all stripes, his electronics books, and electronics workbench.

Not that his house was unpresentable without the extra effort. Of course, not to his eyes, but his guests' eyes were their own business. He made his queen bed every day, covering the sheets and three blankets with a large brown spread with a bear on it. Granted, the sheets and blankets weren't the sort of thing you could bounce a quarter on, but the bear covered them all. He closed all of the drawers in his dresser, closed the closet door where he hung his blue jeans and sweatshirts. In the kitchen, all the dishes except the morning's cereal bowl were washed, dried, and stacked on the open shelves. Of course, the unused serving dishes, an inheritance from a great aunt, would need wiping if he were putting Cheetos into one of them for his guests. Not that he had Cheetos, anyway.

He walked them all through, as a good host would, pointing out the ceiling he had replastered and the breakfast bar he refinished. Of course, like a home of the fifties, the kitchen proved their focal point. Michele took a seat at the breakfast bar. Kevin and Daryl slumped over the table, with Kevin doing most of the slumping. Robert, ever the host, leaned against his kitchen counter in case anyone wanted anything.

* * * *

Kevin had wanted beer, so he insisted on stopping at the gas station on the corner of Page and Woodson. He also insisted Daryl scrunch into the leather passenger seat of his Eclipse, so they stuffed Daryl's bike into the back of Michele's Ford Taurus wagon and followed Robert. Robert's house was only seven or eight miles from Conroy's, so Daryl would have preferred to ride. When he made his initial protest to Kevin, Daryl saw the look on Robert's face. Robert did not want to host two strangers for the extra twenty minutes or so it would take Daryl to ride. So Daryl acquiesced. Which explained why he had gone with Kevin into the convenience mart.

Kevin was suitably disappointed, though, that the gas station did not carry anything more exotic than Michelob as far as beer was concerned. Unfortunately, he then got another bright idea.

"Let's get some Colt .45," he said, pulling a couple of tall boys from the cooler.

"What?" Daryl said.

"Colt .45," Kevin repeated, deepening his voice and affecting an Ebonics accent. "Better than the Silver Bullet is the big bad gun that shoots it." He was entirely too comfortable announcing this in the middle of the convenience store, in the middle of the day.

Daryl wondered if he should try to remember how to operate a manual transmission so he could steer Kevin's Spyder between all the telephone poles between here and Robert's house. "Get what you want," he said, and he grabbed two two-liter bottles of Mountain Dew. They made it to Robert's safely, but not necessarily comfortably.

Unfortunately for Daryl, the group gravitated toward the kitchen instead of the living room, where Robert's entertainment center included a buffet of video game systems. A Tandy Color Computer scoreboard tennis/hockey/handball Pong knock-off, an Atari 2600, an Intellivision, and a Colecovision as well as a Nintendo, an Atari Jaguar, and a PlayStation. Robert hooked them up with a master switch to his large television. Daryl thought it was the bomb, and he let Robert know every time he came over to try to get the 30,000 points on Keystone Kops he would have needed in 1984 to get an Activision patch. Robert had a windbreaker full of the patches, for River Raid, Keystone Kops, Pitfall!, Megamania, Frostbite, and a dozen other classics, in the closet. Daryl envied the windbreaker.

In the kitchen, Robert took up position defending his refrigerator. He offered Kevin a 32-ounce Cardinals souvenir cup for his first Colt .45. Fortunately, Kevin left the accent in the convenience store, and he declined, drinking the malt liquor from the oversized can with oversized relish. Michele let Robert pull her a glass of water from his water purifier. Daryl drank his Mountain Dew right from the bottle.

"So how do we steal the gold?" Kevin followed the question with another slug from the beer.

"Steal what gold?" Michele said. "Are you serious?"

"He's as serious as he is intoxicated," Daryl diagnosed.

"Definitely more, but I am working to bring that ratio into proper balance," Kevin drank another mouthful.

Daryl wondered if Kevin was the type to crush the can on his forehead and decided that he would probably not in this company. Probably did in college, though. "Were you a Greek?" he said to Kevin.

"Sigma Ep at SIUE, you bet. Want to see me crush the can on my forehead? Let me finish it first."

Robert snorted lightly, discreetly. Of course, the private school kids like him called it "soooo-ey," as befit a podunk state school in Illinois. But he didn't mention it here.

"But seriously, we need to get that damn gold bar. It's worth millions, and we could melt it down, untraceable, and split it in four. Beats to hell the severance package nTropics gave us."

"He's talking about the nTropics gold bar, a piece of sunken treasure that JD bought sometime after the IPO, when his options made him a paper billionaire." Daryl responded to Michele's continuing quizzical look.

"Hell, it's right in the logo," Kevin said, mercifully crumpling and twisting the can in his hands. "Hit me with another, eh, Robert?"

Robert drew one of the remaining beer cans from the refrigerator. "It's the gold bar in the logo," he said. Michele had been hired sometime last winter, after the big August auction which spawned a press release and a segment on several tabloid news magazines. "Last August, JD bought a gold bar, and he made a big deal of saying that if the gold bar had been on a trip booked by nTropics, it would not have been on the bottom of the ocean for a hundred years. He had the infrastructure department come out to his house and put a live Web feed of that bar on nTropics. As long as the site's live, he said, nTropics provided the best service for its customers. And so much blah blah blah."

"You help them with that blah blah blah?" Daryl said to Kevin.

"Not me. Too expensive. Although I understand our hits went way up after."

"What about the actual sales?" Michele said.

Kevin shrugged.

"So it's still live?" she said.

23

"What?" Kevin retaliated.

"The gold bar site."

"Sure," Daryl answered, to Robert's chagrin.

"I remember the meetings, and the pages of message text. Dozens of pages of what our corporate message was. Just one sentence zingers, things we hit over and over in ads and in articles. nTropics gets you where you want to go. You can take us anywhere. And so on and so on. You can take us right to the unemployment line."

"So you want to steal the gold bar?" Michele said. Daryl could not read her, to determine how seriously she was entertaining the notion.

"Damn straight," Kevin said. "I think he owes it to us."

"Were you that close to vesting?" Daryl said.

"About two months."

"Me, too," Daryl said. "We started around the same time."

"And we all ended at exactly the same time," Michele said.

"So let's get the bar." Kevin said. "We could just break in and take it, and that would be a couple million each, and we'd be set."

"I don't think of Potosi Correctional Center as 'set,'" Daryl said.

"We'd be smart about it," Kevin argued.

"How would we do it, bright boy?"

"Just break in to his house. I don't know if he's got some security system," Kevin said. He added a thoughtful pause by swallowing about ten ounces of beer. Grasping the can by the bottom, he crashed it against his forehead, recoiling from the blow. The can crumpled slightly, but did not flatten. "Shot," he said, probably meaning the obscenity instead.

"Shouldn't you squeeze it a little first?" Daryl offered.

"Oh, yeah." Kevin said. "I got too excited. Maybe I'll remember after the next one." He motioned to Robert, who reluctantly produced another can.

"Since we're planning to elude the police, should we not practice?" Daryl said.

"What?" Michele said.

"You never know when to duck and when to jump," Robert said. "But you can always try, my boy."

"What are you talking about?" Michele said.

"Keystone Kops. You ever have an Atari?" Daryl said.

"I can whip your ass at Warlords," Kevin warned them.

"Right now, I don't think you could tell a potentiometer from a pot to piss in," Robert said, regretting it the minute he did.

"A what?" Kevin said.

"My brother did," Michele said, and Daryl smiled.

"Let's play," he said.

*   *   *   *   *

Kevin could not defeat anyone but himself at Warlords, and Daryl had smirked several times when he got close to 30,000 points and when he jumped both moving shopping carts and ducked both flying toy airplanes to catch the crook and break the 30K barrier with the time bonus. Michele posed surprising resistance at Combat, Space War, and Boxing, of all things. Not to mention her facility with the Nintendo or PlayStation controllers. Robert and Daryl approved, and Kevin thoughtfully snored, his back against the loveseat and his mouth opened wide.

Daryl and Robert wrestled Kevin onto the sofa and threw an afghan, made by Robert's sister, who was a crochet fanatic, he mentioned, over Kevin's snoring form.

They ended up in the kitchen again, all three of them around the table. Robert produced a previously unannounced bottle of Amaretto, and they were all drinking sours.

"So do you guys think Kevin will really try it?" Michele said.

"What, stealing the gold bar?" Daryl said. "It probably not even worth the millions he says it is."

"Besides," Robert said, "You wouldn't want to just force the door with a pinch bar. The cops would be out looking for you, then. You'd want to steal the bar and not even let Donnelly know it's gone."

"What, like Indiana Jones?" Daryl said.

"Yeah, like that," Robert said.

"You think you could do it?" Michele said.

"I don't know. But a lot of crooks get away every day, and they're not as smart as me." Robert could not believe he said that. He got a bag of pretzels from the top of his refrigerator, although the bread would probably hit the queue in his stomach after the two whiskey drinks he already had, atop a couple of beers and a glass of Mountain Dew. He hoped he would not vomit.

"What, you think I am mad? Listen to how carefully I planned it out," Daryl said.

"You think I am crazy?" Robert said.

Daryl abruptly went from smirk to serious. "No, not too bad. No more than anyone in the industry."

"You just need to case his house, get an idea of his habits, you know, and you'll find his weakness. Something he does that you can exploit. A window he leaves unlocked. A basement door that doesn't always close all the way."

"Yeah, kinda like running scripts on a system that check all the known security holes to see what patches the admin hasn't installed." Daryl nodded.

"Before people had white collars, they were doing it to one another," Robert blurted. He almost leaped from his seat with that prophetic statement and went to the refrigerator. Kevin's penultimate malt liquor was in there. "You want to split this?" he said to Daryl, and a belated glance to Michele to include her.

"Sure," Daryl said, biting off his impulse to recreate Kevin's accent from the convenience store.

"No, thanks," Michele said.

"So it's like live-action hacking," Daryl said.

"Yes! Something like that." Robert poured the Colt .45 into two tumblers, set one in front of Daryl, set his near his empty chair, and continued pacing.

"You ever do any live action role-playing?" Daryl said.

"What, like that vampire stuff? No way."

"When I was at Wisconsin, some guys I was in a group with talked about how they used to do it in the steam tunnels, walk around and play D&D until some kid disappeared or something." Daryl mused.

"I did some Mage when I was in college," Michele said. "At Archon, over in Collinsville."

"You played Mage?" Daryl said. Robert paused. An enchantress.

"Yeah, who hasn't?"

"I haven't. I never played a White Wolf game," Robert said, and regretted it.

"So you're a virgin. That doesn't bother me. Besides, I only played that one time, and it was because my boyfriend wanted to go to the convention, so I went with him. No big deal."

"We'd have to cover our tracks, though, just as if they were keeping logs," Daryl said.

Robert slapped his hand on the table. "That's what I said!' And since his hand was near his glass of beer, he took a drink of it. And grimaced. He really hoped he would not vomit.

"So what I would do," Daryl said, "is get an idea of where he lives. You said off of Litzsinger?"

"Just east of Lindbergh, right by that school where you can't go east on Litzsinger. You have to come west from Brentwood Boulevard."

"What municipality is that?"

"I don't know. Huntleigh?"

"Huntleigh?" Michele said. "I've never heard of that."

"It's between Frontenac and Kirkwood on Lindbergh. It's got about four hundred people, and it's nothing but lots of trees and big houses, so you never hear of it." Robert thought about how it looked on his street guide. Mid-County was a jumble of streets and interstates, and then it struck Huntleigh, between Highway 40 and Interstate 44. Suddenly, a few lines from the artery stretched into the unbroken blocks of land. It wasn't green like a park, and that's how you knew that's where the big houses were.

"I've never seen that area," Michele said.

"It's really nice," Robert offered.

"You guys want to go see it?" Daryl said.

"It's a little dark for that," Robert said.

"Isn't it the right time to case a joint?" Daryl said.

"Intoxicated, in Huntleigh, at night? Not unless you want to case the inside of a Clayton jail cell."

"You guys are too much," Michele said. "I should go home about now."

"You probably shouldn't drive," Robert said, and in a lightning second a fantasy unfolded: Daryl on the couch and Michele in the guest bed down the hall, slipping into his bedroom. Of course, he did not know her that well, and she probably did not find him that attractive, but Robert enjoyed the split second and knew he'd spend more time later thinking about it intricately.

"I'll be fine, boys," she said, pushing herself away from the table. "I've only had two drinks."

"We'll walk you to your car, then," Robert said.

"I am a big girl," Michele ruffled.

"You're a woman," Robert said, hoping he was not displaying his attraction so much as to be creepy, "but this is Overland, and it's a little after eleven."

So they walked her out to the her wagon and saw her off. As they stepped back onto the concrete slab which served as Robert's front porch, Daryl missed his bike. It wasn't leaning against the siding next to the door; instead, he realized, it was still in the back of Michele's wagon, and her taillights disappeared around the corner at the end of the block. "Can I crash here tonight?" he said.

"Sure," Robert said. "We'll go look at JD's tomorrow morning, then."

Daryl doubted it. "Sure," he said anyway.

* * * * *

27

They were talking a little foolish, Michele thought as she drifted to a stop in the left turn lane on Woodson, preparing to hop onto Page and from then onto I-170. Her University City duplex was only about twenty minutes away, down the highway and down Delmar. It might have been shorter to just take Woodson to Delmar, but she preferred the quickness of the intracity highway to dark, unknown streets at night. So she pulled into the left turn lane.

A pair of headlights drifted into her rearview mirror, and Michele automatically checked her mirror to make sure he stopped behind her and to ensure no one got out and approached her car. A handlebar of Daryl's bike poked up into her view, and she cursed lightly in her mind. She thought about turning around, but she was getting drowsy. Not to mention if she would ever find Robert's house in the dark, or ever again without someone in the passenger seat.

She'd see them at…. Well, no, she thought, I guess I'll see them in the morning.

Planning and Casing Donnelly's

Tuesday, the twenty-second of October, dawned earlier than Robert would have expected. Last night's school-night consumption of alcohol. Of course, it wasn't a school night, because he did not have a day job anymore, but Robert was still surprised somewhat that the sun was up when he awakened at 9:30. More surprised that he slept that late.

He heard movement in his house, and remembered he had guests. He kicked himself free from the tangle of the bedspread and threw his feet over the edge of the bed. He quickly looked down at the jeans he had slept in. Good enough for another day, he thought, and then he wondered what his guests were getting into.

Kevin sprawled in almost the same position where they left him. The living room, devoid of windows by a previous owner's renovation design which cut the living room in half to make room for a spare bedroom, was the darkest room in the house. Robert knew when he poked his head around the corner to look into that bedroom that Daryl wouldn't be there. After all, he had heard someone in the basement, and if it wasn't Daryl, well. Since Daryl wasn't in the bedroom, Robert wasn't going to stop back in his bedroom to get the Glock out of his alarm clock/gun safe.

"Good morning, sir," Daryl said.

"Hey. How'd you do that?" Robert asked. Daryl was on Robert's computer with an Internet browser open.

"Do what?"

"Log into my account?"

"I'm not logged into your account."

Robert's silence expressed his disbelief, or his disproval, or something with a dis in it.

"Look, you leave it sitting here with the password protection on your screen saver," Daryl said. "So all I have to do is shut the thing off, log in as guest, and set up a connection to my ISP. It's not brain surgery. I don't even have to look at your hard drive and root through your bank statements."

"I never store personal banking information on my computer. Or credit cards for that matter," Robert stiffened.

"Of course not. However, I have been here overnight, alone with that, too," Daryl said, hooking a thumb in the direction of the beige steel file cabinet on the wall opposite the computer.

"There's nothing in there, either." Robert said.

Daryl turned away from the computer for the first time. "You don't keep personal information in your file cabinet?"

"If you were an identity thief, breaking in here to get my stats, where would you go first?"

"You think an identity thief's going to break in? There are much easier ways to glean your personal information, you know."

"You don't plan for your enemy's intentions, but for his capacities."

"You da monster!" Daryl shook his head. "You know what I have been looking at?"

The monitor depicted an online magazine of some sort, with a discolored mustard menu bar down the right side and a layered ad in the middle. "What?" Robert asked.

"This is *St. Louis Architecture's* Web site. Seems here we have an article about the Bemertons' house, a two story colonial in Huntleigh. It has six full bathrooms, three half bathrooms, and only six bedrooms, which means you have to invite extra guests over just to piss." Daryl clicked a link, popping a photograph into a new browser window. "Look at that sick amalgamation of columns and commonplace."

"Who are the Bemertons?"

"George Bemerton was a respected pathologist at Washington University. Judith Bemerton was the daughter of a brick magnate, of all things."

The third-to-bottom step creaked to announce Kevin. "George and Judy? Like the Jetsons?" he asked.

"George and Judith Bemerton. George retired two years ago, and they decided to move to one of their Florida properties."

"So?" Kevin said.

"And two years ago, they sold it to John Donnelly." Robert surmised.

"Bingo! Fresh out of his previous success at Aquatech, flush with a golden parachute, John Donnelly bought it for four million, two hundred and fifty thousand. Last year, it was assessed at four million, seven hundred and fifty thousand dollars. A mere mortal, paying a one million dollar down payment, would have to pay thirty-five thousand dollars a month on a thirty year mortgage to own it."

"How did you get all that stuff?" Kevin said.

"I got his address from nTropics, and then I used St. Louis County's Department of Revenue to check the property." He ALT+TABbed to another browser. "Here you have a list of improvements and a rough sketch of the major living areas. However, it also displays the last time it was sold. So I rooted around in some realtor's database, and I came up with the Bemertons' name. And I Googled them and got this article."

"How many Web browsers you have open?" Kevin peered at the task bar, shoved oddly onto the right side. Daryl always marked his machines this way, Robert knew.

"Six or seven." He cycled through them. "Google results, Revenue.StLouisCo.Com, Realtor.Com, a little 360 tour, a little advertisement," which he promptly tapped closed with an ALT+F4, "An old cached copy of Wash U's faculty list, an old *Post-Dispatch* article about Bemertons' retirement, and their address in Fort Lauderdale."

"That's great," Kevin said. "Did the Blues win last night?"

"Yes, of course they did; they were playing Nashville. But that's beside the point." Daryl switched to a smaller window, depicting a darkly paneled foyer. A set of stairs led upward onto a sunlit landing. Beyond the far wall, a bright kitchen gleamed with salable freshness. The view slowly panned to the right, exposing a dark and serious living room, designed exclusively for entertaining foreign dignitaries. An imposing wooden-looking door scrolled from the right, flanked by large windows which cast glistening beams on the hardwood flooring. Robert hoped they would be heavy glass, and wired to the gills. No point in putting a solid wood door up if it's attached to single panes of glass. The wall opposite was dark wood panel as well, probably real wood, broken only by a keypad. A door on the left wall led into a study or library type of room, a table and bookshelf the only discernible features. The camera continued its scroll back to the stairs and kitchen.

"Whoa! Hold it," Robert said. "Pan back the other way."

Daryl grabbed the mouse, clicked and dragged the cursor on the window to start the pan the other way. "What's up?"

"Hold it," Robert said. The view paused on the wall to the left of the entrance doors. The little keypad displayed, a stark break of off white on the dark panel. "That's not too bright," Robert said.

"What?" Kevin said.

"The alarm keypad. It's direct line of sight with the windows on either side of the door."

"So what?" Kevin said. "It's good to have an alarm. You got to have the keypad by the door so you can key in your code before it goes off."

"It's not good to have it where someone outside could see you do it."

"Cripes, to protect yourself from the mailman? What are you, paranoid?"

"You don't plan for what people might do, you plan for what they can do," Robert repeated. At least, it seemed to him that he was repeating it, mainly because it seemed like it was common sense to him, something Kevin's father probably should have told him.

"He's paranoid, but he's right, too," Daryl said. "You can be both, and in the twenty-first century, it happens more and more."

"You know which room he's got it in?" Robert said.

"Are you talking about the gold bar?" Kevin said.

"For security's sake, I would put it in the basement somewhere, center of the house. Of course, you couldn't get to it in a fire." Daryl drummed his fingertips on the very edge of his keyboard just beneath the space bar.

"Unless he's got a safe room somewhere?"

"Safe room?" Daryl said.

"They're all the rage. A fire-proof, bomb-proof room you can go into and lock yourself in. Helpful for home intrusion, too. A lot of government officials and heads of multinational corporations have them now, to prevent terrorist groups from breaking in and holding their families hostage," Robert explained.

"You think Donnelly's got one?" Daryl said.

"Probably not, but we ought to check."

"Who wired his house?" Kevin said.

"What, it was January, wasn't it?" Daryl said.

Robert cycled through the list of previous system administrators through his head, settling on a blond flattop, Van Dyked, and slightly overweight picture. "Eddie Bennett," he said. Eddie had been working on a book about tending to your computers, and he had left in February to begin a business as an independent consultant. Give him thirty K a year and he would keep your business's network humming. Robert wondered if you could write a book and work a hundred hours a week, and doubted it.

"If he had his way, he'd run it right to one of the outside rooms so he would not have to pull cable through the whole house." Daryl shook his head. Amateur.

"Hell, I wouldn't want someone poking holes into the walls and ceilings of my new billion dollar home, either," Kevin agreed.

A computer speaker next to the computer made a single ding, even though Daryl had not touched the keyboard. Robert started and felt a momentary sense of panic, but of course they had not done anything but speculated so far. He doubted if Daryl had used an invisible proxy server to get to the sites still open on the computer. Of course, they had done nothing wrong, so he had nothing to fear; however, these thoughts did pop into his mind, rapidly.

"Who is it?" Daryl said.

"What?" Kevin said.

Robert grabbed a remote control from the desk beside the computer. A small television in the corner buzzed and its picture expanded into a brunette woman on a porch. "It's Michele," he said. The picture did include Michele, on what you could recognize as Robert's porch only after you knew what it was. It caught Michele at a three-quarter angle, not quite overhead and not eye level. You couldn't see down the front of a dress, if someone knocking on the door was wearing one. Robert had put the mini camera in at the edge of the roof and angled it precisely for that reason, regardless of what the camera manufacturers said, wink wink nudge nudge, in their incessant pop-under ads. You could stick them anywhere, they intimated, including the bedroom, not that we're encouraging that!

"Ah," Daryl said. Michele leaned Daryl's bike against the side of the porch and hesitated before reaching for the doorbell. The doorbell rang precisely when her finger hit the button.

"You've got a camera on your front door?" Kevin said.

Robert clicked the television off. "Yes."

Robert looked through the peephole. Michele was staring at the siding somewhere off to the left of the door. When Robert started twisting the deadbolt embedded in the red steel door, her eyes centered on the door. "Good morning," Robert said as he swung the door open.

"Hi, I brought Daryl's bike back. Is he still here?" Michele said. More importantly, she thought, is Kevin still here? Of course he was; his Eclipse was still parked two houses down and across the street.

"Yes, come on in." Robert stepped aside and gestured inward.

Michele had worn a sweatshirt and a pair of jeans this morning, this being the first of her many stops on the first day of the next section of the rest of her life. She had to stop at the copy shop on Big Bend and Forest Park Parkway, and the post office, and what the hell, the U City Library to pick up the books which would not only inspire into her to new career heights, but would offer insights about the 1989 job market in case she wanted the historical perspective. And the latest Carlotta Carlyle novel. When she saw Kevin, though, she wished she had put on a base of makeup. "What are you guys up to?" She hoped they were not still talking foolish like last night.

"I was just going to suggest we drive by John Donnelly's house to take a look at it," Daryl said. "He's in the office by now."

"It wouldn't be a bad idea," Robert said. "You want to come?"

"I have some errands to run," Michele parried.

"Well, we're not all going to fit into my car," Kevin said. "Are you sure you're not in, Michele? It's only an hour. Besides, you're already an accessory, and if you haven't turned us in by now, you're going to the pen with us."

"Well," Michele said.

Kevin knew he had her. "We'll take you out to lunch, too."

"I guess...."

"Great!" Daryl said. "I just need a few things."

Kevin stiffened with a sudden thought. "Hey, is it such a good idea to drive up there?"

Robert watched Michele for panic. "Would it be a good idea to break in there?"

"We could go in at night, when no one could see us."

Robert shook his head. Michele took in the conversation with slight interest on her face, but nothing to indicate a tightening or a terror. "If we went at night," Robert said, "we'd be much more suspicious. And if you're thinking about breaking in without looking it over first, this is not an unalarmed middle school out in Jefferson County."

They piled into Michele's wagon, Kevin in the front seat beside her. Robert and Daryl buckled themselves into opposite ends of the bench seat. Daryl spread his trove of maps and house plans on the seat between them. "Go down 170 to Eager, and make a right. Make a left to take Brentwood south to Litzsinger, and make a right. It'll be a couple of miles and on the left."

"Give me those directions as they become more relevant," Michele said. "I'm not going to remember them all in that order now."

*   *   *   *

The houses were far apart on Litzsinger, hidden from the road by trees, shrubs, and design, so the occasional mailbox erupting from the underbrush surprised Michele. The house was on her side, so she was moving a little slower than the speed limit to watch for the mailboxes and for the house numbers. Fortunately, none of the area's residents had appeared on her tail in their Mercedes and Infiniti sport utility vehicles used neither for sport nor utility in this ZIP code.

My, she was tasting a little bitter ember in her thoughts this morning, but she had awakened without a job for the first time since college and did not care for it. At seven o'clock, too. Her natural sleeping rhythm, to which she reverted on weekends and vacations to which she had adhered during college, was a late rise, around ten o'clock, a nap in the afternoon, and then working or reading or whatever until two or three. She'd often thought a job in Information Technology would give her that sort of flexibility like it seemed to give so many. Unfortunately, she was not an eccentric guru; she was a replaceable, and now replaced, a cog in the less technical and more fluffy world of marketing. Hence, the 8:30 to 5:30 grind every day. Hence, she had become conditioned to waking up before the alarm at 7. Hence, she had awakened this morning, much before the alarm which she had set for 8:30 to compensate for her late night and to give her a head start on the job hunt. But waking up like it was a regular work day only reminded her she was out of a job, and damn it, she was not comfortable with it.

"There it is," Robert said.

Michele saw the brick mailbox waiting patiently at the end of a long driveway. On a narrow, less-traveled road such as this, it was a good idea to encase your mailbox in brick. Local teenagers, even those in this area, loved their "mailbox baseball," wherein a passenger of a moving vehicle sat in a car window, swinging a baseball bat at unprotected mailboxes. Well, probably not the teenagers from this area—Huntleigh looked like the sort of area filled with people who were too busy working on careers to make love. But teenagers from the surrounding communities, from Frontenac, Creve Coeur, and Sunset Hills, could certainly find their way up here to do their gleeful young vandalism.

"Pull in, pull in," Robert said, and Michele sensed he was gesturing to encourage her.

"What," Michele said, "into the driveway?" She stepped on the brakes.

"Yes," Daryl said from the other side. "Go on up, no one's home."

"Go," Robert said. Michele stopping in the road would be eminently suspicious.

Michele shook her head and turned hard onto the asphalt driveway. It curved slightly, passing the mailbox and some lilacs. Between some

35

firs, they caught their first glimpse of John Donnelly's house. Manse, Michele thought. What would John Donnelly have named his estate, had he thought to name it? Probably something suggested by a consultant, which would ring with the falsity of New York creative inbreeding.

"All the way?" she said. As it neared the house, the drive circled an elaborately-sculpted set of dormant flora, undoubtedly done by freelance landscapers. She could not imagine John Donnelly kneeling in his Dockers, digging his manicured fingers in the dirt.

"Stop by the front door," Daryl said.

The house was brick, an imposing block with wings to either side. An elaborate awning, held in place with columns, covered the slab of concrete which stretched the length of the block portion of the house. It wasn't much to call a porch, but St. Louis, for the most part, was not a society that emphasized or used front porches. As they reached the circle, Michele could see that the asphalt gave way to brick.

"Who's going to the door?" Daryl said.

Robert thought it would have been much more natural for Kevin or Daryl, as Michele had opted for a counterclockwise rotation of the circle, presenting the passenger side of the car. Of course, the more natural was not what necessarily went through their heads. Michele had pulled in not as though she was going in, though; the passenger side would have been more natural. She did not pull into the asphalt extension that led to the four car garage, either. Although Robert had seen no groundskeepers through the trees, he wouldn't be sure until he got out of the car. Michele stiffened. Daryl must have asked because he did not want to go, and who knows what Kevin would do. "I'll go." Robert snapped out of the seatbelt and out the door.

The Donnelly estate was quiet. No traffic noise from Litzsinger or any other thoroughfare. No deep, insect-like buzzing from a groundskeeper on the back forty. Robert seemed to remember that Donnelly was single, so that hopefully meant that no one was home. He hopped up the step to the porch and went to the front door. Glass panels flanked the door, triple weight security glass from the look of them, and a doorbell to the right of the glass. Robert hit the bell and could not hear it ring inside. Quality construction.

He stuck his hands behind his back and stepped away, emoting patiently waiting for the master of the house. His left wrist felt the moisture where the right hand clasped it. At ease, he thought, I am no trouble. If someone opens the door, I am fucked. Selling magazines with a carload? Taking a survey? Fucked. He flicked his eyes up to the porch roof, two stories up. No birds' nests, no CCTV cameras looking back at him, no bumps which might be mini-cameras. Of course, if they were, he was staring right up into them; he fought the urge to hide his face with a downward look, which might seem incongruous to passersby, if they could see through shrubs and across acres. And it had been long enough from the first doorbell ring.

He rang the bell again, dragging his finger off of the button and hopefully smearing the print. He pressed both hands against his head, but not against the glass, to peer inside. Beyond the glass and a Protected by Peerless Security Systems sticker, Robert saw the foyer. The alarm pad was right where he expected it. Although he could not clearly read the letters, he counted five spots of light on the readout. Enough to spell ARMED. Or READY. Or JOHND, for that matter. A little table against a wall to the right. Small rug on the floor. Deadbolt on the door. Four inches of frame between the door and the window. He turned and shrugged to the car, expressing that Andy wasn't answering the door. That would have made a good story, that he was looking for Andy, but he would probably not have thought the story up if someone had opened the door and challenged him.

"What was that all about?" Kevin said.

"What do you mean?" Robert clicked the seat belt back on.

"You looked almost disappointed that nobody answered."

"I have no idea where Andy is. He said he'd be home," Robert said. "We can go now."

Michele stepped on the accelerator as though she had longed for the opportunity.

"Who the hell is Andy?" Kevin asked.

"Andy was Robert's cover story," Daryl surmised. "What did you see?"

"Alarm pad is still where we expected it," Robert said. Daryl nodded and circled something on a sheet of paper. "Area rug, small table to the right of the doorway to the living room. Stairs up uncarpeted. Louis XIV chair on the landing. No cameras on the porch that I could see. Peerless Security sticker in the window. Deadbolt locked, solid frame, security windows. All the outward signs of security," Robert reported.

"You looked for cameras?" Michele said.

"Turn left onto Litzsinger," Robert instructed. He wanted to make sure that anyone east of Donnelly's only saw them once, not that it would matter, really.

"Of course he did. He's got some of his own. We saw you this morning before you rang the bell." Kevin said.

"The blinds to the sitting room, just east of the foyer, were drawn, but most of the other rooms facing the driveway were open, and most of them had drapes. Did you see the cables running up the outside?" Daryl said.

"No," Robert admitted.

"Probably T1, or ISDN. Buried from the street, but run through the wall at the house. That might bite into the resale. To the east of the sitting room window, so I would guess there's a closet there, with a server and a firewall."

"You think a firewall?" Robert said.

"I would. If not, that's easier."

"So what's your plan, boys?" Michele said. They were passing some sort of parochial school where Litzsinger bottlenecked and met Lindbergh. Turning right onto Lindbergh, probably too close to a full-size pickup. Of course, they couldn't be serious about breaking in, but it did pose an interesting problem to think about. David Albernathy would probably never find himself planning a heist, but a writer should, like a martial artist, aim for a spot beyond the target. The next novel.

"Guys?" Kevin said.

"It's like we said last night. We've got to get in and get it out with anyone knowing." Robert explained, again.

"How would you do that?" Michele said.

"Let me think about it."

After the Casing Planning

When Michele looked closer, she saw that the exterior of Robert's house differed somewhat from his neighbors'. The wooden siding, real wood, Michele discovered by touching it and feeling the rough edge ripe for splinters, displayed a fresh coat of deep green paint. White trim surrounded updated windows. Small chrysanthemums lined the edge of his porch, neat enough to indicate he cut them back in the winter. More than she expected.

As she crossed the threshold, she glanced upward at the roof of the porch. No closed-circuit televisions cameras peering back at her. Robert had taken the time to paint the roof of his porch. So many people did not. Michele wondered if he had done it himself, and suspected he would have trusted no one else to do it. She had just met Robert yesterday, and she was pretty sure she had him pegged. Paranoid, cautious, reserved, she thought, would be the three adjectives that would creep into her narrative describing him.

"Have you got a plan yet?" Kevin said.

"Give me a minute," Robert said.

"Okay if I use your computer?" Daryl started down the stairs.

"I guess," Robert said.

Downstairs, Daryl powered up the machine. Michele looked over the room and settled into a chair at Robert's work bench. Robert paced. He thought it better that way. If he were to sit down, his knee would begin bouncing, he knew, with the excess energy he got when he was excitedly thinking. He didn't want to let on that he was excited, and the knee bouncing would do it more than the pacing, but not by much.

Kevin joined them, the last of the Colt .45s in his hand. "Got it yet?" He sat on the steps and popped open his malt liquor.

"So we have to get into his house without him knowing we were in there, and substitute another gold bar for the real one. How do you think we could best do that?" Robert assumed what he hoped would be a Socratic stance. He was just stalling because he had no ideas of his own.

"We pick the locks?" Michele said.

"Can you pick a lock?" Robert said.

"I haven't," she admitted.

"I used to pick my mother's lockbox when I was in junior high," Kevin said.

"Really?"

"Sure, she had stock certificates and birth certificates and credit cards in there. I once got the credit card out and logged into this one porn Web site. A couple of buddies and me, on a sleepover, did little sleeping." Kevin snorted. "Of course, she saw the credit card statement and called the company. She ended up disputing the charge with her credit card, and because the charge came from a porn company, she ended up never having to pay it. I only did it once, though, because I was scared she would catch on."

"You're lucky she only got billed once," Daryl said. "A lot of those companies double charge because they think you're afraid to dispute it."

"Spoken like a man with experience," Kevin said.

"Or someone who reads CNET," Daryl said.

"What kind of lock?" Robert said.

"What?" Kevin said.

"How many pins and tumblers?" Robert said.

"I don't know. I just got out a bobby pin and a file, like I saw in a comic book, and I wiggled it until I could turn the lock with the file."

"So you're probably not up to a deadbolt like I saw today. Lockpicking's out." Robert paced again.

"We could find a lockpick," Kevin said.

"There are four of us already. How many would you like to have to trust?"

Daryl whistled. "Damn, you know the story on this bar?"

"What bar?" Kevin said.

"The gold bar," Daryl said. "The one in John Donnelly's parlor."

"What about it?" Michele said.

Daryl gestured at the monitor. A photograph of the gold bar from various angles, along with its weight and measurements displayed. "Here's the information from the auction house. Seems our boy was lying at the bottom of the Atlantic over a hundred years."

"So what's it worth?" Kevin said.

"Looks like it was about twenty-five pounds. Carried upon the S.S. Central America, which was coming from the California gold rush.

Sold for six million dollars. Plus fees, of course," Daryl said. He scrolled down, reading to himself.

"That's one point five mil each," Kevin lowered his voice. His face was somewhere between stunned and thoughtful, and Robert expected that thoughtful might be giving him too much credit. "I could pay my car off."

"One million dollars?" Michele said. "That's not much."

"One and a half million dollars," Daryl said.

"Not much?" Robert said.

"Not for a lifetime, but for one night's work," Kevin said. "You could buy a nice house with that. Out in Frontenac or Chesterfield. Or thirty houses like this."

"Not like this," Robert said. He'd put a lot of work into this house, damn it, and Kevin had no idea of what work meant.

"Near enough. Or a house in U City where you live, and a car. Or you could take a year off and bum around the world, or to Colorado. Right, Daryl?" Kevin said.

"We wouldn't get six million for a stolen gold bar," Daryl said. "We're not going to auction it off."

"We couldn't fence it for a quarter that," Michele said. "I've read a lot of crime fiction," she added when she realized that Robert and Kevin were staring at her. At least, it felt like they were staring at her.

"We'd be better of melting it down and selling it," Daryl agreed. "That comes to about sixty-four thousand each."

"What?" Kevin said.

"This gold bar is stamped and numbered. Unless you're an expert thief with a connection you can trust to fence it, we'd be a lot safer not trying to sell it as-is. Gold's got a low melting point. We could melt it down, divide it up, cast it as jewelry, and sell it. Actually, if we cast it as jewelry, we could get more than the market rate for it. I haven't made anything in a while, so I am not sure how good it would be, but that's a better idea." Daryl tapped at the keyboard some more.

"Besides, it's not about the money," Kevin said. He stood. "It's about what John Donnelly did to us. Damn it, we were working hard for nTropics.com. I was, anyway. And I was just about to vest. I took that job for less than I could at ImaTech Studios because I wanted to cash in on the stock options thing. And then the Internet thing went south, and everyone else ran for graphics and advertising companies. I thought we were on the right track when the travel sector started pulling out, and now this. John fucking Donnelly's made his mint already, and part of it's sitting in that house. I don't know how damn many stock options he's got, and how much money he's going to make offa firing us, but I damn sure want some revenge. This's better than keying his Lexus, and even if it's only worth a couple thousand bucks, I'm going to put it on my dresser and every day look at it and know I got him." Kevin gestured with his malt liquor can as he spoke. Robert was impressed with the passion with which the marketeer spoke, but doubted that General Patton ever finished a pep talk by taking a slug from an eight percent alcohol canteen.

Daryl applauded politely, lightly, without spinning in the chair. "That may well be, but I don't think a sixty-four thousand dollar risk against a twenty year sentence is a good example of risk analysis."

"You mean, you're not going to go through with it?" Michele said.

"Not if there's a chance to get caught."

"That's a given," Robert said. "I have no hubris; I have no idea what I'm doing, and I am not going inside for this."

"What do you think, Michele?" Kevin said.

"It depends on our plan," Michele said. She knew immediately when she said "our" what she was thinking. In a certain sense, it seemed like a prank, but she rationally knew it was more than that. Not that they were thinking or talking rationally. She couldn't tell about Robert or Daryl, though. They seemed to be running some sort of internal checksums every step of the way, and if it got too dangerous, she knew they'd stop and back off. She felt security in that.

"What is our plan?" Kevin said.

"We were getting to that," Robert said. "We're not picking his lock."

"So how do we get in? Tunnel?" Kevin said.

"That would leave a mark," Daryl said.

"We could break one of his windows and replace it on the way out," Kevin said.

Robert was impressed. Now he was thinking the right way. Of course, it could be his infinite monkey moment, the one time the random firing of his synapses produced a useful thought. "With triple weight windows, we'd have to get some extra thick cut glass, cut to measure. We'll need to go out again, probably tomorrow, to measure the pane we're going to break," he offered.

"Peerless," Daryl said.

"Oh! You're right," Robert reigned himself in.

"What's that?" Kevin sipped his beer contentedly while Robert proved that Kevin Horton was, in fact, a genius. A criminal mastermind. Or at least not as dumb as they thought.

"The alarm," Robert reminded him. Or hoped he was reminding Kevin. If Kevin had been paying attention.

"The windows are wired?" Kevin hoped they didn't think he overlooked that.

"Probably. He's got the windows wired, certainly in the gold room anyway." Daryl called up Peerless's Web site and looked it over.

"There's no way we'd ever guess his code word anyway." Robert said.

"Code word?" Michele said.

"The alarm company probably has a code word for John Donnelly. Whenever his alarm goes off, they'll call him. If whoever answers does not provide said word, the wrath of God and the St. Louis County Police Department falls on them." Daryl tabbed to a hyperlink on the site and pressed ENTER.

Robert would never get used to how quickly he could do that without the mouse. "St. Louis County?" he said.

"You're right; Huntleigh might rent its police protection from Ladue," Daryl conceded.

"Frontenac, actually," Robert said.

"At any rate, it would only give us a couple of minutes before armed men busted in with nothing better to do than to subdue us and put us in the new jail in Clayton," Daryl concluded.

"Okay, so we better not break a window. Which leaves us the front door," Robert said.

"We could freeze the lock and knob with liquid nitrogen until it contracts from the cold, stick a screwdriver in between the plates of the lock, and give the door a quick kick. It'll pop open without leaving a mark," Kevin said.

"Way to go MacGyver," Daryl said. "Where'd you come up with that?"

"Hey, you guys aren't the only ones with fingers on the steady pulse of the underworld," Kevin said.

"Wasn't that in *The Dark Side of Saint Jude*?" Michele said.

"Hey, it worked," Kevin defended himself.

"What's that?" Daryl said.

"It was a film noir movie from 1971. Main character, Jude Lawless, was a thief trying to go straight, but the Mafia wanted him to do a job for them. He ends up breaking into the U.N. using that trick and getting some diplomatic documents, which the Mafia needs to do some export scam. Jude, or Saint Jude as the mafiosos call him, ends up screwing them, and the woman with whom he had become involved turns out to be a mafioso plant who was going to eliminate him when he finished. He gets the drop on her and cripples her and ends up on the run at the end of the movie," Michele explained. She was surprised

43

Kevin had seen it, as it had not been a hyped video release. As a matter of fact, she had gotten it at the U-City Blockbuster, whose offerings aimed to slake the odd thirsts of the young, edgy, urban crowd that rented videos there. Edgy, urban, and renting videos. Suburban self-banished like her.

"I saw part of it on Cinemax one night," Kevin admitted. "During Noir by Noir West Week."

"I saw the lock. It's a high quality steel lock. Even if we had a canister of liquid nitrogen, which is not available in most common drug stores, I don't think it would shrink enough for us to get a screwdriver in," Robert said, hoping it sounded more diplomatic than it probably did. He wished Daryl would pipe up an idea. He was afraid Kevin's next idea would be that they start working very feverishly on a time machine, travel forward to a future time, move the time machine to the latitude and longitude where the Donnelly house stood, and travel backward to get the gold bar.

"We should just get a key," Daryl said. He spun around and looked at Robert. Robert lacked the initial spark, he knew, but could be good when pointed in a direction. He hoped, because he sure didn't have any ideas.

"Who would have a key?" Michele said. Of course, John Donnelly would, but they couldn't get that.

"The realtor might," Daryl said.

"How long ago did you say he bought it?" Robert said.

"Two years," Daryl said. He'd remember everything he'd learned about the Bemertons and the transaction for a long time. It overloaded his brain with trivia, this retention capacity of his, but it made him popular among his family whenever the church's Trivia Night came around. Between him, his mother, Aunt Tiff, and Uncle Ross, they had won three of the last five.

"We'd have to find that realtor or realty office, and somehow find out if they have the key. I don't think they do, and even if they did, John Donnelly might have changed the locks by now," Robert said. Of course, that had been the very first thing he had done when he had taken possession of this place. On his way back from the title company in University City, he had stopped at the hardware store at Midland and Woodson and bought a brand new set of exterior knobs, including high quality locks, and deadbolts. He only unlocked the house with the keys that they had given him once. He changed the knobs and locks with the screwdrivers in his trunk even before he drove the rented truck over with his possessions. Robert stopped; he had unconsciously begun pacing again, and he stopped to say, "But you know who does have a

44

key?"

"Who?" Daryl said.

"John Donnelly," Michele said. Of course he would have a key.

"Exactly!" Robert said. "We're breaking into his house; why not use his key?"

"Damn right!" Kevin said. His own key, to get his own gold bar. Better and better.

"How the hell are you going to get his key?" Daryl said.

"Recreate it from a laser photo image of the bulge in his pocket?" Kevin joked. He recognized the role he was playing in the group, the dreamer, the visionary leader, and the cohesive force that kept them together with laughter. Every group needed a leader who could get the best from his men, and they would certainly respect a little self-deprecating humor.

"He'll give them to us," Robert smirked. Oh, how simple it would be.

"He will?" Daryl said. Robert had hit upon a plan, Daryl knew, something which reached deep into the well of the strange plans for which Robert would never fall, but that someone else would because he was not building n-tier security lifestyle.

"Well, not to us," Robert said. "But to whom would he give his keys?"

"His girlfriend?" Kevin said.

"Or boyfriend," Michele added, not only because she had made that mistake in the past but also because this was the twenty-first century, and if she did not add that, someone could get sued. Well, not now, of course, but it would be good to keep in touch with the legal lowest common denominator for her next employer. "Or his mechanic, if he was getting his car serviced."

"Who else?" Daryl said.

"A valet." Robert smirked again.

"A valet?" Kevin said.

"What happens when you come to an upscale restaurant, and there's a guy with a tasseled vest there?"

"I don't know," Kevin admitted.

"A lot of people give that person car keys. It's called the valet scam. Some guy puts on a vest, stands in front of a venue where you expect to see a valet. Someone pulls up, hands off the keys, and the con artist has a brand new car, plus whatever cargo's in the cabin and the trunk."

"You want to steal his car?" Michele said. "What good does that do?"

"Of course, we don't want his car. But if he were to give us his keys, we'd have the capacity to get into his house," Daryl said.

"Unless he was going to a play or something that took three hours, we'd be in trouble. It would have to be a good play, too, or we'd be nailed if he walked out in the middle," Kevin said.

"Does John Donnelly like the theatre?" Robert looked to Kevin, who cast eyes down on the candy-striped carpet. Daryl shrugged. Michele met his gaze, but with wide brown eyes that waited for an answer. "I guess that's a no, or at least enough uncertainty to qualify as a no." He paced for a minute. "But we don't need to constrain ourselves within the time he's at his location. If we get his keys, we can make some copies in a short period of time. Especially if we split the keys up."

"Okay…." Daryl said.

"So what do we do, follow him to a restaurant?" Kevin said.

"No, we can't follow him to a restaurant. We have to set it up somehow."

"You want us to take him to lunch?" Kevin said. "Maybe pretend we're analysts happy about his latest round of layoffs?"

"He's joking," Robert ended a moment of surprised silence. "That would interject us into his life prominently. It would be better for us to determine where he's going to go and be set up for him there."

"Oh, sure, no problem," Daryl said. He rat-a-tat-tatted at the keyboard with a determined touch-typing stroke befitting an Olympian. Hey, they were pushing chess as an Olympic sport again. Would simple office duties and innocuous deportments like mall walking be far behind? Maybe next time they were in Florida.

"What?" Robert cast his shadow over Daryl's shoulder. A little download box opened on the screen, and its progress bar zipped to one hundred percent before Robert could make out a file name. "What are you doing? What did you put on my machine?"

"Relax, it's a little utility I've used. It's sitting on a server in the Netherlands where I park some files. My files. It's safe."

"What is it?" Robert said.

"It's a dictionary password executable. It takes an IP address and form information from a Web site and fires words from a dictionary file to the Web server. I'll use the proxy server again," Daryl said. As his fingers poked the keys, the nTropics main page popped into a browser window. Daryl tabbed several times, too fast for Robert to even follow the grey box on the hyperlinks, and Daryl clacked SPACE. A bio page popped up, displaying John Donnelly's grinning visage and information about why he was uniquely qualified to figurehead a string of Information Technology companies, of which nTropics was the latest but probably not the last.

"Won't they catch your IP from this?" Robert said.

"Oh, I'm not launching the attack now," Daryl said. "You see how they list John Donnelly's e-mail here, along with the rest of the board and the C-star-Os and VPs?"

"They're very proactive," Kevin said.

"nTropics offers not only an easy-to-use customer interface on the Web, but also an easy-to-contact leadership open to questions and comments from investors and customers," Michele quoted. She was not reading the screen, but looking thoughtfully at the sound-absorbent ceiling tiles. "You think the Swedes will give a Nobel prize for Corporate Pap in our lifetimes?"

"So what does that mean?" Robert said.

"It says they're ripe for another attack," Daryl said. "I told Eddie all about when he switched over to Exchange. I told him he should create a separate account if marketing was so damn intent to put their e-mail addresses on the Web. He could have created CEO@nTropics.com, abstracting it and forwarding the mail to Donnelly's account. That way, he could put extra security on the CEO box."

"What's your point?" Kevin said.

He tabbed backwards to the URL bar and typed another nTropics address. A login screen appeared. "Of course, I also told Eddie he ought to change the Web front end for Outlook from the default URL, too."

"So you're going to spread out your password assault," Robert said.

"Bingo! We'll hit everyone on the company bios page."

"Listen, guys, I know I'm slow, but I am a couple steps behind you here," Kevin said.

"Daryl's going to break into John Donnelly's Outlook at nTropics and see if he's got anything scheduled we can use."

"Won't they get suspicious about everyone's Calendar being cracked into at the same time?" Michele leaned forward.

"Ah, that's the beauty of this executable. When it hits the password, it flags it, but continues with the list anyway. That way, it looks as though security's not actually been breached, as though some script kiddie was goofing around."

"You sound pretty familiar with it. You write it?" Kevin said.

"Writing stuff like this is against the law," Daryl said.

"Companies get attacked all the time," Robert said. "You think the twins will figure it out?"

"What, Bert and Ernie?" Daryl did not have much respect for the two network administrators currently acting as nTropics stalwart defenses. "There's not a lot to find out. It'll look like a routine Web scan. If they bother to look at the Web server logs. If they know where they are." Which, of course, Daryl doubted, since not only had they not changed the Web server name or instituted the dummy mail boxes, but they had waited until nTropics had been hit by two e-mail viruses to put in a filter. And they had still not disabled VBS functionality on the workstations, which would prevent repeat stupiders from firing more useless scripts. He used an eldritch Windows key combo, hitting the little Open-Apple-away-from-Apple plus an E to open up a Windows Explorer. He tabbed through the file system and hit ENTER. His little executable fired off, opening a DOS window and scrolling lines of text.

"This assumes, of course, that you can find his password in the dictionary," Kevin said.

"Even today, most people use words they can remember, which means words in the dictionary or names. The dictionary database this executable uses includes common personal names, family names from the online white pages, Spanish words, and a collection of fictional character names from novels and short stories." Daryl leaned back in the chair. "This'll probably take an hour or two," he said.

"We did promise Michele lunch," Kevin said. "You guys like Mexican?"

Of course I do, Michele thought, but Kevin would not remember the conversation from a department lunch four months ago. They had spoken of their shared fondness of Mexican food, although Kevin did not know the difference between flour and corn tortillas. He had mentioned a place here in Overland and offered to take her sometime. Today would probably be that sometime, but she had hoped for different circumstances when he mentioned it.

"Sure," Daryl said.

"It's okay to leave that?" Robert said.

"It's my Internet account with an DHCP IP address assigned at login," Daryl said, "and it's running through a Web anonymizer and a proxy server. We're safe enough unless someone starts tracking MAC addresses, and even then, it's started now. I wouldn't set you up."

But it is running on my machine, Robert thought, and I am ultimately on the hook. He slowly clenched and unclenched his fists, inconspicuously, he hoped. I'm on the hook now, he said, and he trusted Daryl more than most members of his family. He leaned over Daryl and clicked off the monitor to save power. It didn't hurt to eliminate the Van Eck emissions, either. "Let's eat," he said.

The Hack Results and Independent Reactions

Daryl clicked the monitor back on. He felt a little numb in the fingertips, but Kevin had insisted on a second pitcher of margaritas. Actually, Kevin had insisted on a third, but wiser voices had prevailed. Although Michele's was probably the wisest of all, since she only had a half because she was driving. Margaritas on tres burritos. Actually, underneath and on top the burritos, making a Mexican sandwich. If they drank margaritas at lunch, Daryl knew why the Latin world needed a siesta.

The monitor buzzed to light. The system tray had a little computer in it, indicating they still had a connection.

"Well?" Kevin said.

"Well?" Daryl replied. He hit the Windows key and R to open a Run… dialog box and typed the command to open the log file from his little utility.

"Give him a minute," Robert said.

Windows' Notepad popped open the text file. It contained fourteen lines, one for each address on the nTropics biography page. "It's a simple comma-delimited file," Daryl said. "User name comma password. The smart ones are just user name comma. That means that the password wasn't in the lists of words." He touched his finger on the screen at the first line. "John Donnelly's not one of the smart ones. It's Appelbaum"

"Apple bomb? What the fuck's an apple bomb?" Kevin said.

"Appelbaum. It's a last name," Robert said. "That must have come from the White Pages, right?"

"Must have," Daryl said. Of the fourteen, he noted, nine had passwords in their comma-delimited list. If he were a clumsy, random, blaster of a hacker, he would use a script to import the nine into the next script and launch a bunch of bots or do some other nefarious activity with the knowledge. But this little application was elegant, the weapon of a Jedi.

"Appelbaum?" Kevin said. He carefully walked over to the stairs and lowered himself to sit.

"I really hope that's not his mother's maiden name," Robert said.

"Kinda like having a vanity plate with your Social Security Number, ain't it?" Daryl said.

"Could be a favorite teacher," Michele said, "or an ex-girlfriend."

"None of our business," Daryl said. He opened the Start menu and navigated with mnemonic keys, pressing the first letter or underlined letter, so quickly that Robert could not see what Daryl was doing, but Robert saw the splash of the Recycle Bin and then Defrag condensing his hard drive. Inwardly, Robert sighed with relief. Daryl had deleted the log file and the hacker application and was taking the first steps of removing it from the hard drive forever.

"I assume you overwrite the sectors of the drive regularly?" Daryl said.

"Twice a week," Robert admitted. He had SystemWorks, and Peter Norton's minions had included the same program, they said, the NSA used to overwrite hard drives. Robert's small hard drives only took four hours, so he did it on Monday and Thursday nights.

"So what now?" Kevin said.

"Now," Daryl launched a browser, "we set our browser to nTropics' Web front-end for Microsoft Outlook, type JDonnelly in the User Name edit box, type Appelbaum in the password box, and click **Login**." On the monitor, the hourglass appeared. After a moment, it disappeared, and a Web approximation of the Microsoft Outlook window appeared.

"Microsoft is such shitty security," Kevin said.

He was parroting what he heard on the evening news, Daryl thought. "What you're seeing is not Microsoft's fault; simple passwords are user error. Now, watch me click **Calendar**."

The right half of the Web page changed to display today in John Donnelly's business life. "Oh, got a meeting with Dawson, Curtiss and Dunston this afternoon. Hope they can pour some money into the biz."

"What's he got for the tomorrow through Friday?" Robert said.

Daryl changed the calendar view to a week. Monday morning, Staff Cuts, 9:30. A good beginning to another busy day. Tuesday, arrive at eight, meeting with heads of departments 9:00, half hour with head of HR at 10:30. "Bingo," Daryl said. "11:00 through 2:00 tomorrow, lunch with Ed Muskel at Martello's, on South Central in Clayton." Of course it would be in tony Clayton, St. Louis's uppercrust downtown-away-from-downtown. A small copse of high rise buildings in the mostly flat plain of St. Louis County. Of course, the restaurant was within sight of the county jail, but he wouldn't mention that.

"That's right between the newspaper shop and Hoover's Oak Door." Robert said.

Daryl clicked the button to advance to the next week. "Holy Toledo," Daryl said. "You see that?"

"Yes," Robert said.

"What?" Michele got up leaned over the monitor with the boys like teens around the peephole into the girls' shower. That was a good metaphor, she thought; I ought to remember that.

"He's going to New York next Monday," Daryl said. "He's got Monday through Thursday marked as Out of Office."

"So? He's always going somewhere," Kevin said.

"Out of Office also means Out of House," Robert said.

"All right, so he's going to be at Martello's tomorrow at 11:30. What now?" Michele said.

"Okay, tomorrow, at 11:20, one of us is standing outside Martello's in a valet uniform. John Donnelly drives up, give that person his keys. Valet parks the car on the street and divides keys among four people. Four people go off in cardinal directions and copy all the keys on the ring. Everyone brings the keys back and the valet reassembles the key ring, and waits for John Donnelly to come out. Just like that." Robert started pacing.

"Why divide them into four?" Kevin blinked and furrowed his dark brows. Robert assumed those brows indicated a blond dye job, but maybe Kevin's head was sun-bleached from riding around in his convertible. Kevin did that all year round, but fortunately Missouri was not Saskatchewan.

"We don't want to go to a hardware store and have them make a copy of everything on a key ring," Robert said. "Besides, it's faster if we divide it up and go to different shops." He was estimating probably a dozen keys. One or two for the car could be eliminated. Probably one, something with a big plastic end which contained an implanted microchip. A couple for the house, a safety deposit box, a girlfriend's house and car, a couple for work. How many keys could one man have? If only they had time for due diligence.

"You want someone in the restaurant?" Daryl said.

"That's probably a good idea," Robert said. "Okay, someone in the restaurant to keep an eye on Donnelly. Who's got cell phones?"

"Me," Daryl said.

"I have one," Michele said. It was at the bottom of her purse, usually on, but seldom ringing.

"Who doesn't have a cell phone?" Kevin asked.

"I don't," Robert said. "Daryl, let me borrow yours. I'll be the valet; I've got an old vest that I can make into a valet's uniform. Michele, you want to have lunch at Martello's tomorrow? Make a reservation or get a table for two; one of the guys will come and get you when it's safe. You guys, be ready to go when I break apart the key ring."

"You probably want me on the inside," Daryl said.

"Why?" Robert said.

"I don't have a car," Daryl reminded him.

Of course not, Robert said, but his first instinct had been to offer the woman the least work. Sexist, he reminded himself. "Okay, Michele, I'll need your phone to coordinate."

"You want mine?" Kevin offered.

"I might need you to handle some special duties," Robert said. Actually, he meant I trust you least and want you on a leash of some sort.

"Okay," Kevin agreed.

"Daryl, find a list of hardware stores near the restaurant," Robert said.

"O Captain, my captain," Daryl said, but he turned to the keyboard and banged on the keys with the one hundred words per minute pace he prided himself on. "Okay, I got a couple near Clayton. Not a lot in Clayton proper, but some in nearby municipalities which should be reachable in ten minutes or less."

"Okay," Robert said. "Break the list down, and print them out. We don't know how many keys we'll each have, but try to keep it to two or three per shop."

Daryl clicked a couple more times on the keyboard, paused for a couple of seconds, and rattled the keyboard anew. "Okay," he said.

Robert's default printer, an old dot matrix, began chattering on the tractor-fed paper. It'd been built before any of them, except maybe Michele, had graduated from college, but Robert appreciated the sound of the pins striking the paper, and he had bought the printer and a hundred ribbons cheaply at a flea market. Better than a sixty dollar inkjet printer and a hundred cartridges at fifty dollars each, Robert thought, but not many people would calculate it that way. Robert was amazed that Daryl had created three different text files from the addresses he had found and had printed each on a separate page. Robert tore them from the printer as they came out. "Wow," Robert admitted. "Okay, here's one for each of us. Let's exchange cell numbers and meet here tomorrow at ten o'clock. Agreed?"

They agreed. Michele, Daryl, and Kevin disbursed their cell phone numbers.

"All right! I got nothing but good feelings about this," Kevin said. "I will see you guys tomorrow!"

Robert listened while Kevin went up the stairs. "Do you think it's a good plan?" Robert said to Michele.

"I guess the best plans are the ones that work," Michele reached deeply to the David Albernathy within her. Stoic and pragmatic. Unafraid.

"So we'll see you tomorrow?" Daryl said.

"Yeah," Michele said. "You guys seem to have all the angles covered. I'll be here tomorrow."

*   *   *   *

Kevin headed west on Page, cutting through pseudo-industrialized Overland. A lot of rusting tin-sided two-bay garages punctuated by the occasional house converted into a consignment shop or printing outfit passed down like an heirloom to a new generation that felt more trapped by its existence than its father did.

This gold bar thing was looking better and better, he thought. Sure, it might only be worth a couple of thousand, but that would be nice. His bank account had been floating at about one hundred dollars, give or take a week's groceries, and the severance package would cover another month's rent. That gave him six weeks to find a job, and it was damn tight out there.

It had been damn tight out there when he landed the job at nTropics. That had been too close. The telecommunications company he had been working for, the Great Nameless Backbone, cut some marketing positions when its stock price stagnated under ten dollars a share. It hadn't been just marketing, it had been eighteen percent of the whole company except vice-presidencies. After he kicked around for about three months, shooting resumes and returning the phone calls of every garage-based recruiter in the county, he missed a rent payment. Before he could miss another, though, he went to his parents' house in Crestwood, drove through the pillared gates of their upper-middle-class enclave, and asked his father for a loan. His old man sat in his well-worn blue plush La-Z-Boy, his legs not elevated in recognition of the somber occasion.

"If you can't find anything, you can always come back to the shop," Robert Horton, Junior, told his son, who was not Robert Horton

III.

In other circumstances, Kevin might have told his father what he thought of the machine shop. He'd spent the summers throughout college there, sweating in the one hundred and twenty degree heat of RHC Fabricators. Amid the clanging that made its way past the cheapest OSHA-compliant ear plugs available, working ten hour shifts and fighting to keep his wits about him and his hands out of the drill press when it came down, Kevin vowed he'd never do that again, that he'd be the first college-educated Horton to do something besides run a blue-collar union shop.

However, since he was asking for a loan of some four figures, he didn't want to be impolite, even though Kevin suspected his father would loan him the money anyway. "Thanks, but I want to do something outside the family business. I don't want the guys on the floor to get upset that the boss's college puke son was taking over."

"Boss put his puke son through college so he could run the business," his father said.

Kevin had felt his whole stomach quiver. His father had put his son through college to take up the family business, but Robert III had also wanted something more, so his quest for excellence ended in an ROTC commission and a downed plane which carried him and twenty-three men he was training to the great metal shop in the sky, where Kevin's brother's bit of Heaven might contain the molten scents that make another man's hell.

Although his father had come across with the loan, and even though Kevin had paid it back as quickly as possible when he landed the nTropics job, Kevin knew that going back again would lead to a job at RHC Fabricators, an end to the life Kevin knew and wanted, and the beginning of a life that top-ended at one hundred or so thousand a year with sixty-five hour work weeks capped with a bowling team and a softball league. And dozens of people who would mistakenly call him Robert.

No, he wouldn't go back to that dark living room that clung to him, with its heavy drapes, dark paneling, and marble hearth. Instead, he'd get in on the Donnelly caper, turning the bunch of misfits into a crack criminal outfit. Of course, Robert, Junior, would not be proud if he knew, but he had always extolled the virtue of being the best. He'd never know, Kevin thought, because Kevin would keep the ship running smoothly and adjust their course to avoid icebergs.

He glanced at the dashboard clock. It was 3:30, and soon the good people of the world would be getting out of work.

He had time before Renee, the girl across the breezeway from his apartment door, would be coming home. She worked at a consulting company in Maryland Heights, about eight blocks from their apartment complex, and she loved to walk home when the weather was nice. Renee Vu was her Americanized name, but she was originally from the People's Republic of China. Although he wasn't sure if that was China or Taiwan, Kevin knew that one of these days she'd let him take her out to dinner. Was she a virgin? Kevin didn't know whether he'd prefer that or not.

However, she would not be getting home for two hours. Hey, a mastermind of crime would scope out the targets for tomorrow, so Kevin pulled into a strip mall parking lot to turn around and head back towards the hardware shops near Clayton.

* * * *

Daryl cruised to the corner of Lackland and Ashby and waited for the light to change. Serious sports bikers pretended that they had a right to the road and would zoom into the left turn lane to turn with the light, but Daryl knew his limitations. He was a pedestrian on wheels, nothing more than an inconvenience to the hurried and discourteous vehicular commuters that clogged and coursed through the St. Louis streets.

He'd left Robert to his own devices at five o'clock. Robert had walked him out, setting the alarm and locking the front door. Daryl could guess where Robert was going. Daryl wouldn't have minded riding along, but five o'clock would give barely him enough daylight to get home from Robert's. It would be about an hour ride, and Daryl wanted the time to think.

Robert was sure that his valet ploy would work to get the keys to John Donnelly's house. The whole thing relied on social engineering, and that had never been Daryl's strong suit nor favorite method of attack. He could always count on the abstract stupidity of humanity, but somehow doing it face-to-face seemed to rub the target's face in it.

Daryl wondered what he thought he was doing. The light changed and he rolled into the intersection. He shouldn't have offered to sit inside the restaurant, but somehow it didn't seem as illegal as running around copying John Donnelly's keys. He'd never done anything really illegal in his life. An underage drink or two, but that was hardly wrong. Of course, he'd done his share of hacking, phreaking, and cracking, but nothing to hurt anyone or make money off of it. More exploratory, to see what systems were out there and if he could circumvent them. He was very good at the game of chess, Professor

Falken, you better believe it.

He slid up a driveway and onto the clear sidewalk, away from the swishing tires and impatient fenders. Of course, assuming they managed to break into John Donnelly's house and steal this bar of gold, it was hardly like they would make a mint off of it. Hell, he'd probably give his share to the Kirkwood YMCA to buy them a decent computer in their computer center. If his share came to that much.

So tomorrow he'd sit in the darkness eating the cheapest thing Martello's had, some bowl of spaghetti or pasta e fagioli, and he'd watch John Donnelly eat. If they managed to get keys without getting Robert thrown in the county slam....

Wow, Robert really put himself on the line. Uncharacteristic, maybe, but he probably didn't trust any of the others to pull it off. Daryl smiled and hoped they would, for Robert's sake.

* * * *

Michele highlighted a whole scene in the novel and hit CTRL+X. Cynthia had the opportunity to study abroad, an application really, and she had learned at the last minute she didn't qualify because she did not have enough credits to count as a junior. So of course she called David right up, and he came over to comfort her. Platonically, of course, because although this took place on pages ninety-three and ninety-four of the manuscript, the love between the twenty-year-old college student and the former Marine was supposed to smolder at this point.

Some smoldering. She almost needed a case cutter to get through the cardboard. The older ex-military college employee/school girl romance seemed a lot fresher six years ago when the seed of the idea began to germinate. Of course, the problems of college seemed so much more relevant when she entered the Writing and Literature program. After five years in the Marines, would David really be drawn to the innocence of Cynthia Thomkins? Who the hell believes in virginal and attractive college juniors anymore? Christ knows they hadn't eight years ago.

No, Cynthia was just the equivalent of some townie that David might have screwed in his young Marine zeal. Probably not just screwed, given David, but they probably didn't exchange Christmas greetings after David left. Or would they?

Michele drummed her fingers on the edge of the desk for a minute before standing up from the computer. Its latent whine of fans and processors would one day drive her mad, but not before she got more coffee. She stepped around the breakfast bar and into the kitchen where her old steel Cory percolator kept some coffee warm. She was no coffee connoisseur, with number four filters dripping Alpine mountain water over premium Brazilian grounds; she was an addict. She poured a cup into her comfortable Webster University mug and leaned back onto her counter, savoring the warmth of the porcelain in her hands.

Frodo grunted as he hopped into the kitchen to sniff at her feet. Michele put her coffee on the counter and leaned forward to stroke the Angora's ears, but he grunted and hopped back towards the living room. Onward to more of his rabbit projects, which mostly involved hopping around and sniffing. But it kept him occupied. "You know, if I don't get another job soon, I'm going to have to eat you," she promised. Sometime she had picked up her father's common refrain to her choice in pets, and she repeated it often. He would have known how to do it, how to skin and clean a rabbit, but that was not the sort of thing you passed on to a daughter, so he had not, and now that knowledge was gone with him. But not the threat to all pet rabbits.

What about tomorrow, she asked herself.

Tomorrow she'd make some keys, maybe, if everyone else followed through. If this silly plan worked. Robert and Daryl seemed to know what they were doing, but she imagined most of the things they came up with were part logic, part chutzpah.

*　　*　　*　　*

Robert got home at about 8:20. After walking Daryl to the road at 5:00, he'd hopped into his 1984 Toyota Tercel and headed for Clayton. Although he had known where to place the little red star for Martello's in the abstract map of Clayton in his head, he didn't have a real concrete sense of how the buildings on Central fit together. So he went to Clayton. The restaurant shared a building with the newspaper shop and had four floors of offices above it. A narrow, but clean, alley separated Martello's from the next building. The back faced a narrow alley with dumpsters and a walled parking lot. Robert parked on the street and walked both alleys and spent a cup of latte's worth of time in the coffee shop across Central watching the traffic around Martello's.

After his trip to Clayton, Robert stopped for dinner at another Italian place in eastern Creve Coeur. The restaurant, a member of a small upscale chain, not only offered delicious Italian food, but also the opportunity to observe a third-party valet operation. The restaurant hired an outside company to handle valet parking in the lot it shared with a movie theater; Robert assumed they got a rate and their valets got a small hourly wage plus tips. Robert did not use them, but sat in the early autumn chill with his restaurant pager to watch them work. All the valets wore to denote them as legitimate valets were red vests with ornate buttons and a name plate. And like lemmings, most people just hopped out of their cars and left their keys for the valet. Before the valet got in, though, he handed the driver a ticket. When a driver returned, he presented this ticket and the valet returned the car. And just once, Robert saw the ticket fall from the valet's grasp as he threaded his way through the lot. When Robert came out and followed the same path in a roundabout detour to his car, the ticket was still there.

Robert smoothed the ticket out and placed it on the dresser in his guest bedroom. He fingered through the accumulated clothing in his guest bedroom's closet, which contained mostly stuff he had outgrown or whose usefulness he outlived. For example, he had both his high school and college gowns hanging in the very left side back of the closet, where the light would not reach them. Of course, back there among them he had the suit he had worn to his mother's wedding. He had not worn it since the twelfth grade, but it was a nice enough suit, and he did not want to get rid of it just yet. Someday, when he was out of room, he'd donate it to the veterans' group, but not today.

Robert shoved everything hard to the right to illuminate the closet contents with the light from the guest bedroom. His fingers lit upon a light medium blue vest and took it out. He had worn the vest for two years of high school when he was working for the local off, off-chain grocery store as a bagger, or what they would come to call a utility clerk. It wasn't maroon, like those used by Morgen Valet Service, but it would do. Or John Donnelly would not give him the keys. Or John Donnelly would not give him the car keys, would call the police, and Robert would explain it to a pair of detectives over a conference table.

Clifton, the other bagger at the grocery strore, thought the vests made them look like the flying monkeys out of *The Wizard of Oz*, doing the bidding of the evil witch Sondra Silverman. Robert had no problems with Ms. Silverman, and no problems with the duties of the job, but he knew he was not going to be a lifer, unlike maybe Clifton. Heck, he even liked wearing the vest. It was something like a uniform, and it made him stand out as someone who could help the customer.

Robert pulled the vest out of the closet and took it off the hanger. With the vest in hand, he shoved all of the clothing back to its original position, into the mothballed dark. He put the hanger to the extreme right, handy for when he needed to hang something back in this closet. Like this vest when he was done with it tomorrow. Or maybe not.

Robert sat at the sewing machine in his guest room. It had been his grandmother's, and since no one else in the family sewed, he got it as default furniture for his new house. It came in handy, though, and Robert was growing fond of it. Although he was not an artist with it yet, he managed to save on some clothing bills with judicious repairs and alterations. Robert sprung the machine from the bowels of the cabinet.

The vest had plain blue plastic buttons. First thing, he would replace those with some more elaborate gold buttons. Second thing.... Robert looked at it, imagined the vest with the gold buttons. If it were a jacket, of course, he would want some tassels on the shoulders, but it was just a vest. Too much would make him look like a bellhop. Like Ms. Silverman, Mr. or Mrs. Morgen did not go to extremes when clothing the employees. Just some gold buttons and a name plate and he would be set. Robert took the scissors out of the sewing machine cabinet's drawer and snipped off the blue buttons.

After he sewed the new buttons on, Robert took another look at the vest. Plain, but elegant, he thought, or hoped. He debated whether to put on the name of the fictitious parking company. Probably not, as the anonymity would prevent anyone from remembering him. He threaded some blue thread into the machine and touched up a few frayed seams.

He reached back into his closet and felt through it, looking for the old delivery uniform. He'd never worn it professionally, of course, but he'd bought it at a yard sale as part of a lot. He wanted to buy just a couple of shirts and a jacket, but the woman running the sale was pushing to unload an ex-husband's leftovers, and Robert got the uniform and eight ties as well, no extra charge. The shirt of the uniform still had a name plate pinned to it. With a set of dark slacks, white shirt, tie, and dress shoes, tomorrow Robert would become Richard, the valet.

He'd never talked to John Donnelly one on one, and that was to his advantage. He'd be in the uniform, and he'd gel his hair up a little, and that ought to be enough to disguise him. Too much disguise would complicate things unnecessarily.

Tomorrow, John Donnelly would give him his car keys. He would divide them equally between Michele, Kevin, and himself. He would make copies of the keys he had. He would reassemble the keys and then bring John Donnelly his car back, and no one would know.

Not that he slept any better thinking that.

The Morning They Get the Keys

Daryl knocked on Robert's door at 9:30, as promised. Robert answered the door, fully dressed except for the vest, and shaven. Of course, Daryl had never seen Robert unshaven, and Daryl wondered if his developer friend even had to shave every day yet. Some guys never do.

"Good morning." Robert motioned Daryl in. Daryl was dressed nicely, too, wearing slacks, a white shirt, and a tie. Robert was amazed that Daryl could ride a bike looking like that. Robert cast a glance over the quiet street, packed with small houses and crumbling retaining walls. No one about.

"Coffee?" Robert said. He was proud of the little Braun coffee maker he had, a ten cup number four cone. He used brown filters because he had heard they were the best. Of course, he had heard that from the same subscription coffee service that had sent him the coffee maker, but they kept him stocked with almost all the gourmet mocha coffee he could drink for only twenty-some dollars a month, so he gave them the benefit of the doubt.

"Nah," Daryl said. "Caffeine's a diuretic, and the last thing I want is to need to pee every ten minutes between 10 and 1."

"Good point." Robert poured himself a cup anyway, his third of the day.

"So do you think the others will show?" Daryl said.

"If they don't, it will be up to me to copy the keys. I suppose I could guess which on the ring are house keys, but it might be tight if it's a quick lunch."

"I guess so," Daryl said. He couldn't believe Robert would go through with it if the others didn't show.

"Michele's here," Robert said, relieved. He had not wanted to seem irresolute.

"I didn't hear the bell." Daryl was surprised by the announcement.

"She just went down the road. I guess she's going to turn around down the block and park in front of my house. I saw the reflection of her wagon in the Alfressons' dining room window," Robert nodded at his kitchen window.

"Ah," Daryl said. Sure enough, he heard a car pull up out front and turn off, followed quickly by a car door. "Aren't you going to meet her at the door?"

"No. If I meet her at the door, she might suspect I have been watching." Even though I have been watching, Robert thought. The best watchers remain unobserved.

Robert got up when Michele rang the bell. Daryl followed. Michele stood on the porch, watching Kevin walk across the street from his parked car. Robert ushered them into the basement.

"So, let's hear it," Kevin said. "You guys have worked out the plan to the minute, right? Good job. What do we have to do?"

"Well," Robert said, waiting for Daryl to interject if he had any better idea. Of course, last night they had not discussed anything, but Robert was affording him any opportunity to interject. Or any of them for that matter, although Robert did not expect to hear nor expect to agree with any suggestions Kevin or Michele made. "Here's what we're going to do," he began to pace.

Robert noted they took up the same positions, almost, as last night. Daryl sat in the chair at the computer, Michele sat at the bench. Instead of sitting on the steps, though, Kevin leaned on the workbench. A little closer to Michele than Robert would have liked, but that was their business.

"All right. You guys know what John Donnelly drives?" Robert said.

"A BMW 328i, green with cream seats and a rear spoiler, Missouri plate NTRPX," Daryl offered. Of course, Robert thought, Daryl had run a DMV check for Donnelly. Or he had checked the DMV's computers himself. "I could see it from my cubicle," Daryl explained.

Good lesson in that, Robert thought. Keep it simple. "Have you seen it, Michele?"

"Yes, I have. Why?" she said.

"Good. At about ten thirty, you're going to be watching for John Donnelly to come out of the nTropics lot. Call Daryl's cell phone when Donnelly gets into his car, and again when he gets near Clayton."

"I thought you were going to take my cell phone," she said.

"Not right away. Daryl, I'll drive you into Clayton and I'll drop you off on the corner of Central and Maryland, and you have to walk a half block. I'll park on Forsyth between Bemiston and Central. There's an alley that runs right up behind the restaurant and an alley next to the restaurant. I'll go into the coffee shop across from Martello's. Daryl, you should go into that coffee shop before me. I'll sit at another table. When Michele calls to say Donnelly's leaving, answer and say, 'Oh, hi there!' loud enough for me to hear. When you do, I'll leave the coffee shop, go get the vest, and get ready.

"When Michele calls a second time, get out of the coffee shop fast and get over to Martello's. That'll be my sign that he's coming. I'll take up position and get his keys."

"Where am I?" Kevin said.

"Park on the street on the northwest corner of Bemiston and Forsyth, facing south on Bemiston. There's a fire hydrant there, so use it if you have to. I'll give you your keys as I drop Donnelly's car in the lot on the corner of Forsyth and Bemiston."

"What about me?" Michele said.

"I want you parked on Forsyth just west of Central on the north side. I'll stop and give you your keys and get your phone. Now, when you're done copying keys, you can find me on the corner of Maryland and Bemiston. I'll be sitting on a half wall, reading a magazine. Give me the original keys and walk around the block to where you parked your cars. I call Daryl on his cell phone and he comes out of the restaurant, and we regroup here." Robert brushed his hands together to indicate that was that. His palms were moist. He put them in his pockets and squeezed the napkins.

"Should we synchronize watches?" Kevin smirked.

"That's not a bad idea," Daryl said.

"That might be a little much," Robert said. "However, I have 10:06, so you know where your watch stands in relation to mine. Anyone have any questions?" He looked them over, wondering what they thought, and if they could do it.

"What if he doesn't use valet service?" Michele said.

Robert pursed his lips and squeezed the napkins, but stopped when he realized what an odd sight that must present. "The two dangers of failure in the plan come at the beginning and the end, really. If he doesn't give me his car keys, I walk away, Daryl has lunch, I send you guys on your way, and that's it. More problematic, though, is if we get the keys but he comes out before we're done with them. If this happens, Daryl calls me on the cell phone and we just keep going. John Donnelly might not ever know exactly what happened to his keys, but we're done."

"It's the Blue Screen Of Death," Daryl said. "We can't recover from that."

"Not a good idea to try," Robert acknowledged. "All right, Kevin, what are you doing?"

"What?" Kevin said. He put the electronic thing back down quickly. He was just twiddling a circuit board of some sort. He had put his hand on it as he leaned on the bench. It wasn't a computer card because it didn't have the one side that sticks into the back end of the computer and into the motherboard. Or not one he had seen before. It wasn't delicate, was it? Or dangerous?

"What are you supposed to do as part of the plan?" Daryl said. Robert was having them recite their parts back. Good call.

"I sit in my car at the corner of Bemiston and Forsyth, copy the keys, and drop them off to you on Maryland and Bemiston. I got it." They didn't need to drill it into him. He might not be a card-carrying Acme Super-Genius like these guys, but he wasn't stupid.

"Michele?" Robert said.

"I wait for John Donnelly. When he leaves, I call Daryl. When we get near Clayton, I call Daryl again. Then I wait for you at Forsyth and Central, and then I drop the keys off with you at Maryland and Bemiston." Michele frowned. "What if he doesn't go into nTropics and just goes to the restaurant?"

"If he doesn't leave by ten to eleven, call Daryl and tell him. He can grab me, and we can let Kevin know on the way out. No pain, no gain, no loss." Robert said.

"What, am I waiting in my car for over an hour?" Kevin said. "That's not exactly fair. Why don't I follow JD from nTropics?"

"Your car is not inconspicuous," Daryl said. "Isn't that why you bought it?"

"There are a lot of Eclipses out there," Kevin pled.

"There are a lot of Porsches, too, but you notice every one you see, don't you?" Daryl replied.

"Besides, you wouldn't want to make Michele do that, would you? That's unsportsmanlike," Robert said.

Michele felt the heat rising into her face and prepared the usual responses to sexism, but Daryl offered a slightly theatrical wink. Of course, they were only trying to convince Kevin that they had given Kevin the proper role, but she still didn't fit the role of the dainty princess to be guarded.

"All right, fine," Kevin conceded. Of course, he had not thought of it that way, and he really wouldn't want to make a girl do the heavy lifting, He's stop for something to eat on the way and he'd be all right. Maybe now that he was laid off, and soon to be rich, he'd have the time in the mornings to eat something for breakfast. Eat and dress well— that would be the life.

"Everyone have his or her list?" Robert said. His hardware shops were tucked into his back pocket. Michele nodded, but Kevin looked slightly blanker than normal. "Your hardware list? Is this yours, then?" Robert proffered a folded printed copy. He had printed second copies for everyone, but he might as well save face for Kevin. Kevin nodded and took the folded paper. "We should all leave, then," Robert said. "Plan to meet back here by two o'clock at the latest."

*   *   *   *

Robert dropped off Daryl as planned and parked his car on Meramac just south of Forsyth. It was one block west of where Michele would park and pointing in the direction of Brentwood and his share of hardware stores. It would take him eight minutes to get to the first one, and then four minutes to get to the second, and then seven minutes to get to the third, and then four minutes to get to the fourth, and then seven minutes back to park on Maryland or just off of Maryland. He had spent about twenty minutes last night, going over the routes. When he lit upon a route he liked, he drove it, in the dark of one o'clock this morning.

The route he planned followed a circle and ensured he would only have to make right turns. Left turns into traffic could add a significant percentage to the thirty minutes he allocated. At one o'clock, he had not had to contend with traffic signals, but he had added thirty seconds for each that he passed through. He would not hit most of them, or have to wait a full cycle for most of them, but it gave him a time estimate.

Of course, if he had world enough and time, he would have tried alternate routes and seen the traffic signal cycles firsthand. But he had not, and he would make do with this route. So he parked on Meramac, facing south toward Brentwood.

He carried the vest, rolled tightly into a ball, into the coffee shop. Daryl was sitting in the corner, pouring over a spread *Riverfront Times*, the local alternative weekly. He had his back three quarters of the way to the door, but Robert guessed he was watching out of the corner of his eye. Robert went to the counter and ordered a cup of house coffee without refills. Of course, the chain did not offer refills like a local coffee shop might have, but Robert specified just the same, and regretted that he indicated that he was not planning to be there a while. Not that it mattered to anyone else. He took his clear glass mug of dark roast to a table by the window and sat so that he was looking out across Central at Martello's. It was ten twenty-six.

* * * *

Daryl's phone vibrated in his front pants pocket. He fished it out and flipped it open. "Hello?" he said, raising his voice unnaturally. He hoped it sounded natural to everyone but Robert.

"It's Michele," Michele said.

"Oh, hi there!" Daryl cued.

"John Donnelly got to nTropics right after I did, but he just grabbed some stuff and we're on our way. I'm headed east on Olive at about Lindbergh."

"That's great," Daryl said.

* * * *

Robert looked at his watch when Daryl spoke into his flip-phone. 10:46. Kevin should be grudgingly in place, he thought. Robert lifted the coffee cup and swallowed the remaining two swallows of rather warm coffee more quickly than he would have liked. However, he was late for something important. He hoped to exude that, anyway. Robert got up and went out the door.

He turned left, cutting up the block at a measured pace. Not a hurried pace, but not a window-shopping saunter, either, he thought. Enough to bring him to the corner of Central and Maryland in approximately two minutes, about a minute or two to the alley, and about a minute thirty down the alley again. He casually shrugged on the vest. He was about to come onto duty for the lunch crowd. The backdoor of Martello's was closed, the dumpster closed and neat, with no rotting vegetables on the pavement around it.

As he strolled down the alley, he looked across the parking lot on Forsyth and Bemiston. It was an hourly lot, which kept away the full-time Clayton employees. Robert counted three open spots he could see over the wall, which was a good sign there'd be room for the Beemer. Best of all, Kevin Horton sat behind the driver's seat of his car, watching this row of buildings, too carefully for Robert's taste. Robert thought he saw Kevin perk up when he saw Robert in the alley. Of course, if the alternative was between Kevin being there and Kevin being too attentive.... Robert wasn't sure.

At 10:52, Robert stepped into the feeder alley. He put his hands in his pockets, gripping the napkins. He wanted to look like he was on break or waiting to start his shift. Most of the time, people came outside to smoke. He hadn't thought of that until now, but he felt bare without a cigarette prop. It was all in his head, he assured himself. He did not notice anyone paying him undue attention. Of course, anyone

66

looking at him suspiciously would be paying him due attention since he was up to no good. He didn't know how he felt about that, really, thinking of himself as a bad guy. On the road to hardened felondom, one had to start with the first. From here on out, they would be much easier, and it was better to get past the shame inherent in traditional morality.

He squeezed the napkins again and looked at his watch. 10:53. On paper, or at least on the timetable in his head, the plan mapped out so nicely. A little schedule, one line per item. 10:46, leave coffee shop, 10:48 turn corner, 10:50 turn up side alley. He had failed to account for the long minutes between the lines on the schedule. Stratocumulus clouds drifted westward, indicating a cool front coming through. Donnelly better get here before the temperature dropped too much from the unseasonable late summer temperatures returned to earth. Robert shifted his weight on his legs and watched the coffee shop door.

*   *   *   *

Daryl's phone vibrated again on the tabletop. As he flipped it open, he glanced at the time. 10:58, or by 11:01 by Robert's watch. "Hello?" he said.

"We're on Hanley at Delmar," Michele said.

"How are you?" Daryl got up from his chair and closed the paper, leaving it face up on the table for the next patron.

"I've stayed several car lengths back; I don't think he's made me." Michele, gripping the wheel loosely with her right hand, wondered if that's how the pros really talked. The amateurs certainly did.

"Great!" Daryl pushed through the single glass door into the foyer, and then beyond, into the grey cloudshine. Robert leaned against the news shop's wall just deep enough inside the alley that only someone directly across the street would see him. None of the passersby paid any attention to Robert.

"You need a ride back to Robert's?" Michele said.

"I was going to ride with Bob," Daryl said. None of the passersby paid him any attention, either, as he stepped to the curb to jaywalk. At the first opportunity, he did so.

"He could be a while. Why don't you meet me at that coffee shop after you leave Martello's?"

"I just left there. Why don't we meet at the Bread Co.?" Daryl said.

"More coffee, though?" Michele said.

"Yes'm," Daryl said. "I'm here now, and I'll see you there later.

67

Bye." Without waiting for Michele to respond, he flipped the phone shut and pulled open the heavy eight-paneled door. He hoped she hadn't thought he was at the Bread Company.

Martello's interior was slightly dimmer than the overcast outside. Dark wood paneling, deep red tablecloths, and dark chairs and booth seats absorbed almost all light offered by the indirect fixtures allotted to each table. A nice, open floor plan, without the twists and turns and half walls that restaurateurs believed could separate smoke from air. Only one other table was taken so far, and Daryl would have the pick of the lot, or whatever the maître d' picked for him.

"How many, sir?" the maître d' said. A stocky older gentleman with dark hair parted from a high forehead.

You're not in Applebee's anymore, Toto, Daryl thought. "Two," he improvised to the gentleman thumbing the menus in the stand's pocket.

"This way, sir," the gentleman said. He selected a table far from the door, in a corner, with two extra sets of silverware. "Would you care to order a drink or an appetizer while you await your party?"

"Bring me a cola," Daryl said. He had eight dollars in his pocket, and he wondered if he could afford a salad with his soda. Or if he could afford the soda.

Telling the maître d' that he was waiting to meet someone—now that was a stroke of inspiration. He could leave abruptly, indignantly when his party did not show up. He would have to learn to trust his instincts more. He'd get out of here with nothing more on his tab than a soda and maybe a salad. He opened the menu and glanced over it. Just a soda.

*   *   *   *

Robert waited a minute and a half after Daryl went into the restaurant to reluctantly push himself away from the wall. His watch said 11:05. The top of the hour could mean he was going on duty at 11, for the lunch crowd. Rock on!

He took his hands from his pockets and wiped them on his trouser legs purposefully, and stepped onto the sidewalk. If he were coming to the restaurant, he'd swing by it first and look for a close parking spot and would then start a circling search pattern for something nearby. This whole plan hinged on John Donnelly following a similar habit. Of course, the plan so far hinged upon a series of happenstances and things falling like tumblers into place around them. It would also take some effort and silence on the part of almost strangers, and even then had little chance of success. He probably ought to focus on the concrete details of the task at hand and only the task at hand, whatever that might be in the grander plan.

Robert felt the heat in his face when he recognized the green BMW coming around the corner on Bemiston. The plate matched, he could see from his position in the center of the sidewalk. He was really glad that Martello's didn't have a front window.

John Donnelly slowed as he approached the restaurant. Robert assumed JD was looking him over, so he tried to look official and busy. His heart jackhammered and he wanted to dry his hands on the napkins again, but he wasn't sure that would look appropriate. Besides, you don't shake hands with a valet. So he didn't dry his hands and concentrated on not flushing or perspiring too much, knowing that the concentration would probably serve just the opposite.

John Donnelly stopped in front of the restaurant, and it was show time. Robert bounded between the parked cars. Energetically, he hoped, a perky member of the service industry-like. John Donnelly opened his door, so there was no way Robert could be accused of breaking and entering or carjacking. He drew the Morgen Valet Service ticket from his vest pocket.

"Dining this morning, sir?" Robert said. Actually, he projected a little more than he should have. He practically shouted it into JD's face as he got out of the car. Too perky, he thought.

"Yes," John Donnelly said.

Robert saw no glimmer of recognition. Why would John Donnelly remember him? Robert was but one of many expendable, replaceable cogs in his machine. "Wonderful, sir." Robert offered the claim check to John Donnelly and slid behind the wheel. He'd never driven a BMW before, but guessed it would be like any other car. He was glad it was not a stick-shift, because he hadn't driven one in a while and did not want to peel out or pop the clutch. Valets drove all kinds of cars all the time. As he put it into drive and hit the gas, he saw John Donnelly in the passenger side mirror stepping through the parked cars and toward the restaurant without a care in the world. Thank you, good sir.

It had crossed Robert's mind to take John Donnelly's car as he went to get his share of keys copied, but that was fraught with danger. He could get into a traffic accident. He could get pulled over. John Donnelly could check his odometer compulsively. No, he'd use his own car for the change.

Robert fingered the key ring in the ignition and was pleasantly surprised when its jingle was highly pitched. Not that many keys, probably a dozen or so. As he drove, he began to unbutton the vest.

He got to the lot, took the ticket from the automatic gate, and parked. He slid off the vest before getting out of the car. He had thought about leaving the vest in the car, but if they did not make it back in time, it would be evidence for the police. They might make fingerprints on the buttons or even the fabric, and he didn't want to waste time being careful with it. It would be the only physical evidence to back up JD's story if he came out before Robert was back. He rolled the vest, wiped the wheel and gear shift with the tail of the fabric, and used the ball to pull open the door.

Kevin was definitely perked up now, Robert could see. The parking lot attendant in the glass booth was reading a paper and only glanced once to assure himself that Robert was a patron and not some random malfeasant looking for a CD player from one of the cars.

As he walked to Kevin's car, Robert fingered the keys. Eleven on the ring, counting the two with the BMW logo. Nine keys remained. Two were too small to be anything but padlocks. Gym and shed, maybe. That left seven for the three of them. Robert drew a small pack of adhesive dot stickers from his wallet. They had fallen out of a book he bought at a yard sale. Someone had been using them as a bookmark, and Robert had placed them in a stationery drawer in case he needed them. Today, he needed them. He had numbered each sticker one through twenty-three after using the twenty-fourth, or perhaps the zeroth if the stickers were a 0-based index, to make sure the adhesive still worked and would stick to a key. He numbered the keys on the ring and took the ones to copy off the ring.

He opened Kevin's passenger door and got in. "We lucked out. He doesn't have many keys."

"Wow, he just gave them to you?" Kevin said.

"Drive. Go west down Forsyth, turn north on Meramac, and drop me off by the corner," Robert said. "Here are your two keys." Robert put them into the cup holder in the console between him and Kevin.

Kevin pulled away from the curb. "Maybe I should get into that valet scam if I don't get another job soon. Can I borrow that vest?"

"No," Robert said. "Remember, corner of Maryland and Bemiston, and don't take too long."

"I got it." Kevin pulled to the curb at the specified corner.

Michele watched Robert approach her car. She reached over and unlocked the passenger door when he neared. She had the printed list of hardware stores on her dashboard. "You get two." Robert handed her numbers six and eight. "Good luck. Drop me by my car on Meramac."

At 11:11, she did.

Returning the Keys

Robert parked on Bemiston north of Maryland. Clayton's downtown ended abruptly a half block north of Maryland, where a wall and gateposts beside Bemiston explicitly indicated that business was on the south side, and the convenient, urbanesque two- and three-story condominium and house living were on the north side. Robert parked on the business side. No doubt, Clayton had a residents' watch in effect, and someone would tow his Tercel.

Robert grabbed the fast food bag and vest from his passenger seat and crossed Maryland. The office building contained an engineering firm, a promotional agency, and various other interests. Any one of which, or none of which, Robert could be dressed for if he only had a jacket. He didn't have a jacket, but he did have lunch. So Robert sat down on the wall, opened the bag, and started eating his processed chicken.

It was eleven forty-nine. He had missed his mark by eight minutes, but part of that was stopping for the food. He'd probably look better eating his lunch before he went to work, so he stopped and went inside. Early lunchers were starting to crowd the drive thru, but Robert was able to get counter service quickly, and he ordered something he saw was ready. He probably ought to not improvise so freely, he realized. The others counted on him. And the chicken was old.

At eleven fifty, he spotted Michele striding west on Maryland. He was people-watching, he assured everyone around him, he hoped, and his glance did not linger over her longer than the normal male-female appraisal, he hoped. She was wearing a dark-colored skirt, snug on her womanly hips, that only showed her calves. Capped with an evergreen, long-sleeved blouse. Robert wished he knew enough about fashion to know what her clothing indicated about how she saw herself, but he didn't, and he didn't plan to start reading the slicks to learn. Maybe he would ask her. She moved smoothly, lightly athletically down the street. He expected she had seen him but was not looking at him as she walked up the road.

Robert hoped that was just long enough for sizing up an attractive woman. He trailed his glance along the far side of Maryland and up a block or two. Nothing. He had a piece of chicken and looked over his shoulder. Kevin was walking up Bemiston rapidly. Robert's heart started to beat faster. It probably wasn't a good thing for both Michele and Kevin to show up at the same time to give Robert something. That would look eminently suspicious. Michele reached the corner of the building across the street and turned to go inside. Robert was certain it was Michele, he thought.

Robert was right where he was supposed to be, Kevin saw, and he was relieved. Not that he would have ever been on the hook if this little scam went south. After all, Robert was the one making contact. Kevin was an accessory, though, but that was only if Robert talked. And he probably would, cutting a deal for himself at their expense. Kevin understood, and he would have done the same thing if it came down to it.

Robert had stopped for lunch, Kevin saw. Robert probably would have blown a gasket if he'd stopped for something to eat. Kevin stood beside him at the wall. "Can I have one of those?" he said.

Robert looked up suddenly. "Roger! Hey, it's good to see you, man."

Roger? Oh, right. Kevin got it. He was Roger. A code name. "Stevie, Stevie, Stevie. What brings you here? Can I have a nugget?" He wasn't kidding about the nugget. He had skipped breakfast, opting instead to roll out of bed, shower, shave, and be on time this morning.

"You bet." Robert offered the box of chicken to him. Kevin took a pair of nuggets and ate them quickly. "Fifty cents a nugget," Robert said.

"What?" Kevin, or Roger (he reminded himself) said.

"Reach into your pocket and dig out a bunch of quarters. Hand them to me." Robert said. Maybe that was too metaphorical for Kevin to pick up, but he had handled the name thing very well.

"All right, all right. And here I thought we were old friends," Kevin said. He reached into his right pants pocket and took out the four keys there. He better not really want quarters, Kevin thought, and he dropped the keys into Robert's palm.

Robert pocketed the keys. Maybe Kevin wasn't as dumb as a post. "Hey, friends are friends, but nuggets are nuggets."

That probably belonged in a commercial somewhere, Kevin thought. Maybe that's where Robert got it. "All right, all right," Kevin said. He wondered if he could get another nugget, but that would cost him real money.

All right, move along, Robert thought. "Where are you headed?"

"Eh?" Kevin said. Where was he headed? Robert was asking for a cover story. Some sort of improvisation test, Kevin guessed. "Oh, you mean why am I here in Clayton. I went over to the shoe store," he offered, "but I couldn't find the sneakers I wanted."

"You could have parked in their lot," Robert said.

Parry/riposte, Kevin thought. Just like fencing class back at Ladue Horton Watkins High School. The mad Hungarian professor, some Olympian or something, ran the community college class like it was Eastern Bloc life-or-death. Hell, Kevin had only taken it to add some spice to his life, to make him that complete and interesting package women would want. All he got was a couple of welts on the chest and finally understanding what the hell riposte meant. And that touché sometimes hurt if your opponent whipped the foil blade. "But they sometimes check to see your receipt and charge you money if you didn't buy anything. Defending their parking turf from freeloaders, you know. And since I wasn't sure they had the Nikes I wanted, I didn't want to risk it. A quarter in a parking meter's better than a four dollar pair of shoelaces." Riposte. Robert was doing his best to make this fun, he thought.

"Ah," Robert acknowledged. This role-playing must only be an extra step from scamming women for Kevin, he thought.

"I better get back to my car before that quarter turns into a ticket," Kevin said. "Thanks for the nuggets." He headed off westward on Maryland. Of course he was headed toward his parked car somewhere down Maryland, so he couldn't turn back and head down Bemiston, right?

"See ya." Robert watched Kevin head the proper way down Maryland, not heading right back to his car. People kept passing. Four people came out of the building, a woman and a man individually and two men together, to smoke cigarettes outside the doors. Nobody paid any attention whatsoever to Robert and Kevin, and that was almost worse than everyone staring. Professional law enforcement would not be obvious, and Robert had not had the extensive experience with them that he could make a cop straight away. Best plan, of course, would be to assume they're all cops.

Two minutes passed before Michele stepped out of the door across the street. 12:06. John Donnelly had been in the restaurant almost an hour. As an executive, of course he was not constrained to the thirty minutes or an hour an employee of nTropics had for lunch, hunched over his or her desk eating a frozen microwaved dinner for lunch and writing e-mail in a futile attempt to remain employed. However, with travel time to and from Creve Coeur, time was growing tight, or at least Robert thought so. Of course, Robert would feel a damn sight a lot better about the whole bit in an hour if they succeeded. The Don't Walk sign that held Michele on the other side of the street didn't help. He put the empty chicken container back into the paper bag and wiped his hands, including the palms, on the napkins as though it were nothing.

After an eternity that lasted 20 seconds, Michele started to cross. Robert watched her cross, watching longer than he had watched others approach, but it would be according to plan. Or at least the new plan. She stepped onto the curb lightly. "Hey, Trish!" Robert called. He wondered if she'd get it as quickly as Kevin had, and hoped she would. She looked at him. "Patricia Gonsalez," he said. "Steve Casper. We went to high school together?" He supposed every city had its peccadilloes, its little flairs of the quaint. Whenever St. Louisians accumulated, the bar, the coffeehouse table, or on the street, they asked each other The Question. Where did you go to high school? Even those who had moved beyond the cliques of socs and goths, onto the trade associations and lingering collegiate drinking circles, somehow calculated and stratified the respondent based on the response.

"Steve?" Michele said.

"We were in English III together. I sat one row over and behind you."

"Oh, right, how are you?" Michele came over.

Robert stood up. Without heels, she was about his height, five eight. "I am well. I haven't seen you in forever. What are you doing these days?"

"I'm looking for work," Michele admitted. Robert was certainly playing this up. Nobody was going to pay any attention if she just gave him the keys.

"A lot of people are," Robert said. "Hey, have you got a pen and some paper? I'll give you my number, and you can give me a call if you want."

"Sure," she said. That was her cue to fumble in her purse for the keys, she bet. She opened her slim bag and got out an envelope and a pen, slipping the keys into the envelope so that Robert could see what she'd done. Absolutely smooth and fluid, she surprised herself.

Robert smiled. She was clever, and he was impressed with her improvisation. He held the envelope in his left hand, tipping it to slide the keys into his palm. He wrote Steve Casper on the envelope and his phone number. He could have written a phony, but maybe she would call it sometime. He doubted it, but if he had written a phony she would never have gotten him if she did call it. He hoped his face wasn't flushing. "Hey, it's good to see you, but I've got to get back to work. Give me a call and we can go for coffee sometime." He passed the envelope back to her, waved, and started down Bemiston. He'd cut down an alley and be back in his position when John Donnelly came out.

As he walked, he thumbed the keys back onto John Donnelly's ring, using the numbered tags to guide him. After arranging the keys, he took off the labels, balled them, and put them into his left pocket. He rubbed the head of each key to remove any lingering adhesive and put Donnelly's ring into his right pocket.

He then collected all loose keys into a small plastic bag and sealed it with its zipper strip and put them, along with his keys, into his left pocket. It wasn't the most flattering arrangement for the line of his slacks, but he was on the clock and not trying to make the cover of *GQ*. At 12:10, he was back in the alley without a buzz from Daryl.

* * * *

The waiter's stops at the table grew more frequent as the lunch hour approached and arrived. "Would you like to order an appetizer, sir? Shall I bring you another drink?" Beneath the polite questions, of course, the waiter was implying that Daryl better spend some money or hit the road. His table was prime real estate now, ripe for generating real revenue, not for a young man who had paced himself on a first two and a half dollar soda so that he could stretch a second into his second hour of residence.

John Donnelly and his two associates ate appetizers at 11:15, salads at 11:35, and got their main courses at 11:50. From what Daryl could see from across the crowding restaurant, John Donnelly was having some pasta with white sauce. One of his associates, the older of the two, was having something parmesan. The younger was having something red. Daryl envied them their lunch.

The three made a matched set of young yuppies. John Donnelly, with his brushed back brown hair and capped teeth, might have shared a barber with these guys. At least they were straight yuppies, Daryl thought, and not the sort to wear Bermuda shorts and Birkenstocks to affect their business meetings. John Donnelly did talk while chewing, though, shattering any illusions of gentility Daryl might have harbored.

To keep from staring, Daryl looked again over the warm, wooden interior of the building. They must have spent a fortune at the Hunting

Lodge Depot store. Even his continuing quips, made mentally for none but himself, were distracting him from the growing claustrophobia he was feeling, surrounded by others with whom he did not belong. He was not a member of the upscale Clayton eating crowd. He could gather fabulous wealth, theoretically, with his computer skills and genius, by being in the right company at the right time more likely, but he was pretty sure that he would feel the same way. Money couldn't change a man that way, he suspected.

The cell phone vibrating in his pocket greatly relieved Daryl. "Hello?" he said.

"We got them," Robert said.

"Great. I'll see you soon," Daryl said.

"Wait, Daryl. You've got to let me know when he's coming out," Robert said.

"I've been in here for over an hour doing nothing but drinking a soda. I'm not going to sit here waiting for another hour for nothing!" Daryl motioned to the waiter, who anticipated the result of the heated cell phone call and produced the check presently.

"Daryl, come on, cut me a break. You're going to leave me hanging out here with nothing."

"Perhaps, but I'd rather not discuss that right now," Daryl said, slapping his phone shut. The waiter, lingering at the edge of another table, finished pouring water for a couple of slacker yuppies, slappies essentially, and went away. Daryl flipped open the leather binder for the bill and slipped all eight of his singles into it.

He charted an advance path through the occupied tables and half-strewn chairs to the door. He didn't want to avoid Donnelly so much as to go out of his way to the wide path by the bar. Instead, he wove to a close pass that would take him behind John Donnelly, with a table of three lunching, business casual women as a buffer. He slowly wound his way through the tables and chairs, avoiding any incidental contact or attention, sometimes waving his gangly arms to keep his balance as he tried a particularly difficult contortion or step between. As he brushed the chair of a businesswoman, she cleared her throat. Daryl's mind recoiled, trying to recall if he had brushed any particular part of her that would constitute sexual assault.

Daryl thought himself home free when he neared the maître d' stand. He'd passed Donnelly's table unseen. Nothing but a gracious but regretful maître d' and the thick wooden door stood between him and fresh, clean air.

Unfortunately, at that moment, the woman who would have most likely been called Woman #2 in the movie version of *The Great Geek*

Caper promoted herself in the credits to Choking Woman. The woman he had brushed must have inhaled when she should have swallowed, laughed with her mouth full, spoken with her mouth full, forgotten to chew thirty times, or done one of the varied things mothers tried to nettle out of their children. She cleared her throat desperately, coughed slightly, and graduated into a full-blown choke.

Daryl turned when he realized what the sound was, and his eyes flickered over the room. Other patrons, too, turned to look at this woman, her face beginning to redden in contrast with her blonde hair, her hands splayed on the table on either side of her plate, her companions gaping. The waiters froze in their places. The manager stepped from the kitchen and paused, probably wondering if a 911 call would clear his establishment of liability and not liking the odds. A heartbeat, and then another, and probably ten passed. They weren't going to do anything, Daryl knew, and she wasn't going to get any better.

Daryl crossed the distance in another heartbeat—he could tell because he heard his own—and pulled the woman's chair out, tipping it forward as he did so. He caught her in her panicked fall forward with his arms around her pouched stomach. Although he didn't get his hands cupped properly immediately, he dug his thumb into her diaphragm. On the second thrust, his hands slipped into a tight clasp. On the fourth, about another fifteen of Daryl's quickening heartbeats, the woman expelled a tiny morsel of beef, about a cubic centimeter, not much really, but enough to be a deadly portion. The woman instantly relaxed as her chest swelled, and Daryl let go.

The restaurant erupted into applause. Daryl felt himself grow hot with the recognition. So much for inconspicuous. He managed a smile, an aw-shucks smile, so he stopped it. His eyes met John Donnelly's, and he saw recognition in them. Then one of the woman's companions grasped her arm, and the other threw her arms around Daryl and squeezed. "Thank you, thank you," she said.

Karen, her name was, the woman he Heimliched, he gathered from the woman comforting her. Karen gathered her wind. The maître d' reached Daryl before the manager, but both of them extolled his virtues and even threw in the word "hero" for good measure. Hardly a hero, he knew, because he knew why he was there. John Donnelly joined the group of six patrons congratulating Daryl on his remarkable ability. When Daryl's hand, somehow outstretched to meet the others' in the group, pressed into John Donnelly's charismatic palm, John Donnelly looked into Daryl's eyes and said, "I know you, don't I?"

"You're John Donnelly, right?" Daryl sobered up somewhat. His breathing and heart rate were up.

"That's right. Where do I know you from?" Donnelly said. He seemed pleased to know celebrity, or maybe just quantity.

"Weren't you with Aquatech?" Daryl said. Donnelly seemed reluctant to let go of his hand, but Daryl pulled away, hopefully inconspicuously.

"Yes! About a year ago. Did you work there?" Donnelly said.

"Sort of," Daryl said. Best to obfuscate this as best he could. "I am a consultant."

"Really? Who are you with?" Donnelly pressed.

"Belfour and Roark," Daryl picked a name from a business card he had received at an earlier job fair. "I do some C++, some Java, and some VB."

"A Renaissance developer," Donnelly said. "I'm with a company called nTropics now. We might be looking for some Java people. Here, take my card. Why don't you call us when your current assignment's up, and we'll see if we can use you. How's that?" Donnelly drew a card from a simple, if you could call leather simple, business card holder.

"Sure." Daryl took the card.

"I'm sorry, I can't remember your name," Donnelly admitted.

Daryl paused for a moment. An alias should have his initials in case he was wearing something monogrammed, not that he owned anything monogrammed anyway. "Dale," he said simply.

"Well, Dale, any time you need a job, like I said, nTropics has one for you," Donnelly promised, and Daryl thanked him.

Daryl shook a couple more hands, got two more pats on the back and a thump on the back, and Karen thanked him as well, not only for herself but for her husband and two-year-old daughter. After that small eternity, some hundred slowing heartbeats and diminishing praise from the maître d', Daryl pushed through the door. It was 12:13 by his watch. His lungs expanded with the cool, clean air. Thank you, he thought to no one in particular.

* * * *

In the alley, Robert was working the napkins quite a bit. With Daryl outside the restaurant, he'd have no way of knowing when John Donnelly would be coming out so he could get into position. He had thought of that, another improvisation, but they had not agreed on it beforehand, so Daryl was rebelling now. He was off the hook, and now Robert was really, really on the hook.

He couldn't stand in front of the restaurant, or other people might expect him to park for them. Or someone from Martello's might come out and bust him. If he wasn't out front when John Donnelly came out and John Donnelly went looking for the valet, he was busted. He might as well walk now, he was that busted.

He pushed himself away from the wall with his elbows and was preparing to calmly run for it when the phone in his pocket chirped.

"Yes?" he said.

"Daryl here. I'm across Central in front of the Japanese restaurant. It looked like his group was working on coffee, so you have a couple of minutes. We can chat for a couple of minutes while we wait, and I'll keep an eye out for him when he comes out. You copy the keys?"

"Yes, we did."

"I think I might have caused some trouble," Daryl admitted. "Whoa, his buddies are coming out. Looks like they've left him. They're walking down the block, so he's either squaring the check or going to the bathroom. I think you're up."

"Thanks." Robert snapped the phone shut and shoved it into his pocket.

He turned the corner and took a position flanking the door, on the opposite side of its opening so that people inside the restaurant would not see him when the door opened. He barely touched the brick wall when door opened, so he straightened right up and was looking at John Donnelly's back. Or it looked a lot like John Donnelly's back, although Robert had not seen him from this angle. He squelched the native doubt. "Sir, can I get your car?"

Donnelly wheeled. "Yes, thanks."

"Your ticket, sir?" Robert was going to be a stickler for detail, since a legitimate valet had better.

"Oh, yes." Donnelly took the slightly rumpled ticket from his back pocket.

"Thank you, sir. I shall be right back."

"Where did you put it?"

"Sir?"

"Where did you park my car?" Donnelly slowed the pace so that a day laborer could understand him. Or maybe Robert was just sensitive to the CEO's treatment of the lesser mortals these days.

"It's in a lot on Bemiston, sir. I'll go get it for you. I will be but a moment."

"No, that's all right. I will go get it myself, thanks. Where can I get my keys?" Donnelly held his hands.

"No, sir, I will go get it." Robert knew he was flushing. "It's my job. And although we have a deal with the parking lot, it's not prepaid; I have to show my ID to take your car out, or else you have to pay for parking for your lunch. It's all right, I will go get it for you, you just wait here a moment." When Donnelly did not protest immediately, which means before Robert could inhale after his rapid-fire paragraph, Robert bolted, or only walked quickly down the alley to get the car.

Crap, crap, crap. Should he have let Donnelly get the car? Robert did not know to what lengths a valet's professionalism would have taken him. Actually, it probably all depended on the valet, and Robert knew he would be exactly the kind of valet, well, that he was being, sort of. He took a couple of deep breaths as he walked, got into the car, paid the parking lot attendant $4.00, and brought the BMW around.

Donnelly waited for Robert to stop before stepping between the parked cars. Robert left the keys in the steering column and held the door for the client.

"Thanks a lot," Donnelly said, slipping a five dollar bill into Robert's clammy hand before driving off.

Robert looked into his hand as he walked out of the street and into the alley. His life of crime was paying off already. He was already a dollar ahead.

We've Got the Keys. Now What?

Michele was sipping a chocolate coffee thing in the St. Louis Bread Company. No whipped cream, Daryl thought. She was more manly than he was. She glanced up and saw Daryl approaching.

"Well, how'd we do?" she said.

"Okay, I guess," he said. "I left Robert with JD. He's in capable hands." He sat on the chair opposite Michele.

"That easily?" Michele couldn't believe it. This sort of thing didn't happen every day, did it? Maybe she ought to write caper novels and not spend her time trying to grasp and recreate the subtle idiosyncrasies of serious characters in literary fiction.

"Boggles the mind, doesn't it?" Daryl agreed.

"I can't believe he just gave his keys to Robert."

"Our civilization is built on trust," Daryl explained. "Just like you trusted that coffee jerk behind the counter wouldn't sprinkle rat poison in your coffee or that he washed the cup before he gave it to you. So John Donnelly thought the guy with the valet vest and valet ticket was a valet."

"That's pretty cynical. Or are you paranoid?" Michele probed.

"Not like Robert. And not like it's paranoid. It's risk assessment, kind of, in everything you do. Odds are pretty good if it walks like a valet, talks like a valet, in most cases, it is a valet."

"Is Robert really paranoid?"

"Probably not. Paranoia's clinically a form of schizophrenia, and Robert's not lost his grip on reality that I have seen yet. Excuse me," Daryl said, pulling a vibrating cell phone from his pocket and placing it on the table. It vibrated on the table, threatening to walk its way off the table. "Nah, Robert just has a risk threshold lower than most people, and he's very conscious of it."

"Do you want to get that?" Michele said.

"It's Robert asking where I am," Daryl predicted. "Hang on." He flipped the phone open. "Hello?" he said. "I'm at Bread Co. with

Michele. No thanks, she'll give me a ride back. Yes, we're leaving now. We'll see you in a little bit, okay?" He closed the phone.

Michele shotgunned her cup of still-hot coffee. "Let's go," she said. "I'm parked right here, and I have a receipt," she said.

"Did you know Robert before you guys worked at nTropics?" Michele eased her car into the Clayton traffic.

"Nah, we just started having lunch together, and then we started hanging out. nTropics is Robert's first IT job."

"But not yours?" Michele said.

"Nah, I have been around. I've done some computer assembly, some repairs. Actually worked in a CompUSA once, for a month, until the manager came down on me for not trying hard enough to sell worthless warranties. But enough about me. nTropics your first IT gig?"

"Yes, but not my first marketing thing. I have been out of school for four years, doing menial mental labor and temping. Did you go to school?" Michele already knew what made her tick.

"Not much. I did some time at UMSL, but I didn't like the commute. So I stopped going. I got a job in a South City computer sweatshop down off Compton and have been moving up ever since. Of course, nTropics was supposed to be my last job, with the stock options. You know the stock split three times since I was working there, so I was set for life if the stock went to forty dollars a share. Oh, well. I have a bit of savings and a youthful joie de vivre. You okay?"

"I have a month's worth of expenses with the severance I got. I'm hoping it won't last that long, my unemployment, I mean."

"Are you calling all of your contacts?" Daryl said.

"I don't have that many contacts," Michele admitted. "I haven't liked most of the people with whom I have worked." Michele wondered if Daryl was deftly turning the conversation back upon her like she was trying to do to him. Probably not, she thought, because he might not be a scholar of human behavior like she wanted to be. Probably just conversational.

*   *   *   *

Robert didn't want to admit that he was disappointed that Daryl was riding back with Michele, and he didn't have to. Still, he was crestfallen, slightly.

Kevin was waiting at the curb when Robert got back. Kevin bounced from the sports car and met Robert on his walk. "We got them, hey?"

"Hey." Robert rattled his keys in his lock and turned the corner. Shielding his right hand with his left, he punched his four-digit pass code into the beeping alarm control panel.

"Great. So it's that easy, hey? Now we just go get the bar? Shit!" Robert led Kevin into his kitchen. "Can I get you something to drink?" Robert said.

"It's not too early for beer," Kevin acknowledged.

"We drank that all," Robert said.

"I'll run out and get some," Kevin said.

"Why don't we wait for the others to get here," Robert said. He sat at his breakfast bar and drew the plastic bag of keys out of his pocket. He spread the keys on the bar in front of him and looked them over. Seven keys. Three with triangle heads and four with circular heads. Robert aligned them on the countertop. Two of the triangle heads had similar patterns in the notches, so they were probably related.

Kevin stood opposite Robert and studied the keys as well. "So one of those opens John Donnelly's front door, eh?"

"Probably these two," Robert said, pointing to the two with similar cuts. "One for the deadbolt and one for the regular lock."

"Mine's not like that," Kevin said. "I have one key that fits my deadbolt and my knob."

"I don't," Robert said. "Because I don't want someone who comes up with one of my keys to be able to get in."

"Who's going to get just one of your keys?" Kevin said.

"You don't plan for the intent, just the capability," Robert reprised. Of course, he had thought of that, too, after he had installed the locks. But what was done, was done, and he kept the two keys separated on his key ring. Who knows, maybe the extra few seconds would be those seconds where one of his neighbors would say, "Hey, who are you, and why are you going in Robert's house?" Of course, these days neighbors did not know each other's name, and no one would probably give it a second look.

The doorbell rang. Robert stood and switched on the 12" television on the counter. Daryl looked up at the camera. Michele stood on the porch behind him, running her fingers on the pillar holding the porch roof.

"You are too much," Kevin said.

Robert let them in.

"John Donnelly saw me," Daryl said.

"What?" Robert said.

"The woman at the table next to Donnelly tried to digest her food through her lungs," Daryl said. "So I Heimliched her."

"She what?" Kevin said.

"She choked. Nobody else helped?" Robert said.

"Nobody else would have figured out what was going on and remembered their eleventh grade health lessons in time," Daryl acknowledged.

"And he saw you?" Michele said.

"Everyone in the restaurant saw me," Daryl said. "They all wanted to shake my hand and thank me. They're glad to know someone like me is dining near them, so that they don't have to bother to learn to deal with crises on their own, and if they start to choke, I'll be there."

"You should have let her choke," Kevin said. After all, then maybe they would learn to do the choke thing. He tried to remember, was that the one where you counted three fingers under the ribs to look for the Phylum Process? Maybe he should go to the Red Cross for a refresher.

"Kevin!" Michele said.

"No, probably not," Kevin admitted.

"So what do we do about it?" Michele said. Maybe this was the end of it, then. But it was just now getting interesting.

"We don't expose Daryl where Donnelly might see him again," Robert said.

"What about you?" Kevin said.

"Probably not," Robert admitted. "But he saw a valet, and not necessarily me."

"He recognized me," Daryl said.

"What?" Robert said. Did Donnelly know Daryl knew Robert Davies, the Web developer? Probably not.

"I told him I worked with him at Aquatech, and that my name was Dale. He acted as though he remembered that, so I guess he was bluffing."

"Dale? Good work," Robert admitted. Dale sounded a lot like Daryl. A good fake name sounds a lot like your real name, and Daryl obviously knew it.

"He bought it?" Kevin said.

Daryl shrugged. "He seemed to."

"Whew," Kevin said. For their plan to go awry on such a simple detail would be bad. Of course, they better plan ahead more than this for the next steps. "So what's next?" he said.

"Next, we determine John Donnelly's secret code number and get into his house, swap the gold bar with a fake, melt it down, and cast it into jewelry we can sell. Right?" Michele said. She, too, found the first draft of an outline the easiest. She could fill in the capital letters beneath the Roman numerals, too, but she had trouble placing details beneath them.

"Details?" Kevin said.

"TBD," Daryl said.

"I have to work tonight," Robert admitted. "At three."

"Three?" Kevin said. "You didn't get off that early from nTropics."

"I called the manager and let her know I could come in earlier," Robert explained.

"So you need us to ditch?" Daryl said.

"I have to start getting ready soon."

"These are the keys?" Kevin pointed to the keys on the countertop. When Robert nodded, Kevin began brushing them into a pile. "Why don't I hold onto them tonight?"

Robert was perfectly content to let Kevin take the incriminating evidence with him, but Daryl was not.

"Why don't you leave them here, and we'll get together after Robert's off. What time are you off?" Daryl said.

"10. I will get home about 10:30." Robert admitted, saddened when Kevin stopped collecting the keys.

"I thought you said you worked near here. Why does it take you thirty minutes to drive home?" Kevin said.

"I walk to work," Robert said. Rule number 567, have at least one job you could walk to in case your car ever broke down and you could not afford to fix it. He never expected to have that problem in the Information Technology field, but no one ever expects the Spanish Inquisition. Rule number 567. Maybe he ought to start capturing his rules and numbering them.

"Really?" Michele said.

Robert thought she sounded impressed, but of course he would hope that. "Yes. It's only about a mile and a half."

"So we meet back here at about ten thirty?" Kevin said.

Robert's house wasn't the most centrally-located, he knew. However, it was the best equipped for illicit activity. He wondered if the NSA or the FBI knew it, much less the zealous Overland Police. "I guess. Daryl?"

"Sure. I'll go up to the library."

"We can get some dinner and catch a movie," Kevin offered.

"I have some research to conduct," Daryl said.

"Cool. You up for it, Michele?" Kevin said.

"I can't, tonight," Michele said. IntraTemps had called her back this morning already, and she had scheduled an appointment tomorrow at eight to meet them in their Chesterfield office.

"Date?" Kevin said. He was somewhat disappointed with her for not being dedicated to the cause enough to dump a date, but would he have turned away Renee? Nah.

"Job interview tomorrow morning," Michele admitted.

"Already?" Robert hadn't even updated his resume, with all this nefarious activity afoot.

"I guess they're looking for someone with my skill set," Michele said.

"What's that?" Kevin demanded. Anything she had done at nTropics, he had done, too. With more diplomacy, he thought.

"Everything," Michele said. "I had four years as an undergrad and three years of grad school to work at a number of lower white collar jobs. The sort of thing a temp agency wants."

"We won't need you tonight," Daryl said. "This will be mostly a bull session, probably with the emphasis on bull."

Robert wondered what repartee they had developed on the ride from Clayton. "We'll run the ideas by you tomorrow. How's that sound? You want to meet at noon?" he said. "Will you be done by then?"

"I should be," Michele said. "Okay. Here?"

"Sounds good," Robert said. We'll do lunch. "So you guys will be back tonight, and I'll see you tomorrow, Michele," he clarified, and when the three others affirmed, he led them out.

*   *   *   *

Robert walked quickly through his Overland neighborhood, scanning around him every minute or so to make sure no one was climbing dangerously out of cars or coming perilously off of porches. No one had, really, but he had seen and met the eyes of every single person, duo, and trio he had ever encountered on the street. When he met younger people, he would dip his hand into his jacket pocket in the autumn or winter or loop his thumb into his right pants pocket in the spring and summer. Not that he was carrying, of course, anything more dangerous than a pocket knife with a one inch blade. Well, legally dangerous. He carried a tape measure key chain that had his video shop keys, when he was acting as manager, and the tape measure would turn the key chain into a pretty effective flail or garrote. Not that he ever tried in a real life situation, but he could pull the tape in two and a half seconds.

Not that anyone ever came from their porches or cars. The smaller houses of Overland nestled against each other so that all neighbors would know what evil lie in the actions of the others. If one neighbor liked to grow pot in the attic, the others would know about it. That was a pardonable sin; if one neighbor liked to sell pot, inviting suburban traffic to clog the narrow inner ring suburban streets or draw the wrong element to the region, one or more neighbors would huddle behind the miniblinds of their front upstairs bedrooms to watch the Overland Police arrive with several units to discourage that behavior. Life in the small houses, with the fenced yards and zoysia mingled with Bluegrass would go on.

Robert walked through his neighborhood, with his hands in his pockets to keep them warm from the October light chill. It was down to the lower fifties so far this year. Robert was only challenged by a few dogs out for their last runs of the evening, notably the two Dalmatians on the corner of Lackland and Goodale and the Rottweiler behind the eight foot tall privacy fence halfway down the block on Burns. Each night that he worked, Robert was glad for the eight foot privacy fence behind the two-story wood frame house. Although he had studied at the Bujinkan dojo for a year, he'd never had to try his reflexes against a hundred and fifty canine pounds. Or much else for that matter.

Daryl awaited him, sitting on the edge of the porch and watching the neighborhood sleep. Robert's porch light backlit Daryl, but Robert's neighbors would not call the Muni tins, Robert's pet name for municipality police, for a man sitting on Robert's porch. He wasn't there for drugs; Robert was such a nice boy. Or at least he always was polite, but short, with them. Maybe he was one of the nice ones you never suspect. Maybe he ought to be more gregarious with them. Like Ted Bundy. "Hey," Robert said when he came up the walk.

"How was work?" Daryl said.

"About the same as every night, really." Robert unlocked and deactivated. "It's not a lot of work, but it gives me a lot of time to think."

"Think about what?" Daryl said.

"Most nights, not a lot. How I would react to different things, or if I found myself in certain situations, mostly plots from Star Trek or novels I am reading. Tonight, however, I had something else in mind."

"Me, too," Daryl said.

"Coffee?" Robert put his jacket into the hall closet.

"No thanks," Daryl said. "So what did you think about tonight?"

"What we have to do now that we have John Donnelly's keys." Robert flipped the light on in the basement.

"What do we have to do?" Daryl said.

"We need to do two things before we go into Donnelly's house next week. We need to get his pass code to shut off the alarm, and we need to create a replica of the gold bar. A bag of sand won't convince anyone on live Internet feed." Robert said.

"Okay," Daryl said. He pulled the folded printouts from his back pocket. "I went to the library and poked around on the Internet." He unfolded the papers and passed them to Robert. "The auction house placed pretty exact specifications in their online brochure for the auction where Donnelly bought the bar."

Photos, printed with a fading toner cartridge that left a black graduated streak on the right side, displayed six sides of the bar. Text described the weight of the bar at 390.10 ounces of 903 Fine gold. "Cool. You have the URL?"

"I mailed it to my Hotmail account." Daryl said. Using a Web-based free e-mail service, he had sent an e-mail containing the Web addresses of sites he had found. Since he sent them to a Web-based e-mail service, he'd have them available to at any computer with a Web connection. Like Robert's computer here.

"That's not encrypted," Robert said. That information would be coming to his computer unencrypted, which meant anyone with a subpoena could see that he was looking at the statistics of John Donnelly's gold bar.

"It's just a URL," Daryl said.

"It's not secure."

"I'll tunnel and no one will see it on your ISP logs. How's that?" Daryl shook his head.

"Fine," Robert said.

"For someone who's so not into risks, aren't you taking a mighty big one ringleading this little expedition?"

Robert's throat closed briefly. "I'm not the ringleader." Would that entail an extra charge?

"The hell you're not. You came up with the valet scam." Daryl didn't know where this confrontational urge came from.

"Yes, I did, but that's because I knew about it. That doesn't make me the leader." Robert thought Daryl seemed to have some passive aggressive response to the whole Hotmail thing.

"So who does that make the leader? Kevin?" Daryl asked.

"I thought we were all partners," Robert said quietly.

"So what are you in it for?" Daryl said.

"Same as you, I guess. To see if it could be done."

"And to make sure that it's done right," Daryl said. "You're an aesthete."

The doorbell rang. The television displayed Kevin, lit by the porch light.

"Hey, guys," Kevin said when Robert opened the door. "I brought the beer." He held up a case of generic beer, bearing only a white label and the word **BEER**. Kevin hadn't believed they still made it, but when he went into the Overland super-discount grocery store, he found some in a cooler in the back. He had stopped in to see what sort of groceries he would have to grow accustomed to if this little operation failed, and he was not happy with the selection. However, he would remember the **BEER** beer as a good joke to serve at parties when he was rich. And, he thought, why not start tonight? Just to taste it and see if anything could be worse than Bud Light. "We can drink fiscally responsibly."

"No more malt liquor?" Robert said.

"Variety is the spice of poverty," Kevin said. He went into the kitchen and put his beer in the refrigerator, pausing to pull a white can from the cardboard box. "So what do you gentlemen have?" he joined Robert and Daryl in the basement.

"We think our next steps are to create a fake gold bar and to get JD's pass key number," Daryl recapped.

"That sounds harder than the keys," Kevin said.

"Yes, and no," Robert said. "It's not a simple scam, but it's not impossible."

"You've already got an idea," Daryl said.

"It's only because of the lax security sense exercised by whoever installed his keypad. It's on the wall opposite the door. Maybe it was installed before the glass opposite the door sides, but it offers us a clear insight into what his code is. We can see what he punches into the keypad and use it ourselves."

"You mean, have one of us stake it out, with binoculars and a notepad?" Kevin popped the top on his **BEER** and took a sip. He made a face to telegraph his displeasure and his normally higher standards. Definitely worse than Bud Light. It tasted like slightly brewed well water. He might have to drink a whole twelve-pack for a buzz.

"Something like that," Robert said. "A zoom camera would be better, though, because it would more inconspicuous than one of us sitting in a tree." Of course, he had run through the possibilities behind the veneered counter, ringing up the occasional made-for-video thriller for suburban husbands who convinced themselves that they watched these movies for the suspense or even the violence, not for the sexual situations and nudity. This predilection towards masculine Thanatos urges explained why they picked, more often than not, the boxes

89

depicting a woman in a negligee as viewed through blinds instead of *Reservoir Dogs*.

"You mean like what you have on your porch?" Kevin swallowed more of the **BEER**. If you drank it quickly, it didn't taste as bad. Well, it probably still tasted as bad, but not for as long, which was just as good.

"Something like that," Robert said. "With a better zoom." He opened a cabinet at the base of the bookshelves and took out a mini-camera. "Something like this."

"How many of those do you have?" Daryl said.

"I have three extras." Robert didn't exactly answer the question. He didn't include the two on his garage; the one on his back porch, although they could surmise that from the one on the front porch; one on either side of the house; of course, the one on the front porch, which the others knew about now; and the one with the pan and tilt he put in the kitchen. He'd bought a special six-pack deal of the standard cameras and had gotten four more advanced models later, when they came out and the camera company had recognized and rewarded a loyal customer.

"You like them so much. You buy the company?" Kevin said.

"This one zooms up to ten times," Robert said. "We'll put it in the shrubs at the center of his circle and focus it on the keypad. John Donnelly's right handed, right? So we'll place it on the right edge of the circle so his body doesn't block his hand. We'll have a limited pan and tilt with this base. We'll bury the very bottom of the base for stability since we cannot bolt it to anything."

"Don't we need a television?" Daryl said.

"I have a special USB adapter. It will fit into a laptop."

"Are you going to bury the laptop, too?" Kevin said.

"It doesn't have to be with the camera; just within a couple hundred feet. We could put it the laptop anywhere. I've got a superslim laptop we can use." Robert put the camera down on the workbench. "The laptop has a DVD burner in it, so we could just capture the time when Donnelly was there to and burn the video to DVD. Next morning, we gather the equipment and the DVD and replay it, watching where John Donnelly hits the keys."

"Couldn't we just set up a live video stream?" Kevin said.

"Sure. We could just dig a T3 line right up to our hidden laptop," Daryl said. "Or piggyback off of a wireless connection from his neighbors, if any, and leave a record of it in ISP logs."

"Sorry," Kevin said. "I am not a guru like you guys. I'm only good for one thing. Who else needs a beer?"

"I'll try that simplistic brew," Daryl said. "I hope it tastes as badly as you're letting on."

"Worse," Kevin said. He clambered up the stairs.

"One for me, too," Robert said. A beer that tasted worse than beer would surely pace him better than normal.

"So what do you do for a battery?" Daryl said.

"The laptop's good for eight hours. The camera can go on a battery pack for about ten."

"So you want to set it to go when we put it in and let it run?"

"That's a little tricky on the timing," Robert said. "We'd have to wait until later in the day to put it in then. If we had more time, we could case John Donnelly to see his home arrival habits. We're cutting it thin as it is. Normally, an operation like this would take months to plan. What's our hurry?"

"Months? That would be boring," Kevin said. He handed **BEER**s to the guys and opened his. "Besides that, I can't wait months. I need money soon, or else I am going to have get another real job. Getting canned by nTropics set back the odometer on my dreams of wealth, man." He sat slowly on the step. "I don't have two weeks."

"You're putting an awful lot on this heist. We probably won't even go all the way through with it, you know. Any moment it looks like we're going to get caught, or even looks like there's a chance we might get caught, and we walk." Daryl opened his can of beer and tasted it. No worse than store brand cola.

"All the more reason to find out sooner rather than later," Kevin said.

"That makes sense," Robert said. He had not expected reason from Kevin. "I guess I had been planning with those prerequisites in mind, which is why I did this all with stuff on hand.

"We have two other things to consider," Robert continued. "We need a replacement for the gold bar, and we need to cover ourselves when we make the switch. Daryl, you've got the dimensions. Now we need to know how to make a replacement."

"Well, casting one out of gold is out," Daryl said. "May I?" he gestured at Robert's computer. When Robert nodded, Daryl logged in and connected to his Internet Service Provider.

"What about pyrite? Fool's gold? Can we make a fake from that?" Robert said.

"Cheaper to electroplate some steel," Kevin said.

"Electroplate?" Robert said.

"Sure. Pick up scrap steel for a couple of bucks and a couple ounces of gold or gold jewelry. Fashion the steel as you will. Create an electroplating tank. Pour solution into tank. Sand or file gold into solution. Drop in steel bar, turn on the electricity, and bam, you've got a gold bar," Kevin said. He finished his beer.

"How do you know that?" Daryl said. His fingers rattled on the keyboard like rain on a tin roof.

"My name's not fucking Robert, but I still know something about metalworking." Kevin said.

"What?" Robert said.

"RHC Fabricators. My old man's metal shop. I worked there a couple of summers." Kevin stood up. "Maybe I ought to bring the beers down here. You ready, Robert?" he said.

"Sure."

"Can I run some stuff off your printer?" Daryl said.

"What do you have?"

"Some diagrams for an electroplating tank. A quick glance over the principles says Kevin's right."

"Of course I'm right." Kevin reappeared at the top of the stairs as the printer began rattling out the pages. "You guys don't give me any credit. Just because I'm not a techno guru, you think I'm worth less than you are. But don't worry, I get that a lot, and in a lot of disciplines. It just makes me look even better when I surprise you."

"For a minute, I thought you were going to start weeping in your generic beer," Daryl said.

"Not yet. Give me a couple more," Kevin said.

"All right," Robert said. "We electroplate a steel bar. That leaves one small detail. We need to make the switch seamless to the thousands of Internet viewers. Ideas?"

"How about the *Speed* trick?" Kevin said. "You cut a loop of the existing feed and run it over and over until we've got the gold?"

"Call it up," Robert told Daryl.

Daryl's keys danced upon the keyboard. "You got it, chief." The Web page displayed on the screen.

Robert leaned over his shoulder. Kevin stood slowly and walked as tentatively as a tightrope walker to place a hand on the back of Daryl's chair.

"If nTropics had booked this travel....this gold bar would have been in North Carolina on time...." the banner explained in expensive custom font. An image displayed under the banner. Text explained the origin of the ingot in the California Gold Rush and its ill-fated passage on the *S.S. Central America*, ad absurdum. Written with a marketer's eye to fluff and blind eye to detail, it disappeared off the screen. "Angie wrote that," Kevin said.

Robert tapped the image. The gold bar, aligned on a forest green velvet background. The image didn't hint at anything else in the room. However, imposed on the image, a date and time stamp incremented in slow, dial-up connection jerks. "That's a problem."

"What if we create a movie for the time and substitute the movie for the feed?" Kevin said.

"I'm not that good with any video editors. You?" Daryl said.

"No," Kevin admitted.

"I'll just bring it down," Daryl said.

"Down?" Kevin said.

"Just bring the site down," Daryl said. "That's the easiest thing to do. No worries, no log files explaining that someone was mucking with the feed, nothing."

"Denial of Service?" Kevin said.

"No," Robert said. "That's an obvious attack."

"Besides, I don't have bots out there on the Internet awaiting my every command. I'll find something. Some router will fail or exactly wrong set of circumstances will cause it to come down."

"Like what?" Kevin said.

"I don't know yet. I'll have to snoop a bit. Give me a day or so."

"All right," Robert said. He looked at the empty beer in his hand, again. How many was that, he wondered. Two or three. Like the two or three things they needed to plan. "We've got the basics set up. We'll try to get his pass code. Then we electroplate a fake ingot, and crash the live Internet feed."

"Shit, this was just like college. Sitting around all night, drinking beer, and figuring this stuff all out. Man, I love you guys," Kevin said, with sincerity only slightly enhanced by the **BEER**.

"You don't have to love us. You only have to work with us." When he said it, Robert realized he sounded like a ringleader.

The Morning After the Plan, Lunch, and Metal Hunting

Robert was the first awake. He looked at his alarm clock gun safe. 8:06. He was sleeping late these days.

He moved quietly through the household. The guest bed bore a lump beneath the spread. Daryl's feet, he assumed, since he could not verify without stepping into the room the owner of the lump, nor if it was only pillows designed to make a lump. However, he trusted Daryl, and Daryl had slurred a good night before carefully feeling his way into that bedroom. No reason to expect anyone but Daryl. Robert had consumed four, or five, cans of generic grain alcohol before going to bed. Maybe he ought to stop for another glass of water. He wasn't experiencing any of the traditional signs of dehydration, but he never liked to tempt fate.

He drew a glass of water from the bathroom tap slowly, so as to not disturb his guests. He was not quite ready to entertain them yet. He wanted to take a look on the Internet and see what he could learn about electroplating. He allotted a half hour to perform his searching before he made the awake noises, the morning shower and shaving, that would awaken Kevin and Daryl.

He hit the IntraTemps site first, to find out some information about this place Michele was interviewing. A West County address, a building in the rapidly developing corridor that followed Highway 40 west from Clayton. Their site claimed they could place IT and other professionals, but Robert had never run across a consultant from them, so he suspected they were wishfully thinking. Too bad about Michele. Daryl and he'd have no trouble getting into something in the IT industry because they had necessary skills; however, in a down economy, IT companies would not be hiring the auxiliary resources.

Robert quickly hit some metalsmith Web sites. One provided him with a detailed diagram for an electroplating tank. Robert printed the schematic. It matched Daryl's from the night before.

From beneath his workbench, he took a plastic tub he sometimes used to hold cleaning solutions. He tugged on the grey cabinet door, forcing the thick wood to part. The paint was scraping off where the door met the face. Robert was glad no one was downstairs yet, to see that he had not planed the door or realigned the hinges and had not repainted the worn spot. He might have time to do that between things this week. He'd make sure they did not see the flaw.

He took out one of his extra power supplies and put it on the bench. He had to tap the door on the offending corner to close it flush, but when it was closed, an observer could not tell it was off unless he or she measured the gap between the face and door, and because it was the back corner that rubbed, the observer would not measure much indeed. That explained why Robert had forgotten it except on those occasions when he needed to get into that cabinet, which was only once a month, if that.

Robert drew an electrician's Phillips screwdriver from the rack mounted on the bench. Don't try this at home, he thought, avoiding the capacitors that had enough juice in them to kill a man. Although it was only a 150 watt power supply, scavenged from an old dinosaur machine, Robert gave it proper respect until he discharged the caps.

Daryl came down the steps. "Good morning, sunshine."

"Good morning," Robert said.

"Building an electroplate tank?"

"Yes," Robert said. He wasn't bothering with eye contact.

"Hey," Kevin added, coming down the stairs. "Whoa, good job," he said when he saw what Robert was working on.

"That will work?" Daryl said.

"Looks like it. That's direct current coming out, right?"

"Anode," Robert said, touching the rubber-coated shaft of the screwdriver to a wire on the extending from the front of the power supply. He touched another wire. "Cathode," he said. Well, not exactly that easy, he knew, because each of the wires had positive and negative leads coming from it. However, if Kevin didn't know by looking a +12v from a −12v, Robert wasn't going to bother educating him right this minute.

"Cool. You have any solution?" Kevin said.

"I don't have any electrolyte solution," Robert said, "nor do we have any gold."

"I don't have any gold," Kevin said. "I don't look good in jewelry." His look was more rugged, less refined than gold or silver would indicate. He had once worn a pewter dragon pendant on a steel chain a couple years back, but they weren't stealing a pewter bar, so it wouldn't do them any good, if he could even find it in his dresser.

"Me, either," Daryl said. "You have enough old computers lying around. We can get the gold from the contacts."

Robert put down his screwdriver and turned on the stool. "That's spread pretty thin. It could take us a day or two to come up with a half an ounce."

"Michele's probably got something," Daryl said.

"She doesn't wear much, either," Kevin said. "I've seen a silver ring, but no gold. No earrings."

"She'll be glad you noticed," Daryl said.

Robert hadn't noticed.

"We could grab something at a pawn shop," Kevin said. "There's always fairly cheap low quality gold in a pawn shop. We don't have to put 900 gold on the bar. Anyone that inspects the thing's going to know it's a fake anyway."

"Sounds good to me," Daryl said.

"But," Kevin hesitated, "I don't have enough in my account to get the steel or the jewelry." He hoped this would be the most expensive part of it.

"Of course not," Daryl said. "How much do you think we'll need?"

"I don't know. I don't expect more than a hundred for both. Most of that's for the gold."

"Let's go get them," Daryl said. "You know any good pawn shops?"

"Two over on Woodson, but I would prefer you went somewhere further afield," Robert said.

"You?" Daryl said.

"I am going to finish this, and then I am going to configure the camera and laptop. We should install them this afternoon," Robert said. And he had a lunch date, although she might not know it.

"All right. Let's go," Kevin said. "I know a pawn shop down in Lemay. Is that far enough?"

"Yes," Robert said.

"I'll need to stop at an ATM," Daryl said.

"How long will it take you?" Robert said. It was nine forty-five already. So much for the half hour. He still had time to shower and shave, though.

"We'll be back by two. How's that?" Kevin said.

"Good enough," Robert said. "Try to be earlier than that so we have time to set up the system."

* * * *

By 12:15, Robert had not only turned the power supply into a variable voltage rectifier, but had also had showered, shaved, and put on a nice denim-collared shirt that might set off his pale blue eyes. Of course, the shirt was blue, but darker than his pale eyes. Would they clash? The same color was not good, he had sensed from the way others talked around it. Nobody ever showed him the proper charts, so he never picked up whatever skill everyone else seemed to have. At least the slacks were grey, probably not a problem.

He put the cod into a lukewarm oven to keep it warm. He hoped she liked seafood. Fish tacos were uncommon enough to be noticeable, but quick enough to prepare in thirty minutes. He hoped Michele would notice it enough to be impressed, but not enough to think he was going to any lengths for her. Maybe it was a little more than he would have eaten on his own, but he had company coming. And he had to use the cod before the weekend.

He had planned to be just finishing his lunch serendipitously at about the time that Michele was scheduled to arrive so that she would see him finish up and he could set an extra plate for her. However, since she was ten minutes late so far, he put the fish in the oven and spent a few minutes shredding extra lettuce and chopping tomatoes until Michele arrived.

Robert answered the door when she rang. He hoped he did not smell too much of cod. Michele, still dressed from her interview, came in. She had added extra curl to her hair and makeup, to great effect, Robert thought.

"Hi. Where are the guys?" Michele had not seen Kevin's car outside, but Daryl's bike was chained around a porch upright, so she had felt much better about knocking on Robert's door. Come to think of it, he had only explicitly told her to be there at noon.

"They're out buying steel and gold," Robert said. "I've made some lunch. Are you hungry?" He wondered if he should offer to take her suit jacket or not, and decided not. Don't bow and scrape, he reminded himself.

"What do you have?" Michele said. How long would Daryl and Kevin be gone?

"I've made some fish for fish tacos," Robert said.

"Fish tacos?" Michele said.

"Yes. With soft tortillas. Is that okay?"

"Yeah. You didn't go through any trouble?"

"Oh, no. I had some fish to get rid of, and tacos are a scalable meal. When Daryl and Kevin get back, they can eat whatever we have left cut with veggies." He drew four plates from the shelves to emphasize the group. He took the pan of fish from the oven and stacked it upon a cast iron trivet on the counter. "Guest first," he said.

"I've never had fish tacos," Michele admitted. She slipped her jacket off and folded it over a chair.

"Just like regular tacos," Robert said, drawing a plate from the stack and proffering it. "Except that fish is better for you. Brain food. That's why I cook it every chance I get; I need all the help I can get." As he said it, he felt foolish, wondering if she'd see his self-deprecating humor as a weakness. Maybe it was.

Michele took the plate and lifted the lid over the tortillas. He had a tortilla holder, for crying out loud. A little wooden pedestal and glass dome over the top. She expected that sort of showy propriety from Kevin, out to impress the stream of women visiting his apartment for a home-cooked meal and a one night stand. Did Robert have a stream of women coming through here, too?

"I know, but the cheese tray keeps the tortillas warm. I take the ceramic insert out of the base and put it in the oven for a little while to warm it. It transfers the heat to the tortillas," Robert admitted. She had paused a millisecond while holding the lid, and he wanted to defend himself immediately.

"Cheese tray?" Michele said.

"I bought it at an estate sale," Robert explained. "It was made in 1964 by Carlton Industries, a little manufacturing company in Peoria, Illinois. Underneath the tortillas, it has a ceramic insert that depicts a barn scene. I warmed the ceramic insert to keep the tortillas warm." The estate sales admission probably told Michele he was cheap.

Michele took a warm tortilla from the stack. "Is the base walnut?" These things were always walnut, and Robert seemed to take some pride from knowing the cheese tray's history. The tortilla was warm, though. Robert might never host a cheese party in his life, but he was getting use from the cheese tray.

"I am pretty sure," Robert said. "The collectors' Internet sites say it is." He picked the dome up when Michele put it down and took a tortilla.

"How much did you pay for it?" Michele fished, for lack of a better term, a few pieces of the finely cut cod chunks from their pan.

"A dollar," Robert said. "A lot of estate sales let the small stuff go cheaply. As long as the mahogany buffet goes for seven hundred dollars, they're happy."

"Did you plan to serve cheese on it when you bought it?" Michele said.

"I knew I would serve something on it," Robert said. He had little in the nice things department, and he was only now starting to accrue them.

Michele nodded and finished making a fish taco and sat at the table. Robert sat beside her, not across from her.

"So did you like *The Dark Side of Saint Jude?*" Robert said.

She hated it when people asked her a question right when she took a bite of something, but the bite was not bad. The cod did not taste particularly fishy, so she forgave him somewhat. "Well, I thought Jude probably had more options than simply following the Mafia's orders. I mean, the guy's trying to go straight, but he lets himself get sucked into something based on a woman with whom he's only recently gotten involved? He never mentioned he was a burglar, and suddenly she needed someone to break into a Mafia business to get something for her? I had some trouble with that," she said. How would Robert handle that? Had he seen the movie?

"You don't think a man would risk himself for the mere chance that she was telling the truth?" Robert said.

A perfect way to parry with a question, Michele thought. "Why would he?"

"He almost got shot on the Pomari job," Robert said. "So he wanted to go straight. He took a leap of faith using the remainder of the mob's stake in getting a decent suit for job interviews. Why wouldn't he take a leap of faith on Elena?" Robert said.

"Elena had never said anything about herself," Michele said. "All of her speech had been directed toward her goal. Why would he trust her?"

"Maybe Jude was a romantic," Robert said.

He had seen it, Michele thought, suddenly guilty herself.

"Or maybe he had no idea how normal people behave or court," Robert concluded.

"When did you see it?" Not changing the subject, Michele thought, but more skewing it to her liking.

"I borrowed it one night this spring," Robert said. He had made it through the comedies last winter and had started the suspense in March. By late March or early April, he had hit D in the alphabetical organization of the shelves. At his peak, he was watching twelve videos a week, but the weather was bad last winter.

"You get to borrow free movies?" Michele said.

"Donna, the owner, says an educated clerk leads to happier customers," Robert said. He decided not to mention his anal methodology.

"So, do you like noir?" Michele said.

"Well, that depends," Robert said. "When you mean. Things like Quentin Tarentino, not really. They're just slasher films with bullets. Most of the stuff that's noir from 1970 on is like that, to a matter of degree, I think. I prefer the forties and early fifties, when Bogart and Ladd were at their peaks."

"Really?" Michele wondered if she should mention the Bogart retrospective at the Tivoli, but decided that would sound too much like an invitation to a date.

* * * *

"So, are you interested in Michele?" Daryl said as Kevin piloted the sports car down the lightly trafficked I-270 toward Lemay. He had run his automated teller machine card for $200. He didn't think it would be a bad idea to have an extra hundred beyond what Kevin thought it would cost, and if he had overage, good. He could buy paper goods necessary for the proper continued functioning of his apartment.

"What?" Kevin said.

"Are you going to take Michele around the world?" Daryl said.

"You mean, what? Date her? Hook up?" Kevin didn't glance over to see if Daryl was serious. He couldn't be.

"Both B and C," Daryl said. "Or B or C. One of the above."

"Not really," Kevin said. "Why, has she been asking about me?"

"Not really," Daryl riposted. "I was just wondering. She's one of the only women I have seen you spend more than twelve hours total with that you didn't either find a total dog or that you didn't try to hump."

"Ouch," Kevin said. A lot of his male friends were jealous of the attention women paid him, so he was used to the jabs. "I mean, she's okay, but she's not my type, you know?"

"Sure," Daryl said. If Kevin wasn't interested in her, maybe Daryl would ask her out after this whole affair was over. To Agostino's or Tony's, somewhere he could afford if he was a millionaire. Why stop there? Why not fly her to New York or Paris? Or Denver? Inwardly, he snickered. When he was a millionaire. When this little thing made them all millionaires, and Michele would be unimpressed with the millions. "I wonder if Robert's having any luck with her."

"Robert?"

"He did invite her over for lunch and then send us out," Daryl said.

"The stud!" Kevin smiled. He'd wondered about Robert's taste in women, or if he had any taste at all. Michele was definitely choice. Or prime. Whichever was the second best.

Robert was hardly the stud, Daryl said, but Robert was probably a step ahead of him.

"You think that's what he's in it for?" Kevin said.

"In it?" Daryl said.

"Stealing the gold bar," Kevin responded. He nosed the Eclipse into the exit lane. The exit ramp for the connecting interstate was a relatively new tangle of fly-overs and intermingling lanes of traffic. Why not just put a seventy-mile-an-hour traffic circle in the middle and really thin the population? He'd seen too many befuddled old domestic claptraps merging at thirty miles an hour and trying to commit suicide on the front of his car. However, he'd rode this roller coaster plenty of times going to see his aunt in Carondolet, so he navigated with the smooth efficiency his 200 horses gave him.

"To impress Michele?" Daryl hadn't thought of that. Robert had not mentioned a lot about women around Daryl. When they first started hanging out, Daryl wondered if he'd have to recalibrate his gaydar, but Robert never hit on him, and eventually mentioned a girl he had dated some years ago. "I doubt it."

"He's not in it for the money," Kevin said.

"No, he's in it because he's curious to see if we can do it," Daryl said.

"And you?" Kevin said.

"I'm curious to see if we can do it."

"Money will be nice, too," Kevin said.

"Probably should not spend it all at once," Daryl said. "Put most of it in a box and spend a little for the rest of your life."

"What if I launder it?" Kevin said.

"You know any syndicate types?" Daryl said. "You don't have to launder it if you bring it in slowly. Like a hundred dollars a month."

"What's the fun in that? What's the point in being rich if you don't spend it?"

"It's not to worry about it. Most rich people don't live in mansions and ride in stretch limos. Most of them don't spend as much as they take in."

"Sheesh. Thanks for the lesson. If I snatch the gold bar out of your hand, will I become a wealthy man?"

Daryl shook his head and looked out the window. Kevin exited on Bayless Avenue, where Interstate 55 met a metal recycling facility. Kevin pulled his car into the driveway and past the weight scale shack. He parked beside another trailer marked **Office**. "You hang out here,"

Kevin opened the door. "Give me sixty dollars," he said.

Daryl pulled three twenties from the roll in his pants pocket.

"Be right back," Kevin said, and he closed the door. He went up the wooden steps to the trailer door and went in.

Daryl watched a car come into the recycling center and back to a concrete dock. A young man, sporting what looked like a dirty dirty blond ponytail, popped the trunk and threw several bags onto the dock. An employee, dressed in a stained blue thermal coverall, put the bags on a digital scale. Behind the scale, a mountain of aluminum cans extended out of sight and to the limits of Daryl's imagination. The young man slammed the trunk, crossed flannel-encrusted arms, and waited for the employee to jot the weight on the slip. When he got it, he drove off. Daryl remembered being left in the car once when his mother went grocery shopping. Only once.

Kevin hadn't even offered to leave the radio on for him. He probably didn't want Daryl to drive off with his pride, but Daryl wouldn't know how to handle the amalgamated shifter. Was it a stick? Was it automagic? Who knew?

Daryl tried the glove box. Kevin didn't lock it; who did? A six pack box of condoms, open and missing a condom. Daryl glanced over the leather interior of the car, its two-plus-two seater design broken by a painful shifter. Interesting configuration for amoration. Kevin also carried a map of St. Louis, a travel guide to St. Louis, and the manual for his Eclipse Spyder GT, courtesy of Kirkwood Mitsubishi. A pen and a pack of stick gum at the back, the gum unyieldingly stale in its wrapper.

In the console between the seats, Daryl spied Kevin's cruising CDs which apparently included Dar Williams and Skid Row. Which would you play first for seduction? Kevin also carried a few extra dimes, nickels, and pennies, undoubtedly drive-thru remainders.

A cart scuttled through the trailers and mounds. Kevin came out of the door, smiled and said something to someone inside. Another employee, dressed in a similar coverall but yellow-orange, hopped from the cart and lifted a crate from the back of the cart. Kevin opened the trunk of the car. "Sure that's fine, thanks," Kevin said.

"You're welcome," the employee said.

Daryl closed the console at the same time Kevin closed the trunk. Kevin said something unintelligible and hopped into the car, leaving the employee to scuttle back into the pre-apocalyptic waste of his vocation.

"You know, we have too much," Kevin said. "Steel's lighter than gold for its size."

"Is it?" Daryl said.

"So we have extra. That's better than the opposite, I guess." He backed the Eclipse from the trailer. "The pawnshop's just a little ways down the road."

Kevin could have said "At the end of the road," because the pawnshop lay at the end of Bayless, at the top of the T intersection with Lemay Ferry. At nights, he remembered, they parked cars on the sidewalk in front of it to prevent smash-n-grabbers' automobiles from getting a running start down Bayless and crashing through the barred windows to the guns and ammunition beyond. Of course, he'd never been in there—when he needed to hock the CD player to make it to another job's payday, he used a shop up in Overland, off of Page, but Robert didn't want them to visit the familiar, or the nearby. Kevin had, of course, seen this Lemay shop a year ago in the spring, so about a year and a half ago. Melanie lived around the corner in a tiny house on Wachtel. The walls almost pressed against the walls of her elderly parents' house, but Melanie had not awakened them. He pulled around to park at the curb, almost where the owner of the pawnshop would place the station wagons tonight.

"I've never been in a pawnshop," Daryl admitted.

"Great place to get deals on electronics," Kevin said. He didn't know what Daryl would think about the kind of people that hocked stuff in pawnshops. Hell, he didn't think much of most people he saw in the pawnshop on Page that were in there the one time he went. A little lower class than he was, but he was only hocking once. It wasn't like he was selling plasma or anything.

The pawnshop was lit and organized well, with glass counter fixtures showing the smaller, pocket-sized electronics. The counters formed a U with the bottom of the U at the back wall of the shop. Rifles in locked racks lined the walls behind the counters. Kevin hesitated, so Daryl followed the one counter to the interior wall. Daryl looked at the pistols and gold chains under the glass.

The proprietor stood from a stool, placing a newspaper the corner of the counter. "Can I help you gentlemen?" he said.

"Gold," Kevin said, coming forward to review the contents of the case. Within, he saw a number of chains and several rings, all upon a black velvet background.

"Something for you, or something for a friend?" the man said, drawing a set of keys from his pants pocket. He put a key in the back of the counter, but didn't turn it. Daryl wondered what Robert would have thought of that, if the man had some security provisions in place should Kevin and Daryl turn out to be bad men. Daryl was probably spending too much time with Robert if he was thinking along those lines. Besides, he and Kevin probably looked as harmless as they were.

"Let's see that one," Kevin said, gesturing at a plain, medium weight chain with no pendant.

The proprietor turned the key, lifted the back of the cabinet, and took out the chain Kevin had indicated. He placed the chain on the countertop and left his furry hands nearby.

Kevin hefted it and looked at it. "That's about right," he said. They could file it down and get a couple millimeters of coverage over a decent facsimile gold bar with this necklace. He twisted the little paper price tag over. "Ninety-five dollars!"

The proprietor did not play along. "That's a little much, don't you think?" Kevin continued.

"That's exactly the right price, I think, otherwise I wouldn't have put ninety-five dollars on it," the man said. He rubbed a heavy grey sideburn.

"Look at that," Kevin said, turning to show it to Daryl. Not that he had to turn far, because Daryl was standing beside him.

"Sir," the man behind the counter said, gesturing, "Please give me the chain."

Oh, shit, Daryl thought. Is Kevin going to try to boost the necklace?

The guy jumped pretty quick for the necklace. He thinks I'm trying to steal it! It amused Kevin momentarily, but he handed the necklace to the owner. "How about sixty dollars?" Kevin said.

The owner straightened the necklace and spread it on the velvet. "It's ninety-five dollars," he repeated. "You couldn't find it anywhere else for a better price."

"That's fine," Daryl said, pulling the roll from his pocket. "I'll take it."

"You will?" the man said.

Daryl fanned five twenties for him.

"Ninety-five plus tax," the man said.

"I think I can handle that," Daryl said. He fanned an extra twenty and rolled the extras into his pocket again.

"All right, then," the man said, taking the chain out of the case.

Kevin was silent until they closed the car doors and he turned the ignition key. "I'm surprised he wasn't negotiating. Maybe I should have looked at some of the other chains before I started haggling," he said as he pulled into traffic.

"This will be enough?" Daryl pulled the chain from the box the pawnbroker had provided.

"Should be, if we can file it into dust. Mostly, anyway." Kevin smirked. "Now we're off to plant the cameras, the wonderful cameras of ours," he sang, trying to mimic Judy Garland from *The Wizard of Oz*. Not bad, he thought.

"If it's okay, I'd like to make a stop first," Daryl said.

Planting the Cameras

Kevin didn't know how long it would be before they'd be familiar enough to just walk into Robert's house and say, "Hey," like he did with some of his old friends from college, a bunch of guys that lived over in the Illinois suburbs now, a hop, skip, and river away. Of course, he didn't see them all that often anymore, and the guys who were married managed to hook up with wives that didn't like college buddies stopping over, walking right in, and saying, "Hey." When they got onto Robert's porch, Daryl knocked, and if Daryl was still knocking, Kevin figured he'd better remember to knock. He shifted the old crate the junkyard had given him, clinking the steel.

Robert opened the door and held it for Kevin. "You might as well put that in the basement right away," he said about the crate. "I've made fish tacos in the kitchen, and they're still warm," he said.

"Fish tacos?" Kevin said. "You made fish tacos?" He shook his head as he carried the crate into the basement.

Daryl put the bag on the table and took out the necklace. "What do you think?" he said to Michele.

Michele took the necklace and felt its weight and texture. "A little plain. It needs a pendant," she judged. She didn't wear many necklaces, and certainly nothing this plain without an accent. A little more braid, maybe.

"It would have been a shame to waste a good pendant, too," Daryl said. He left Michele with her orange juice and the gold while he assembled a fish taco under Robert's careful scrutiny.

Kevin shook his head as he came into the kitchen. "Fish tacos. I can barely keep from burning down my apartment building with my wok, and you're making fish tacos. How do you do it?" He washed his hands in the kitchen sink and dried them on a dish towel hanging from the oven's handle. Come on, man, tell her something like you learned it from a master chef in Japan when you were studying a broad. Or since she knows your name, maybe something believable.

"I got it out of a cookbook," Robert said. He took the dish towel from the oven handle and tossed it onto the counter to remind himself to launder it.

"Camera ready?" Daryl said.

"All set. I have the laptop configured, too, and a fresh DVD for the image. I have them in a backpack, ready to go. As soon as you finish lunch, we can go." Robert said. After Kevin fixed a plate of lukewarm fish, Robert began cleaning the dishes.

"So what's the plan?" Kevin said.

He was between bites and almost with his mouth full. Only a quick swallow kept Kevin from sharing his mastication results, Daryl noticed. "Almost the same as yesterday. Two teams. Kevin, you will drive by nTropics to make sure he's there, and call us to let us know that we're clear. When we get your call, we'll plant the camera and get out of there as quickly as we can," Daryl said. He finished a paragraph of speech, so he ought to have time for a bite. The fish tacos tasted like fish salad with a stiffening tortilla wrap. Somewhat like a regular taco.

"Kevin, park across the street in the CMI lot so you can see his car. If he leaves, call us immediately." Robert got another dish towel from the drawer beside the sink to dry the dishes.

"Why do I get to sit and wait?" The tacos weren't bad, but they weren't enough to bribe him.

"We're switching off cars," Robert said. "Michele was outside nTropics yesterday. We don't want to have anyone inside see the same car more than once, especially if someone might recognize it."

"You've got a car," Kevin said. Certainly they didn't just want him out of the way, where he could do no damage.

"It's my camera and laptop," Robert said. "I have to set it up in case we have any trouble."

"If you want to drive us, you and Michele could swap cars. Let her drive your car over to nTropics, and you drive hers. Can you drive a manual transmission, Michele?" Daryl said.

"Sure," Michele said. Was Daryl suggesting it seriously or was he trying to convince, or even manipulate Kevin? Very interesting.

"Hey, no problem, I can do it. Who should I call?" Kevin was glad they thought it all out.

"Michele," Robert said. He and Daryl would set the computer and camera up, and Michele would wait in the car. He thought about his little leather-bound computer toolkit and whether he should bring it as well. Probably not. If this did not install in a couple of minutes, a lawn of a mansion in the middle of Huntleigh was not the best workbench upon which to troubleshoot the difficulty. So he let it go.

"Great," Kevin said. He took another bite of taco. Not damn bad. Maybe he'd get Robert to give him the recipe or the name of the cookbook. He'd tried to cook a couple of things with his limited experience and with his limited stock of ingredients and pots. Jambalaya had proven more difficult than spicy lalidope, pronounced lah-lee-dope, a dish his grandmother had made from hamburger and leftover canned vegetables from the refrigerator. Fish tacos were, what, some kind of seafood, fresh vegetables, sour cream, and tortillas. Certainly he could make that, and cooking in would save a couple bucks on dinner. Not to mention it was closer to the bedroom.

"Finish your lunch and we can go," Daryl said.

*   *   *   *

"Let me see it," Daryl said.

"See what?" Robert said from the back seat of Michele's station wagon.

"The laptop."

Robert unzipped the backpack and pulled out the old black laptop. A simple Pentium, before the Pentium II, but with MMX technology. The masses would consider this machine anachronistic or would simply refuse to use it, like a spoiled child who didn't like a toy. However, with the right emulators and non-Windows operating system upon it, a developer could tightly code some precision applications that used less than six megs of RAM per `Window` or `Panel` object and less than twenty megs of storage for a typical install, and with these applications conquer the world. Or at least the code for John Donnelly's alarm system. Robert passed the laptop to Daryl with a cord. "Plug it into the car's accessory port. We don't want to run down the battery."

"Right." Daryl plugged it in, opened the screen, and started it up. "Linux, good man," he said. "I didn't know there was a Linux version of the camera software."

"There's not," Robert said, "But I've got an emulator daemon that handles all the calls as if…."

"Shouldn't Kevin have called by now?" Michele said. She tapped her fingers on the wheel. She had parked in a strip mall parking lot on Brentwood to wait for Kevin's call. She had done that ten minutes ago and had been content to watch traffic and listen to the news on the radio. But the CBS news had come and gone, replaced by local news and a forecast for a cool night, but no precipitation.

"Probably," Daryl said. "He had a shorter drive than we did."

"Well," Michele said, preparing to explain that Kevin sometimes

109

had a roundabout way to go that made no sense to normal people, and that perhaps she should have driven Robert's car if the car thing was really an issue, but her cell phone chirped before she could begin. "Hello?" she said.

* * * *

Kevin turned the Dokken down when he got into the office park containing the nTropics building. He did the same thing when he pulled into the apartment complex where he lived, and the street where his parents lived. Sometimes, when he was looking for an address or a street name, he did the same thing, as if the sound were interfering with his vision. Maybe he just didn't want people seeing him acting like he didn't know where he was going. He certainly didn't want to draw any attention to himself now.

The office park didn't have very many trees or tall shrubs, but it's not like he was going to hide behind them with a red sports car. Still, he felt very conspicuous, and he knew they were probably right to not want him to follow Donnelly yesterday. He wondered if Donnelly had ever seen his car, because if he had, certainly he would remember it. Maybe not the license plate, and Kevin was really glad he hadn't thought of a good vanity plate.

He drove past the nTropics parking lot, planning to turn into the Custom Mailing, Incorporated, parking lot. But the Beemer was not in its accustomed spot, four slots from the door and against the street. Donnelly always parked there, except when he was somewhere else. Apparently, he was somewhere else. Instead of going right, into the CMI lot, Kevin improvised with an abrupt braking and jerk of the wheel to the left.

Kevin pulled behind the nTropics building, where trucks would go if they ever had anything to deliver to the elevated concrete loading docks. Since no trucks did, some nTropics employees parked there to be closer to their departments than the lower lot. Kevin eased his car between the phone poles, dumpsters, and parked employee cars. John Donnelly had not parked behind the building today, if ever.

The alley behind nTropics crossed the lower lot before depositing Kevin back on the street. He slowed through the lower lot, looking both for the Beemer and for employees who might recognize him. He wondered if Robert or Daryl would have taken the risk, going driving through the very lot of the company that had fired them? Probably not, but didn't that mean he was braver than they were, like Daniel or Homer or the guy that had his men rope him to something so he could hear the songs of the, what were they, Harpies? Probably not; just luckier that no one was going out to lunch or a doctor's appointment or to get a CD from his car.

Brave or lucky, Kevin hung a left and slowly drove past the nTropics lot. No one he knew came out, but he saw no green Beemer among the Toyotas, Hyundais, and Dodge pick-ups. He made another left and cruised the white-collar ranks of nTropics cars, the importance of people's cars growing the closer he got to the main entrance. Well, if the developers in the lower lot were blue collar, that is. Nothing in the middle management collection of Miatas and Audi TTs and Expeditions and Mountaineers.

Kevin turned right this time, into the CMI lot. He found a parking spot marked visitor, somewhat hidden from the nTropics front door by a dead bush. Of course, it was dead now, but Kevin remembered the bush had some kind of purple flowers on it. More than once he had planned to snitch a flower from it for Amy last spring, or Melissa in August, but he hadn't gotten across the street. The parking spot was marked **VISITOR** in faded paint, but Kevin was just visiting.

*   *   *   *

"You're sure?" Michele twisted the phone from her mouth. "Donnelly's not at nTropics," she announced to the car.

"What?" Robert said.

"He didn't have anything on his calendar, did he?" Daryl said.

Robert shrugged. They hadn't looked for today, an oversight he would try to correct in the future.

"What do we do?" Michele said. "I just asked," she said into the phone.

Daryl made eye contact with Robert before he spoke. "We go home," he said. No point in making Kevin sit conspicuously in a parking lot in Creve Coeur while they did the same here in Brentwood.

"Should we call nTropics to see if he's in? Maybe his car's in the shop," Michele said to Daryl and Robert.

"No," Robert said. "Too risky. Charlene might recognize our voices, or they might log ANI information in the PBX." A good ploy, though, and he was impressed.

"Annie?" Michele said.

"Automated Number Identification," Daryl said. "The computer equivalent of caller ID. There's little risk of that."

"But it's too much risk," Robert asserted.

Daryl inwardly shook his head, trying to keep the appropriate muscles from following through on the impulse. "Abort," he said with a shrug. Robert Davies was a good canary in a coal mine for subterfuge and criminal endeavors. If he got nervous, they all better get out, because he could smell the gases they could not. Daryl hoped it wouldn't kill him, though.

"We're not going in," Michele said into the phone. "I'm going to drop Robert and Daryl back at Robert's place. Right." She flipped the phone closed and placed it on the little shelf in her dashboard. "He said he'll meet you back at your house." She started the car and put it into gear. "Does this mean it's over?"

"We'll have to reassess," Daryl said.

"We could see about tomorrow. Or set him up with a tail tonight, if he goes out," Robert thought out loud.

"Do you trust any of us as a tail?" Michele'd never tailed anyone before, but she'd seen how it was done. Well, read how it was done, but she knew it would be harder in practice than in prose. David Albernathy wouldn't know how to tail anyone, either, since he'd not had to do it in the MPs. Maybe if he was a cop, or a private investigator instead of a campus security guard chasing undergraduate idealizations of Michele at 20.

Robert thought it over. Daryl didn't drive, Kevin drove a sports car, probably aggressively. Michele was asking, which might indicate self-doubt on her part. That left him, and he could probably do it if they needed a tail. Well, maybe not. "No," he admitted. Daryl said nothing.

"So tomorrow's our last chance?" Michele said.

"It's a little early to say that," Daryl said. Did they have enough cohesiveness to hold itself together if things didn't go entirely their way? Probably not. Kevin would get bored. Michele would get another job. He and Robert, maybe, could see this through to completion, but Daryl knew he was just as susceptible to a different shiny objective diverting his attention as the next guy.

"It might be," Robert said.

Of course, Daryl thought, Robert was ever the optimist. Or parsing her question to recognize the "our" as the key to the whole statement.

The phone rang, vibrating and threatening to topple from the shelf onto which Michele had put it. Daryl grabbed it as Michele completed her turn into traffic and proffered it to her a ring later, when the car's trajectory was stable in a lane.

"Hello," Michele said, one hand on the wheel and one on the phone. This criminal enterprise was making her live dangerously. Normally, she didn't answer or make calls when she was driving, but this made two days in a row.

"You're sure?" Michele said. "Okay, hang on." She raised her voice for Daryl and Robert. "Kevin says John Donnelly came up the drive as he was leaving. He must have been to a late lunch or something."

"An executive, coming back from lunch at 2:30? I am shocked, shocked!" Daryl said. Perhaps he and Robert would have help after all.

"Kevin's sure?" Robert said.

"He's turning around and going to check to see if he parked, what?" Michele said, then asked. "Kevin says he's parked in his normal spot and is going into the building."

"Donnelly, not Kevin, I hope," Daryl said.

"Yes," Michele said.

"Turn around," Robert said. "Let do it."

"We're going in," Michele said. She sounded utterly professional with it. She wondered if she should develop some slight code phrases, nothing like "The Fox is going into the hen house," but something slightly obfuscated. Probably not, she thought, flipping the phone closed and putting it onto the shelf again as she signaled for a left turn.

* * * *

Huntleigh was very, very quiet, Robert noted, and that might be worth something. Probably not a million or three dollars. From his house, he could hear the obscure traffic sounds of Page Avenue, I-170, and Lackland, all diffused into a slight shush sound at the edge of consciousness whenever he was outdoors. Here, in Huntleigh, nothing. An infrequent car on Litzsinger, but that's all.

Michele had pulled to the side of the circle closest to the house, which meant furthest from the street, as Robert recommended. She had the cell phone in her jacket pocket and her hands in the pockets to keep them warm.

"So what's the range we need this laptop in?" Daryl said.

"Just a couple hundred yards," Robert said. "Don't worry about it right this minute." He had put a fresh set of batteries into the camera. Robert unfolded the camera base and snapped the camera into its mount. The base was solid, with a single stem attaching the camera instead of a tripod configuration. Robert stepped over whatever dried and brittle flora John Donnelly had his landscapers place in his driveway circle. The center, about two square feet, was clear. He knelt in the clear space, carefully not crushing the valued topiary. He placed the camera in the remaining brambles, closest to the house. He set the camera on its pan and tilt, ready to receive its remote commands. "Plug the laptop into the accessory port," he said.

"Roger that," Daryl said. He opened the driver side door and sat on the seat, snaking the cable into the cigarette lighter again. "Ready," he said.

Robert plugged the other end of the cable into the laptop. He flipped the top open and booted it.

Michele held the cell phone tightly in her right hand, ready if it began ringing. She'd set it to vibrate instead of ring when she got out of the car. She didn't think the silence would be a requirement out here, but she wanted to contribute something. Daryl watched over Robert's shoulder as he began typing. Michele heard the faintest sound of motors and gears. She had to strain to pick the camera and its tripod out of the surrounding brush, but, so she probably only imagined she could see the camera move slightly.

"A little to the left," Daryl said.

Michele turned to look over Robert's other shoulder. Robert was using a cursor and the laptop's touch pad to align a photo in the middle of the screen. The photograph centered on the windows on the right side of the door. The cursor on the screen turned to a plus sign, and the image focused on the wall behind the door. And then, barely, a keypad.

"Can you get any tighter?" Daryl said.

"That's it," Robert said. "The camera's at the end of its range."

"Can we move it closer?" Daryl said.

"To conceal it, we'd have to mount it on the porch roof, and we don't have the time nor the tools to affix it properly. Besides, that would leave permanent marks and physical evidence," Robert said.

"Isn't John Donnelly right handed?" Michele said. "Shouldn't you angle in from the other side?"

Robert's heart swelled with pride. She was thinking logically, but missed one step. "Because he's right handed, he'd block the other side with his body as he extended his right hand to tap in the code. While he might block the code with his hand, he'd certainly block with his body if we picked the other side," Robert said.

"Excellent deduction, Watson," Daryl said. "You're making a lot of assumptions."

"If I'm wrong, we can get other positions in the IT field," Robert said. He opened the drive and triple-checked the disc in it. He tapped the tray to shut it. He disconnected the laptop's power cable.

"Where do we go with the laptop?" Daryl said.

"Look around," Robert said. "We've got to lay it flat, but it can be anywhere on this side of the house."

"What about under that lilac bush?" Michele said, gesturing to a bush centered in the expanse of lawn between the road and the lawn. The Donnelly estate, if it warranted estate status, featured a number of bushes placed sporadically upon the lawn, but together they would present a sight and noise break between the road and the house. The closest bush, a lilac, she thought, was a couple paces off the driveway. Donnelly, or his staff, wouldn't bother with it any more this autumn.

"That's a lilac?" Daryl said.

"It's not at its best in late October," Michele said.

"That should work." Robert said. "Michele, pull your car around so that you're about halfway down the driveway."

Michele and Daryl got into her car and she did as instructed. Robert trotted to the lilac, carrying the laptop carefully. When he got there, he opened the laptop, tapped a few commands, and closed the laptop. Not all the way, Daryl noted. Robert loped to the rear passenger door and got in. Michele didn't need direction; she stepped lightly onto the gas when the door clicked shut.

"The disc can hold approximately fifteen hours of video, but the laptop's batteries will only last about eight hours, or until about midnight. We can retrieve the equipment tomorrow," Robert said. "This car's not in the video if someone else recovers the disc." Robert clicked his seatbelt.

"So we're all set?" Michele said.

"We'll find out tomorrow," Daryl said.

Getting the Code

The next morning, Robert, Daryl, and Kevin sat in Michele's car, waiting for Michele's call to confirm Donnelly was at nTropics. Robert wasn't entirely comfortable behind the wheel of the voluminous station wagon parked suspiciously in the parking lot on Brentwood Boulevard. At eleven o'clock in the morning, the traffic was picking up for lunch. He had parked on a side street south of Litzsinger, performing a clumsy Y turn in a driveway so they'd be facing Brentwood. They'd only been there three minutes, but Robert could feel his skin prickling with tension.

"Relax," Kevin said. He'd called shotgun, so he was watching Robert fidget in the driver's seat. Personally, he couldn't remember the last time he'd ridden in a station wagon. Probably 1982.

"I am relaxed," Daryl said from the back seat.

"I'll relax when we're browsing the disc at my house," Robert said. He could feel eyes from behind curtains upon him, even if they weren't there. He hadn't seen the Neighborhood Watch warning sign at the end of the street, so they were probably safe. He'd rather leave, though. It was different with him behind the wheel.

"You ought to...." Kevin started, but his phone rang.

Robert turned the ignition key. It probably would have helped if they had been doing something with a map, or at least talking animatedly. Perhaps he should have pressed the cell phone against his ear as a cover story.

"Hi, Michele," Kevin said.

Robert levered the steering column-mounted shifter into drive and pulled into the street. Whatever Michele was saying, they were leaving.

"Sure, that's great. Will you meet us back at Robert's in, what," Kevin lifted the phone from his mouth. "How long will this take us?" he said to the passengers.

"Better make it an hour," Daryl said.

117

"Thirty-five minutes," Robert said. "Seven minutes to John Donnelly's, five minutes on site, twenty minutes back."

"That's thirty-two minutes," Daryl said.

"Insurance," Robert said.

"About a half hour," Kevin told Michele. "There's lunch involved. Come on." He lifted the phone again. "Lunch, right?"

"For someone out of work, you sure want to eat out a lot," Daryl said.

"Robert's got something, right?"

"Frozen pizza," Robert said. He didn't feel like discussing this now, when he was trying to move to the left lane on a busy street and avoiding all the Volvos that decided, suddenly and without using their blinkers, to turn into the Subway parking lot.

"Italian," Kevin said to Michele. "You bet. See you." He hung up the phone. "She'll be there."

* * * *

Robert turned the car slowly into the driveway, hoping to not underestimate the length of the car's nose or the pivot point of the vehicle, either brushing the bushes and scratching Michele's paint or bouncing the rear tire over the curb and into the grass, leaving a tire track in the soft earth.

Robert parked at the top of the circle as he had directed Michele to the day before. He pulled the keys from the ignition even as he was opening the door. "I'll get the camera," he said. "Daryl, you get the laptop. Kevin, you're on the phone."

"Right," Daryl said. He started walking toward the lilac, but noticed Robert was moving quickly, so he began to jog.

"You want me to call Michele?" Kevin leaned across the roof of the car.

"No," Robert said. He took off his jacket and spread it in the dirt at the circle's center before stepping onto the jacket. Not exactly Raleigh, but Sir Walter had spread more time in prison than Robert intended for himself.

Daryl snatched the laptop and brought it back when he saw Robert, crouching on his coat and digging with his fingers to free the base of the camera. "You are nuts, you know that? Nuts."

Robert stood with the camera and base in hand. "Perhaps," he said. "Just be sure to testify that I am NGRI when the time comes." He picked up his jacket and wrapped the camera in it. It was cool enough that he would notice it if he had any distance to go, but hopefully he'd only be walking between the car and his house, and not somewhere between where the car broke down and his house. Hopefully the jacket would pad the camera and camouflage it if they were stopped by a police officer on the way back to his apartment. Although three young men might have perfectly good reasons for having a pan, tilt, and zoom miniature camera with them in a car on a day when the normal people of the world were working, they just as easily might not. Of all the things to pop like flashbulbs in the officer's imagination, getting the key code to steal several million dollars' worth of gold from a former employer probably ranked low on the list. Given the current climate, it probably carried the lightest sentence of all possible intrigues.

Kevin looked at his fat sports watch. "Two minutes, thirty-six seconds. You, gentlemen, are professionals." He held the roof to swing himself into the passenger seat. "Let's roll," he said.

Daryl slipped into the back seat from the driver's side. Robert handed him the camera package. "One minute," he told the two in the car before closing the door on Daryl. With the others safely in the car, he trotted to the lilac bush and to the circle, scanning for anything forensic they might have missed. He didn't have enough time to look for traces of his fabric in the bushes, but at least he saw no paper nor plastic nor silicon on the ground. Even if they left traces of fabric, maybe the Federal Bureau of Investigation would assume it belonged to the landscapers. Too much to really hope for, really. If only they had known the style of uniforms Donnelly's landscapers wore. Robert pulled Michele's car keys from his pants pocket and slid into the car, starting it efficiently.

"All clear, boss?" Daryl said.

"Yes," Robert said. "They won't be looking for evidence for some time. By the time Donnelly needs to sell the bar, hopefully anything we left behind get trimmed and mulched by then."

"What makes you think we left something behind?" Kevin said. He'd only stood on the driveway and leaned on the car. Anything he'd left would be traveling with them. Unless he'd stood in a special mud or something, leaving a special mixture of red mud, clay, and lawn fertilizer only used by his apartment complex. He hadn't stepped in dog crap, had he? He would have smelled it by now, before leaving any on Donnelly's driveway. Hanging out with Robert was really starting to get to him.

"You always leave something behind," Daryl said. Cryptic and prophetic. He should have squinted his eyes like Clint Eastwood when he said it. Definitely a movie tagline in that.

119

*   *   *   *

Michele guided Robert's car to Overland in fewer than thirty minutes. She didn't want to sit in front of Robert's house for fifteen minutes, so she drove a couple of blocks down the street, looking at the houses. Most were as small as Robert's, although some of the bungalows had a second floor. Most dated from the first half of the twentieth century, so many had rec rooms and maybe a bedroom in the basements, finished by veterans and their younger siblings in the long, lazy decades after World War II.

The houses definitely had enough room for a single person. In the early half of the twentieth century, she thought, it was room enough for a small family, but times have changed. Now, each child needs his or her own bedroom with room for a full bed and an entertainment center.

She turned left at the corner of Tennyson and Hood. The yard of an aging elementary school held a google of children from the neighborhood. They still would know bunk beds and younger siblings beneath them in the night, looking down from their beds and out the windows into the streets in which they played street hockey and rode Big Wheels by day.

Michele knew she was projecting again; kids these days did not ride Big Wheels, and from what she had seen in her neighborhood, did not play much outside, either. She was projecting her own childhood into this pastoral scene and idealizing them all. Moving from base to base with her parents whenever her father had finished a tour or got promoted or whatever spurred the dislocation of a young girl from her small off-base bedroom would never match the experience of a kid growing up in an Overland neighborhood for any number of years that needed two hands to count.

Maybe that's the essence of being a writer, Michele thought, a deep dissatisfaction with some aspect of one's own youth and direction that you want to recapture and alter through a fictional alter-ego. Maybe she wanted the foolish young Cynthia to tame David Albernathy, to settle him down from his nomadic ex-military lifestyle.

As if she had never had the Electra complex epiphany before. Michele squealed out of the stop sign by the school, somewhat startled and not sure if she had stopped for longer than normal or not. If it came down to it, she could blame lack of familiarity with the Tercel.

She turned the corner again and started up the next block. Across the field just outside the schoolyard fence, Michele saw her car driving in the same direction she was. She glanced at her watch. On time, no less. She drove down the block with less reflection and more acceleration, turning the corner at an uncontrolled intersection with but the most judicious use of brakes and tight cornering. Robert's junk bucket of a car was in good shape. Better than hers, probably. She wondered if he worked on it himself and suspected he did.

Robert had parked her car on the opposite side of the street from his apartment. He was climbing up onto his porch with something wrapped in his jacket. To Michele, it certainly looked like something suspicious. Not long enough for a rifle, too long for a pistol. Maybe a sawed-off shotgun. Of course, she wouldn't mention it to him. She smiled, though, at the mindset she was developing. A former MP would certainly look around suspiciously like this. Now, if only she could come up with something better for David Albernathy to do than fawn over Cynthia.

Kevin waited for her at the edge of the lawn. "Hey," he said.

She met him and they walked up the sidewalk. "How'd it go?"

"Like a precision machine," Kevin said. "Robert kept us on a short leash."

"Good," she said.

Daryl was holding the door for them.

"Pizza's in the freezer," Robert said from the bottom of the basement stairs, and he disappeared into the basement.

"That's Italian?" Michele tried to keep her voice from dropping at the end. She had wondered what Robert would do for an encore.

"It's the only Italian I cook," Kevin said. He opened the freezer in the kitchen. "Delivery? No, it's da freezer!"

Michele shook her head and followed Daryl and Robert downstairs.

"I've got VideoMash installed on my main box," Robert said. He unwrapped the camera and folded his jacket over the edge of the chair at his workbench. He'd have to wash the jacket and clean off the camera and camera base. Right now, though, he was more interested in what was on the disc.

Daryl logged into Robert's computer with his username. He wondered if he could guess Robert's password. Probably not. Maybe Robert didn't have his box locked down as much as he should, either. It would pose an interesting challenge, anyway. But his username logged right in, displaying the dark background and centrifugal alignment of icons and shortcuts.

He opened the tray and put in the disc from the laptop. Because it was not executable, it didn't autorun for him, annoying him with the system lag and intrusive install or run screen. He selected **Start > Programs > MyMediaCo** (he guessed) **> VideoMash**.

The application opened up. Daryl clicked the **File** menu. No

121

recent files in the list, but an **Open** command. On a lark, he pressed **CTRL+ESC** to open the **Start** menu and hit **D** to review the recent documents list. Nothing displayed on the menu but the files he'd opened recently. Of course, it was tied to his user name. He **ALT+TAB**bed to get back to the video editing application.

Daryl felt Robert's shadow fall on him and glanced peripherally. Robert was right over his left shoulder. Michele was standing just beyond. Certainly she'd seen his little detour into the **Start** menu, but she probably didn't recognize it as nosing around. Or did she?

On the screen, the video started playing, somewhat choppily.

"I had it set to recording twenty frames per second to save space," Robert said. "Coupled with the access time to the drive, it's not going to be pretty."

"As long as it's clear," Daryl said.

"It's not too bad. Here," Robert said, taking the mouse and lassoing the door with the selection line in the screen. A dashed, color-changing rectangle surrounded the door. Robert clicked a menu command, and the selected region zoomed to fill the window. It was much grainier, with pixels the size of gnats.

"Can we fast forward?" Michele said.

"If not, it's going to be a long night, and Robert doesn't have a pizza for dinner," Kevin said from the stairs. "What have we got?"

Robert bent over the table to better work the mouse. Daryl stood to let the captain have the conn. Robert, recognizing the gesture, sat down. Any time a tech support person offers to let you drive, you should feel honored, he thought. He clicked one of the iconic little buttons at the bottom, a double forward arrow so stylized that it was hardly recognizable.

On the screen, the picture might have moved more quickly, but nothing changed. Pixels flickered for no good reason. After a minute, Robert clicked the icon again to double the advancing speed. The door darkened.

"Shit. It's getting dark, and he hasn't come home," Kevin said. Unless Robert had night vision on the camera, they weren't getting anything from this picture. He didn't put it past Robert, though. If anyone would have military surplus night vision gear, it would be him. "You have night vision on this thing?"

"Not on this thing," Robert said. He didn't have any night vision gear, truth be told, but why ruin a perfectly useful preconception? "However...." After a few seconds, as the picture darkened further, the window brightened in contrast to the exterior of the doors. "John Donnelly leaves his foyer light on all day," Robert said.

"How did you know that?" Michele said.

"He went to the door and looked in," Daryl said. "Nice job."

"Oh, yeah," Kevin said. Robert didn't miss anything. "Do you have a photographic memory?" he said. People with photographic memories made him somewhat uneasy. If he were in the X-Men comic, he'd be one of the people voting for the Mutant Registration Act.

"No," Robert said. "It's called synthetic thought."

"Which reminds me," Kevin said. "We've got no beer."

"Do we need beer at noon?" Daryl said.

"It's well after noon," Kevin said.

Daryl didn't have a snappy comeback for Kevin, and before he could lamely try to one-up him with something, a dark form obscured the camera view. The picture flickered and clarified, with a man quickly in the middle of the frame and then exit stage right.

"That's him!" Kevin said.

"You have a gift for the obvious. Slow it down. Rewind," Daryl said.

"Wait a moment," Robert said, and he let the scene play out for a couple of seconds before he clicked it to a halt.

"Why'd you let it run?" Michele said.

"Just because," Robert said. Focused as they were on the door and the keypad beyond, they'd have had no way to know if the person in the frame was John Donnelly. The person, John Donnelly or not, did not panic after visiting the keypad, nor run screaming back out. Odds were, then, that he or she had entered the right code phrase. From the **Edit** menu, he selected **Cut > End**.

"What are you doing?" Kevin said.

So little trust, Robert thought, and knew he would have asked the same questions. "I've trimmed the rest of the file from this block." He double-clicked the reverse button to replay the person in reverse and, after the person disappeared, cut to the start. From the **File** menu, he selected **Save As** and put the file on his hard drive. He'd delete the file later, overwrite it, and break the disc into six pieces to dump in a trash can in a fast food restaurant somewhere. Or six fast food restaurants. Sometimes, Robert even amused himself with his little plans. "Now we can watch the person entering the code without the chance of overshooting it and having to look for it again through the whole file."

Robert clicked the play button without the fast-forward. The dark shape filled the screen. Robert clicked a smaller button, and the video slowed. The shape appeared and paused before the door.

"He's unlocking the door," Kevin said. Donnelly didn't even know he was on camera. How could he? Was Kevin on camera right now, in Robert's basement? He suppressed the urge to look around. Robert would never have put the camera where he could see it, anyway. On the computer monitor, Donnelly went into the house. "He's in. And now, the moment we've been waiting for."

Robert clicked the slow button until the frames were playing individually. The dark shape on the screen was a shadow of a man, really. Robert couldn't testify the shape was even John Donnelly; the magnification and the poor lighting blurred the image to make the subject incomprehensible. The subject, however, was not the target of their camera inquiry. Or the target was not the subject of their inquiry.

"He's there, and there's the code," Kevin said. The figure on the screen stopped at the far wall and touched the keypad. The display of the alarm center changed. "Disarmed."

"What did he type?" Michele said.

"I don't know yet," Daryl said. "Robert?"

"We'll have to watch it more than once to see. Watch the way his hand moves; you won't actually see which key he presses," Robert said. He clicked to reverse the video, pausing it before the shape got to the keypad.

"All right," Daryl said. He took a pen from a crowded vertical pen holder and tapped on the screen where the keypad was. "Keep your eyes on this." Subtle color changes indicated the different buttons, a lighter shade of tan than the keypad itself. And the keypad was only a few shades darker than the off-white walls. Daryl lowered the tip of the pen to the desk. "Roll 'em."

Robert played the video again.

When Donnelly's hand met the screen, Daryl tapped the pen on the desk in the quick rhythm of the fingers on the keyboard. The fingers started lower left and progressed upward and to the right.

"Seven," Kevin said.

"Seven four," Daryl said.

"He's hitting both of them with his index finger," Robert said. He replayed the sequence.

"Seven four," Daryl said, tapping the pen, and then tapping the pen twice more without vocalization.

"I think the third number is one or two," Michele said.

"Probably two because he's moved from his index finger to the middle finger," Robert said.

"Could be," Daryl said.

"The fourth number is hard because his hand obscures it," Robert said. He replayed the sequence.

"Seven four two," Kevin and Daryl said together to the tapping of the pen.

"I didn't see it," Michele said. Kevin and Daryl shrugged.

Robert played the sequence over. "He's switching to another finger," he said. He played the sequence again. "Looks like his ring finger," Robert said. "Do you guys see it?"

"I guess," Kevin said.

"I'm not sure how you can even tell which finger he's using," Daryl said.

"Watch the shape of his hand as he moves it," Robert said, and he replayed the video.

"Sure," Daryl said. Robert must have eyes like a hawk, or be really used to watching the subtle differences presented by a digital camera.

"If he's going to the third finger, it's probably a number in the third column," Robert said. If it were in the middle column, he'd use one of the first two fingers. Robert tried it out on his desktop. He would definitely use the ring finger for a three or six. Maybe the little finger for a nine? "Does John Donnelly play the guitar?" he said.

"What?" Kevin said.

"If he plays guitar, he might use the last finger for a nine," Robert said. "Guitar players have greater finger strength in their ring and last fingers."

"That's playing the odds, to be sure," Daryl said. He didn't know if JD played the guitar, and he was certainly not going to break into his house based on an assumption that his guitar playing influenced the pattern through which he typed in his pass code. "Actually, that's nuts."

"All right, we have a one in three chance, then," Robert said. "It's 7423, 7426, or 7429. Can you guys see the last number clearly?" He clicked the rewind button on the screen.

"7426," Michele said.

"What?" Robert said.

"That's Donnelly's extension at nTropics. We saw it the other day when we were on the Web site. Plus, I had to call him a couple of times," Michele said.

"You called John Donnelly?" Kevin said.

Robert minimized the video software. "Daryl, proxy us," he said, standing to let Daryl drive.

Daryl sat in the chair and opened the Web browser.

"A couple of times, I provided him with some notes and a set of points for him to cover at conferences," Michele said.

"You wrote John Donnelly's speeches?" Kevin said.

125

"Not well enough," Michele said.

"She's right," Daryl said. "7426 is his extension." He gestured to the Web page containing the contact information.

"Maybe Appelbaum is his mother's maiden name," Robert said, incredulously.

Preparing for the Break-In
and Making the Bar

Robert closed the video software, deleted the movie files, ejected the disc, and emptied the computer's recycle bin without sitting down. He took the disc to the workbench. He drew a pair of tin snips from a drawer and cut the disc in half.

"What are you doing?" Kevin said.

"Destroying evidence," Robert said.

"What's next?" Michele said.

"Now we perform some alchemy," Daryl said.

Robert lifted the wooden crate of steel onto the workbench. "What do you need to shape this into a facsimile of the gold bar?" he said.

"I could use a furnace and a forge. Ideally, I would melt the steel and mold the bar."

"A furnace and forge?" Robert said. "I was under the impression it would not take that much."

"What, did you think I could do it with a torch and a hammer?" Kevin said.

"Yes," Daryl said. When Kevin had mentioned it, it had sounded that easy. Or maybe they had wanted it to be that easy.

"You're not going to get a uniform appearance unless you melt the steel," Kevin said. "It'll be a big kludge if you just fuse it with a torch. Besides, no worries. We can use my father's shop."

"Do you often use your father's shop to work on sculptures?" Robert said.

"No, I don't do sculpture," Kevin said.

"Then it's not a good idea for you to go this one special time," Daryl said.

"What?" Kevin said.

"Because your father might take note and ask what you're doing. We're not going to your father's shop." Even as a last resort, Robert thought. He shook his head and swallowed, feeling the ripple all the way down to his stomach. The whole plan was highly contingent, but somehow he had expected to complete the mission.

"Where else can we go to do it?" Michele never worked with metal, even in high school shop. All woodworking in a room full of guys. She'd thought of a sculpture class in college, but opted for drama instead. Writing drama was like writing anything else, and watching drama was much like watching anything else. "Can we rent a forge somewhere?"

"No," Kevin said. "It's not like a backhoe."

"St. Louis Community College has one," Michele said. "They use it for sculpture classes." She had also thought about taking a continuing education sculpture class down at MIT, Meramac In Town or Mom, I Tried, or so people sometimes called St. Louis Community College's Kirkwood campus.

"They only let students currently enrolled in a metal shop or sculpture class in," Kevin said. "I took a metal shop class through them as a high school extension course, and we needed student ID to get in. They checked us against a class roster."

"Could we fake a student ID?" Michele said. In *The Fugitive,* Harrison Ford used some self-laminating sheets and a razor blade. They wouldn't need to be that detailed. "If Kevin's still got his, all he'd have to do is replace the date sticker. We could get one from a current student.

"We could eat some oranges and make some IDs," Daryl said.

"Except that we'd have to fake a class roster," Robert said.

"We could snatch a copy of the existing roster and fake a name that's on the roster," Kevin said. He'd kept the ID, along with other mementos of his high school days, in an old Converse box on the shelf in his closet. He'd meant to get rid of them, the notes passed in class that said Candice did like him after all, the letter he got for Distributive Education Clubs of America, and the little medal he got for his Rotary Club speaking competition. Whenever he moved, though, he always put them in a box, and when he was seriously cleaning his apartment, he often opened the box before tossing it and started reading the notes. By the time he was done, having fingered the knit letter and the medal and reviewed how much better he looked than he did in the high school ID and the community college ID, he didn't have the heart to throw them out. Maybe someday a wife could do it for him.

"We don't have to go through all that trouble," Daryl said, smiling.

"What?" Michele said.

"The SCA has a forge over in Illinois. We can go over there and do it."

"The SCA?" Kevin said.

"The Society for Creative Anachronism," Michele said. "I didn't think of them."

"Are you a member?" Daryl said.

"No, not really. I dated a guy who was into it," Michele admitted. Ryan had been plotting his ascent to grand wizard or whatever they had in the kingdom of Camdenton. He'd also been into weirder things, which was why she'd told him he'd be better off without her after six weeks of courtship.

"What's the Society for...whatever," Kevin said.

"Essentially they run around, pretending they're in the Middle Ages. They've got the United States cut up into a bunch of fantasy kingdoms and have mock little wars with each other using swords and shields," Michele explained.

"And armor," Daryl said. "And when the subjects of the Barony of the Three Rivers need arms, they are welcome to some of the facilities maintained by the Barony of the Shattered Crystal. This includes The Forge, a metal shop in Edwardsville."

"You're kidding, right?" Kevin said. "What, a smithy? In Edwardsville?"

"Essentially, yes." Daryl said.

"They have the facilities Kevin needs?" Robert said.

"Yes," Daryl said.

"So, you know some people with the SCA?" Robert's shoulders and body felt much lighter.

"Well, I was in the SCA until a year ago," Daryl said. "My paid membership's lapsed, but I have been to the Forge, and I've still got a breastplate there. Baron Edward Darkhorse should let me in."

"Edward Darkhorse?" Kevin said.

"His real name's Andy Gibbon. I've got his number at my apartment. So there's your furnace and all the Borax you need. What do you think?" Daryl said.

"How do we get in?" Robert said.

"We'll tell Andy we're coming, and he'll let us have the run of the place. On any given night, two or three people are there, working on their armor. Typically, a senior SCA guy's in, helping people out. I'll make like I am finishing off my breastplate, and Kevin here can shape steel he brings into the bar." Daryl smiled.

"About that shape," Kevin said. "Do we have the shape? I mean, we know it's rectangular, but...."

"We're going to determine the measurements this afternoon, of

129

course," Daryl said. He gestured at the computer. "May I?"

Robert nodded.

Daryl tapped on the keyboard, logging out of Robert's account and logging in with the new `Daryl` account. Once the machine displayed the desktop, Daryl hit the Windows+R, popping open the **Run...** dialog box. He typed `iexplore` and hit ENTER to start Microsoft's Web browser. He preferred Netscape Navigator back in the day, and although Robert had the latest hep alternative installed, Daryl knew its limitations. Not that they'd be doing anything besides looking at HTML pages, but it was habit, he knew, and not Microsoft's patented Fear-Uncertainty-Doubt affecting his mind. Damn them for being good at something, he thought.

He typed an address in the URL bar. "It's still using the proxy server," he explained.

"Okay," Robert said.

"What are you doing now?" Kevin said. "The Web's going to make my bar for me?"

"Almost," Daryl said. The Web page displayed the auction house's information about the gold bar, including its size in inches. Daryl wrote the measurements on a piece of scrap paper. "Now, when we look at these photographs, we can gauge the distance between the edge of the letters and the edge of the bar. When we compute the percentage of the bar used by each letter, we can guess the spacing of the letters."

"Hang on, I have a calculator," Robert said. He opened the upper left drawer of the desk and brushed aside a set of loose pencils. He'd kept the old Texas Instruments statistic calculator his mother had bought him in high school. Reluctantly, though; he still had the second-hand slide rule she had bought first. A little too frugal at times, but she had managed to raise him and his sister on an office manager's salary. He kept the slide rule clean and practiced on it. Partly as a tribute to his mother, and partly in case civilization collapsed and he could no longer find the watch battery for the calculator. He smirked and pulled the calculator box from its drawer. He slid it out and turned it on.

"You guys are going to triangulate the size of the bars from the photos?" Kevin said.

"You have a better idea?" Daryl said. Personally, he was all ears. He'd rather not count the pixels and project the measurements, but he wasn't sure they had another way, unless they went in beforehand to measure. He looked over to Robert, whose blue eyes were fixed intently upon Kevin. Robert would never agree to that second risk, Daryl thought. He was probably right.

"No," Kevin admitted.

Amazing, Michele thought as Robert and Daryl bent over their computer screen, calculator, and paper. Robert opened up his graphics editor, and he and Daryl argued a bit about procedures and surmises. Michele wondered what it would have been like to go to school with these guys. She would never have given them the time of day in high school. Would she have been more open-minded in college? The English program had divorced her from exposure to many other types of people, so by sophomore year, she'd never have seen them except passing them in the campus library. Astounding.

She looked around the room again, over the wood paneling a notch above the cheap brown paneling that fit into so many basement rec rooms. She didn't know what kind of paneling it was, but it had knots and different gradients of grain in it. Had Robert refinished this room by himself? It wouldn't have surprised her if he did.

"I get it," Kevin said. "You're measuring counting the pixels across and then using the photographs to calculate ratios for the letter widths, computing the inches using those ratios."

"Of course," Robert said.

"That's not really trig," Kevin said. He was glad, because he had never cared for Mr. Houston's math classes. He'd had Algebra II and Trigonometry in Main 132, sitting in the row by the windows that faced the bare brick exterior wall of the Science building. Mr. Houston adorned his walls with Navy airplanes instead of cats hanging from trees with inspirational sayings, but Kevin had heard Houston worked for McDonnell Douglas back in the day. Between the walls and the math, the semester and a half of fifty minute increments would have been wasted without Cyndi sitting in the next row, one seat in front of him, and Todd sitting in the same row, one seat behind him. Between those two, he worked on a lot of English skills with notes passed back and forth, and a little French with Cyndi once. But after eight years, he still knew trig when he saw it, or didn't see it.

"Not yet, anyway," Daryl said. He tapped a couple floats into the calculator. Then he realized only a developer would hit the decimal point button and call a number a float. To regular people, numbers without decimal points were the same as numbers with decimal points in them.

It took them three scratch sheets of paper and several columns of numbers, but Robert and Daryl created relatively detailed measurements for John Donnelly's gold bar. Kevin had some input into the final sheet of paper, which offered measurements he could use in a designed blueprint format. Robert knew enough about architectural drawings, mostly culled from old handyman magazines, to see the similarity. He folded the last piece of paper up and passed it to Kevin. "You're handling this," Robert said. "You hold onto the plans." He'd shred the intermediate steps and disperse them as well.

"All right. When can we get to this SCA place?" he said.

"I need to call Darkhorse and see when they're open. They should have unlocked the Forge by now; it's mostly open at night and on the weekends because most of the SCA members do have real jobs," Daryl said. "I don't have his number on me; I'll have to stop at the apartment."

"I have to work tonight," Robert said. "I cannot go."

"Call in sick," Kevin said.

"I'm not sick," Robert said. He had accrued three weeks of sick time at a part-time job by espousing the philosophy that even if he was sick, as long as he could stand at the counter, holding himself up with both hands if need be, he was not sick enough to call in. Not that he ever did, of course, although he did drive to the video shop on more than one occasion. When all was said and done, though, he had dragged himself into nTropics without a sick day and only three days of paid vacation for two years and ten months. Dedication had not earned him an extra minute of severance pay. Still, Robert knew that Donna was different slightly from a corporation. *Little cos good, big corps bad, the sheep repeated.*

"We don't all need to go," Daryl said. "I can go, and you need to go. Michele, would you like to go?"

"Sure," Michele said. It had been a while since Ryan had taken her to an outing, down in Jefferson Barracks Park. The full SCA members dressed in medieval apparel, with all the ruffle and tights that tunics and leggings afforded. Michele had seen herself in one of the full-length dresses, forest green and fetching, awaiting a knight. Of course, back in the Middle Ages, a woman of her age then would have been an aged mother or a crone. That was four years ago.

"So we'll meet you here tonight at 10:30?" Daryl said.

"Is that necessary?" Robert said.

"We can look over the bar and plan our entry," Daryl said. "We haven't much time. Plus, Kevin will need your tools to make the letters."

"Won't they have the tools at the forge?" Kevin said.

"You don't want to make an exact replica there," Daryl said. "Just the basic shape. You can put the letters in here, so they don't know what you're doing exactly."

"Okay," Robert said. At the SCA forge, they would not have a

132

chance to measure the bar as precisely as they wanted. Certainly not without drawing attention to what they were doing. "We'll meet here at 10:30."

* * * *

Michele wondered if she could charge mileage against the eventual take of the gold bar. After all, she was doing much of the driving, but she couldn't blame them. She often drove when she collected more than one person for a social occasion, such as happy hour at work. She often found herself behind the wheel to take grad students or coffeehouse dates to whatever cultural event passed for simulated romance among the cultural elite-in-training. Or the pre-tenured, anyway. For too many years, she'd been the girl with the car, and with maintenance considerations and fuel concerns therein. Of course, charging $.29 a mile against a million dollars would be petty.

"Take Lindbergh down to Washington and make a left," Daryl said. "I'm in the apartments right behind the bank."

Michele followed the instructions and parked on the street where Daryl directed. The trio climbed a couple of cement steps and veered right at an encircled tangle of marigold remains. If she were the landlord, she would never have left the marigolds to rot all winter; surely someone could have pulled them up when they started going brown. Of course, with the St. Louis climate, that might not have been until November in some years, but this year had been unseasonably cool since September. Michele didn't like marigolds anyway, so if she were the landlord, she would begirth the apartments with something more colorful than marigolds.

Daryl pulled open the unsecured outer door and led them a set of stairs. The owners also didn't bother with niceties, like walls; they had only slapped a coat of paint on the cinderblock.

Daryl had his keys in his hand and inserted his key into his lock smoothly, with one stroke. He flipped the switch by the door, lighting the floor lamp in the corner. It didn't provide much light, certainly not enough to compensate for the healthy darkness provided by the drapes he had hung over the windows in the living room, and in every room, actually.

"This place is a cave," Kevin said. First, he noticed the wall-coverings. Instead of pictures, posters, or the normal things, Daryl covered his walls with blankets, it looked like.

"I like it dark," Daryl said. "I'm a geek." He preferred to think of his wall hangings as tapestries, as though his home really was his

133

castle. Upon his living room walls, he had an actual tapestry thing he'd bought at a flea market; a Pink Floyd The Wall three by four silk screen; and a king-sized blanket, depicting a tiger, he'd received as a gift. He liked to think that the coverings added a layer of insulation, that they kept the heating bills down in the winter, but in truth they probably just kept it dark. He wouldn't let them into his computer room, where a life-sized white Elvis silhouette on unframed velvet covered the wall opposite his computers. He couldn't explain it to them. On the rare occasions when he spun around in his chair to rest his eyes from a late night session or to seek an idea and he saw it, he had trouble explaining it to himself.

"I hear you," Kevin said. The sofa was something out of a Goodwill store, bearing a windmill print and some woodsy things. He sat in it. The cushions were soft, and snap-on pads fit over the heavy wooden armrests. Otherwise, a girl could bang her head. Not that Daryl encountered that problem often, but Kevin decorated his own apartment chivalrously.

Michele saw Kevin perch on the sofa and decided to examine the bookcase contents instead of sitting next to him. Daryl had a set of World Book encyclopedias and all of the annual updates until 1988. Certainly, he had a story behind them. Probably an aunt and uncle that bought them for Daryl's cousins until they were in high school, she thought, or did Daryl's parents favor an older sibling? Aside from the encyclopedias, Daryl had some paperback novels, from *Neuromancer* to *Mona Lisa Overdrive* and several lesser-known cyberpunk pieces. He also had *Frankenstein* by Mary Shelley in hardback, and not an illustrated classic. Score one for Daryl, she thought.

"Hang on a second," Daryl said. He kept his address book in his computer room, the second bedroom of his apartment. He figured the "hang on a second" would keep them from seeing the mess in his computer room, including the paper plates that were over the rim of his little waste can and the printouts spilling from the top of his three mismatched desks. He found the address book in the center drawer of his writing desk. He flipped through to the D section, where he did find the listing for `Edward Darkhorse (Andy)`. He quickly memorized the number, put the old-fashioned pen and ink address book away, and went back into the living room.

"I've got it," Daryl announced. He picked up the phone on the dining room wall and dialed Andy's number. "Andy," he said when Edward Darkhorse answered. Should he have asked for Edward? Daryl wondered. Andy would get him in less trouble, he thought, if Andy's mother were to answer the phone.

Daryl's kitchen was pretty standard, Michele noticed. Daryl hadn't hung more dark fabrics in the kitchen, which indicated he didn't go there much. Or so she thought. A paneled wainscoting over the bottom half of the walls met wallpaper extending from the ceiling. Daryl spoke into a simple touch-tone phone on the wall. He had dialed and reached someone. Michele didn't pay full attention to the vetteral utterances that comprised Daryl's end of the conversation. He wasn't writing anything down, though, so she hoped he knew where it was.

"Great, we'll be on our way in about an hour," Daryl said. Edward Darkhorse had granted permission for him to show some outsiders the forge and to pick up the breastplate Daryl had been working on. Of course, Daryl could use a set of pauldrons and greaves, Edward said, as wells as a girth and some leggings. If he was going to fight any mock wars. Of course, Daryl would have preferred a castle, perhaps an armada, or a couple arquebus instead. He told Andy he'd bring them over this evening and hung up. "We're cleared," Daryl announced.

*   *   *   *

Once you crossed the river into Illinois, the scenery flattened into sameness, with plains occasionally broken by a copse of deciduous trees. At least the growing development added something, nudging the family and corporate farms further inland, replacing rows of corn and grain with rows of cheap used cars and subdivision houses. Michele didn't make it over very frequently.

Daryl guided them to Edwardsville, home to a Southern Illinois University and not much else, although its Chamber of Commerce might disagree. Michele took the Illinois State Highway 157 exit from Interstate 270 and wound northward. Somewhere ahead, the campus lie off to the left; however, Daryl had her turn right before the campus, before the sign that proclaimed Edwardsville the home of some obscure Illinois governor. Michele was glad to follow the directions, not only because Daryl was good at them, but it interrupted Kevin's narratives.

"Turn right here, onto Industrial," Daryl said.

Michele turned right where he indicated. The industrial park had honest names, at least. They'd turned off 157 onto Commercial Drive, and they'd crossed Technical Drive before reaching Industrial Court. Too many builders had tried to dress up their 80's and 90's equivalents of the Quonset hut communities with street names like ice cream flavors. The industrial park contained the requisite brown brick buildings near the highway, offering two IT firms, a vending company, and three companies with androgynous names that could have fit any

135

industry. After they passed Technical Drive, however, a number of steel buildings housed fleets of industrial equipment.

"You've been here before?" Kevin said.

"No," Daryl admitted. "Last time I went to the Forge, it was in someone's basement. Darkhorse told me how to get here."

"You memorized the instructions?" Michele slowed so that Daryl could have a look at the buildings as they passed; Industrial Court was not very long, and she hoped he'd see the address they wanted. She didn't want to have to drive another forty-five minutes back to Kirkwood so Daryl could get the phone number again and confirm directions.

"It's only three steps," Daryl said. "North on 157, East on Commercial, South on Industrial. Pull into this lot, the Carbondale Molding building."

"That's four steps," Kevin said.

"No, that's three steps," Daryl said, "Unless you want to count the desired result as the ultimate step. I don't; in a recipe, you don't put 'Eat cake' in the directions, do you?"

"I don't see it," Michele said. The Carbondale Molding facility, ironically located some miles north of the burg for which it was named, was a tall, but single story structure bearing brown concrete walls and a set of high windows that let the sun in, but did not let the workers stare out. A door, flanked by glass, faced the street at the northern corner of the western wall, probably leading to the reception area. Steel double doors in the north wall led into the guts of the building, probably reserved for the worker ants. A sign directed receiving traffic around back. The parking lot was empty. Carbondale Molding must be a one-shift shop, much to Carbondale's chagrin. Maybe it needed a state grant to waste.

"Go right here," Daryl said.

Michele followed the front parking lot of the building. At the southern edge of the building, a secondary parking lot extended to the left. More importantly, several cars nestled the building on its south wall, huddled around another set of double-steel doors, one of which was propped open. "Park?" she said.

Daryl nodded. "They sublet a part of the building."

Michele parked next to a blue compact pickup and they got out. Kevin pulled his box of scrap metal from the station wagon's back and carried it. Daryl led them in, leaving Michele nothing but to follow them in. Kevin carried the box easily. Michele remembered how his arms swelled against his short sleeved shirts last summer, and how she and Angie had asked him on several occasions to carry boxes of paper from the supply closet just to see that.

She hesitated just outside the door. Although the day was chilly enough for her light blue coat, she could feel the warmth coming from the open door, and she could hear the clanging of hammers on steel. Through those doors a men's world lay, and she didn't know how comfortable she'd be there. It was not unlike her first day of shop class, when she was just an awkward sophomore, unsure of herself and afraid her braces would make her unkissable if she saw a guy in class she wanted to try to kiss her. She stepped forward quickly, hoping that the men did not see her hesitation; she wasn't a gawky teenager anymore.

The interior was darker than the outside, no matter what the architect intended with the high windows. The beginning of October twilight negated both the windows and the few fluorescent lights high overhead. Only half were lit, which meant somewhere someone had not flipped all available switches. Probably another developer who liked the dark.

Michele felt the weight of heat upon her face and hair as she stepped into the room. A large furnace showed fire through a small hole, augmenting the unnatural light and casting some flickering shadows across the nearby work benches. Like sub, sub demons, a few slacker-generation youth banged hammers on steel to atone for their sins. Or their lack of a better thing to do on Friday night.

A man in a sleeveless shirt plunged a bent sheet of metal into a tub of water to punctuate her thought. Michele gasped inwardly when she realized his hair was grey curls, not blond, and that his sleeveless arms were probably better than Kevin's. A dark spot, either a tattoo or a bruise, colored the top of his right bicep. Not a slacker, a boomer, Michele thought. She wondered what Angie would say. Actually, Angie would probably mention her husband had arms like that when he played softball and hockey, but not since he discovered multi-media online role-playing games.

"Alden Wolfheart," someone else said.

"Edward," Daryl said. He deepened his voice as though on stage, which he was, in essence. The SCA was all theater, all the time. Mostly.

A red-haired man came around a workbench. His long, wavy hair was tightly pulled back in a ponytail behind him. He wore a denim jacket with the sleeves shoved up over his elbows. He stuck out a slender hand, far more slender than Michele would have expected for a husky man. She wondered if he played piano. When Daryl held out his hand, Edward grasped Daryl's wrist. "Well met by firelight."

Michele winced.

Daryl grabbed Andy's wrist much as Andy had his. "It had been too long since we fought shoulder to shoulder."

"These are your fellows?" Andy/Edward said.

"Indeed. Kevin Halefellow and Michele Darklocks." Daryl said. "Kevin has brought steel to forge tonight."

"Well and good, well and good," Edward said. "And you? Will you complete your armor? For when the horn of the King of Meriedies blows again on the field...."

"We shall see, we shall see," Daryl said. His voice lightened. "May Kevin use your facilities?"

"What do you need?" The red-haired man's voice lightened to match Daryl's. Michele wondered if Daryl would call him 'Andy' now.

"Kevin?" Daryl said.

"I just need to shape a bar, really," Kevin said. "It's for a class project."

"A bar?" Edward/Andy said.

"I see what I need." Kevin said.

"You've worked with metal before?"

"I am in a class," Kevin said.

"All right, then," Andy said. "Help yourself, but don't hurt yourself."

Kevin set the box of steel on a workbench and looked around. Daryl walked off with Andy. Michele put her hands into her pockets and teetered on the balls of her feet for a minute. The guy in the sleeveless shirt held a set of tongs into the furnace and withdrew a plate of metal. Michele considered going over and talking to him, trying to determine what sort of man retained his enthusiasm for knights and swords to his age. She had enough on her lab clipboard, trying to figure out her three compatriots. With nothing else to do, Michele followed Kevin around a table of what looked like, and very well might have been, medieval tools or torture devices.

Kevin balanced the box of steel on his hip and the edge of a table as he cleared some space. He'd never been here before, Michele thought, and he's making himself at home. That was his whole world; everything served his purposes. Michele never felt that comfortable, that easily. Kevin shoved the box onto the new clearing on the table. He opened the top and started rummaging through it. Michele leaned her backside on the edge of another table.

Kevin wasn't sure if he'd mislead them or not; he hadn't said he'd be able to mold the steel. Now that he was here, though, he'd have to make a show of it. Perhaps he could fuse the steel and blend the seams, but he didn't really know how to work with a forge. I mean, it's not like he was making a sword, right? Kevin pulled the assorted pieces and chunks of broken steel from the corrugated cardboard crate and spread them on the desk. At the bottom of the box, he found his salvation.

It looked like a cut from a steel beam of some sort. Kevin laid his hand upon the top, pleased to see the piece was longer than the span from his fingertips to his palm, roughly seven inches. He took the beam bit from the box, shoving the box aside and bulldozing some room in front of him. The table contained a set of hammers, but no ruler or tape measure. "You see a ruler?" he said to Michele.

Michele looked over the bench she had leaned on. It had some power tools bolted to the top of the table. Nothing resembling a ruler, she thought. She looked closer at the base of one set of gears and belts. The base bore a stamp of a ruler, probably important to the function of the machine. "Here's one," Michele said.

"Great!" Kevin said. He brought the beamlet and measured it. Nine and a half by five by six. It wasn't forty pounds of steel, but it slightly larger than the measurements that Robert had made him memorize. Give or take a freaking millimeter. Kevin remembered the tolerances allowed by many of the things he machined and milled in his father's metal shop. Within a hundredth of an inch would be no trouble at the RHC plant. But these SCA guys were trying to recreate something out of the middle ages. At least they had a good milling machine, to which the ruler was attached.

"What?" Michele said.

"This was cut from a beam, probably from a building demolished in the building frenzy at the turn of the century," Kevin said, and he would have elaborated, giving a chronology or archeology of the building from which the beam had been cut, but he realized Michele worked in the same department he did, so he cut it short. "We can just trim this piece to match."

"Okay," Michele said. Kevin knew what he was doing, but he wasn't good at simplifying things. Which is why he was a marketing assistant, and not a technical writer.

Michele watched Kevin mark the bar and measure it again. He drew lines with a straight edge that tapered the beam into an ingot. He started a motor on the machine in front of him and started pressing the metal bar against some moving part—Michele couldn't see it, but she could hear the collision of steel and something stronger. She watched Kevin's long fingers precisely, steadily moving on the steel and the machine.

"Don't tell OSHA, okay?" Kevin shouted over the machine.

"What?" Michele said.

Kevin nodded at a sign on the rear of the machine. Red text on a yellow background warned them, next to an internationally approved icon, that eye protection was required using this machine.

Michele nodded. She looked over the other three people working with metals. They were working with far cruder implements—the hammers and the fire, mostly. She wondered if they would use eye protection. She raked her eyes over the tops of the nearby benches. No goggles in sight, so either The Forge expected SCA members to bring their own, or the SCA members were not too worried about eye injuries. Or, Michele thought, perhaps most SCA members wore glasses.

Kevin turned the steel ninety degrees and began pushing it slowly into the machine again. Michele didn't expect him to stick the tongue out of the corner of his mouth, and he didn't. He looked intently, but not intensely, at the steel in front of him, not particularly concerned that the machine could capture one of his fingers. Michele wondered what would happen if it did. She pictured Kevin losing his middle finger. No, his left ring finger. That would be much more poetic and metaphoric. Would he highlight it, or hide it, from the string of women who would only come to know too late, like little Missy, the woman he would meet at the gym. Did Kevin go to the gym? Of course he did. Little Missy, the junior college tech support bunny, who knew only enough to frustrate those who got her Level 1 tech support. Of course, no one ever got frustrated with Missy because her voice was quite perky, so the poor Level 2 guys caught hell when she offered the customer a remedy. Missy, who owned a parrot because her high school crush had given it to her. Missy, working out at the gym because they told her it was good for her, not that she ever noticed— her metabolism kept her ultra-thin anyway. The kind of lightly bubble-headed blonde Kevin liked before the accident, but now.... Would she see past the disfiguration, to see the man beyond? Would Kevin?

"Hey, guys," Daryl said.

Michele started. She'd been a little into that imagination trip.

"Hey," Kevin said over the machine.

"How's it going?" Daryl said.

"Almost done," Kevin said, turning the bar again.

"That fast?" Daryl said. "What about molding, and fire, and everything else?"

Kevin flipped a switch on the side of the machine. The wheels and belts within spun down with a diminishing whine. "That's it. There's no molding or cutting since we had a piece I could mill down. It was a little bigger than John Donnelly's gold bar, so I just cut it to size. No molding needed."

"Could you have done this at Robert's house?" Daryl said.

Kevin thought about it. He hadn't sorted the metal by shape and size, and probably ought have before dragging them out here. "I don't know," he said. "It depends on what tools and equipment he has at home. It's better to do something like this where you have all the resources at hand," he added.

"It's only been twenty minutes," Michele said.

"We've got a lot of extra steel," Daryl said.

"We can leave it for these guys. It's scrap," Kevin said. They'd never notice extra scrap, would they? He didn't want to lug it back, and certainly none of them wanted any scrap steel, like the incriminating bar, laying around.

"You can make a dagger blade from this one," Michele said, picking up a long, mostly flat piece. It was longer than her hand. She envisioned an ivory handle with an elaborate Celtic weave. However, its sole function would be to explain their visit and time spent.

"A dagger blade?" Kevin said.

"How's it going?" Andy appeared behind Daryl.

"We were talking about the dagger Kevin needs to make," Daryl said. "Could you show him how to use the forge to hammer a blade from this?" He took the metal from Michele.

"Sure! You'll need to come over here, though. I hope you're not afraid of fire," Andy said.

Kevin didn't appreciate the condescending chuckle, nor wasting time making a blade. "I haven't been burned so far," he warned Daryl and Michele, and he wondered if they got the message.

Before the Break-In

Michele pulled the car into the parking lot of the video store and engineering firm. "Please don't drink that in the car," Michele said. If Kevin spilled any beer back there, she'd never get the smell out. She couldn't think of a way to explain that to Aunt Catherine when Michele shuttled her to dinner. Aunt Catherine might be nearing eighty, Michele's great aunt actually, but she had a nose that could tell if a man had been in the car with cologne. Spilled beer might kill her.

"I was just looking at it," Kevin thought. He was counting the words on the Rolling Rock Extra Pale label. He wondered if he should count the name of the beer. That would throw it over 33.

"There's nothing on the back of the label," Daryl said. "No need to view it from the inside."

"Yet," Kevin said. He'd convinced Michele to stop at a Schnuck's grocery store after they had dinner in the Central West End at a little café he'd recommended. He'd hoped to see Trisha, since she had an apartment nearby, but he hadn't. Food was good, though, and he had seen a guy named Doug who he'd met at a party once.

"Do you always drink this much?" Michele said.

"No," Kevin said. He paused a beat, then two. "Sometimes I drink a lot." He smiled, but Michele wasn't looking at him in the rearview mirror.

"We're hardly in normal circumstances," Daryl said. "The last few days have been like Spring Break in college." He wondered if that made him an enabler, but since he was drinking with Kevin, he was enabling himself, too. That probably made it a rationalization instead.

Robert stepped out of the darkened store with an older woman. As she locked the door, he swept his eyes over the parking lot, nodding at Michele's car, but keeping his eyes moving to the corner of the building and the sidewalks on either side of the street. He accompanied the woman to one of the two other cars in the parking lot, an old Mazda sedan, and watched while she got in. He said something to her and came over to Michele's car, opening the rear passenger door when he recognized his place.

"Hey, stud, older women make beautiful lovers, they understand," Kevin said.

Robert closed the door softly, glancing at Michele for her reaction. She had none, of course, but he could hope. "That's the owner of the store," he said.

"I would never have expected a relationship with a co-worker from you, Robert!" Kevin said. "Or is she using her position of power to position you?"

"She's not," Robert said. "Well?"

"Well?" Kevin said.

"Show him the bar," Daryl said.

"Right," Kevin said. He put the beer back into the twelve pack and picked the bar up off of the floor. "How's this?" He offered it to Robert with one hand, knowing Robert would be surprised by the weight.

"It's not twenty-five pounds," Robert said. Kevin had probably expected him to drop the bar, but he kept it up with one hand after an initial dip, at least he kept it up with one hand long enough to bring it to the other so he could hold it for close inspection.

"Gold's more dense than steel," Daryl reminded him.

"So how did you put the letters into it? You didn't do it at the SCA, did you?" Robert said.

"I've got my methods," Kevin said.

"What he means is he's got some engraving tools in his apartment," Daryl said.

"Four cutters and some lubricant to keep the tips cool," Michele said. She'd applied them where he was cutting so that he could keep cutting, with a cool blade. She'd trusted Kevin to not amputate any of her typing fingers. He'd done a good job. He followed the instructions mapped out on Daryl's scratch paper perfectly.

"It looks right," Robert said. Daryl would have kept Kevin honest. He desperately wanted to measure the letters with his micrometers, but deep down knew that they'd be imperfect to the slightest degree, and they'd be imperfect copies of their imperfect guessing. Robert resolved not to measure when he was pacing tonight.

"It is right," Kevin said.

"So what now?" Michele said.

"Now, we perfect our plan," Robert said.

"And drink," Kevin said.

"And drink," Daryl seconded.

*   *   *   *

Robert carried the bar into his basement. Kevin had chosen to carry the beer into the kitchen, so he let Robert take possession of his proud contribution. Robert set it on the bench next to the electroplating equipment. Funny, it was only a power supply and a bucket yesterday, but today it was "electroplating equipment." He felt like MacGyver, but better equipped.

"May I?" Daryl gestured toward the computer. Robert nodded.

Kevin stormed down the stairs, four open bottles of Rolling Rock in hand. He passed them out like campaign fliers, Michele thought, but she took one anyway.

"Would anyone like a glass?" Robert said, especially to Michele. She didn't, and neither did anyone else.

"Okay, we've got to sand the necklace into powder and we can plate it," Kevin said.

"I've already got that," Robert said. He picked up a sealed bowl behind the electroplate tank. He opened the lid slowly so to not spill the contents, couple of cubic inches of gold dust.

"Did you sand that all down before you went to work?" Kevin said.

Robert briefly thought of retaining the mystique. "I have a grinder," Robert said. "And a pair of pliers."

Kevin smiled. He hadn't thought of that. Less time with sandpaper and more time for the beer. "Cool. You have some electrolyte solution?"

Robert pointed to the bottle behind the power supply. He'd picked some up immediately after they'd left him this afternoon.

"Wow, this is just like a cooking show. And in the next step, we'll need some finely chopped carrots, which we happen to have right here." Kevin said. "Well, let's do it. Is this power supply plugged in?"

"Yes," Robert said. The cord from the back led to the outlet beneath the work bench, if Kevin had bothered to look.

"All right, then." Kevin looked over the bench and took the insulated gloves he knew would be there, putting them on the edge of the bench. He poured the gold dust from the bowl into the bucket first and then poured the electrolyte solution over it. The motion of the liquid would help create the suspension more quickly than the other way around; regardless, Kevin took a screwdriver and stirred the mix. "Which is anode, and which is cathode?" he said.

"Red is positive, black is negative," Robert said. He'd slit the wire bundles coming from the power supply, removed the computeresque plugs from each end, and had bundled the positive wires and negative wires into two separate strands. He'd used two different colors of electrical tape to binds the colors and had capped each strand with a metal connector.

"Just like a stereo," Kevin said. "Cool."

Michele moved so she could see over Kevin and Robert what they were doing, and not so close as to be dangerous. She watched Kevin's hands and compared them to Robert's. Kevin's were longer, of course, because he was taller; Robert's had strange texture to the backs, with veins and tendons exposed. She wondered if he clenched his fists a lot to make them prominent, if they were the most exposed thing about him. If he were a character in her novel, they would be, and it would mean something.

Kevin put on the insulated gloves. He put the steel bar into the electroplating tank. "This will be basic physics at work, friends," he said. He adjusted the bar in the tank. He placed the red-taped wire loosely in the solution. He lay the black wire on the top of the submerged steel bar. "The electrons will flow from one pole, the anode here in the solution, to the negative pole, which is touching the thing we want to plate. When the electrons travel, they'll hop on bits of gold, like little ferries, and when the electrons get to the steel bar, the gold sticks to the steel."

"Elementally, my dear Watson," Daryl said. He'd spun the chair to watch what they were doing, but he couldn't see through the thicket of bodies.

Kevin turned the power switch on. It didn't make any sound at all, but he watched the bar change colors until it was a bright gold. He turned the switch off and waited a few seconds before reaching into the tank. He took out the bar and displayed it.

"Damn," Daryl said.

"Of course," Kevin said, turning the bar to display two silver spots where the bar had touched the bottom of the tank, "I'll have to turn it and apply more gold to cover these, but the edges will be nice and even when I polish it. Walla!" He put the bar back into the solution and applied more voltage.

"That's great," Michele said, and she meant it. Robert had built an electroplating system in his basement. He couldn't have used it, well, probably not as easily as Kevin used it, but he built it. Kevin, on the other hand, could not have built it, but he could use it. Robert could craft jewelry as a hobby. Didn't Daryl already say he knew how to do that?

Kevin turned off the voltage and took the bar from the tank. He shook it twice to get most of the water off it and set it, base down, on the workbench. He took off the gloves and brushed his hands.

Robert looked at the bar. "Hang on a second," he said. He paused to pick up the printed photographs of the bar, taken from the auction house's Web sites and printed in high quality dot matrix. Robert compared the photographs to the real bar. Robert would not have not known the bar before him differed from the one on the paper. "Good work," he said. He tried to balance his appreciation against how impressed he was that Kevin actually did it. He should remember in his assessments of other people that sometimes they had hidden skills you would not expect, and not to underestimate them.

"So now what?" Kevin said.

"Monday morning, we use the keys to enter John Donnelly's house, we type 7426 into his keypad to disarm his alarms, we bring down the cameras on the Web page, we exchange the bar, we rearm his alarm, and we leave with the gold bar," Robert said. He didn't number the steps or tick them off on his fingers, but the order was clear.

"What do you mean, we?" Kevin said.

"We have three teams," Robert said. "Daryl will handle the live Internet feed, right, Daryl?"

"Sure," Daryl said, tapping on Robert's keyboard. "I have the perfect idea. I'll attack the routers at nTropics' ISP. They have an old patch on them, which leads them to a certain fundamental flaw wherein a malicious user can force a reboot. Of course, the reboot looks like a software error on their part, so nTropics will never know that anything happened. The outage should last about ten minutes, and I can kick it off the minute you need it."

"Okay," Robert said. "We'll need a driver to drop off the insertion team and to pick it up. We don't want a car sitting in the driveway, and we need two people to go in."

"I suppose I get to drive," Michele said.

"Thanks for volunteering," Robert said. "Kevin, you and I go in and exchange the bar."

"What?" Kevin said.

"Michele drops us off, we tell Daryl to drop the routers, and when he says it's clear, we exchange the bar. Then Michele picks us up." Robert thought the plan sounded good.

"Why do I have to go in?" Kevin'd made the bar. He didn't have to go into the house. "I can drive."

"Listen," Robert said. "Do you want to make Michele or me carry that fake bar, or the real one? You're the biggest mule we have, and we need you to haul it."

Kevin looked at Robert's arms and at Michele. He didn't like the thought of actually breaking in, because that was flat out a felony, but Robert was right, he was the best man for the job. The strong, silent type. "Okay, boss," he said. "But I want a gun."

"A what?" Michele said.

"A gun," Kevin said. "Listen, I am going to be breaking and entering here. If someone starts shooting at me, I want to defend myself."

"You won't need a gun," Daryl said. "What are you going to shoot?"

"Nothing," Kevin said. He could almost feel the weight of a big nine millimeter in the small of his back. He'd wear a flannel shirt open over a T-shirt so nobody would see it. Probably the old Metallica shirt that Miguel loaned him and he never returned. Because it wasn't his shirt, nobody could trace it to him. Of course, he'd have to wear the flannel shirt his Aunt Gwendolyn insisted upon buying him every second Christmas, but flannel shirts were a dime a dozen. Metallica shirts were unique.

"So you don't need a gun," Robert said.

"Carrying a gun while you're committing a burglary is an additional felony count," Michele said. She remembered reading about it in the paper and researching it. David Albernathy would have to leave his pistol behind whenever he planned to burglarize the apartment of a suspect. Of course, David Albernathy wouldn't do anything like that in *Sonnet 127*. He's too busy wooing Cynthia clumsily. However, in *A Sordid Boon*, which Michele didn't start writing beyond an idea and a partial outline, he'd have plenty of opportunity. Maybe she ought to work on that one first; she was certainly garnering experience for crime fiction.

"What?" Kevin said.

"I am afraid so," Robert said. Michele had seized the right tactic, he thought. "If you have an unlicensed firearm on you when you commit a crime, it's automatically a felony. Or an additional felony."

"Shit," Kevin said. He really liked the thought of packing heat, but he didn't like the thought of prison. Actually, he could go to prison anyway. "So what's the difference between one felony and two?"

"Fifteen years in the state prison," Michele said.

"We're not going to get caught, right?" Kevin said. "So what's the big deal?"

"What is the big deal?" Daryl said. "Is it some sort of penis thing?"

"I got the penis thing covered with the red sports car," Kevin said.

"My father's got a Glock in his home office. I'll just borrow that. No worries."

"No worries? You're off your nut," Daryl said.

Shit, Robert thought. "I have a clean gun," Robert said. He had a Heym Detective Special .22 in his laundry room safe. He'd bought it from a guy he'd worked with, a guy he trusted enough to expect it had never been used in a crime and that it wasn't stolen. The guy had been hard up for money, and Robert preferred to give Ben ten more dollars than the pawn shop would have. He cleaned it every time he fired it at the range, so it was clean. Hopefully, Kevin would take the bait and think he meant some underworld password for unregistered and hence, more desirable.

"Clean?" Kevin said. That fit his ideal better; an unregistered, disposable handgun. He wondered if he was going too gangsta, or just enough.

"Spotless," Robert said.

"You're not serious," Michele said.

"It's better than him trying to steal his father's gun, isn't it?" Robert said.

"Marginally," Michele said. She met Robert's eyes and tried to sound what lay beneath their placid blue/grey waters.

"Yes," Daryl said. Robert would probably hand him a pellet gun.

"Okay," Kevin said. He could compromise.

"You guys are nuts," Michele said.

"We're the ones going in," Robert said. "There's no danger to you."

"Since you guys asked," Daryl said, looking again at the computer screen, "John Donnelly's on American flight 334 to Dallas tomorrow at 9:20 am."

"You've got his itinerary?" Michele said.

"He uses nTropics," Daryl said. "Of course I do."

"Can you find out if he's on the flight?" Robert said.

"Sure, he'll check in at the airport. I'll have to hit the airline's site, not nTropics, but I can probably get in," Daryl said. He'd prodded Trans World Airlines some many years ago; he wondered if American just imported all user names and passwords, or if they created them anew, with the merger.

"All right. You do that. We'll be on our way there. Call us when you're sure he's on the flight, and we'll go in," Robert said. "We'll meet here tomorrow at nine o'clock. Everyone good with that?"

"How about I don't?" Daryl said. "I'll go to the County Library headquarters instead. You don't want me to launch an attack from your

149

home computer. I'll use the Internet computers they've got there."

"All right. Kevin? Michele?" Robert said.

"Okay," Michele said.

"What?" Kevin said. He'd thought he'd drink some beer and crash here again.

"Meet here in the morning. We've got a big day tomorrow. We should all try to get seven hours of sleep," Robert said.

"I'll see you guys tomorrow then," Michele said.

"So where's this gun?" Kevin said.

"I'll have it tomorrow," Robert said. "You don't want to get pulled over with it in your car, and I don't want you holding up any convenience stores tonight."

"Good enough," Michele said. "I'll see you guys in the morning." She put her sparsely sipped beer on the workbench and headed out.

Robert grabbed her bottle and followed Michele upstairs, hoping to lead the others up.

Kevin brought his empty bottle and put it on the counter. "All right, then. I'll leave the beer here so we can celebrate tomorrow afternoon. You want a ride, Daryl?"

"Can you run me home, Robert?" Daryl said.

Robert glanced at the clock and calculated how much sleep he'd get with a round trip ride to Kirkwood. "Yes," Robert said.

* * * *

"So it's Monday," Daryl said. He watched the dark, wooded silences of Ladue pass on Lindbergh. At the intersections of Ladue Road and Conway, gas stations and slightly upscale chain restaurants punctuated the gloom, but passed into darkness when Robert accelerated from the green lights.

"Yes," Robert said.

"Do you think it will go smoothly?" Daryl said.

"It has so far," Robert said.

"Do you think we'll get the bar?" Daryl said.

"We should," Robert said. Somehow, though, he couldn't quite imagine that soon he'd be a millionaire. Or any better off than he was today.

"Okay," Daryl said.

"You'll be ready?" Robert said.

"Sure," Daryl said. "You?"

"Yes," Robert said.

"All right," Daryl said. "Call me when you're at his house, and I'll drop the router. You'll have about a minute and a half to make the switch, and that should be plenty."

"I'll call you when we're in the room with the bar."

"All right. Keep me on the line while you make the switch. As soon as you're out of there, I'll leave the library and meet you at your house. Okay?"

"All right," Robert said. He accelerated a little abruptly into the left turn, screeching his wheels. He turned a block north of Daryl's street, as usual, so he could drop Daryl at the walk to his apartments instead of making him cross the road. Besides, Robert preferred to make a right to get back onto Lindbergh.

Daryl didn't say anything until Robert stopped in front of his apartment building. "Thanks," he said, and he got out.

"You're welcome," Robert said before Daryl shut the door. He watched Daryl climb the steps and circle the darkened marigolds. When Daryl reached the outer door to his apartment, Robert let go of the snow brush/ice scraper he kept behind his passenger seat. Maybe a thug would laugh when he raised it, and maybe the person whom he would save would think it queer, but the handle was a solid plastic rod. Robert would use it like a han bo with a point—the ice scraper—at the end. He grabbed the shifter with his newly freed hand and put the car into drive.

*   *   *   *

Michele got her hand vacuum out and took care of some of Frodo's litter box misses. He was eighty percent trained, and still he was better than Bilbo had been. Every night when she got home from work, or had gotten home from work (she remembered), she'd vacuumed the day's accumulated fecal balls. She'd never have tolerated a dog that crapped on the floor or a cat that peed on the bed, but somehow, the discrete, distinct balls seemed less dirty. Of course, she vacuumed them before anyone came to her place, not that anyone beside her mother had bothered to come by.

Her answering machine light didn't blink. So much for the marketability of her resume. The economic climate didn't seem so downtrodden a week ago, when she was employed. Of course, she'd been laid off three days ago. Even in the height of the information technology feeding frenzy, she'd needed more than a week to convince an HR specialist that written communication, as a skill, was really as desirable as the television news said.

Michele sat at her computer desk and tapped her mouse to break

151

out of the screen saver. The text on the screen depicted, again, David Albernathy and Cynthia in medias res. Michele traced over some of the purple prose. She snorted, saved, and closed the window.

She opened a new window. David was an ex-Marine, stoic and fit. A child of a broken home who found his structure in his disciplined lifestyle. He deserved better than to be a cardboard character in a dime romance novel that took half a decade to write. She closed the Microsoft Word document, making sure she saved it, and created a new document based upon her fiction template.

Instead, she could make David a recent graduate of the St. Louis Police Academy and assigned to Town and Country as a patrolman. He'd be unhappy to be assigned to a municipality with no action, instead of one of the northern municipalities where Saturdays might erupt in gunfire. She could set him up with a locked room mystery, wherein an executive from a local leader in the biochemical industry was found in his own bed, dead from unknown assailants. Assailants who were former employees. Who finagled the executive's keys and got his alarm code using trickery. She smirked. Write what you know.

* * * *

Sunday night, Kevin raised his glass of Sam Adams and smiled. Rachel did the same. "May your future rise up to meet you," Kevin said. He clinked glasses with the natural blonde next to him at the bar and drank.

"You're damn upbeat," she said. She fumbled a vanilla cigar from a leather case.

"I have not yet lost a job and not gotten a promotion from it," Kevin said.

"Times have changed," Rachel said. "You don't always get what you expect these days?"

"You can't always get what you want, but if you try sometimes, you get what you need," Kevin said.

"You and Mick," Rachel said.

Kevin felt damn smart whenever he quoted something and someone else knew what he was talking about. "Yeah," he said. He put the empty glass on the bar. His third of the night. He had about two more drinks' worth of cash in his wallet, and then he'd walk across the four lane undivided, but not entirely busy, stretch of road to his apartment. On the other hand, he could include Rachel, one more beer for each of them, and instead he could walk her to her apartment in the complex next to the pizzeria/bar. He watched her twist a dirty blonde curl and stretch it away from her round cheek. On the other hand, he had a big day tomorrow, and he only had enough for two drinks.

"So what is it you need?" Rachel said.

"I need to own a place like this," Kevin said. "Or just a bar. Something with deep wood paneling and polished brass."

"That's classier than the places you like to hang out," Rachel said. "You're a Hot Shots kind of guy. Something with pool tables and all the big screens your walls could hold."

Kevin frowned at his empty glass. The bartender brought him another glass of beer, but didn't take the empty one away. "That's what I can afford now," he said. "But when I get my money…"

"What money's that? When your parents die?" Rachel stopped toying with her hair long enough to light another vanilla cigar.

"I'll get my own money," Kevin said. He turned away from the sweet stink of the cigar. He'd heard they tasted great when you smoke them, but that the aftertaste was nasty. Rachel covered the aftertaste by chain smoking them. He sure as hell didn't want to kiss a woman like that again, and he didn't particularly want to look at her now. He caught sight of the clock above the restroom corridor. Ah, relief! "Shit! I have to get out of here. I've got an early appointment." He drank his full beer.

"An appointment?" Rachel said. Her voice trailed lower with disappointment.

"Business," Kevin said. "Good night." He walked carefully out the door, across the road, down the block, and into the second breezeway. Inside his apartment, he debated whether to put on music, what mood he was in, and whether he was anything without his parents' money until he fell asleep without even brushing his teeth.

* * * *

Daryl had Sundaynitis. Daryl wasn't tired, and he didn't feel like sitting down at his computer for a quick session of killing things on the Internet. A quick session might be four hours, and he didn't want to be up all night.

Instead, he ran his fingers on the white-veneered bookshelf in his living room that housed his video collection. He ran his fingertip over the library: four videocassettes containing the first season of the *Buffy the Vampire Slayer*; the two unlabeled cassettes for whatever he had wanted to tape from television back when he lived with Donny and Steve, which contained parts of a couple *Star Trek: The Next Generation* episodes; and nineteen previously viewed videocassettes, aligned by title, from *Battlefield: Earth* to *Weird Al's Video Hits*.

He settled on *Robin Hood*, the Kevin Costner version, and popped it into his video cassette recorder. Habitually, he turned the VCR on before the television so by the time the old nineteen inch picture tube warmed up, he'd be watching an FBI warning and not a bunch of snow. His mother kept offering him an old rabbit ear antenna so he could at least get the basic channels, but he told her they wouldn't do any good through the thick cinderblock walls. In reality, he was somewhat proud to not have a television and not know what was going on in popular culture. Except he read some of the entertainment Web sites and knew anyway, without having to spend the time on it. Entertainment Web sites were kind of like Cliff Notes for television, sadly enough.

Daryl settled into his sofa and stretched his feet out, looping one leg over the back of the sofa. He'd seen the movie two dozen times. The first scene in the movie took place in a prison, a prison for the Christian infidels in the holy land. Daryl tried to imagine the inside of the state penitentiary down in Potosi. Wasn't it Potosi? Certainly it wouldn't be like Oz, which was bleak, according to what he read on the entertainment sites.

Daryl's chin settled toward his chest comfortably. Robert Hood and his merry band. Merry little band, indeed. What would he do with a million bucks? Did he need a million dollars? Robin Hood didn't want all the wealth that Nottingham stole or that King Richard wanted to dish out; he just wanted to avenge his father. Daryl smirked. He had nothing to avenge. Although McDonnell, then Boeing, might have driven, or flown, his father up the wall, Boeing hadn't hung him in the courtyard for Daryl to find.

Daryl watched as Robin Hood divested some of Prince John's gold to provide food for the oppressed people of England. His eyes drifted over the room. He didn't need a million dollars. He had enough for any man his age, a bank account which would keep him in his apartment for several months and enough skill to be assured he'd have some kind of job any time he wanted it. Even if he just worked at a car wash or something.

He wondered who could use a million dollars, or whatever his cut was? He'd worked some with Habitat for Humanity in St. Charles. He thought about sending them some money, but he could hardly write them a check with his new found wealth. He thought again about the little computer lab in the YMCA across the street. He'd seen the computer lab when he'd gone over on one week when he'd thought about getting into better shape. Old, donated equipment then, and that was last year.

He could order them a number of new Dells, workstations and servers. He smiled and closed his eyes to imagine how they would deal with the sudden boxes from California. He could write out the machine specs and send money orders bought with his ill-gotten gains to buy the computers. He smiled, and then he slept with the television still displaying the movie.

*   *   *   *

Robert walked from his bedroom, into his kitchen, and then into the basement. He thought about hitting the Internet to check the specs of the bar one more time, but he had already done that once with his micrometer. He'd been surprised how precisely it matched the specifications, varying only by a couple microns from the blueprints they'd drawn up. He'd hoped their speculative specs were fairly accurate.

He walked back upstairs, through the kitchen lit only by the rear porch light shining through the opaque curtains, and into his bedroom. He'd set out his clothing for the morning. His dresser held a pair of blue jeans, a tee shirt, a baseball cap, and a pair of medium-sized cotton work gloves. A backpack with a GenCon logo, on the floor beside the dresser, held whatever small things he thought of, as he thought of them. He'd put a legal pad, a pencil, a pair of rulers, and John Donnelly's new bar into it.

He took the revolver from the bag again, opened the cylinder and examined the chambers. He spun the cylinder and closed it and put it back in the bag.

He took his wallet from the fake book on the little bookshelf under the window. Inside, a slip of paper said, "Erika (636) 842-7426." Robert slid it into the wallet pocket and put the wallet back on the shelf inside *Birds of North America*. Robert had felt somewhat bad about using the router to remove the glued pages so he could put his wallet in it, and he really felt bad about what it did to the router. But he cleaned the router, and the book was an actual book, not an obvious fake from a mail order catalogue.

He imagined himself trying creative visualization like the texts said. He visualized turning the key, walking in, typing in the pass code, turning to the left, and calling Daryl. Daryl would call them from the library when the site was down, and they would switch the bars. Then they'd call Michele and wait about five minutes for her to pick them up. Should he drive the route tonight and clock it? He looked at the clock. Two o'clock. He'd be too suspicious driving around Huntleigh at this time of night.

He'd have three or four hours of sleep. Enough for a day with two finals, enough for a day of ten hours at a computer screen. Should be plenty of sleep for a felony, too. Robert walked from the bedroom to the living room. He hadn't vacuumed the cushions in his couch since September, he remembered. He got the vacuum from the closet and assembled the attachments. As he vacuumed, he really tried to creatively visualize tomorrow, but the alarm code kept being wrong or John Donnelly kept coming back for his shaving kit.

Once Onto the Breach

Robert poured his fifth cup of coffee at 8:37. The sun wasn't out, which wasn't a bad omen, but if it rained, they risked tracking in mud, water, and leaves. Assuming, of course, the others arrived and they got into John Donnelly's house.

Robert sipped from his coffee, draining it as it cooled. He wore the outfit he'd laid out. He'd put his wallet in his pocket, and then he'd taken it out, wondering if he should carry ID, and then he'd decided if they were busted, they were busted. The wallet rested on his left thigh, the slightly tight jeans keeping everything in check. He'd put a belt on and had hung his multi-tool on it, just in case. He had pliers, blades, scissors, saw, bottle opener, and a toothpick at his disposal. He had no idea what he could use them for, but he had them if he needed them.

Robert rubbed moist palms together to dry them. At least the warm coffee cup was keeping him from clammy, he thought. He finished the cup at 8:53. If he drank two more, he wouldn't have enough to offer Michele and Kevin when they came. He poured one more cup, leaving two and some for his guests.

He put the coffee on the table and looked out his kitchen's side window. Robert saw the headlights and grille of Michele's wagon reflected in his neighbor's window. She doesn't want to come in, Robert thought. I've made her uncomfortable. What did I do this time? As he started replaying the contact they'd had in the last few days, a red flash showed between the edges of the houses and braked suddenly. Kevin had arrived, and at 8:57.

Robert ushered them into the kitchen. Michele was wearing jeans and a sweatshirt. Kevin had on a tour shirt and a flannel shirt.

"Coffee?" Robert said.

"Do we have time?" Michele said.

"Where's the gun?" Kevin said.

"Hang on a minute, Kevin," Robert said. He turned to Michele. "We should. The flight's scheduled to leave in twenty minutes, which

157

means it's probably thirty before Daryl can confirm Donnelly's on the plane. So we've got time for a cup if you'd like one."

"No, thank you," Michele said.

"I don't need any coffee," Kevin said. "I would like to see the gun, though."

"All right," Robert said. He opened the bag and took out the revolver. "It's a small caliber double-action revolver. Do you know what that means?"

"Small hole and the bullet rattles around inside the target," Kevin said.

Robert sighed in relief as much as in exasperation. Kevin had no clue about guns. "No, double action means you don't pull the hammer back before you fire it. When you pull the trigger, the hammer goes back and the cylinder rotates to present a chamber with a round in it. This is the safety," Robert said. He held the pistol to sideways, making sure to point it away from Michele. She was paying as much attention as Kevin was.

"What caliber is it?" Michele said.

".22," Robert said.

"Can I hold it?" Michele said.

"Okay," Robert said. He held the pistol out, butt first to Michele.

Michele took it carefully, aiming the muzzle towards the same point on the wall as Robert had. Her father had taken her shooting once at the range down in Maplewood, but she had been fourteen at the time and terrified of guns. Not the sound of guns, for the ear protection muffled that, but in the thought that she could quite inadvertently injure herself, her father, or the guy two booths over.

Still, she'd read enough in the Writer's Digest guide book to weapons to get started, and then in a handgun collector's primer to tell the difference between a revolver and a semiautomatic and how to open the cylinder.

Robert watched Michele handle the gun confidently. He wondered if she had her own gun or guns. If she did, she probably wouldn't be uncomfortable coming into Robert's house by herself. Michele opened the cylinder and looked into the chambers. She met his eyes, but didn't say anything as she snapped the gun shut. Michele offered it back to him, and he took it. He offered it to Kevin.

"Cool," Kevin said. He lifted the gun, checking its weight and balance and looking down the sight. "Works for me," he said, tucking it into the waistband of his pants in the back and pulling the shirts over it. "Can you see it?"

"No," Michele said. No wonder characters always carried guns in the small of their backs.

"Great. Are you guys ready?" Kevin said.

"Hang on," Robert said. Beneath the coffee, his intestines suddenly knotted or unknotted. When he returned from the bathroom, he said, "You guys want to go before we leave?"

"You're just like my mother," Kevin said. "Except she doesn't break into people's houses when they're on vacation."

"John Donnelly's not on vacation. Have you got gloves?" Robert said.

"Sure," Kevin said. He took out his latex gloves. He had a whole box of them under his sink, originally bought for housecleaning. He hadn't bothered with them when cleaning, but little did he know he'd need them with a quick career change.

"All right. Grab the bag." Robert waited for Kevin to pick up the backpack, activated his alarm, and ushered them out the door.

Kevin plunged into the back seat of the car and regretted it. The seat drove the butt and one or two sharper points of the gun into his spine. "Shit!" he said, taking it out and putting it on the seat next to him.

Robert looked back at Kevin as Michele pulled away from the curb. "Get that under something," he said. "Don't leave it in plain sight. Give me your phone."

"Why do you get my phone?" Kevin shoved the gun under the backpack.

"Because you're carrying the other stuff," Robert said.

Kevin handed the phone over. Robert opened it and dialed Daryl's number. "Hey, do you have a passenger list yet?" Robert said. "Okay, call Kevin's phone when it comes in. Okay."

"What did he say?" Michele said. The clock on her dashboard said 9:18, but she knew it was about four minutes slow because it said :56 whenever the CBS news came on KMOX.

"It takes them a couple minutes to get the passenger list together. He said the flight began boarding on time and is departing, but it will take a few minutes before he'll know. Is this on ring or vibrate?" Robert said.

"Ring," Kevin said.

"So where do I go?" Michele pictured herself driving around long blocks in Huntleigh, past immaculately white rail fences, discreet trees and shrubs, and the bored police cruiser with a friendly, polite officer. Right from the academy, the young man would be pleasantly surprised to pull over a blue Taurus wagon full of a gun, a gold bar, and a conspiracy.

"Drive towards John Donnelly's house. We're about fifteen or twenty minutes away. Daryl ought to know by now," Robert said. He passed the cell phone back to Kevin. "Set it to vibrate."

Kevin set the phone to vibrate and passed it back. He felt the bag through its nylon blend. "What else is in there?" he opened the sack without waiting for an answer.

Michele concentrated on her driving. She wondered how nervous the others were. Beside her, Robert kept rubbing his thighs and shuffling his feet. Behind her, Kevin was ruffling through things and wondering aloud where Robert put the lock picks, stethoscope, pinch bar, and other good stuff. She wondered if he was just not smart enough to be scared.

Robert took the phone from his lap. "Yes?" he said tersely. "You're sure? Well, that'll have to do," Robert admitted. "I'll call when we're in." He turned a little in the seat to face both Michele and Kevin as best he could. "The computer says John Donnelly's on the plane. Are you guys ready? This is the last chance to back out." Robert swallowed a couple of times. He hoped he'd slowed the words to normal speed instead of sounding like a speeded tape. At least his voice hadn't cracked.

"Sure," Michele said.

"You bet," Kevin said. "You bet I am ready, not you bet I want to back out."

Michele made the right turn onto Litzsinger. She kept her foot hovering on the accelerator, touching it lightly enough to goose it to 35 miles per hour and no further. At each intersection and driveway, she scanned for police cruisers.

Robert rubbed his palms on his pants again and tugged at the seatbelt a little to loosen its pressure on his abdomen. He would put the phone in his back pocket when he got out of the car, he thought; it will fit better there. He pulled John Donnelly's keys to the top of his right pants pocket so he could take them out more quickly.

Kevin zipped the backpack closed with a dramatic, audible flourish. He took his gloves from his pocket and put them on, snapping them like he'd seen in a Woody Woodpecker cartoon. He slid the gun from underneath the backpack and picked it up with a gloved hand. Crap, he thought, I've touched it without the gloves on. So he wiped it down with the front hem of his flannel shirt, being very gingerly near the trigger.

"You've got your cell phone on?" Robert said.

"Yes," Michele said. She would have tapped her purse tucked behind the driver's seat, but she didn't like to remove her hands from the wheel when driving under the influence of stress. She turned into the empty driveway and pulled to the top of the circle.

"Get it out and wait for our call. Don't go too far." Robert was opening his door a fraction of a second before the car came to a complete halt. He got out, jammed the phone in his pocket, and drew the keys and his wallet simultaneously. "See you in a few."

Kevin got out of the car and put the gun under his shirts. He then bent over to get the backpack.

Robert felt bubbles shifting in his belly when he saw Kevin lean over, printing the pistol for all to see, but he didn't say anything. Instead, he fumbled Erika's phone number out.

Kevin stood up and slung the backpack over his shoulder. Its weight rested on the gun, so he shifted the backpack a little left. He shut his door softly, so softly he had to tap it to latch it all the way.

Michele pulled the purse up onto the passenger seat, unzipped it with one hand, and spilled its contents onto the seat. When the second door closed, she was proud she didn't peel out.

Robert watched Michele travel down the driveway. She looked calm, but if she didn't return, they could put the backpack, with the bar in it, under a short blue spruce halfway to the street. They could come back for the gold later, after they had walked back to Robert's house.

"If you miss her that much already, you're in love," Kevin said.

"Let's go inside," Robert said. He turned on his heels. He looked around as he did, looking for the shape and color of a person against the convenient foliage. He didn't see anyone.

"You're the boss," Kevin admitted. With a final thunk of shocks on concrete, Michele's car turned out of the driveway and accelerated eastbound on Litzsinger.

Robert climbed the stairs confidently, rifling through the keys. He found a likely candidate and tried one in both the deadbolt lock and the door knob lock. It didn't fit. The second one didn't fit, either, and Robert's mouth dried. He didn't want to shake, he didn't want Kevin to see his hands shake, and he didn't think he was shaking too much when the third key fit the deadbolt and the door knob. He unlocked both and dropped the keys into his pocket. Kevin made an impatient gesture, rolling his hands at the wrists. Robert made sure he was holding the paper so he could read it. "Are you ready?" he said.

"Yes," Kevin said. He breathed a couple of times, deeply, to make sure he was ready.

Robert put on his work gloves, transferring the paper carefully and looking around for witnesses. "Gloves," he said.

Kevin rubbed the latexed palms together to indicate their presence.

"Here we go," Robert said. He hoped Kevin wouldn't take all the exposition for reluctance. He turned the knob. It felt slippery, intangible, under his cottoned fingertips. Across the foyer, the alarm keypad beeped rhythmically. To Robert, it might as well have been a klaxon, a great AROOOOGA! AROOOOGA! Three steps took him across the hardwood foyer to the keypad. He looked at the paper in his left hand to double-check the number he memorized the night before.

Carefully, aiming his fingertips within the gloves at the small buttons, Robert typed in the last four digits of Erika's phone number. He paused a beat, less than the interval between the beeps, and pressed the **ENTER** button. An interval passed without a beep. **DISARMED**, the little green letters on the display read. Robert inhaled, deconstricting his chest.

"Good job!" Kevin said.

"You can close the door now," Robert said.

"Right," Kevin said. He closed the door behind them.

Robert felt his intestines burble when the door snicked shut. The foyer was hardwood and wainscoting, with dark paneling topped by white wallpaper with an elaborate floral print. On the south side of the foyer, opposite the doorway, a staircase ascended, carpeted and turning at a landing. The landing had a Victorian chair, a wayside for people who were tired from the climb. A hallway extended beside the stairway about fifty feet, with two doorways visible on the left and one on the right before the hallway curved right. To the east, a solid door with a metal knob with lock. To the west, an open doorway led to a living room, or "great room" as they called them in the million dollar plus homes. Robert looked up for motion sensors, but he didn't see anything. Robert stepped through the western doorway.

"Isn't that the room over there?" Kevin gestured toward the big door with the lock on it, but Robert wasn't looking. "Where are you going?"

"I am getting an idea of the house's layout," Robert said. He always turned right at estate sales to ensure he saw every open room in the house. He saw no reason to break with habit just because the occupant whose valuables he would get for a steal was still alive. His intestines tickled. His torso, from chest to pelvis, tightened in response. The great room was about 15 feet long, extending west from the foyer, by 25 feet wide. The only other exit opened on the south end of the west wall, a corridor extending west out of sight. Centered on the south wall, windows looked out to the well-lit back yard. A simple marble fireplace dominated the west wall. White wainscot gave way to blood red paint on the walls. Robert smirked inwardly. All he needed was a pencil, some graph paper, and a d12, and he could be in the basement of a house on Sappington, worrying about what would happen to his fourteenth level cleric. As long as the hallway didn't hold a mind flayer, their low level party ought to be all right.

Kevin looked over the room and approved. A fine leather couch and loveseat, facing the fireplace. A tasteful sound system, including a Nakamichi receiver, a Pioneer 5 disc DVD changer, a Kenwood 200 CD changer, a Bose 101 bookshelf unit, and a 5 speaker Klipsch reference series set. The rig was a couple years old, but it would get the job done. Kevin would have put a gas fireplace in, but he wasn't very good at making a wood fire. Maybe the snap, crackle, and pop of wood added something to the ambience. And the smell, and sparks. Maybe when he had a million dollars, he'd set up a scientific environment and test whether women preferred natural fireplaces enough to make them worthwhile.

At the edge of his hearing, Robert detected a scrape of some sort, a sound not made by his or Kevin's thighs passing in a step. "Shh," Robert said. "Do you hear something?"

Kevin thought he had been fairly quiet to begin with. He stopped, and frowned to indicate his concentration.

Robert concentrated. Then his intestines reshuffled their contents loudly.

"Was that you?" Kevin said.

"That's not what I heard," Robert said. It might have been the wind blowing trees against the roof or windows. Most likely it was not a blue dragon. He stepped into the corridor. Robert remembered what he'd seen from the outside; a wide house. The first door on the right was a bathroom. He ran a series of scenarios through his head and stepped into it. "Give me a moment," Robert said.

Kevin tried not to pay attention to the sounds in the bathroom; instead, he looked at the hallway's decoration. The half wood paneling continued, but a wallpaper took over for the bright red paint, something blue with a print to it. John Donnelly wasn't the sort to hang pictures outside his bathroom door. Neither was he.

Robert opened the door to the restroom. He'd forgone the fan since they were the only ones who'd be in the house for a couple days. He hoped Kevin wouldn't recoil. "All right," he said. He looked into the two rooms at the end of the hallway. A bedroom and a bedroom used as a storeroom. Robert led them back to the foyer and down the corridor past the stairs.

The first doorway on the right opened into a closet for overcoats, umbrellas, and canes. The second opened into a half bath. The kitchen opened to the left, along with what the realtor probably termed the cozy breakfast nook. The corridor expanded into a sunroom, or three-season room, a four-season room, an all-season steel-belted radial room, or whatever the realtors called them this year. Robert called the three walls of windows facing the secluded backyard a security nightmare, but Robert didn't sell many houses.

Robert stepped into the kitchen. The range fit into an island centered in the kitchen. The countertops, steel that matched the doors of the industrial-sized refrigerator, glistened. Donnelly probably didn't chop or spill much on them. Under the top cabinet, nestled neatly against the edge of the pantry, the microwave probably saw most of the duty. Against the east wall, the breakfast nook sported a booth, a table, and two chairs. A door on the west wall led to the basement, Robert surmised. Another heavy wooden door, set in the southern wall, barred them from the former formal dining room. Robert tried the knob. It was locked.

Kevin liked the kitchen, too. Well-lit, shiny, and clean, ready to present. Kevin didn't see a wok, but that probably meant John Donnelly knew how to cook, too. He wondered if Donnelly had any parties and how to get invited. Imitating Robert, he opened the pantry. "Look at this pantry," he said. A walk-in pantry, no less, filled with a broom, several kinds of canned fruits and vegetables, dry goods, dog food, and a couple of boxes of snack crackers. "Maybe it's a converted bedroom." He crossed to the large refrigerator, its door unblemished by an ice or water tap. What did a CEO keep in his refrigerator? The usual condiments, an open bottle of red Missouri wine, a can of biscuits, and a large volume of cool air. Nothing in Tupperware or old Cool Whip tubs covered with tin foil, and no fresh vegetables. Kevin didn't want to see the frozen pizzas, so he didn't even bother with the side-by-side freezer.

"Locked, huh?" Kevin said to Robert.

"Yeah, but we should have the key," Robert said. He froze, keys half sorted in his hand, when he heard a sudden arrhythmic ticking. "What's that?" he said.

"It came from this closet," Kevin said. He'd heard it, too, like water dripping. Perhaps John Donnelly had left something leaking in the closet, or exposed water pipes were condensing, or something. He opened the door.

"Don't open that!" Robert said, and it was too late.

Kevin saw it wasn't a closet, but the basement steps; they went down to the right. The ticking increased as the light chased the shadows from the top of the stairs. A low growl started, and Kevin leapt backwards from the doorway, brushing the island and jamming steel into his back. Kevin wrapped his hands around the butt of the pistol and regained his balance even as the snarling dog reached the top step and turned on him.

He pointed the gun at the white blur as it reached his feet and pawed and gnashed at his ankles.

"What are you...." Robert said.

Kevin pulled the trigger. He saw the cylinder spin, watched the hammer come back and snap forward, and heard the revolver click. The gun made no other sound, and the dog continued to nip at the cuffs of his pants. He pulled the trigger again and it clicked empty again. "What the fuck?" he said. He stamped his foot to get the dog off him.

"Good work. You have successfully killed the savage Bichon Frise, and probably shot yourself in the process," Robert said. He stepped forward and extended a hand for the gun.

"You gave me an empty gun," Kevin said. He swung his arm with the revolver towards Robert.

Too much for Robert's taste. "Don't point that at me!" Robert said. He swept the gun's arc past with an open left hand and punched Kevin's funny bone. The gun clattered to the floor loudly. "I couldn't trust you with a loaded gun. You've proved my point. You shot John Donnelly's dog in the middle of John Donnelly's kitchen. I think John Donnelly might have discovered, then, someone was in his house at some point."

"The dog attacked me," Kevin said. He rubbed his numb arm with his good arm.

"It's a toy dog," Robert said. "It couldn't have hurt you that badly."

"I didn't know it was just one," Kevin said. "For all I knew, it was a pack of six or seven of them, and they could have all been rabid."

"I doubt it," Robert said. The dog had stopped attacking Kevin long enough to tremble and growl, standing in one place. "Bang!" Robert shouted at the dog. The dog started, urinated, and retreated to growl from a more defensible position beneath the table. Robert picked the gun up from the floor. "That didn't scare you, did it?" he said to Kevin.

"I'll be all right," Kevin said.

"We better get it back into the basement," Robert said. "And we have to clean up this mess." At the edge of hearing, he thought, he heard the crunch of tires on asphalt and the muted shriek of a complete stop.

"What's Michele doing back?" Kevin said.

The Bichon yarp-yarped and scrabbled toenails on tile before scooting out the kitchen door, headed for the foyer.

"That's not Michele," Robert said. Someone put a key into the lock. "Pantry," he said.

"Why not the..." Kevin said.

Because someone at the front door will see us crossing the hall, Robert thought, but he couldn't articulate the thought as quickly as he would have liked. "Pantry," he whispered harshly. The cleaning lady! Nothing was dusty, nothing was dirty, and Robert should have known that Donnelly didn't do his own cleaning. Because Robert didn't trust a stranger, bonded or not, in his house when he wasn't there, he'd forgotten some people, especially of the CEO set, would. He began ushering Kevin to the pantry. He pulled the door mostly closed behind him, leaving a crack through which he could listen.

The front door opened. "Prince Hal!" a woman's voice said. "Johnny left you out? He must know you're such a good boy! Yes, you are. Are you coming to Aunt Melanie's house today? Yes, you are." The dog yipped happily. "Let's go get your things!"

Heavy footsteps thumped down the corridor, occasionally ticking heels onto hardwood between the area rugs. Robert's shoulder muscles seized painfully when the footsteps ticked into the kitchen. He heard Kevin's breathing stop. The pantry was as dark as the inside of Robert's eyelids; he closed them to hear better and then opened them and saw no difference.

"Oh, Hal, you've had an accident! But you were a good boy to have the accident on the tile, yes, you were!"

Robert froze. He tried to remember if he saw a paper towel dispenser on the counter or cabinets somewhere. Robert didn't keep his paper towels in the pantry, and he really hoped Donnelly didn't either. He had the gun now, so it was his extra felony rap if she opened the door. Maybe they could knock her down and get the hell out of there before she saw them. Several seconds passed without a sudden exposure to light, and Robert guessed the paper towels were elsewhere.

"There," the woman's voice said. The dog started scratching at the door to the pantry and whimpering. Robert felt warm suddenly and hoped he had not evacuated himself. His fingers hurt around the grip of the revolver in his right hand and the door knob in his left. He held the door tightly against its jamb with the door knob still turned.

"You want a treat, Hal? Look what Auntie brought for you," she said. The dog retreated from the door and crunched on something. "Where's your food dish, little Hotspur? Did Daddy put you down in the basement after all and not close the door all the way? Your daddy must have been in some hurry this morning! He didn't even set the alarm. But you were on duty, weren't you? Yes, you were."

The woman's footsteps clopped down the stairs. Robert pushed the door open slowly, until he saw the dog's snout. The dog snarled and tried to put its nose in the crack. Robert quickly pulled the door closed, as silently as he could, and he let the knob turn. He flexed his hand to reduce the cramping in the fingers.

"Go!" Kevin whispered.

"Go where?" Robert whispered back. "Wherever we go, the dog will chase us."

"It's better than staying in here," Kevin said. He shifted his weight quietly. He had run his fingers over the edges of the shelves nearest to him and contemplated sitting, or at least leaning, on the shelf. He knew Robert wasn't leaning on anything, though, and if Robert didn't need to, he wouldn't.

"I doubt it," Robert said. The woman's steps ascended the basement stairs, and Robert suppressed the urge to shush Kevin.

"Well little man, we're ready. You want to go see Falstaff and Mercutio? I told them you were coming!" Her voice rose as she neared the door, and Robert found himself leaning backward. He could feel the air compressing between him and Kevin, so he stopped before he bumped him. The dog made an impatient noise. Then, the woman and the dog together tick-tick-ticked out of the kitchen and down the corridor. The woman said something else that Robert couldn't catch, no matter how many combinations he tried the unintelligible syllables. Then, the front door thudded shut. At least Robert thought it might be the front door. Or the raging Bichon knocked her down. Robert pressed the light button on his watch, careful not to scrape the barrel of the gun on the pantry door.

"That was her leaving, right?" Kevin said. "Let's go."

"Give her two minutes to load the dog and drive off. In case she's forgotten something." Robert said.

Kevin thought that sounded reasonable, so he didn't say anything. He thought about Lacey, a girl he'd known some years before. Her parents had a kitchen with a range in the island, just like John Donnelly. He didn't know if they had a deep, dark pantry with enough room in it for two, and had he thought of it, he and Lacey could have checked into it.

Robert put the gun into his waistband, brushing Kevin and startling him in the process. "Sorry," Robert said. He looked at his watch. It had only been a minute thirty-six, but Robert turned the knob and admitted the sunshine. He pulled John Donnelly's keys out again and

167

tried the unknown keys in the lock. One of them fit, and Robert turned the knob.

The former formal dining room was a little smaller than the living room, probably eighteen by sixteen, or some other offset rectangle size. Robert could have imagined how it looked in previous years, with mahogany or other deep, dark wood furniture: A table with room for ten or twelve; a buffet along the east wall; a china cabinet in the southeast corner. Light chintz or lace curtains to let in natural light the better to highlight the fine china in the cabinet and the intricate crochet or knit table cloth.

John Donnelly didn't have an eye for tradition. Heavy drapes pulled tight over the windows admitted no sunlight. Only a blue halogen floor lamp and the door from the kitchen lit the room. Upon the eastern wall, he'd placed two cubicle walls with a cubicle desk hanging from them. Beneath the desk, two tower-cased machines whirred happily. On the desk, a KVM switch hooked the two machines to a single Keyboard/Video/Mouse combination. Donnelly had sprung for a large monitor for his home as well, along with a split keyboard for proper ergonomics. nTropics probably splurged for him, and the corners cut were he, Daryl, Michele, and Kevin, Robert thought.

Donnelly must not have many people over, Kevin thought when he saw what Donnelly had done to the dining room. The dining room is a focal point to a party, a convenient place for people to sit down face to face for a game or just to bullshit. John Donnelly's dining room didn't even look like a dining room; it looked like work, except Donnelly hadn't even personalized this cube-away-from-cube with Dilberts or Far Sides. Maybe he didn't spend much time here, Kevin thought. Why, then, buy a big house? Kevin managed to not spend time at home with a much smaller abode.

In the corner of the cubicle desks, the gold bar sat on the green velvet background. The background acted as a floor for the bar and was tacked to the cubicle wall. The camera, set upon a tripod, faced the bar and the background. The whole set-up was angled away from the center of the room so that people could move in and out of the room without interrupting the live feed. Robert appreciated that. He dug into his pocket and pulled out the cell phone. He dialed Daryl's number while keeping an eye on Kevin.

* * * *

Daryl looked over the other computers at the librarians behind the counter. He'd chosen the machine with its monitor facing the library stacks to mask what he was doing from inquisitive eyes. The librarians didn't like it when you rebooted their Internet computers, logged in using Safe Mode, and did naughty things to get a user account and a Telnet client. He did those naughty things beginning at nine o'clock. He figured it would take him about ten minutes. He typed the first command he'd use into the Telnet window on the PC and then changed over to the Web browser to look at Dice.com. Just like any other out-of-work techie would do at this hour, Daryl thought, although he personally wouldn't hire an out-of-work techie that lacked his or her own personal computer. What sort of dedication was that?

Daryl had run through all of Dice's job listings by 9:22. He'd last spoken to Robert at about 9:30, about twenty minutes ago. He reviewed stltoday.com, the local paper's contemptible Web site, and discovered that the Blues were primed for another run at the Stanley Cup. Except they were primed for the 100 meter dash, and the Stanley Cup was a 4 by 400 meter relay, Daryl thought.

He looked at his watch. He'd overstayed the thirty minutes the library allocated patrons for the Internet computers. A guy with a mullet sat at a machine, probably looking for the Van Halen official fan club site or reading the article on the Blues. Opposite Daryl, a young woman sat at a machine and kept her eyes locked onto her monitor. Her eyes moved back and forth as she read, which indicated a lot of text. Her mouth didn't move. Just his type.

With one computer open, the librarians wouldn't run him off unless someone took the open computer and a complainer wanted his. Still, Daryl kept an eye on the man and women behind the counter, reorganizing the books and stamping the morning's magazines.

His phone vibrated while he was waiting for the first stock reports from the morning to load. "Hello?" he said.

*   *   *   *

"We're here. Do your thing. Don't hang up; let us know when you're ready," Robert said into the phone. "Put the backpack on the floor and open it," he said to Kevin.

"All right," Kevin said. He set the backpack on the floor on its back and pulled both zippers to their ends. He flipped the flap open. The bar was at the very bottom, flanked by the other equipment. Kevin lifted the bar out. It looked a lot like the bar on the desk, all right. He was proud.

"Don't get too close," Robert said. "Daryl's just now taking care of it."

Kevin leaned back, even though he hadn't thought he was that close to the camera or the real gold bar. Robert just wanted to feel like he was in charge, Kevin thought. He'd keep Robert happy by letting him think he was.

"All right, thanks. Talk to you later," Robert said. He hit the **NO** button and stuck the phone in his pocket. "Daryl says we have about a minute and a half before everything comes up. The picture's down." He sneaked a glance at his watch. 9:59:14, roughly.

"No problem," Kevin said. He lifted the fake bar over the desk.

"Hold on," Robert said. He reached into the backpack for two wooden rulers. "We'll line it up precisely."

"You're going to measure it from the edge of the desk?" Kevin said. "We've only got a minute."

"No," Robert said. Carefully, he aligned the edge of one ruler with the long edge of the gold bar. He aligned the edge of the second ruler with the short side, making sure to square the ruler corners. With both hands, he lifted John Donnelly's gold from the velvet background. "Put that bar on it so that the text is facing the camera." He put the gold bar into the backpack.

Kevin set the fake gold bar in the rulers and nudged it into place, carefully so that the velvet didn't bunch between the bar and the guides. After he aligned them, he picked up the rulers and brushed his fingers on the velvet to make sure the rulers didn't leave an impression. He also took care to not leave impressions with his fingers.

Robert looked at the setup. "Good work," he said. His watch said 10:00:22. He took the phone out again and dialed.

* * * *

Michele turned onto Lindbergh and then onto Clayton Road. She thought about her route, taking Lindbergh to Clayton to McKnight to Manchester. She planned overlapping circles, doing right-turning loops so that she'd never have to drive down the same road twice, and yet she'd be within minutes of John Donnelly's house. She wished that she'd thought to bring a street guide, or at least look at one before starting out. How would Robert have handled this? WWRD?

Michele followed Clayton Road past its allocation of wide lawns and narrow asphalt driveways and newly constructed, old-look schools and churches. The getaway driver always gets shorted in the movies and in books. A walk-on character, just one step above an extra. The driver could easily be the mastermind of the crime. After all the driver really risks nothing. Just drives, or parks the car, and doesn't commit anything but conspiracy until the accomplices hop into the car.

David Albernathy would never be a getaway driver; she'd built him too much into a law enforcement type. She could create some tension between him and a criminal mastermind, acting as the getaway driver in a robbery. Perhaps Cynthia could be that mastermind; but Cynthia was a kid, an upper class college girl trying to grow up; Michele couldn't imagine her any other way. Instead, she'd need a new character, a rougher-edged woman with a sketchy past. Karen Mulvaney, third generation Irish-American, ten years out of high school and out of a job. Michele smiled as she turned onto McKnight Road.

She tried to keep focus on her new idea, but kept sneaking a glance at the dashboard clock. Somehow, she'd gotten the impression it would only take a couple of minutes for them to switch the bars; however, it had been almost twenty minutes. Her next set of circles would take her up Lindbergh to Conway, over to Ballas and back down. The job might be going badly. If they weren't ready on the next lap, she'd swing by on Litzsinger to see if there were police cars out front. Or she could call Daryl, but that would tie up her cell phone if Robert tried to call.

Karen would have outfitted them with headset radios. Could she scramble them or encrypt the transmissions? Or would that make the authorities more curious and suspicious?

The cell phone rang, and Michele scrambled to pick it up from the dashboard and press the appropriate button while simultaneously braking for a stoplight.

"Robert?" she said. "I'm on my way."

She looked at the street sign of the cross street. Bopp, pronounced with the long O sound, just like it's spelled. That should get her up to Litzsinger, she thought, and she turned right.

*   *   *   *

"Melanie reset the alarm when she went out," Robert said. He looked at the alarm keypad. ARMED.

"Who?" Kevin said. The backpack rested more easily on his back without the gun back there, but he wouldn't admit it to Robert. At least the gold bar didn't make the bag any heavier.

"The woman who came for the dog." Robert disarmed the alarm again. "We'll reset it when we go out."

"Okay," Kevin said. He started for the door.

"We'll wait in here until she pulls into the driveway," Robert said.

171

"We don't want to be seen out there, especially if Melanie comes back."

A car swished up the driveway. Robert peeked through the windows flanking the doorway. "It's Michele. Go," he said.

Kevin went out the door and into Michele's backseat.

Robert typed the code in again and pressed ARM. The keypad beeped and started flashing letters. Robert stepped quickly out of the door and pulled it closed. He locked the door, checked to make sure it was locked, and took off his gloves before getting into Michele's car.

A Ruse is Exposed

Michele waited for Robert to close the door and fasten his seatbelt. She calmly, slowly, turned the car around the circle and down the driveway. "You've got it?" Michele said.

"Right in here." Kevin tapped the bag and took hold of the zipper.

"Don't get it out in the car," Robert said. He passed the pistol between the front seats, keeping it low. "Put this in there with it."

"What happened?" Michele turned onto Litzsinger and only then allowed herself the luxury of speed to take them away from the scene of the crime. She checked her rearview mirror, but no one was behind her, and no one was in front of her or coming in her direction.

"John Donnelly, apparently, has a little dog. Kevin tried to shoot it," Robert said.

"You tried to shoot the dog?" Michele said.

"It attacked me," Kevin said. He secured the handgun as directed. "I overreacted. When I was younger, I had a bad experience with dogs, okay?"

"With dogs?" Michele checked the speedometer again, making sure she stayed relatively close to 35. The sooner she had the bar out of her car, the happier she would be.

"When I was about ten, I had a bunch of dogs attack me, okay? Biting and trying to knock me down. I had to run three blocks to get away from them. I could have gotten seriously hurt. So when a dog runs up to me, I get excited."

"How many dogs?" Robert said.

"Six or seven," Kevin said. "I was too busy running to count."

"How big were they? Robert said.

"Different sizes. They were a wild pack."

"What kinds of dogs?" Robert said.

"Terriers, I think, and some hounds."

"Pit bulls?" Michele said.

"No," Kevin admitted. "The little square ones."

173

"You were chased by a bunch of Scotties for three blocks and you were traumatized forever?" Michele said. "You almost struck a telling blow for humanity today. Good thing it wasn't loaded, or you'd still be mopping."

Robert got out Kevin's cell phone and dialed Daryl's number. "This is Robert. We're on our way to my place. How long until you can make it? We'll see you then." He hung up and passed the phone back to Kevin. "He'll be about thirty minutes," Robert said.

*   *   *   *

Michele didn't want to open the backpack until Daryl got to Robert's house, so she told Kevin not to. Daryl had been instrumental in their plan, and he should be present at the unveiling. Kevin contented himself with a bottle of Rolling Rock. Michele declined another cup of coffee, but Robert put a pot on to brew while they were waiting. They didn't have long to wait.

Daryl knocked on the door about forty minutes after he spoke to Robert, which was late, but he'd had to wait for a freight train to pass on an at-grade crossing at Lindbergh. Although he could have taken a cross street and the overpass just west of Lindbergh, he originally thought it would take longer, and to every minute he invested waiting for the eventual passing of the train, he added the time it would take to go around. The train's total time was about thirteen minutes, which included a stop somewhere eighteen cars beyond Daryl's vantage point in front of the Kirkwood train station. He could have gone around, bicycling up the block, over the overpass, and back down the next block. Observing all stop signs and accounting for discourteous drivers who would have ignored his right-of-way, it would have taken him six or seven minutes to go around. Ergo, he could have saved time at any point up until seven minutes into his waiting. "I had to wait for a train," he said to the trio in the kitchen to avoid being tedious with his explanation.

Kevin unzipped the backpack with gusto. "Ta dah," he said when he flipped the flap over. He made some impressive fanfare music, much as a movie or a symphony might make, when he lifted the bar from the backpack. "It's gold! Gold, my boys! We're rich."

Michele stiffened out of habit at the 'boys' comment, but she didn't say anything out of the same habit. The size of the gold bar stunned her; although it was only as big as the copy they had made, this was real gold, millions of dollars' worth. It didn't belong here, in Robert's plain, rather middle-class kitchen; it belonged in a museum or a vault somewhere.

Daryl whistled. "I wasn't sure you guys had gotten it when the server came back up. I couldn't see a difference in the picture, and I was looking for it."

"We made sure to put it in the same exact spot," Kevin said. He didn't want to ruin the magic by explaining what they'd done behind the curtain.

"Let me see it," Daryl said. Kevin passed the bar over the table. Daryl accepted it, but was startled by its weight. "I thought this was supposed to be heavier. You sure you switched them?"

"I am sure," Kevin said. "You need to work out more."

Daryl looked the bar over carefully. 903 fine gold, 390 ounces. Daryl felt the rounded corners as he turned the bar over, the edges smoothed by a hundred years of salt water. Or not. "Oh, shit," he said.

"What?" Robert said.

Daryl lowered the bar, upside down, to the table, setting it carefully to make sure that the table would hold it and to not scratch the surface. He ran his fingers over the lightly engraved letters on the bottom.

Kevin cocked his head to read what Daryl was pointing to. "All your base are belong to us?" he said.

"What?" Robert said again. He looked at the bar more closely and unsnapped the holster on his multipurpose tool.

Michele's laugh exploded, echoing in the small dining room.

"What's so funny?" Kevin said.

"It's on the bottom. The base. It's a pun."

"The weight's a dead giveaway," Daryl said.

Robert unfolded the flat screwdriver blade from the tool and put it onto the gold bar. He pressed his thumb on the edge of the blade and pushed the screwdriver head. It plowed tiny flakes of gold ahead of a thin, silverish line. "Electroplate?"

"It's a fake?" Kevin said.

"Why would John Donnelly have a fake bar on the Internet?" Michele said. "Does he have the real bar in a vault?"

"It would make sense," Daryl said. "In the old days, you always made copies of your applications and stored the copies somewhere safe. He's probably doing the same thing."

"So we just broke into his house to steal his gold bar, but it's a fake?" Kevin said.

"No, John Donnelly bought an authentic gold bar; they wouldn't have done all the publicity if he hadn't," Michele said. "He bought it from a reputable auction house."

"So what do we do now?" Kevin said.

175

"Whenever they move the bar to dust it or whatever, they'll know; ours didn't have the stuff on the bottom," Michele said. "We have to get it back, or they'll know someone broke in and changed them."

"Someone beat us to it," Robert said. "Someone else stole Donnelly's gold bar."

"What?" Michele said.

"What?" Daryl echoed a millisecond later.

"Why would Donnelly be so careful as to lock up the real gold bar in a vault and then leave the fake one in such lax security? Only if it were bait for some kind of trap. It doesn't make sense," Robert said. "Furthermore, what's the point of the 'All your base are belong to us' on the bottom? That's more of a thumb in the eye than an inside joke."

"So you think someone else stole it?" Daryl said. "That's pretty thin basis for a theory."

"What does that mean, anyway?" Kevin said. "All your base are belong to us?"

"To make a short story long, back in 1989, some gaming company released a game called Zero Wing that was originally made in Japan. Whoever translated the subtitles was not proficient in English, which led to such wonderful declarations as 'All your base are belong to us' and 'someone set us up the bomb'. Someone on the Internet got a hold of it right around the millennium and did a bunch of Photoshop work to put 'All your base are belong to us' on a bunch of ads and billboards. Quite an amusing phenomenon for a day or so," Daryl explained.

"Are you serious?" Kevin said. "Now that makes no sense."

"Do you believe that John Donnelly's sense of humor led him to put that on the bottom of a fake gold bar in his dining room?" Robert said.

"Well, who could have done it?" Michele said.

Daryl pulled out the chair nearest him and sat down. "Well, anyone could have brought the Internet feed down like I did."

"Whoever did it faced the same obstacles we did. To get in the house, to deactivate the alarm, and to disrupt the Internet feed," Robert said. He sat down, too, and looked at Daryl over the other fake gold bar.

"Unless the bar was fake when John Donnelly bought it," Daryl said.

"I don't think John Donnelly would believe the San Francisco mint in 1848 carved 'all your base....'" Although, Robert thought, he did fall for the valet scam. "Plus, to put the inscription into the fake bar, the other thief or thieves had to know which side was face down. Otherwise, the inscription would have been visible to the next person to see the bar."

"So you think someone did it just like we did?" Kevin picked up his beer from the counter and set it on the table before spinning and straddling a chair.

"Probably not exactly the way we did it, but someone probably took the real gold bar from the same spot we took their fake," Robert said.

"It's not been live for a whole year," Kevin said. "Last December, wasn't it?"

"January," Robert corrected. "The site's been live for nine months and two weeks, plus or minus."

"The bar was there before the site went live," Daryl said.

"Good point," Robert said. "If they get it before the site's live, they don't have to bring it down. Any chance we can take a look at the site's log files to see when the down times were? We could narrow down the possibilities there, too."

"Probably not," Daryl said. "Log files that old aren't on mounted drives; typically, it's on a tape somewhere, if they're kept at all."

Michele leaned against the counter. "Do you think it might have been an inside job?"

"Someone with legitimate access to the house would overcome two more of our obstacles," Robert said. "But it couldn't be one time access; this person had to see the bar in its environment and then fabricate a copy."

"Do we qualify as an inside job now that we no longer work for nTropics?" Kevin said.

"It's quite a flight of fancy logic," Daryl said. "We have an insider, with easy access to John Donnelly's house, making a copy of the gold bar and heisting the real one before the Web site goes live."

"A sound argument is one that is internally and logically consistent," Robert said. "A valid argument is one that is internally and logically consistent and that applies to reality. This scenario is perfectly sound."

"So what do we do?" Michele said.

"We need to do some research," Robert said.

"Which means I have to do some research," Daryl said.

"We need to find out when and how the bar was delivered to John Donnelly's house; when and how the room was specially modified with the new doors; when the Web site went up exactly; and what happened between delivery and site going live," Robert said. "This documentation of reality can help prove our scenario valid or invalid."

Daryl leapt from his chair. "To the Geek Cave!" He trotted around

177

the table and down the stairs.

"To the Rolling Rock!" Kevin said. He trotted to the refrigerator and got out a new bottle. "You guys need one?" he said.

"Sure, why not," Michele said. She thought Rolling Rock tasted flat for a mid-tier beer, but if they were going to drink, so was she.

"Okay," Robert said. He took Kevin's old bottle and rinsed it out. Kevin took four bottles from the refrigerator and went downstairs. Daryl was already logging in when Robert followed Michele down.

Robert took a clipboard and legal pad from a cubby. He picked up a pen from the desk and started writing. "Okay, we've got to find out who delivered the bar, who put the doors up, and the timeline from the delivery to the house to when the site went live. Also, you'll want to check the ISP to see if they've preserved the log files." He looked at the abbreviations on the legal pad. Illegible to anyone but him, he hoped. He'd tear it up after they were done and disperse it just to be sure.

"Aye, aye, Captain," Daryl said. His fingers rattled the keyboard. "He bought it in New York from Numismatics Auctions, Inc., last December 22; I guess Donnelly was out there on his vacation. NAI, as they like to call themselves, typically ship through a bonded courier which takes a week or two of business days."

"How did you get that so fast?" Kevin realized he still had Daryl's beer in his hand and felt like the ball game scoreboard's Two Fisted Slobber. He looked at the beer level of both bottles to confirm he had only taken a swig, or at least had taken more of a swig, from the bottle in his right hand and put the other one on the desk by Daryl's left hand so Daryl wouldn't knock it down with explosive mousing. "You da hacking monster!"

"I read the press release on the nTropics Web site and I clicked the link in the About Numismatics Auctions, Incorporated section. They've got information about their preferred shipping methods on the site," Daryl explained. "It's not as though everything I do is hacking."

"Okay. What are you going to do now?" Kevin said.

"Now I am going to see if I can find information about Nationwide Bonded Corp, such as a delivery schedule to see if John Donnelly took delivery from them."

"Is that going to be on the Web?" Michele said.

"Doesn't look like it," Daryl said. He opened a command line window and started typing.

Kevin leaned over Daryl's shoulder and watched Daryl type. He saw a couple of commands he recognized as DOS commands and then a couple of UNIX commands and some from some language he'd never seen before. Welcome messages scrolled up the screen before Kevin could figure out who was welcoming them, and Daryl continued typing even before the welcomes turned cold and the messages warned them that they would be prosecuted and monitored. In that order.

"You're untraceable," Robert said.

"As far as I know, I've never been tracked," Daryl said. He looked over his shoulder at Kevin. "You keeping up?"

"Hell, no," Kevin said. "I don't even think as fast as you're typing."

"All right, let's see what they've got for last December," Daryl said. "Actually, let's see what they have for Donnelly." He typed a complex UNIX command into the command line. Let's see you do that at a Windows command prompt, he thought. "John Donnelly, Litzsinger, January 16."

"January 16? Why did it take them almost a month?" Robert said.

"Holidays," Michele said.

"Or something else," Daryl said. "Who knows? John Donnelly got the bar on January 16. What day was that?"

"Friday," Robert said. "New Year's Day was on Wednesday."

"All right. Now, about the doors," Daryl said.

"How do we find which contractor did them?" Michele said.

"Who does nTropics work for the office?" Kevin said. "He probably had the same people do it. He didn't pay for it."

"He's got a point," Robert said.

"Well, that's no trouble at all," Daryl said. "We'll just look at nTropics' accounting to see if they paid for it. Their records will tell us when the work was done." His fingers found the familiar pathways without Daryl having to direct them. After all, he knew some administrator passwords and didn't have to break them, and he knew the directories he needed without having to list them. Colleen Winters, accountant extraordinaire and unrepentant hoarder of illicit music files, kept a copy of the ledger in her home directory. When the new corporate mandate banned all such repositories of music, Bert blew away everything in Colleen's home directory. Heavy metal, hair metal, hard rock, quarterly expense report summaries, the whole thing. Colleen, naturally, had come to Daryl to recover it all.

Daryl changed over to \cwinters and copied the ledger file, in a roundabout way, to the desktop of Robert's computer. He opened it using Notepad and searched for Westport. The first hit made no sense, so he repeated the search. He repeated the search several times. Each row was separated not by commas but some software-specific formatting characters that made no sense to human eyes. Daryl's eyes found the patterns in the garbage and could quickly deduce relevant information about each hit. Other human-readable strings in each row included a date and some shorthand explanation. Finally, he found the row that said, "JD hse sec doors," garbage, and a date. "January 14," he announced.

"So the construction guys put the doors in before the bar arrived," Robert said. He noted the date on his clipboard and noted his musing. "So did we find out when it went live?"

Daryl switched windows to the Web browser and backed up to the nTropics page. He tabbed to the gold bar's page link and hit ENTER to display the page. Their reasonable facsimile displayed in the center of the Web page. A discrete Web counter at the bottom told them that 4,377,205 people had viewed this page since 14:06 on 01/20.

Robert noted the date on the pad. "So we've got four days between the bar arriving and the site going live. Who's there for that period?"

"John Donnelly," Michele said. Would he have done it for an insurance scam; if so, wouldn't he have needed to pronounce the bar missing? More likely, he'd needed to hock the bar to some underworld type to keep himself living the good life, or to finance a shaky, shady business of some sort. He'd need the fake bar to keep up appearances.

"Whoever does his house cleaning," Robert said.

Michele thought about it briefly. The butler did it? She didn't like it.

"Eddie Bennett," Daryl said.

"Eddie?" Kevin said.

"He was there to hook up the camera and set up the computers," Daryl said. "It could have been him."

"Any other ideas?" Robert said after a minute of silence. He didn't let the next moment of silence go on quite as long as its predecessor. "All right, then. Daryl, why don't you take a look and see if you can find some old log files for the live video feed." Robert looked at his notes. He wondered who Melanie was, and if John Donnelly could really trust her.

"Wow, if this is going to take a while, you mind if I play some video games?" Kevin said.

"Go ahead," Robert said. If he had another computer, he could have begun some research of his own. He watched Kevin climb the stairs and heard him open the refrigerator for another beer.

Michele watched Kevin go. A little dense, the muscle for the job, but sexy as hell, with the confidence a limited intellect provides. Karen would sleep with him if she wanted to, without attachment. No, that was too cowboy and shallow; Karen would sleep with him if she wanted to, and would not like it afterward; she'd push the memory and the distaste deep into that well within her where she stored her pain. Of course, Michele wouldn't sleep with Kevin until he, or she, convinced her that it meant something else to him than just a casual hook-up. At one point, she wouldn't have taken much convincing.

She looked over the others. Karen would trust the technical guy for the most part; his ego made him easy to understand and control, for what little she would need to control him. The other one, what niche would he fill? The organizer, Karen's right hand man? Careful, methodical, and likewise dangerous. Michele thought about whether Robert could double cross her, and Daryl and Kevin. Somehow, she didn't think so.

"I wonder who the woman is that took the dog," Robert said. "That Melanie. Is that Donnelly's sister? She called herself Aunt Melanie."

"Hello, hello," Daryl said.

"What do you have?" Robert said.

"As I suspected, the ISP had no logs that old, so I've wandered back to nTropics. According to Eddie's calendar, he was over there on January 19 and January 20 to set up the computers and take the site live," Daryl said.

"So he was in the house," Michele said. "He had access to the room. The bar was there."

Robert nodded. Opportunity, one of the big trinity of means, motive, and opportunity. "Find out what you can about Eddie Bennett, then." He paced the length of his office and decided that a second lap would look too eager or anxious, so he went upstairs. He was happy to see Kevin was playing Defender on the Atari and not searching Robert's drawers. Robert went into his kitchen and took a beer from the refrigerator and opened it. He hadn't brought the old bottle up with him nor had he asked anyone if they wanted something while he was upstairs, but these would provide him with a good excuse for another trip when he had to move around.

When he went back downstairs, Daryl had a Web-based database interface open. Robert glanced at the contents. Payroll information for Eddie Bennett. "No wonder he left," Robert said.

"They hired him with certs only and no experience, and then they gave him like eight percent raises for the two years he was there," Daryl said. "And when he left, they had to hire two people to replace him."

"Why are you looking at his pay stubs? You don't even know for sure he took the bar," Michele said.

"We're looking at whatever we can," Robert said. "We don't know

181

what might become important."

"Here's his bank information," Daryl said. "We can find out if he's made a deposit for five million dollars in the last few months. That would clinch it. Here's his social security number, in case we want to get credit cards in his name."

"Right there on the Web?" Robert looked closer at the screen, and indeed, Eddie Bennett's ID number was eight digits long. "Crap, mine's up there, too, then."

"Well," Daryl said, "Not right there on the Web." After all, not even Bert and Ernie exposed the Intranet servers to the Internet itself. Of course, there are always ways around those things, especially when you have unlawful carnal knowledge of the network.

"Any chance there'll be some log files on the local machine? Maybe we can look at the Event Viewer and see if the computer itself restarted." Robert said.

"You think they might have just cold rebooted the machine right there?" Daryl said. "I guess that could work." He typed some. "Hello, FTP Server. What are you doing there? I wonder if the twins even looked at this machine when they got hired."

"So you can just log into it?" Michele said. "The machine in John Donnelly's dining room?"

"I just did," Daryl said. "Do you have a broadband connection at home?"

"No," Michele said. She didn't get online at home, really, except to check her mail with her America Online account. She probably wouldn't garner respect from these guys to mention her ISP, so she didn't.

"Too bad," Daryl said. "I could have demonstrated how easy it is."

"What do you have?" Robert said.

"Nothing," Daryl said. "Just a couple of failed services."

"It was worth a shot," Robert said.

"Hello, what do we have here?" Daryl said. "`test1.mpg`, dated January 20."

"Where's that?" Robert said.

"It's in the `\temp` folder. Looks like Eddie forgot to dump it. You mind if I copy this over?"

"How big is it?" Robert said.

"Two megabytes," Daryl said.

"Put it in the `\temp` folder locally," Robert said. "We'll...."

"Delete it when we're done, roger," Daryl said. He spun around in the chair and shook his head. "How are you doing, Michele? Not too bored yet, I hope."

"Fine," Michele said. "I am learning something. So what if Eddie Bennett did steal the bar? What then?"

"Depends on what he did with it, I guess," Daryl said.

Michele nodded. WWKD, she thought. What would Karen do?

"Hey." Kevin stepped off of the bottom step and met Robert's eyes straight off. "I think there's something wrong with your joysticks. I didn't used to be that bad. What's up?"

Daryl glanced over his shoulder. "Done," he said. "Let's see what you've got." He used the Windows Explorer to navigate to the file and double-clicked it. Robert's movie player of choice opened the file in a small window. Daryl wasn't surprised to see it wasn't the Microsoft bundled of joy.

Robert recognized the heavily draped wall of John Donnelly's dining room. "That's the...." he started to say. The camera moved on its vertical axis, showing a blur of the ceiling before it lit upon the gold bar in its corner of the desk. The shot did not match the Web site; the gold bar was not centered, nor was the camera zoomed. The desk was somewhat cluttered, with a pliers and screwdriver lingering at the edge of the velvet. A large toolbox sat at the edge of the frame, to the right of the gold bar; Robert remembered that was the side without the computer equipment. A body stepped into the frame, and a husky arm picked up the pliers and screwdriver and put them into the back pocket of a pair of blue jeans.

"Is that Eddie?" Michele said.

"I think so," Daryl said.

As if to dispel doubt, the body bent at the waist. Eddie Bennett grinned at the camera and patted the gold bar before straightening and moving behind the camera. Slowly, the camera centered on the gold bar and zoomed in, cutting off the periphery. The shot remained on the gold bar framed by its velvet for a moment, and then the media player's logo displayed when the movie finished.

"The toolbox," Robert said. "He carried it out in the toolbox."

"What toolbox?" Kevin said.

"The toolbox that wasn't there this morning," Robert said. "Play it again."

Daryl clicked the mouse button.

"After the camera flips, here, see that toolbox?" Robert said. "Closed. Now, watch what he does with the tools; he doesn't put them in the toolbox, he puts them into his pockets." The video clip finished predictably.

"That could be just his tools," Kevin said.

"It's his second day there," Robert said. "He probably pulled the

183

cables on the 19th and configured the system on the 20th." Robert paced as he spoke, and frankly didn't care if the others guessed he was upset. "I can't believe it."

"You're sounding convinced," Daryl said.

"Check his bank account, see if he made any substantial deposits in the beginning of February," Robert said.

"You mean, break into the bank computers? I am shocked, shocked!" Daryl said. He turned around and closed the media player.

"No wonder he left right after the site went live." Michele said. He had retired in his twenties, the only way a tech employee could after the bubble. Suddenly, it seemed more real to her, the possibility of taking some time off to pursue other opportunities of her own preference. Eddie didn't even have to split it.

"Eddie Bennett." Daryl said. "He seemed like such a nice boy. Quiet."

"Eddie Bennett!" Kevin said. "Who would have thought it?"

Suddenly, Daryl felt light in the arms and belly. His blood sugar bottomed out, again. Of course, he'd had no time for Pop Tarts this morning on his way to the library. "Hey, did we skip lunch?"

"I had two servings from the grain group," Kevin said.

"Why don't you guys go run and get something and bring it back. This might take a while," Daryl said.

* * * *

Michele and Kevin took less than an hour to bring back Jumbo Jacks, fries, soda, and more beer. Kevin calculated they had all afternoon and all night to drink. Four beers wouldn't hold him, much less the others.

Robert took fewer than eight minutes to consume his Jumbo Jack with Cheese, fries, and about sixty percent of his cola. While Daryl tried his hand at various scripts and utilities to garner access to Eddie's bank account, Robert dismantled the electroplating tank, returning it to its component parts and stowing them. He couldn't turn the rectifier back into a power supply and considered dismantling it into its barest components. He decided not to, however, and took it out to his garage. He never could tell when he might need a rectifier.

Since Daryl had Bennett's social security number, he also had his banking identification number, half of the combination that he needed. A simple script could guess the PIN and win! He narrated as he went, his normal operating procedure when working on a problem. Narration, of course, meant he talked to himself. With the others in the room, he'd hoped to elicit a question from the audience to pass the minutes, but the others were too busy eating.

Kevin ate his burger in silence. So quickly they'd gone from almost wealthy to, well, where they were a week ago, but unemployed. He ought to savor this meat, because it was potato soup and Ramen next week. Probably Budweiser, too, which was worse.

"Bingo," Daryl said.

"You got it?" Kevin put the three quarters burger on its wrapper. If he saved it, he could have meat tomorrow, too. He didn't wrap it up.

"You bet." Daryl watched the Welcome screen load, more slowly than normal because of all the relaying and roundabout connections, but the Welcome screen nevertheless.

"Go to the history," Robert said. "Let's see what happened in January and February."

"Right-o," Daryl said. He clicked the History link before the page finished loading the various buttons and mouse-over images that bogged the Web down.

"I miss the corporate Internet connection," Kevin said.

"Hang on," Daryl said. "This is almost like using an old 2400 baud modem. Or a computer without a hard disk drive. You kids these days don't know how lucky you have it. Why, when I was young, I had to dial-up two miles uphill to a single-line message board...."

"His current balance is $4678.04," Michele said. The Web page displayed it in red text at the top of the transactions for the month.

"I hope that's not all he got for the gold," Daryl said. The site constructed a table of transactions for the month. Using Cold Fusion, no less.

"There it is," Robert said. He tapped a line on the screen. "He did get it."

"What, did he make a deposit?" Kevin said.

"On January 21, they deducted the charge for a safe deposit box," Robert said.

"A safe deposit box?" Kevin said.

"He's put it in there to hold it for something," Robert said. "He's renting it quarterly. Go to this month," Robert said.

Daryl clicked as directed. The line occurred on the current month's billing summary.

"He hasn't cancelled it yet," Robert said. "It's probably still there. And that's where we're going to get it."

Another Heist is Required

Daryl exhaled heavily.

Michele looked at the computer screen carefully and then gauged the others' reactions.

"So we get to do a bank job next?" Kevin said. He didn't have a ski mask.

"We're not going to stick up the bank," Robert said. "We're need to get the contents of Eddie's safe deposit box. We're not recreating *Dog Day Afternoon.*"

"How do you break into a safe deposit box?" Kevin said.

"Can you build a gigantic Drill-A-Ma-Tron 5000?" Daryl said. Actually, given the supply of old motors and supplies Robert had in his garage and under his work bench, Daryl could almost see him building some sort of contraption out of an old movie. Robert might already have one or two contraptions under a tarp in the garage, but Daryl didn't think one of them was designed to drill into a bank.

"I don't know," Robert said. "We're not going to stick them up, though; that's a federal crime, and the FBI does spend some time on non-terrorist things."

"Breaking in will be a federal crime, too," Michele said. She tried to remember the employee handbook they'd given her when she did her two weeks at the bank. Of course, the locally owned bank she'd temped at in college had been acquired by a larger regional bank which had been bought out by a national bank based in Delaware. And so on, and so on....

"It's less obvious," Robert said, "if we do it right."

"What do you have in mind?" Daryl said.

"I don't know," Robert said. "Maybe we go in and pick the lock?" After he said it, of course, he remembered none of them could pick locks. Someone had offered that as a suggestion for Donnelly's house and he'd said something along those lines.

"Pick the lock?" Daryl said. "But none of us can pick a lock."

"You want us to pull a valet scam on the bank president?" Kevin said.

Robert put his hands behind his back and paced. He wondered if they could pull something like that off on a bank president. "You remember that a couple years ago, some bank robbers kidnapped bank employees to get their keys?"

"No," Kevin said.

"Well, some bank robbers did just that, kidnapping bank employees and making the employees let the robbers into the banks first thing in the morning. Much like in *Bandits,*" Robert said. "Undoubtedly, banks have taken steps to prevent that, which means bank employees probably won't carry their keys home or have them on their regular key chains. Even bank presidents."

"You can't get into a person's safe deposit box without his or her key," Michele said. The others looked at her, and Michele realized she had seized the conch shell. "Don't you guys have safe deposit boxes?"

"For what?" Kevin said. "I don't have a gold bar."

"Typically one puts other things in them," Daryl said. "Like important paperwork and small valuables you don't want lying around the house. I should get one, but I haven't."

Robert didn't mention the fire safe behind the fake electrical panel in his utility room. He flicked his eyes from Daryl to Michele so that he wouldn't involuntarily look in that direction.

"The bank and bank employees can't open individual boxes. The customer brings her individual key. If the customer loses the key, the bank has to drill out the lock to open the box. So the valet scam won't work," Michele said.

"On the bank employees," Kevin said, "but what about Eddie?" He gestured with the bottle of Rolling Rock and triumphantly swallowed the last of it.

"Eddie knows us," Robert said.

"I don't think Eddie would recognize me," Michele said. "He didn't come up to the Marketing Department too frequently."

"He didn't know much about Macs," Kevin said.

"They don't have valets at TGI Friday's," Daryl said. "It's not as though Eddie Bennett goes places where they have valets, much less that he uses them."

Robert processed the new information. "He's not an executive."

"Do you think he's gone nuts spending money based on his expected cash-out?" Kevin said. "I certainly would." He wondered which four star restaurant he'd hit first, but remembered St. Louis only had one. He wondered which three-and-a-half star restaurant he'd hit second, then.

"We need to find out more about Eddie Bennett. Where does he live? What are his spending habits? Is he working now?" Robert said.

"I'll get right on it, Captain," Daryl said. He started running his fingers over the keyboard.

"What are you doing?" Michele said. "What are your first steps?"

"First, I am going back to nTropics to review the information we know for sure about Eddie, like his address. Then I'll go back to his bank and see what I can learn about his cash flow. The people to whom he sends checks will lead us to his habits. From there, who knows what we will find," Daryl said.

"That sounds a lot like detective work," Michele said. She noticed Daryl used "whom" properly in a sentence.

"More realistically detective work than what you read about or see," Robert said. "No running around pushing mobsters' buttons."

"How do you know where to go, what to do?" Michele said to Daryl.

"Well, I know where he worked and I already know his bank. It's an inside job, so to speak, since I'm not starting out cold. I already know a lot about nTropics' network because I worked there. I know something about his bank's network because, well, I know where certain things are on the Internet. I know where to find the login prompts for several different universities, some banks, and even a DOD workstation."

"Why?" Michele said.

"Everyone needs a hobby," Daryl said. He often thought about it and tried to pinpoint where he'd deviated from the rest of his class. Somewhere around seventh grade he'd started hanging around with the "bad" crowd on America Online, hijacking the occasional account himself. Sometime in the eighth grade he'd gotten banned from AOL, and instead of getting mad at AOL, he got a real ISP and started seeing what else was out there. Once he was off AOL and away from the worse influences, he started hacking not to exploit, but to merely explore. His spelling improved, too.

"It's a good, lucrative hobby," Kevin said. He looked at the other beer bottles in the room. Not even close to empty. "Better than beer drinking, but not as much fun." He started up the stairs for another.

Daryl peeked into the employee database. nTropics kept Eddie's entry, marked inactive, probably in case it could ever figure out who would want to buy a list of its ex-employees. "Eddie lived on Manchester, in Maplewood, when he worked for nTropics," Daryl announced. He wrote the address on a scratch pad. "Now, for the good stuff." He cracked his knuckles.

"The bank?" Michele said.

"The bank," Daryl said. He popped open a terminal window and Telneted to an IP address he knew. Great ASCII art letters, CIS NETWORK, greeted him. Please Enter Login Command, it asked politely. Daryl did.

"How did you know the login?" Michele said.

"When you keep your eyes open on some of the hacking sites, you get to know a couple things the hackers exchange," Daryl said. Of course, hackers didn't routinely exchange testing logins that accidentally made it to production systems. But Daryl had promised Howard, the former systems tester for an old mainframe development shop, that Daryl wouldn't tell another soul about PR0F3SS3R F4LK1N. Of course, he didn't promise Howard he'd never use the login, and he didn't promise Howard to ever stop ragging him about his poor spelling, even in Hackerese. Maybe it was coincidence, but he and Howard didn't talk any more.

"So what are you going to do now?" Michele said.

"Well," Daryl said, "sit down and I'll show you."

Michele pulled a stool over and sat so that she could watch the screen as Daryl typed.

Robert paced a little and tried to convince himself entirely that Daryl was not endangering Robert's computer in any way. He didn't know the ways Daryl could be leaving tracks, but he could imagine tracks. He opened the right drawer on the workbench and scrambled through the collection of old radios, calculators, video games, and other electronica. He took out an old Mr. Microphone, a seventies/early eighties toy fad. Robert had planned to make it into a miniature transmitter. Robert turned his back on Michele and Daryl and hunched over the workbench.

It worked on a similar principle to his cameras, broadcasting a signal an FM radio could pick up. Of course, out of the box, or out of the garage sale without a box and priced at only one dollar, the microphone was a clunky appendage a Solid Gold disco performer would wail into, a microphone trailing a several inch antenna. Robert took out a screwdriver and started opening the casing. He'd see what he could make smaller, perhaps redesigning it to be smaller, and boost its transmission strength. Of course, he could buy transmitters smaller than this, but he wouldn't have made them, have cut and soldered and glued the pieces together. Besides, if he ordered one online, he'd leave tracks, and there's no telling what enterprises were integrating information to use against him in a court of law.

If Robert concentrated very hard on the Mr. Microphone, he almost couldn't hear Daryl describing the illegal things he was doing from Robert's computer.

* * * *

Although Daryl slowed his typing to the sound of a moderate summer shower, Michele couldn't follow what he was typing or the commands he used. He even told her what he was doing and why he was trying it, and a lot of the time whatever he did worked; Michele nodded when he did it, briefly comprehending each step in the chain of events. But when Daryl finished his sketchy notes on the scratch pad, Michele couldn't remember exactly how he'd gotten them. Certainly not well enough to recreate them in a novel. She'd better pack a notebook when it came time for in-depth novel research. Perhaps a video camera, too.

"Well, guys," Daryl said, spinning in the chair. "Here's what we got. He saw Robert at the workbench, but no Kevin. "Where's Kevin?"

"He's asleep on the couch," Robert said. He'd gone to check after Kevin hadn't returned immediately; Kevin had stopped for another beer and had then played some Atari. The next time Robert had gone to check on him, he found Kevin stretched out on the sofa, unconscious. "I'll go get him."

Daryl almost told Robert not to bother, but he let Robert climb the stairs. If Kevin was going to share in the loot, he was sure going to share in the conspiracy. Daryl heard Robert call Kevin's name loudly, using the voice instead of the touch to awaken the sleeping man. Daryl pictured Robert standing to the side, just in case Kevin was one of those violent awakeners. Or would Robert not assume that, thinking Kevin woke up beside more women than violent men? Daryl decided he was being too much the deerstalker cap type and waited.

Kevin followed Robert down, rubbing his gritty eyes. "What's up? What time is it?"

"Six twenty-five," Michele said. Her little Seiko's hands pointed to six and twenty-six, but she always rounded for those whose internal sense of time, or preferred clock or watch, differed.

"All right, here's what I got," Daryl said. "Edward Russell Bennett lives on Manchester Road above a used bookstore in downtown Maplewood. He's not in danger of his apartment being razed for a strip mall only because the Village Elders of Maplewood hope to emulate the success of the U-City Loop in attracting Young Urban Types Living

191

On Daddy, commonly called YUT-LODs. He makes his rent out to Kinison, a company that's trying to move more into the lucrative commercial market, based upon their holding trends and their current properties listings." Daryl looked at the paper.

"Eddie's got no regular deposits coming in, neither direct deposit nor weekly or biweekly deposits like he's got a real job. He's made several large lump sum deposits, on April 14 for $2500, on June 18 for $1800, and on August 17 for $2350, roughly."

"Is he taking payday loans against the money?" Kevin tried to figure what the interest rate would be by the time Eddie sold the bar. When Kevin had taken a payday loan, once, when he was right out of college and working for his father, he'd paid almost ten percent for a week. Suddenly he felt stupid suggesting it.

"More likely consulting," Robert said.

"Probably," Kevin said. He knew Robert'd had it made from high school on. Robert'd known what he was doing early. Robert'd never have found himself one rent payment short of a month.

"Regardless," Daryl said, "He's not renting the safe deposit box quarterly; he's rented it for a year. He only makes payments quarterly, deducted from his account every third month."

"So there's no telling if the bar is still in his safe deposit box," Michele said.

"No," Daryl said.

"What's his last transaction date?" Robert said.

"He withdrew twenty dollars from an ATM three days ago," Daryl said. "Of course, with batch processing, he could have deposited a million dollars yesterday and withdrawn it today, we wouldn't see it." Daryl had taken the Web page as his final answer on that one. An oversight, of course; he could have checked the recent transactions on the account number when he was on the mainframe, but he had looked for more basic information than the check register.

"He couldn't make a large deposit without alerting federal law enforcement," Michele said. "The limit's like ten thousand dollars or something."

"He'd have to deposit smaller amounts and take more time to do it." Robert didn't know much about money laundering. "Do we have any other account numbers for him at other banks? Transfers between them?"

"No," Daryl said.

"He hasn't cleaned out his bank account and he's still paying rent on his apartment, so it's safe to say he has not fled the country," Robert said. "If Eddie put the gold bar in the safe deposit box, it's still there."

"Or he already fenced it and it's full of cash," Michele said.

"That would be less work for us," Kevin said. "So how do you break into a safe deposit box?" Daryl looked down at the notepad and didn't answer. Robert rubbed his hands together and paced. Michele just looked back at him. "Do we drill in? Blast our way in? Eat the locks with acid?" Kevin tried to think of everything he'd seen in the movies, but most bank robbers were looking to get into the vault, which was a much larger target.

"None of us are explosives experts or have a drilling mechanism," Robert said. Of course, he'd had chemistry in college and had a couple of batteries around, but he didn't like the idea of acid.

"We don't have to be subtle, though," Daryl said. "What's Eddie going to do when he finds out it's gone? Call the cops?"

"We still don't want Eddie to know who's got it," Robert said. He envisioned Eddie Bennett with a Glock kicking in the door while Robert was in the kitchen, unarmed. Not to mention that Eddie Bennett, if he determined who had stolen his ill-gotten bar, could easily decide not to reclaim it, but summon the law on those who had it in their possession. Of course, they'd melt the bar down and cast it into jewelry within a day or so, but who knows what evidence the police would find? Robert was careful, but he couldn't think of everything. Of course, Robert knew his limitations, and was the better for it, but he tried hard not to feel comfort in the knowledge and make it into hubris.

Daryl made a thoughtful sound. "You're right."

Michele tried to remember what she'd learned while temping in college. She'd only worked at the counter, as a teller. Still. "We need someone on the inside," she said.

"Inside what?" Kevin said. Then he realized. "You mean someone in the bank?"

Robert shook his head. "We don't want anyone else in on it."

"We don't need anyone else," Michele said. "They use temps in banks. I used to be a temp. I'll go to work there. The safe deposit box attendant's usually a temp. I used to temp at a bank." Michele paused when she realized her arguments were coming a little quickly and not making much sense. She took a deep breath and started trying to marshal her points into paragraphs. "We're not going to get into the safe deposit box using a crowbar, or acid, or a pound of C4. The box is designed to prevent that sort of thing. Not to mention the bank. If I were working in the bank, I could use subterfuge to get into the box."

"What sort of subterfuge?" Robert said.

"I don't know yet," Michele said. She felt her heart beating, rump-thump-thumping beneath her wool jacket. She was surprised they

193

couldn't see it. "Once I am inside, I can find out."

"You think you can handle it?" Kevin said. They'd been pretty light on Michele so far, but it was from Robert's misguided chivalry or chauvinism. As far as Kevin was concerned, Michele could pull her own weight.

"Yes," Michele said. She thought she sounded like she meant it. She hoped she did mean it.

Daryl looked at Robert. As far as he was concerned, he'd let Michele try it. He'd done his bit of social engineering in the restaurant. She could do some. Even if she didn't manage Jedi mind tricks on the bank staff, who knows?

Robert felt the eyes upon him. He didn't have to look down at Daryl, sitting in his chair, at his computer. He didn't have to look at Michele, sitting above Daryl on a stool, nor up at Kevin, standing halfway between the computer and the stairs. Robert looked at the discombobulated microphone on the workbench. If he said no, Michele and Kevin and maybe Daryl would go off on their own. If they got caught, the whole story would come out, including his involvement. If only he could think of something, some way to get the keys directly from Eddie Bennett; but myriad obstacles loomed. Perhaps Michele's insight into banking, coupled with her observations about the particular policies of Eddie's particular branch, could provide something. "All right," he said. He met Michele's eyes. "Try to get hired at the bank for reconnaissance. Just to see what the bank's policies are and what particular things the bank employees and managers do, how they handle things. After you're there for a while, we'll see."

"All right!" Kevin said.

"Give me a second," Daryl said. He spun the chair and began typing.

"Whatcha doing?" Kevin said to Daryl.

"We need to find out what temp agency the bank uses," Daryl said. "I'll tap into their HR or their accounts payable and see who gets the checks."

Michele didn't watch Daryl this time. She felt the urge to pace and wondered if she was picking that up from Robert. She hadn't worked in a bank for almost eight years. She had never expected to go back, but she didn't expect to be out of work, either. She took a deep breath and stopped after a couple steps. She was just going to take a look around inside the bank. No need to do anything illegal, just do a job and collect a paycheck. She looked at the workbench and its contents. While Daryl had been working on the computer, Robert had been working on a circuit board and tangle of wires.

Robert picked up a wire cutter. He could cut the circuit board in half and fold it over, adding wires to connect the leads where he clipped them. Or he could diagram the transistors and capacitors and resistors to determine how to build his own transmitter. He liked that idea better. Besides, Mr. Microphone was a collector's item, worth a mint on eBay.

"What is that?" Michele said.

"A Mr. Microphone, manufactured by Ronco. A toy from the late 70s," Robert said.

"Are you repairing it?" Michele said.

Robert looked at the spread case, contents, and screws set neatly to the side. Of course, she'd think he was troubleshooting it. What fool opens perfectly good equipment? "I am reverse engineering it," he said. He put the wire cutter down. "Looking at it to see how it works. It's a short range FM transmitter, essentially," he explained. Of all the reverse engineering he'd done, he was glad this was the one Michele saw, and he was glad the cartoonish flower that sang "You Are My Sunshine" was dismantled, its cartoonish flower parts in the trash some weeks ago, and its "You Are My Sunshine" parts in a sealed Tupperware container in a drawer.

Suddenly, Michele realized that they were all alike: she liked to see how people worked, what they thought and how they reacted, so she could better recreate facsimiles in her writing; Robert liked to see how electronic things worked, so he could better use them to his own devious ends; Daryl liked to test the limitations of computer systems to see how they fit together, probably for his own curiosity; and Kevin— well, maybe Kevin wanted to see how women worked to better enjoy his Epicurean pursuits, or maybe Kevin just liked to see what came next. Michele thought she ought to write down this sudden epiphany, since she had a burst of uber-lucidity like this once a week, and when she didn't record it, she often forgot. She probably liked the EUREKA! spark every time she covered the same old realizations, so she didn't capture the thoughts and could enjoy the same ones over and over.

"Got it," Daryl said. "Integral Staffing Solutions provides three staffers to the bank, a total of one hundred billable hours a week. Two full time and a part timer. Or some combination."

"Integral?" Kevin said. He pronounced the name carefully, in TAY grull, just like Alan told him. "I know a recruiter over at Integral."

"You what?" Robert said.

"I know a guy over there. Alan Bradford. He's a recruiter," Kevin said. "He owes me a favor. Should I call him up and tell him I want to get a job for this girl I know?"

"How well do you know him?" Robert said. He had a complete set of business trading cards in his drawer, too, sorted alphabetically and with the date and job fair written neatly on the back of each. By some accounts, Robert knew those people, too.

Kevin chuckled. He remembered Alan Bradford, red-haired and needing to shave only once every three days, as a college freshman. Alan's eyes were wide at orientation, as befit his small Catholic high school upbringing. Somehow, he had expected the university to be the same, but the fortuitous presence of Kevin two doors down in Woodland Hall saved Alan's soul. Of course, Kevin had been somewhat wide-eyed at that point—his own upbringing at Lindbergh High under the watchful eyes of his father hadn't been made him quite as self-assured as he had projected. "We were in the same dorm in college," Kevin said.

"Can he place me at the bank?" Michele said.

"Can he hire Michele as a temp?" Robert said. If they asked this guy to place Michele specifically at the bank, it would be very bad. Very bad.

"I introduced him to his wife, so he owes me one," Kevin said. He had, in a roundabout way. Kevin had been the one to approach the trio of au pairs at the trendy Central West End coffee shop. Alan had stood behind him when Kevin started talking to Veronica, the Austrian blonde leader of the three. When it came time for introductions, Alan had insisted upon kissing their hands. Although Veronica had only sunken further into the leather couch and twisted her pretty lips into sophisticated distaste, Katarina, the dark-haired, dark-eyed Ukrainian, had found it charming. That, and Alan was Christian, which was all the rage among a certain healthy sect of females that year. Such as Katarina. "I'll let on that I'm trying to impress Michele."

We know better, Michele thought.

"Hey, I'll call him now," Kevin said. He took his phone from his pocket and auto-dialed number seven.

Robert pushed back from the workbench and began pacing. He would have called Kevin off, but he didn't have any better idea. "Don't tell your friend where to place her," he said.

"What?" Kevin twisted the phone's microphone from his mouth, but turned it back into prime speaking position. "Hi, Kat, is Alan in? Thanks." He looked at Robert and said, "What now?"

"Just tell him to hire her, not where to place her," Robert said.

"Of course not," Kevin said. "Hey, Brad Alanford." He always got Alan's goat when he called Alan that in college. It was a comfortable throwback, a way to remind Alan that they went way back almost ten years. "Hey, you know what nTropics did? Yeah, that included me. No, I got something on the fire, but I could use a favor. I worked with this woman. Yeah, she's hot," Kevin said into the phone.

Really, Michele thought. She certainly ranked cute, or pretty, but as long as she was above 150, certainly not hot. Of course, by her own definition, she hadn't been hot since eighth grade.

"She needs a job, quick, and she's got some temp experience. Sure, she's got a resume. Can I e-mail it to you tomorrow? Man, if I could get her a job, she'd know I was wired. Yeah. Wired to you. You're the CPU, I am the video card, man. You rock! Yeah, sure, how about next Wednesday at the Trainwreck? You going to bring Kat? You know I love her, too, but not like," Kevin sighed theatrically, "Veronica. Yeah, I know it. Next Wednesday, six o'clock. Thanks." He pressed the **END** button.

"Well?" Michele said.

"You're in," Kevin said. "I'll e-mail your resume to him, and he'll find a spot for you." He frowned. "Can we make sure she gets a job at Eddie's bank?" If not, he thought, at least she's got a job. He wondered if his skills could land him a temp position. Perhaps he shouldn't have wasted this favor on Michele.

"We'll see what we can do," Daryl said.

Each Ponders the Next Heist

At eight o'clock, with night thoroughly fallen, Robert found himself alone with only the furnace's throaty murmur. He listened to the furnace, and the silence that enabled him to hear it, for several minutes after listening for Kevin's car to start and drive off down the street. His one vice, at least the one that came to mind at that moment, was his love for a warm house. Rationally, he knew that he could turn the temperature down to sixty for the night, and compensate with an extra blanket and comforter on his bed. He could turn the furnace down during the days, afternoons now, when he went to work. It would save a percentage of his money, more than interest the bank would pay on his savings, but Robert liked the thought of the warmth enveloping him when he stepped through his front doorway after a walk from the video shop or the nearby Save-A-Lot grocery store. The warmth meant home. Like a ticking alarm clock for a new puppy, the furnace's click and hum lulled him to sleep many nights. Robert shook his head and wondered if normal people thought that much about the role of forced air heat in modern civilization. Which is what he romanticized, when you came right down to it.

He drew a glass of water from the kitchen tap and went into his basement. He'd left the Mr. Microphone unassembled so he could diagram its electronic components, so he got out a pad of graph paper and a pencil and began diagramming.

*   *   *   *

Michele fed Frodo and scooped herself three orbs of vanilla ice cream. No toppings, and only vanilla, so it was not much like ice cream at all. The rationalization might have worked if she didn't like vanilla best anyway. Since she did, the calories all counted. Frodo grunted in agreement, or perhaps in pleasure at her mere presence for the first time in twelve hours.

She sat at the kitchen table with her ice cream and dangled her fingers to scratch the passing bunny. She spread the copy of *The Writer* magazine, freshly arrived that day, across the table. She breezed through the letters section to the meaty, how-to articles. "'Incredible? Make It Credible -- Make the fantastic real and draw your readers in,'" she said.

Frodo grunted in response. Michele read through the article, looking for fresh content for her own craft or reminders of things she'd learned in Fiction 074: Plot as Revelation of Character. She gleaned a few tidbits, perhaps eventually worth what she paid for the issue on her subscription.

She rinsed the bowl and put it into the dishwasher, sighed, and looked at the computer reluctantly. Upon it, she had over ten years' accumulation of short stories and notes about David Albernathy, his years in the Marine Corps Recon and the training, the things he'd seen that hardened him to diamond clarity. David Albernathy's life, according to Michele's notes, pretty much rationalized why he'd fall for an innocent little Cynthia, the doe-eyed English major.

Never, in the six years she'd been drafting the novel, had Michele captured any text notes for why this perfect man would want Cynthia.

She opened a new document and looked at the toolbars, the marker that indicated the end of the file. The same as the beginning. She saved the file as KarenHist.

She looked at the stuffed animals on the bookshelves, each with its own story: the bear in overalls Jay gave her in college, when he thought he might win her heart with a sensitivity he displayed for her amid stoicism he puffed for everyone else (one of which was faux, and she'd never cared which); the rabbit Sy had gotten for her at the school picnic in high school, before she'd gotten a real rabbit on her own; the black and white bear, aptly named Theodore, she'd slept with as a child; and four other plush beasts, each bearing a specific memory or a memory cue for an era of her life. She looked at the books behind the animals, the anthology textbooks, the cheap paperback editions of the classics, and the set of 1984 World Book Encyclopedias and yearbooks she inherited from cousins and kept around in case she needed to write period pieces set in the early 1980s. She'd looked at them all for the lifetime of the half-hearted novel she'd been trying to write as a history of....

Well, something. She had notes, and character outlines, as though she were writing a damn paper about something that had already happened.

She saved the file again, this time with the filename KarenNovel.

She'd come up with a better title as she went along. The end of file marker hadn't moved yet, but Michele knew that every moment, every keystroke, she was creating who Karen would be, and who Karen was.

"Karen saw the diamond tiara at the auction, and knew she had to have it for much less than the starting bid of two million dollars," Michele said. Frodo grunted. "Although it was reputed to have belonged to Queen Anne, Karen found the price a bit high, so she thought she might steal it." Then Michele typed it.

*   *   *   *

Kevin had dropped Daryl off in Kirkwood, so of course he discovered that the Hot Shots sports bar and grill he preferred was on his way home if he got off 270 and headed west for fifteen minutes. On his way home as the crow flies, which was good enough for Kevin since it was still early. He only had eleven dollars in his wallet and didn't think it would have been a good idea to stop at the ATM, so he was in for a short night.

He was pleased to see a couple of the people he knew. He had nodded royally to a couple of tables and made his way to the bar. Which is where he had found Amy Wallace.

Amy Wallace was a friend of Rod Whitehall's from college, or a former apartment neighbor. Rail-thin and cute in a repressed librarian sort of way. She had big blue eyes behind huge lenses that seemed to cover her cheeks, too. She sometimes bound her soft, wavy brown hair in a loose ponytail, but tonight she had it rolling down to her shoulders like a downy waterfall. She could dance fairly well, not raunchy but playful, and she often smelled of a light flowery perfume. She worked as a proofreader for a textbook publisher in Maryland Heights but lived in Winchester. Although she said the job was boring at times, she liked reading all the different textbooks and could talk a good engineering, psychology, and medicine at bars. Kevin thought she might be good for him, but he doubted he would be good for her.

"You really didn't lose it if you never had it," Amy said.

Kevin sipped at the Bud he'd had drafted. He might as well start getting used to poverty. His opening line to Amy had been that she could have been drinking with a rich man, but that the Man had taken it away. She thought he meant the stock options he'd lost at nTropics, and he probably ought to let her. "I guess," he said.

"It's like when a great big company goes bankrupt, and all of the employees start weeping about the money they lost in the stock. For the most part, they didn't, really. For example, someone who buys

201

twenty thousand shares of company stock using options whose strike price was fifty cents a share. It costs him $10,000. If the stock price goes to fifty dollars a share, employee has a million theoretical dollars. If the company goes belly up, the employee who has exercised his options is out ten thousand dollars, not a million, contrary to what the media report. That's nine hundred and ninety thousand dollars of theoretical money, and it's not real unless the employee sold the stock." Amy paused to look at Kevin to see if he was listening, to see if he was understanding what she was saying or if he was looking over the crowd. He appeared to be listening, so she continued. "The important thing is, don't give up. You lost that virtual wealth, but you're still young. You've got time." She'd recited the speech to many of her dot-com friends to varying degrees of success. She didn't mind succoring Kevin, though.

"You're right," Kevin said. "It's not as though I went right out and started spending that money. But I would like the aristocrat lifestyle someday." He shrugged. It felt kind of like when the lottery prizes reached multimillion dollar payoffs and Kevin ran a couple of dollars through the computer-generated number pickers. A couple of days of thoughts and maybe a glance at the paper's real estate section with its front page of new mansion offerings. "Now, do you fancy a spot of pocket billiards?"

* * * *

Although Kevin had been reluctant to lose a locked-in drinking companion, Daryl got dropped off, bike and all, at his apartment. Daryl walked the bike up the stairs and into his apartment, where he leaned it on its kickstand in front of sofa. He got a Mountain Dew from his refrigerator and headed for the computer. He had a couple ideas he wanted to run down, and he could do it better without Robert fretting or Michele asking questions over his shoulder, particularly since he didn't know what he'd be doing, much less could he really explain it.

He turned on his Linux box, an old AMD with common peripheral components. When he'd built it, it had just been easier to stick the most readily available video card, modem, and NIC into the box than to put in the best simply because the drivers had been better for the more common components way back when. Now, of course, you could put any souped up hardware in a Linux box, find drivers, and be blasting beasties in online role playing games with full screen animation and beautiful texturing. Still, it was a workhorse, and it offered a robust set of command line utilities and none of the handy identifiers embedded in a Windows operating system. Nowhere did the name Daryl or Simon, much less Daryl Simon, appear on the hard drive or in a FROM THE DESK OF label affixed to the case. A wonderful hacking Clydesdale. He logged in with the root account.

He started by looking for Integral Staffing. He Googled them to get the official Web site and looked it over, visiting a number of pages. Integral didn't list individual positions they had available. The temp and consulting world was premised on the lottery system. Send us your resume, and you might win a paycheck! Of course, if the agency could place you, you were a valued employee. If they thought they could place you, you were a valued prospective employee. If you fell somewhere in between, you were nothing. Thank you, don't call us, we'll call you.

Daryl had made the mistake of trying the consulting route when he first got out of school. He remembered Joyce Wittingstern bubbling about his Philosophy degree complementing his comp sci minor, along with his experience at the computer lab at Saint Louis University. She'd bubbled through his first interview and testing, and then through his communication for his technical interview, and then the bubbling suddenly stopped. Joyce didn't return his calls for two weeks, so Daryl gave up and took a job as a computer operator with a market leader in HR, benefits, and payroll employee services through corporate portals, intranets, and interactive voice response solutions. By the time Joyce called back, burbling again now that she had an opportunity for him and, more importantly, for Joyce's company, Daryl was developing applications and didn't need a consulting position, thank you.

Of course, persons interested in temping with Integral could submit a resume to opportunities@integralstaffingsolutions.com. No doubt an address automatically forwarded to Kevin's friend and all the other recruiters in the house. It kept the junk mail down to the individual boxes, no doubt, and it kept competing firms from hiring away the recruiters.

Once Daryl had located Integral's Web site, he easily gleaned the IP address of their Web server, or firewall protecting the Web server, or router leading to the firewall or Web server. Once he had the number, he had ways of making the computer who answered to that number talk.

So he did. He rattled the door knobs, and eventually one turned. When he opened the door, he found a corridor with numerous doors, each leading to an unlocked room containing file cabinets with employee records, customer information, and a host of music files. Alone in the ill-lit cyber room, Daryl said, "Computer, tell me who is working at the bank now and what you know about that person." In his own room, lit only by a desk lamp and a street lamp outside, Daryl said, "Son, you have to cut down on the cyberpunk novels or you'll really jack in one of these days."

His terminal displayed Jessica Albright's vitals without saying anything back. She'd worked for Integral for about four months. Her first placement had been as a receptionist for a print shop, her second the bank. The recruiter had scored her highly on simple positions in receptionism and financial services; ergo, her position at the bank. She was making one figure an hour, three if you count the decimal places. If Daryl were Jessica, he would. Of course, as a new hire, probably just out of one school or another, she didn't have vacation. Probably not sick leave, either.

Daryl laced his fingers behind his head. The tree between his window and the streetlight moved slightly in the wind. In the summer, the tree blotted out the light entirely, but in the autumn and winter, it offered shadow puppetry on the wall. Daryl watched it a moment, unable to make anything from the shapes. He Googled Jessica Albright St. Louis as a matter of course. The white pages offered an address and phone number. Daryl glanced over the results. A leftover sorority page from last semester. An announcement from an SLU student poetry reading. They might have shared some of the same professors. He clicked the sorority page and found a picture of her at a charity car wash with her sisters. She didn't look bad in cut-offs and a tied-up tee shirt.

Daryl closed the browsers quickly, feeling a twinge of unease or guilt or generic that-ain't-right. Poor Jessie (as the ALT tag of her Web photograph called her). She had no idea how easily Daryl could Web stalk her, and he did know; he also wanted to know more about the blonde with the hose in her hand and the 3.2 GPA at SLU. She ought to be creeped out, unless she too checked her Google occasionally to see what the public, and love-sick computer geeks, could find out about her. Daryl's eyes wandered across his walls and met the silk-screened eyes of the King. "At least I am not itching like a man on a fuzzy tree," Daryl said. "What the heck is a fuzzy tree?"

Daryl started poking around Integral's network and found the employee handbook on a mapped network drive. He used a little tool he had that let him look at Microsoft Word documents even though he was using the forbidden system. Integral offered the standard benefits, but only gave their staffing professionals a week off after a year employment and two weeks after three. Daryl wondered how many employees made it three years.

Daryl scrolled down to the other time off allowed. Three days for bereavement leave for parents and siblings; none for grandparents, aunts, or in-laws. Poor form, Peter! Of course, the document paid some lip service to the Family Medical Leave Act. They allowed off for jury duty, of course, but would fully expect you to shirk your civic duty for your $72 a day in wages and untold wealth of benefits.

The chair squeaked as he leaned back again. The shadows of the tree's arms crossed and recrossed themselves thoughtfully. Daryl looked for a pleasant courtroom scene in them, an aging Southern attorney struggling to his feet to object to something while the jury watched intently. He didn't see it, of course, but if he focused, he could imagine Jessica Albright sitting in a jury box. For half pay, of course, but not at a counter in the bank. He smiled.

Daryl grabbed Jessica's social security number and address from the Integral site and moved on to the St. Louis County Court System computer. These days, government computers were getting more and more secure, but Daryl had time, and he had tools. It wasn't as though he had to smash and grab something from a crowded shop window. With the Internet, he had all the time in the world, and a couple of handy network utilities and password guessers to help him along the way.

Daryl explored the Byzantine, and probably pre-Byzantine, systems in the County Courts. He had to drill down beyond the simple unsecured desktops of employee workstations. Certainly, somewhere, someone would have kept his or her notes in a Word document or a spreadsheet, but Daryl didn't have time to look for it. He did, however, find a server with an interesting database on it.

An Oracle database. Won't break down, can't break in, they had advertised. Lucky Daryl just wanted to peek in. He poked at it to discover its version and patch level. An older version missing a couple critical patches. Governments spent their grants on new whiz bang front ends and initiatives that involved large numbers of connected consultants and maybe even someone who knew technology. Good for him, he thought.

Daryl submitted a few queries to explore the system. Again, he could have saved time had he only known the opaque naming system for workstations in the county system to find whoever was responsible for data administration so that he could find data models or notes on that person's workstation. He didn't, though, but with a quick couple of queries to the system tables, he had a fair idea of the system. More to the point, he could see that Jessie had never served on a St. Louis County Court Jury and that the system had a batch process to prepare mailers for printing. Daryl updated the flag on Jessica Albright's record so that tomorrow morning, a laser printer somewhere in the heart of Clayton would spit out her name and address and a date in the county courthouse in two weeks.

He double-checked his update to the database and then removed the transaction from the database's auditing log. He looked for the usual connection logs on the firewall and machine into which he Telnetted and removed his log entries there. He thought about hunting for other logs, and weighed the time, effort, and chance of leaving more tracks than he already had against his impression of the quality of network administrator you could buy on local government money, and backed out.

He hit Integral again to cover his tracks, but created an account called MSAdmin for later and logged out. He stretched and looked, with surprise, at how light the room had become. He tapped the mouse on his main machine to disengage the screen saver. The clock on the taskbar read 7:36. He had an urgent need to release the three Mountain Dews back into the wild, and then to sleep. So he did both.

Casing the Bank

Michele awakened several minutes before her alarm was set to ring, but she waited in bed habitually anyway. If she were a go-getter, she suspected she would leap out of bed every morning, drink some juice, and go for a run before heading to work. Or start reviewing the correspondence she received overnight, from agents and editors and readers because she had spent the mornings fruitfully instead of just waiting for the alarm to go off. Then the alarm chirped like an arrhythmic sparrow, and Michele got up.

She bathed, shaved her legs, and dressed comfortably. She hadn't any interviews, nor errands to run, so she'd spend the day visiting Monster and every other online job site. Lisa, her friendly neighborhood coffeehouse poet of ill repute and human resources coordinator for a non-profit, compiled a list of resources for Michele when she accepted the job at nTropics. Lisa had suspected that Michele might be on the short list if the economy, or just the company, made a turn for the worse. Michele had already pulled the manila folder out of her file cabinet and looked through it, placing it on her desk for further use.

Michele had finished her morning granola bar, coincidentally the last one in the box she had removed from the desk drawer at nTropics, and was looking over some sales and marketing leads when the phone rang.

Michele smiled once, using what some article had called a radio announcer's trick, before picking up the phone. "Good morning," she said.

"Good morning, is this Michele Is Bert?" a recruiter said.

"Isbert," Michele said.

"I'm sorry, I don't encounter many French names here in St. Louis. My name is Alan Bradford, and I am a recruiter for Integral Staffing Solutions. Kevin Horton passed your name on to me as someone who might be interested in an opportunity as a temporary employee," Alan Bradford said.

"Kevin is a fast worker," Michele said.

Alan Bradford laughed. "He sure can be. I see you have some experience as a temp in your past. Did you enjoy it?"

"Some parts of it," Michele said as she slipped into the phone interview patter.

*   *   *   *

Daryl called ahead and made sure Robert would be home before riding to Overland. He'd gotten up at the crack of noon, consumed some sugar flour puffs, and skipped the shower since he was just seeing Robert. Pedaling up Ballas Road, Daryl thought about what he'd done and how he would break the jury duty trick to Robert. In the glaring light of day, he wondered if he'd been too impulsive. Robert probably would want to deliberate quite a bit. He couldn't think of a better alternative, and he spent much of the ride trying.

Robert ushered Daryl into his kitchen at a little after two o'clock. When Daryl called, he'd said he had something he wanted to talk about in person. Robert had offered to meet him somewhere closer to Kirkwood, but Daryl had wanted the ride. Robert had to work in a little under two hours, so it suited him that he could be at work almost immediately after. He passed the glasses cabinet and the refrigerator and skipped all host decorum. "What's up?"

Daryl took a deep breath. He looked at Robert whose eyes widened like a deer in the headlights. Well, not like a deer in the headlights, but more like an expectant child at Christmas. No, maybe like a.... Well, Daryl couldn't exactly say what he read in Robert's expression. "I selected Jessica Albright for jury duty starting in two weeks," Daryl said.

"Who's Jessica Albright?" Robert said.

"Jessica Albright works for Integral Staffing Solutions, currently assigned to the safe deposit box at the bank. She's not been there long enough to have been the one who handled Eddie; she graduated from SLU in June."

"You got her on jury duty?" Robert said.

"Well, it takes her out of the picture for a limited period in a controlled time frame and we don't have to kidnap her or put her in the hospital," Daryl said. He tried to imagine Kevin with a collapsible baton in his hand, whacking her knee. He didn't like the image.

"How did you do that?" Robert said.

"I just manipulated the database at the county courts. They've probably mailed her notice already," Daryl said. "She's scheduled for two weeks from tomorrow."

"That places us under a time constraint," Robert said. "She's got, what, two or three days that she sits in the county courthouses, maybe more, maybe less."

"I know," Daryl said.

Robert stepped around the breakfast bar. "Can I get you something to drink?" he said, not so much as a proper host. He wanted a destination to keep from looking as though he were pacing. Of course, Daryl probably knew him well enough to know he was, in fact, pacing. When Daryl declined the drink, he abandoned the pretense and began energetic pacing. "So in two weeks, we might have Michele working inside for us. All right, she won't have much lead time. We have two weeks to prepare, but what do we prepare?"

"I don't think Michele can drill the box or carry the gold bar out in her pockets," Daryl said.

"You're right," Robert said. He'd once known a riverboat casino employee. Although Billy had only been a Courtesy Ambassador and not a money tender of any sort, the casino had issued him a uniform which had decorative pockets, but no actual place to put things. The casino forbade him from carrying any of the product—money—with him while he was on duty and subjected him to a couple of random searches. Robert didn't know what the standard was for bank employees, but he couldn't see Michele carrying a backpack out without arousing suspicion.

"So if we were going to have her take it, she'd need a place to put it," Daryl said.

"The trash?" Robert said. Of course, he was copying *Ocean's Eleven*. It didn't turn out well for Sinatra and the boys. "No, never mind. The janitorial staff would certainly notice the sudden weight to the trash, and even if they did not, who knows if a dumpster diver would get it first." Robert imagined a slightly bedraggled member of the lower class rooting through the shredded papers in the bank's dumpster, looking for aluminum and coming up with gold. He tried to keep from finding a metaphor for himself in the image. He failed.

"You know whom we ought to have here?" Daryl said.

"Michele," Robert said. She knew how a bank worked.

"I'll give her a call," Daryl said. He took his phone out of his pants pocket. "What's her number?"

Robert recited the number, including the 314 area code. Too quickly, he thought.

"What should I tell her?" Daryl asked.

"Tell her to meet us here tomorrow," Robert said. "Around eleven o'clock."

Daryl relayed the message and hung up. "All right. I'll call Kevin over, too, but I know you've got to get ready for work. I'll see you tomorrow."

*   *   *   *

Kevin directed the spray from the hose onto the roof of his car. The good people of the world were scrubbing their cars, and although Kevin would have preferred to be drinking beer at noon on a Tuesday, he wanted to at least keep up the appearance of respectability. He liked to wash the Eclipse once a week, too. The suds washed over the passenger side. Kevin expertly angled the nozzle to completely clean the car's surface and avoid getting his shirt wet, which was more important in October than in the summer.

He finished the hatchback and spoiler and draped the hose over the coin box when his phone rang.

"'Ello," he said.

"Hey, Kevin, it's Alan," Alan Bradford said. "I interviewed your girl Michele Isbert today. I'm surprised. She doesn't look like the type you normally go for."

"What type?" Kevin said.

"Usually you go for younger and less mature," Alan said. "The kind typically impressed with a smoothie."

"You're a little married to be jealous," Kevin said.

"You can never be too married," Alan said. "Anyway, it looks like she'll fit in here; I scored her pretty highly for her technical competencies, not necessarily for her choice of men."

"So you think she'll get something?" Kevin said. He wanted to suggest a bank position, but held his tongue.

"It's all up to the computer now," Alan said. "Whenever we have a position opening, our database pops up a list of available candidates and we run down the list."

"So you're out of the loop now?" Kevin said.

"For the most part. I am not a placement specialist. They don't ask us lowly recruiters about the interviewees too frequently after we score them. Sorry I can't help more," Alan said.

"Hey, you've gone above and beyond the call of duty already, man," Kevin said. He climbed into his nice, clean car.

"How are you doing?" Alan said. "Have you got a job yet?"

"I'm working on some leads," Kevin said.

"Well, if you want to temp, let me know. I can score you high on a couple things," Alan said. "Like alcohol tolerance."

"AB hiring taste-testers?" Kevin said. "I'm good. I've always got the metal shop to fall back on."

"Wednesday?" Alan said.

"Wednesday," Kevin said. "I'll talk to you later."

"Later," Alan said.

As Kevin rolled out of the self-service car wash, he was already dialing Daryl's cell phone.

*   *   *   *

Michele's mail didn't hold any job offers, but she didn't get any form letter rejections from employers, either. She tossed the mail on her table beside the groceries and Walgreens necessities she'd picked up. Still too early for the rejections, really. She checked her answering machine. Once, when she'd first entered the workforce, the answering machine's light had blinked almost every day with an opportunity with a company expanding in the St. Louis area. Now that she was looking, they were not. Much like her love life.

In her bedroom mirror, Michele watched herself turn from side to side in the skirt and business jacket combo she'd worn to the Integral job interview today. Professional, assertive. But not slimming. It almost looked like she was wearing the great shoulder pads from the 1980s, her shoulders were so broad. Still, they added to her self-assured business look. Managerial. Too bad she'd wasted the suit on a temp job.

Still, Integral Staffing Solutions was an integral part of the plan they were developing. By concentrating on the interview, and not on the reason for the interview, Michele had remained calm while Alan Bradford had fed her the leading questions. She'd answered well, she thought.

She changed into a loose pair of jeans and a sweatshirt. No blinking light on the machine meant no calls for a movie or dinner out. She needed a night off for a DVD or a book anyway.

But when she came back into the living room, she saw the computer and she felt a not infrequent resolve, a Will-To-Discipline. She creaked into the worn wooden office chair, tapped the mouse to dispel the screen saver, and read what she'd written last.

Steven brushed imaginary creases from the front of the vest. Karen thought the gesture indicated professional pride. Of course, she'd never commend Steven or he would think it a good reason to slough off. She hoped he'd convey the professional pride in front of the hotel where Schofield would be staying.

She'd decided that Karen was reclaiming the tiara for the child of a Holocaust victim who lost the jeweled headpiece to the Nazis. That way, ultimately, Karen could be a heroine, and David could become involved with her with a clear conscience, eventually. Of course, what if the heir was lying? David and Karen could team up to.... She leaned forward in the chair and put her head in her hands as she looked at the Rabbit-A-Day desktop calendar. First she had to get the group to steal the tiara.

Michele straightened and began typing, not quite a full 75 words a minute, but at a more thoughtful speed. She got all the way through the key copying and return when the phone rang.

"Hello?" she said.

"It's Daryl," Daryl said. "Are you busy tomorrow at around 11:00?"

She didn't need to look at the day planner in her purse. She was clear all week unless Integral had a position for her, or the one of the two other places she interviewed suddenly reached a decision. Five days of blank days except for drinks on Friday with Mary, Luisa, and Ellie. "No, what's up?"

"We just wanted to have lunch again. Can you meet us at Robert's?"

"Sure," Michele said.

"Great, I'll see you then," Daryl said.

She thought about Daryl on a car phone. Or a bike phone. She didn't hear any traffic, so he wasn't talking while pedaling along. A safe practice. On her way to the kitchen for the can of soup and quick warm-it-up bagged roll she'd have for dinner, Michele paused beside her flopped-over Frodo and scratched him. He purred, his whiskers vibrating like little plucked guitar strings. "Don't try to pretend you're a cat; you're not fooling anyone," she said again. "You and me tonight, curled up before a computer monitor. What could be better?" she said.

* * * *

Robert locked the door behind him when he got back from work and did his normal perimeter walk, checking to see a spray of glass beneath a window. He didn't find one, but suspected that if he stopped looking, he would find one. He checked the locks on each; of course, they remained locked, for he had checked them before he left. The tour let him assess each room as he entered, the sewing room, his bedroom, the living room, the bathroom, and the kitchen, the dining room, to check their cleanliness. His house, he thought again.

After he completed the walk through, he put turned on the kitchen radio. WSIE, the local jazz station run out of the basement of a university in Illinois, was playing a Tony Bennett bonanza; Tony was singing the 60s pop hit "Blue Moon" and not doing too badly. Robert tore some iceberg lettuce for a salad. Actually, the torn iceberg lettuce was the salad. He salted it and ate it. He looked out at the dark house beside his, his neighbors already in bed so they could be up doing retiree things early in the morning.

Robert wished he could do something about the gold bar probably locked in Eddie Bennett's safe deposit box. Eddie Bennett was probably not related to Tony. Unfortunately, Robert couldn't hack to investigate and he didn't like the thought of staking out Eddie's apartment. He pictured himself in a trenchcoat and fedora, breathing frost in the cool autumn night, as he stood in a doorway beneath the apartment building. Then he saw a group of disenfranchised urban youths accosting him, causing him to either commit assault or assault with a deadly weapon to defend himself. Or a Maplewood cop busting him for loitering. Or the myriad other charges that local, state, and federal legislatures enacted since the 1940s to keep a good noir detective down.

He rinsed the bowl in his sink and then washed it, and all the dishes in his dishwasher, by hand. Although it was 11:30, he knew the earliest he would get to sleep was 2:00. He could pop in a video to pass the time until tomorrow, hopefully directing his thoughts away from the things he had no control over. Of course, he had no control over the movie, either.

His entertainment center, within his living room, contained a cabinet full of videocassettes and DVDs. He looked over his collection of screwball comedies, old detective movies, and sci-fi television series. Nothing would do. He had some unread magazines in his magazine rack, the cullings of his last trip to Barnes and Noble. Nothing grabbed his interest. He closed the cabinet and paced.

He didn't feel like a video game or like surfing the Web. He didn't feel like anything, and it was too early to go to bed. He certainly didn't want to spend any time puzzling over the heist. He preferred to think that his subconscious was a great machine, a black box like a COM object that took a passed parameter or problem, did some magical logic

213

on it, and returned a solution. He never knew if there was logic in it, or just a random number generator. If he waited long enough, something came out, and he could use it or reject it.

Robert got the vacuum cleaner out of the hall closet and ran it. Vacuuming the upstairs, when he included the bedroom, took far less than an hour. Dustmopping the wood floors would take five minutes. Afterwards it would still be too early to go to bed. Some nights stretched on like this, and typically the next day the house was clean. So Robert vacuumed. Then he topped off the soft soap dispensers in the kitchen and bathroom from the jumbo bottle he'd bought at Sam's.

Michele, assuming she got a position with the bank while the regular temp was on jury duty, couldn't put the bar in a backpack and walk out of the bank. She couldn't put it in a trash can because it weighed too much. Anywhere she put it in the bank, they'd have to break into the bank to get it. Except.... Robert smirked and put the jumbo bottle of soap back into his linen closet. Except a safe deposit box. Robert smirked. Frank Sinatra might have been proud.

*　*　*　*

Daryl showed three hours earlier than everyone else at Robert's morning phone call behest. Robert, he could see, had something on his mind. He tried to put his finger exactly on the difference between general anxiety and eager anxiety in Robert, but he couldn't, exactly. Maybe Robert was merely vibrating at a higher frequency than normal. Robert offered him coffee and fell into a pleased silence. "What are you so pleased about?" Daryl said.

"I have a plan," Robert said. "Well, the seedling of a plan." He picked up his cup of warm French Vanilla coffee and sipped it.

"What is it?" Daryl said.

"If Michele's going to swap the bars from inside the bank, she needs two things: she needs Eddie's fake bar in the bank where she can get to it, and she needs somewhere to put the original one. Maybe it's only one thing," Robert said.

"Right," Daryl said. The scent of the French Vanilla made Robert's kitchen more domestic than normal.

"Where's Michele going to be?" Robert said.

"Where?" Daryl said. When, he thought, was a more appropriate question. He assumed Robert had worked his seedling of a plan down to a second-by-second set of gearworks.

"Working the safe deposit boxes," Robert said. "So the best place for the fake gold bar," he paused dramatically, or for about sixteen or

214

seventeen milliseconds, "is in a safe deposit box. Michele can switch them. We'll rent a safe deposit box and put the gold bar in it. Michele can open the box or something and then switch them, and we can take the bar out at our leisure."

"How much coffee have you had?" Daryl said.

"Just a couple of cups, why?" Robert said. "You don't think it's a good idea?"

Daryl considered the goal, ripping off a safe deposit box in a bank, and considering the goal was probably not a good idea in the first place, and thought Robert's plan sounded reasonable. "You think Michele can do it?"

"I don't see why not," Robert said. "It's very white collar." Unlike breaking and entering and attempted caninicide, which Robert considered very blue collar crimes. "We can ask her. She seems okay with it so far." He sipped the rest of the coffee in his cup.

"All right," Daryl said.

Robert poured a new cup of coffee and saw it only left three cups, hardly enough for a guest, so he rinsed the pot and refilled it. Of course, since he was refilling the pot, that meant the few cups he'd already consumed numbered six, plus the new one he poured. Of course, were he an executive, he could count the one he poured as one he consumed, but he wasn't, so he didn't, and Daryl had not pressed for actual enumeration. Maybe six or seven was a lot in three hours, but Robert hadn't thought the idea while buzzing on caffeine, so it wasn't too suspect now. "So what can you find out about the safe deposit boxes?" he said to Daryl, changing the subject within his mind.

"Everything, I guess." Daryl thought about the mainframe interface and didn't know exactly what he could discover unless he tried. "You want me to look now?"

"Yes," Robert said. "Maybe we can rent the box this morning." Actually, he'd hoped so, which is why he'd called Daryl at seven thirty, shaking the night owl from bed and summoning him forth.

"You da boss," Daryl said. He took a cup of the flavored coffee downstairs and logged into Robert's computer.

"Okay, I got it," Daryl said. He looked at the light grey text on the command line interface—the Command Prompt, the operating system called it, burying it several levels deep in the Start menu and not appreciating the simple beauty of words, prompts, and commands scrolling ever upwards. "Eddie's got a large box, number 1197. Numbers run from 1001 to 1200. Obviously, they're following the new checking account numbering convention."

"It would have to be a large box," Robert said. "Can you find an

215

available box of the same size nearby?"

"Hang on," Daryl said. He backed out of the customer view and started poking around the administrator menus. He found one that let him see branch statistics and drilled down. "Okay. A lot of the big boxes are available. 1180, 1182, 1183, 1185, 1187, 1189, 1192, 1195, 1196...."

"Is that the one right next to Eddie's box?" Robert said.

"It's the one preceding it numerically," Daryl said. "How the bank has ordered them, I have no idea. It's a lot of available boxes. Even if we specify which size we want, it's not guaranteed we'll get one close to him."

"Is there a weighted algorithm that determines which one a customer rents?" Robert said.

"There's an editable flag that marks whether the box is rented or not," Daryl said. He tapped the screen. It contained a table with box numbers, account numbers, start date, end date, rented, and last bill date.

"Can you edit it?" Robert said.

Daryl typed 1180R and hit ENTER. The cursor moved up to the RENTED column beside box number 1180. A flashing box displayed over the N as the mainframe and its COBOL or FORTRAN program awaited an administrator's instruction, that somehow, normal batch processing had missed a box that a consumer had already rented.

"So you want to go rent the safe deposit box? I can set all the flags to Y," Daryl said.

"Not right now," Robert said. "Someone else could walk in off the street and get it. I'll give you a call when I get to the bank."

"Are you going now?" Daryl said.

"No time like the present," Robert said. He waited a few seconds for Daryl to react. Instead, Daryl moved through a set of menus on the computer. He liked Daryl well enough, maybe even trusted him, but Robert wasn't about to let Daryl wander about his house while Robert was elsewhere. "Wouldn't it be better if you did that at the library?"

"As in, get the hell out of my house," Daryl said. "Probably." He logged out of the ISP and the workstation. "How are you going to let me know when to make the changes?"

"I'll call you," Robert said.

"You don't have a cell phone," Daryl pointed out.

"Certainly the city of Maplewood has a pay phone somewhere," Robert said.

"Oh, right," Daryl said.

"So it'll be one-way communication. I'll call you when I get to

Maplewood, near the bank. When I call you, block off all boxes but 1196. Do you need me to write the number down?" Robert said.

"1196, I got it. November of my senior year," Daryl said.

"Okay. Two minutes after I call, I'll call back to make sure you're ready. Can you edit all the boxes within that time?"

"You bet," Daryl said.

"All right. I'll call you when I am out of the bank, and you can set the flags back," Robert said. "Except for 1196."

"You bet," Daryl said.

"Let's go," Robert said, and they did, with Robert pointing his car southeasterly and Daryl biking northeast.

*   *   *   *

Robert drove by the bank once and started looking for a pay phone. The local chain supermarket down the street had one outside the front door. Robert parked in the middle of the supermarket lot and walked to the phone. He picked it up, waited for the dial tone, and put some coins into the slot. He put his shoulder against the wall, casually, he hoped, and glanced around to make sure no local hoods were looking for their hook-ups. Of course not. In this day and age, they all had stolen cell phones. He dialed Daryl's cell phone.

"Yes?" Daryl said.

"I'm here. I'll call back in two minutes," Robert said. He shifted so he was leaning on top of the phone, hanging up and looking at his watch. "Where did you say he lived? I tried that. Uh huh," he said to the broken connection, surreptitiously, to see if anyone was waiting for the phone. He didn't see anyone coming nor loitering as though he or she wanted to use the phone, but Robert didn't want to chance hanging up and risking a confrontation. "Listen, tell me again from Manchester and Big Bend. All right, I did that. Right. Right." He spent the next minute and ten seconds getting nondescript directions from the dead line.

With twenty seconds to go, he hung up and fished in his pocket for change among the collection of four quarters, three dimes, a nickel, and his keys. With twelve seconds to go, he dropped the money and started to dial. One final impatient glance at his watch assured him he was on time.

"Yes?" Daryl said.

"You're ready?" Robert said.

"All set here," Daryl assured him.

"I will call you back when I finish," Robert said. He hesitated for a

217

moment. "Thanks," he said, and then he hung up.

Robert decided to leave his car in the supermarket parking lot and walk a block to the bank. He hadn't surveyed the bank, but he expected cameras on the light posts or on the building proper, and he didn't want his car on the tapes. Of course, in a couple minutes, he'd be in the system with social security number and all, but Daryl could probably take care of that. Daryl couldn't erase tapes. Daryl couldn't clean up the paper trail, either, so Robert would have to plan on writing illegibly. Of course, he'd be on tape in the bank, too. Maybe they hadn't upgraded their cameras, he thought. Maybe they'd just have to get it right.

The bank had a small parking lot that they had probably reduced to accommodate the drive-up windows on the west side. It faced south, looking across Manchester, but didn't have many windows to observe the row of shops, but undoubtedly, inside the small shops, the barber, jeweler, and book peddler, could see him.

Robert pulled open the bank's glass door and held it for a young woman with a bar through her lower lip. She struggled a stroller through the door and didn't speak to Robert as she passed. Robert's hand slipped from the door handle too easily, and he hoped no one would want to shake his hand.

Robert's eyes adjusted to the relative dimness inside. The door was not centered on the front wall; instead, it opened at the western side of the building. The room into which he stepped was long and narrow, about eighty feet long. The west wall was ten feet to his left and the east wall of the room fifteen feet to his right.

The teller counter, chest high, ran along the west wall, with money counting and money packaging machines against the exterior wall. Two tellers had open windows to handle customers; three people, bored and herded through a set of poles and vinyl straps, tapped slips in their hands and looked at the walls. Two cameras peered down, with overlapping fields of view, on the teller area.

The wall to the right looked solid and had no doors. Of course, the vault probably lie behind that wall, with its stacks of money and gold bullion, except for the gold bullion in which he was interested. Two more cameras, making sure the whole bank was layered in overlapping video. The building had no guard posted at the entrance, but certainly, somewhere, someone was packing heat, and no doubt eyes were upon Robert now. Robert hoped the moment had not stretched too long, and he crossed the room.

As he passed the tellers to find the personal bankers, Robert saw the room stretched into an L shape. The wall to the right gave way to a small counter. A young woman sat behind it, reading something hidden behind the counter. She looked up as Robert neared. Along the north wall, several offices with President, Senior Loan Officer, and Real Estate Loan Officer had open doors and glass walls that let the bank president and two senior loan officers look out. The offices gave way to cubicles, which gave way to filing cabinets in the northeast corner, spaced around a fire exit.

The center of the room had three desks without walls, two occupied, and a table with a clipboard. Robert looked at the clipboard. **Personal Banker Sign In**. Robert suspected it was not, in fact, for personal bankers to sign in, but for people who wanted to see personal bankers to sign in. He took the pen and wrote his name and the time onto the lines provided.

He put the pen down and straightened up. The young lady behind the counter had returned her eyes to whatever page she was reading. Behind her L shaped counter, Robert saw a set of small rooms with closing doors on the east wall and, behind her, an open door to a room lined with safe deposit boxes. That might make the young woman Jessica Albright.

Robert looked at the short leather chairs apparently designated as the customer waiting area. Or client waiting area. Whichever banks had. Robert, the customer or client, sat in one.

One of the men from the occupied, unwalled desks stood up almost the millisecond Robert sat down. He walked to the table and picked up the clipboard. About five eleven, maybe one hundred and sixty or seventy pounds, Robert estimated. A trim build, dark brown hair, dark brown eyes, thin facial bones. Wearing a polo shirt with no logos, tucked neatly into Dockers, the guy was not carrying. If Robert worked in a bank, he'd carry. Of course, with his ten-year-old Botany 500 striped shirt, buttoned almost all the way up, tucked into his black denim jeans, Robert couldn't think where he'd carry. He'd probably leave it in his desk. "Mr. Davis?" the man said.

"Yes," Robert said. He didn't correct the man. Perhaps the man would remember a man named Davis, and not Robert Davies.

"I'm Jeff Sommers. How can I help you today?" Jeff Sommers said.

"I'd like to open a safe deposit box," Robert said. He followed Jeff Sommers to his desk and sat in Jeff Sommers' customer or client chair.

"We've got numerous sizes of safe deposit box," Jeff Sommers said. "What did you have in mind?"

"What's the largest size you have?" Robert said.

"We have a box that's eight inches tall by ten inches wide and twelve inches deep, which can accommodate several hundred pages of letter-sized paper," Jeff said.

"Is that the largest you have?" Robert said.

"Yes, it is." Jeff said.

"I think I'll need one of those," Robert said. "I'm trying to think how big my lock box is at home, and I think that should hold the contents. How much does it cost?"

"Those boxes rent at $149," Jeff said. He lowered his chin a little to look earnestly at Robert.

"Wow," Robert said. "That's a lot. Is that for a year?"

"Yes, sir, from the date you open it."

"What's the next smaller size?" Robert said.

"We've got one that's eight by four by twelve. It will accommodate several envelopes or folded sheets, or small items of value," Jeff said. "A lot of people like them for antique jewelry or old coins. They rent for $89 a year."

"Hmm, I guess I'll take the bigger one. I've got the usual papers, you know, birth certificate and social security card to go in, and I've got some old coins my father left me." Robert took out his wallet and extracted eight twenty dollar bills. "No sales tax, right?"

"Uh, no," Jeff said. He reached deep into a drawer full of file folders and extracted a handful of bureaucracy. "Do you already have an account with us?"

"No," Robert said. "This will be my first."

"All right," Jeff said. He opened the center drawer in his desk and took out a carbonless form. "I'll need you to fill out an application, a contract, and a signature card," Jeff said. He placed the forms, turned so Robert could read them, and a pen in front of Robert. "If you have or open an account with us, we can automatically bill you for renewal every year, and you save five percent from the price."

Robert picked up the pen. "What if I open an account after I get the safe deposit box? Will I get the discount right away, or can I only get it the next time I renew?"

"Next time you renew, I'm afraid. However, if you want to open an account now," Jeff said, "we can deduct the cost of your safe deposit box from your initial account balance. You've got more than enough to open a basic checking account and have a balance left over."

Not after you've deducted the applicable fees for falling under the minimum balance on my first day with your bank, Robert thought. I'll owe you money. "I don't know. Not today. I'll see what balance I have in my savings account that I might be able to transfer over." He looked over the application form. A standard application, with spaces for social security number, employer, and whatnot. Not much fine print, just the standard waiver that said the signee acknowledged all the information was accurate under penalty of death, dismemberment, and probably a fine. The contract offered the standard stacked deck to the bank. The signature card had a place for his signature as well as a physical description, probably to ensure everyone besides Jeff would know him on sight.

"Whatever you decide," Jeff said.

Robert felt the stare of the young banker on him as he filled out the paperwork. No extra commission today, he thought, although he wasn't sure bankers got commissions. Probably just extra points in the race to move into a cubicle or an office. Robert wrote as illegibly as he could, sticking with the Davis motif in his name. He signed that he hadn't committed any felonies in the completion of the form and handed it to Jeff.

Jeff keyed some information into the workstation. "All right," he said. He took the eight bills Robert had laid on the desk. "Do you have a driver's license or other ID? I'll need to make a photocopy." After Robert produced said identification, Jeff pushed himself away from the desk. "I'll get your keys. One moment."

Robert watched Jeff as he walked to the woman behind the counter. Jeff said something, and the woman took the paper from him. She looked at it, scribbled something onto a card, and typed something into her computer. She stood up and went into the room with the safe deposit boxes. Robert rubbed his palms on the thighs of his jeans and bunched the coarse material.

The woman came out of the safe deposit room with a key. She passed the key to Jeff, who accepted it with a comment and a smile that reaffirmed he was single. The woman behind the counter said something, and Jeff came back to his desk. "All right," Jeff said. "Your box is number 1196. This is your key."

Robert exhaled and let go of his pants leg to accept the key.

"Are you familiar with safe deposit boxes?" Jeff said.

"Somewhat," Robert said.

"When you want to access your box, you need to visit our safe deposit box attendant, who sits at the counter behind you. Jessica can help you. She'll take your key and use both hers and yours to open the box. No one can get into your box without your key. That means you cannot get into your box without your key. If you lose it, we'll have to drill out the lock in your box," Jeff said. "Do you want to place anything in your box today?"

"I didn't bring anything with me," Robert said. "I wasn't sure I'd get one."

"Okay. Is there anything else I can help you with?" Jeff said.

"So I don't have to sign back in with you?" Robert said. "I just have to see the attendant?"

"To get into your safe deposit box, yes. But if you have any other account needs, like when you decide to open that checking account, or if you have any other questions, feel free to stop in. Let me give you my card," Jeff said. He stood and fingered a card from the holder on the desk.

Robert stood with Jeff and accepted the card. "Thanks," he said. Now, don't let him....

Jeff offered his hand. "Thank you for coming by," he said.

Robert pushed the card into his back pocket, rubbing his palm on his backside to dry his hand from moist to partially clammy. "Thanks, Jeff," he said. He turned and walked out of the bank, counting the steps to the doors.

*   *   *   *

Daryl looked at his watch again. Twenty-three minutes. The computer monitor in front of him had page six of seven in Monster.com job ads. He'd dawdled over the first six pages, frequently delving into synonymous job ads, for twenty-three minutes. So far, no one in the library had complained that he'd overstayed a thirty minute period at the computer, but the crowd in the library was picking up. A second window on the computer, stashed on the taskbar and auto-hidden with the taskbar, contained the Telnet connection to the bank computer. He wondered how long it would take for the connection to time out. He ALT+TABbed to the dark terminal screen and looked at the grey text at the bottom of it. No time out message displayed.

Then Daryl knew he was being watched. He turned his head a little to the right and caught a glimpse to confirm and then looked at the man. Sandy blond hair blow dried to the left, purple plastic frames on his glasses slightly angled to mimic horned rims, but not enough to be committed truly to retro styling. Daryl had seen him behind the counter more than once. If you can see them, he thought, they can see you.

"What's that?" the librarian said.

"What?" Daryl said.

"That Web site you're looking at," the librarian said. "How old is that?"

Daryl looked at the terminal window, with its simple text against a dark background. If only it had a weird textured .gif as the

222

background. Of course, the name of the bank displayed on the title of the screen the terminal emulator was presenting. The titlebar of the window had the terminal emulator's name and the connection name. The terminal window, while it had its own toolbar buttons to start the capture buffer, end buffer capture, and create a new connection, lacked an address bar for URLs and the Internet Explorer globe spinning into infinity. The librarian didn't notice the specifics, though. "That's my bank's low resolution interface for low bandwidth connections," Daryl said. The librarian didn't object, didn't rankle, didn't even look like he understood. "I use it when I am on shared computers because it's quicker. I don't know what speed of connection you have here, but I didn't want to hog it with lots of graphics and SSL connectivity."

"We have a broadband connection," the librarian said. "But thanks for thinking of us. Is this site really faster?"

"Sure," Daryl said. "It doesn't have any graphics, which really bogs down any connection you make to the World Wide Web, especially if your browser doesn't cache them." He studied the librarian for any sign of comprehension, or of suspicion. Nothing. "It's direct access to your account, really," Daryl couldn't resist adding. Regret twinged him; would the librarian pick up his meaning?

"Interesting. It's certainly primitive enough," the librarian said. "I wonder if my bank has one of those."

"It probably does, but most of the people, like the tellers and stuff, don't know about them. You have to call their headquarters like you're having trouble with your regular online banking and someone might tell you," Daryl said.

"Cool, thanks," the librarian said. "Have a good day."

"You, too," Daryl said. He watched the librarian straighten some chairs and wander back to the counter. How long had the librarian been watching him? The librarian certainly must recognize him by now—he'd come in several times over the last week. The librarian, once he sat back down so Daryl could only see his head, didn't look at Daryl. Maybe he bought the story. Occam's Razor said the simplest explanation often sufficed; perhaps a simple lie was easier to accept than the reality that Daryl was hacking into the bank using a special CustomerAdmin account he'd set up on all Internet workstations in St. Louis County libraries for the express purpose of making all safe deposit boxes at a single branch of the bank appear to be rented for a simple sliver of a single business day. When he put it that way, Daryl didn't believe it either. Perhaps he'd discovered a secret of social engineering. Make a preposterous plan and a simple lie.

His phone vibrated, finally. "Hello," he said.

"I'm done," Robert said. "I'll be back at my house in thirty minutes."

"You get what you needed?" Daryl said.

"Yes, I did. Thanks."

"I'll see you then," Daryl said. Robert sure could say what he meant without applying a context.

"Yes," Robert said and hung up.

Daryl quickly knocked off the rented flags for all the boxes he'd set to Y and logged out of the system. He logged the computer back into the default user, the patron account that blocked everything but the Internet browser. He stood up and looked at the librarian who'd spoken to him. The man was still engrossed at his desk behind the returns counter. Daryl slipped out as quickly and discreetly as he could.

Preparing for Michele's Heist

Daryl took the extremely scenic route to Robert's house, riding down Midland to a road called Sims, passing Upper Overland, the houses with dignity, character, and a sense of being out of place. He rode back up Lackland, through the strange small town downtown found in many of the smaller municipalities in St. Louis, where independent towns had been assimilated by the expanding suburbs. Kirkwood had one of its own, just a couple blocks from his apartment. Kirkwood's, though, was a booming yuppie mecca, not a rundown strip of cut rate tax preparers, greasy spoons, and bowling supply stores.

As he pumped and coasted, he ran through what he told the librarian. Technically, Telnet kind of was a forerunner of hypertext transfer protocol, so it could conceivably be construed as a primitive Web site. He wasn't comfortable with the rationalization, though; he'd told a falsehood to the man, his second in as many weeks, and not of the "Your haircut looks nice" magnitude. It was a lot different from hacking; hacking wasn't lying to a person, just a computer system. He wasn't being a white hat liar, or even a grey hat.

When he got to Robert's house, Robert let him in and offered him some coffee and then led him into the basement.

Robert picked up the pad of graph paper from the workbench. He'd folded over the Mr. Microphone notes and had mapped out the bank quickly, before his memory had added too many poetic flourishes of inaccuracy. "Here's the bank's layout. I don't have the accurate scale yet, but the proportions are correct."

Daryl looked at the paper. Robert hadn't used architectural symbols like you'd find in house plans; he'd used the symbols from inside the front cover of the Player's Handbook in *Dungeons and Dragons*. The Basic set, no less. Daryl tapped the penciled unbroken line of inner wall to the east. "I'd like to check for secret doors right here," he said.

"I don't have a d6 handy," Robert said. "Listen, the safe deposit boxes look like they're right through this door. Michele will sit at this counter here. When I come in, I talk to her."

"You think you're going to talk to Michele?" Daryl said.

"I don't know," Robert said.

"When are you going to put the gold bar in the safe deposit box?" Daryl said.

"Tomorrow," Robert said.

The doorbell rang. Robert glanced at the television. Michele and Kevin stood on the porch. Kevin looked up in the camera's direction. He's letting my neighbors know about the cameras, Robert thought, and he bounded up the stairs and threw open the front door.

"Hey," Kevin said. "Are you guys ready for lunch? I haven't had anything to eat all day."

"You bet," Daryl said.

"I'll make something," Robert said. "We've got to talk about what Daryl and I have done, and what we've got left to do."

"All right," Kevin said. "You have any steaks?"

"No," Robert said. The others followed him into the kitchen. "Coffee?" he said. The contents of the pot were less than an hour old, plenty fresh for guests. Of course, Robert knew no such concepts— freshness versus scorched—for his own consumption.

He hadn't thought to thaw anything, and he'd nothing in leftovers. He could make them a big salad, except he ate the lettuce last night. He had spaghetti, butter, milk, and bacon. Enough for Spaghetti with Carbonara sauce. "How's spaghetti?" he said.

"Sounds good," Michele said.

"Hey, free is better than good," Kevin said.

Robert filled a pot with water for the spaghetti and got a pan to fry the bacon. "You want to start, Daryl?" he said.

"All right. I got the current Integral temp on jury duty starting two weeks from today," Daryl said. "She'll be out of the office for two days. Or more, I suppose, if she gets scheduled to sit on the Trial of the Century."

"Jury duty? How did you come up with that?" Michele said.

"I read the employee handbook for Integral," Daryl said. "It was either jury duty or National Guard."

"National Guard?" Kevin said.

"Integral's handbook says it lets its employees off for National Guard or military reserve duty," Daryl said. "But Jessica's not in either, so that's not really an option."

"You got her picked for jury duty?" Michele said.

"Sure," Daryl said. "The county's computers are not very secure."

"So how are we sure they're going to hire me and assign me to the bank?" Michele said.

"Hmmm," Daryl said.

Robert drained the bacon and used a saucepan to melt the butter and warm the milk. "You've worked as a temp before. How does that work? How do you get an assignment?"

"The recruiter calls you up and says, 'I've got a position for you,'" Michele said.

"That's all?" Robert said.

"That's all I know," Michele said. She sat forward and put her arms on the table. "I was only a temp."

"You know, when Alan called me, he said it was all up to the computers," Kevin said. He took a hearty swallow of hot coffee, perversely enjoying the burning down his throat and into his stomach.

"The computers?" Daryl said.

"That's what he said." The hot coffee made Kevin's voice huskier. "Hey, baby," he tested. Not deeper, just huskier.

"A database with an application that scores people based on their aptitude for a job?" Robert said.

"Probably," Daryl said.

"Can you rig it?" Kevin said.

"Depends on the set-up and the database. I could probably just boost Michele's scores and lower the other temps' so that her name crops up for a query," Daryl said. "It's no harder than rigging jury duty."

"Good," Kevin said.

"So once I get in, then what?" Michele said.

"We also rented the safe deposit box right next to Eddie's," Robert said. He stirred the spaghetti and lowered the temperature on the sauce.

"Right next to Eddie's?" Michele said.

"Yes," Robert said.

"So you have the key for that one and everything?" Michele said.

"Sure," Robert said. He used the tip of his spoon to cut a piece of spaghetti. He found no resistance, so he turned the burners off and poured the spaghetti into a colander.

"So how do I make the switch?" Michele said.

"Lunch is ready," Robert said.

"You guys don't have a plan yet, do you?" Michele said. She looked at Robert, busying himself over serving dishes, and at Daryl, who met her eyes and shrugged.

"Do you have a plan?" Kevin said.

"I guess not," Michele said.

"I hope this is okay," Robert said. He put plates and silverware in front of everyone and put the pasta in the center of the table.

"What is it?" Kevin dished a pile of the white-sauced spaghetti onto his plate.

"Spaghetti Carbonara," Robert explained.

"It's free," Daryl said.

Robert offered the bowl to Michele before piling the remainder onto his plate. He'd estimated fairly well for four people, assuming no one wanted seconds. He was a little light on the sauce, though.

Michele cut the spaghetti on her plate with her fork. "You know, it takes two keys to open the box. One from the bank employee, and one from the consumer. If we're not going to take Eddie's key from him, we need to have him give me, the bank employee, his key so I can open his box."

"How do we get Eddie to do that?" Kevin swallowed and put another forkful into his mouth.

Michele stirred the pasta on her plate. She took her first bite. Not bad, she thought, chewing slowly to give herself time to think. She swallowed. "Have you ever read Agatha Christie's *Ten Little Indians*?" she said.

"What?" Kevin said.

"In it, there are ten people on an island, right, who've been accused of and cleared of murder, but someone brings them to an island and starts killing them off."

"I think that's *And Then There Were None*," Robert said.

"No, it's *Ten Little Indians*," Michele said.

"The judge did it, right?" Robert said.

"Yes," Michele said. "And then he commits suicide, so investigators don't know what happened until someone finds a message in a bottle that he'd written explaining how he did it all."

"That's *And Then There Were None*," Robert said.

"The title's not important," Michele said. "I was thinking about the ninth murder, the last one he does before he kills himself."

"The girl who hangs herself?" Robert said.

"Murder?" Kevin said. "Isn't that a little drastic?"

"It's not the murder, it's the method," Michele said. "The judge puts a noose and a chair in this woman's room, and she hangs herself."

"So what's your point?" Daryl said.

"So Eddie's guilty of something. We need to use his guilt against him to play into our hands," Michele said.

"You mean, to get him to come to the bank when you're there?" Robert said. "Call him up the days you work there and incite him to take the bar out of the safe deposit box?"

"We don't even have to get him to come there to take it out. Just to check it," Michele said. She paused dramatically and had a bite of pasta. "Say we call him up and tell him that we have stolen the bar out of the safe deposit box."

"We?" Daryl said.

"She means 'we' as in an elaborate, unseen conspiracy of professional thieves," Robert said. "An anonymous call from a pay phone to gloat."

"Right," Michele said.

"So he comes down to the bank. What then?" Daryl said.

"She steals his key and gives him back a fake?" Kevin said.

"She steals his key and gives him back the key to the box next to it," Daryl said.

"That will give him my name when he tries to straighten it out," Robert said. "We don't want him to know I was involved, or Michele was involved. Any ideas, Michele?"

"I wonder how many times Eddie's been to his safe deposit box," Michele said. "If they put their logs onto the computer, could you find out, Daryl?"

"If it's on the computer, sure," Daryl said.

"If he's only been there once or twice before, I can use Robert's key to open Robert's box, pull out the box with the fake gold bar, and give it to Eddie when he comes in. Eddie'll take it to the little depositor room. While he's in there, I can open his box and put its contents into Robert's box, close it up, and when Eddie comes back, put the fake bar into Eddie's box. Of course, if Eddie doesn't have the bar in his box, he'll have a real surprise when he gets a box that weighs more than he's expecting. I'll have a better grasp of whether I can do it after I've seen the bank and the safe deposit boxes," Michele said. All three of the men looked. Their forks weren't moving, and they weren't chewing.

"That's crazy," Kevin said.

"What's crazy about it?" Michele said.

"Switching the boxes while he's not in the room?" Kevin said. "That sounds like a magic trick."

"Can you do it?" Robert said. Michele would be on her own; when he'd gone into John Donnelly's house, he'd had the comfort of Kevin with him, someone to distract him from the acute thought of what he was doing. Michele would only have time to think about what she was doing, to doubt if it were in her nature. It was sure in his.

Michele felt her shoulders and chest tighten under Robert's heavy appraising stare. Easier said than done, she thought. "Yes," she said. Her voice sounded strong and confident, she hoped.

"What if he doesn't go to the bank after we call him?" Kevin said.

"We've not exactly been making the high percentage plays so far," Daryl said.

"If he doesn't, Michele doesn't make the switch and works two or three days at the bank. We can try to come up with something else or give up," Robert said. He didn't like the taste of surrender at the end of the sentence.

* * * *

Daryl looked at Elvis. He'd once owned an oversized pair of sunglasses that Max had bought him the summer Daryl had grown sideburns. Daryl had worn them twice and had opened an extra button on his flannel shirt and said, "Thank you. Thank you very much," with the appropriate theatrical drawl, and Max had called him the Grunge Elvis. Daryl had lost the sunglasses but had gained someone to talk to at one o'clock in the morning, when the Mountain Dew made the little characters dance like motes in his dusty eyes.

"I should have written a script," he said. He'd started at nine o'clock, poking around Integral's systems, looking for the telltale directories that would indicate a particular machine hosted the database.

Once he found the host, he ferreted out the connection information so he could send his own queries to the database through its SOAP interface. Before the advent of Web Services, it was much harder to snoop. Integral, apparently, didn't realize they had a Simple Object Access Protocol service running; its log only showed startup and shutdown messages, and the Integral system administrator didn't lock it down or disable it.

He spent the first hour figuring out the structure of the database, including the relevant tables for employee information and the scoring. He dug into Jessica's record to determine her start date at the bank and looked through database logs preceding it to determine how, exactly, the staffing company picked the best candidate to temp at a safe deposit counter. Whatever query produced Jessie at the head of the list, or near it, would need to provide Michele's name near the top. Once he figured out the criteria the recruiters used, he ran the query to see who was on top and whom Michele had to beat.

Once he had the list of candidates, he created and sent a series of messages to knock down the scores of the candidates above Michele.

He ran the original query a couple more times to check his progress, and then he boosted Michele's scores ever so slightly. Finally, around midnight and two liters of Mountain Dew later, the query listed Michele as the grand champion safe deposit box watcher.

"Of course," he said, "if I had written a script, it might have taken me longer to come up with an algorithm that would have moved Michele up the list without moving those other candidates to the bottom." He tapped his fingers on the desk. The King did not respond. Good sanity check; when Elvis responded, it would be time for vacation.

* * * *

Robert awakened at 7:30. He showered, shaved, made himself breakfast, and wondered how else to fill the time until the afternoon. He didn't think it would be a good idea to go to the bank at the same time as he did yesterday. He didn't want Jeff Sommers to remember him too well.

He watched the clock change to 8:30. Were he still working at nTropics, he'd leave within two minutes to arrive at the office with ten minutes to spare. When he first started at nTropics, he'd left his house at 8:15, but the traffic proved marginally heavier, and he found himself arriving with only a four to seven minute cushion. Eventually, trial and error had led him to the timing he espoused in the last eight months he'd spent at nTropics. He'd work from 8:50 until 1:20. He'd go to lunch after the noon traffic died down so that he could maximize his time home or run errands as needed.

He paused, dish towel and pan in hand. If he still had a day job, he'd run his errands at the same time every day. He rubbed beads of water from the Teflon slowly. So he would have to go to the bank about the same time he went yesterday, as if he took his lunches routinely on the other side of the lunch rush to avoid the traffic. He put the pan back onto its shelf and went downstairs to get the bar.

Robert pulled the old duct tape from the seam in his furnace. The adhesive was provided by some double-stick tape on the underside of the duct tape. Fresh duct tape would be a dead giveaway to someone searching his house, whether a burglar or the police. So each time he put something in the furnace, he meticulously removed the double-sided tape from the bottom of the duct tape and replaced it with new so it would stick and still look old.

He set the tape and unscrewed the screws holding the sheet metal together. He placed them upon the topmost shelf on the set of metal shelving that contained his nonessentials, mostly consisting of magazines he intended to sort and organize someday. He peeled back the sheet metal to expose the A-coil for his air conditioner. Since he preferred not to use the air conditioner, the A-coil compartment made a handy year-round hidden storage facility for items too large for his fire safe behind the fake electronics panel.

Robert took out the nongold bar and set it on the floor. He took out the box containing his grandparents' gold wedding bands, securely preserved for his special day, probably in the far distant future. He wiped the top of the box with his palm and opened it to ensure the contents were safe and untarnished. The matching gold bands, real gold, gleamed in the light of the single incandescent bulb near the furnace. He closed the box and put it back.

He replaced the screws and carefully peeled the double-stick tape from the adhesive side of the duct tape. He carefully aligned new tape on the duct tape and replaced the duct tape over the seam in the furnace. Perhaps no one could tell that someone had recently removed the duct tape. No one would see a disturbance in the surrounding dust since Robert left no surrounding dust. He looked at his hands, clean enough to carry the bar without leaving visible fingerprints on it.

Robert carried Eddie's bar into his office and put it on the workbench. He'd brought down a soft attaché case, and he put the gold bar in it. The weight of the bar caused the bottom of the case to sag perceptibly when Robert picked it up. Robert measured the inside dimensions of the bottom of the bag and cut a small piece of 1/8" plywood to fit. He put the plywood in first and then put the bar atop it. When he picked up the case, it didn't sag. If one didn't look too closely at the handles, one might never suspect the case weighed as much as it did.

Robert checked the clock. Plenty of time to get to the bank. He put a pair of work gloves and an alcohol-based monitor swab in the case with the bar and topped the collection off with three stock reports and a United States Saving Bond, just in case anyone saw him open it. He set the case beside the door, put a collared shirt over his tee shirt, and picked the case up on his way out.

His dashboard clock displayed 10:47 when Robert parked at the meter on Manchester Road in front of a real estate brokerage a half block east of the bank. Robert fed the meter, crossed at the corner, and walked to the bank. He didn't notice being noticed, which was the best he could hope for.

Robert entered the bank and didn't pause today. He passed the tellers and ignored the personal banker sign-up table. Instead, he veered right and stood before the L shaped counter and the young woman behind it. "Hello," Robert said. He didn't put much behind it; his voice sounded nervous. "I'd like to put something in my safe deposit box," he said, getting a little vocalization into the sentence but not so much as to shout, or sound like he was compensating for being nervous. Maybe the young lady was used to having that impact on young men; after all, she was quite pretty.

Blonde hair, large brown eyes, and pleasantly round cheeks that smiled before her lips did. "Hi. This is your first time here, isn't it?" she said.

"Yes," Robert said.

"I could tell. Normally, people just say, 'Give me a card.'" She opened a drawer beneath the counter and took out a small, green printed card. Behind the counter, a computer monitor sat recessed and angled upward slightly. Upon it, Robert could see the telltale colors and blocky menu bars for the *St. Louis Post-Dispatch's* Web site. "You'll need to fill out this card to log your visit. You just need to sign your name and put your box number on it; I can date it and put your time in for you." She handed the card to Robert and then put a pen on the counter for him.

"Thanks," Robert said. He wrote his box number on it and signed his name illegibly. He also dated it. Any time he signed anything, he filled in all the blanks. He passed the card back to the woman and put the pen back on the counter.

The woman looked at the card and compared it to his signature card. It passed, and he apparently passed, because she slipped the little card into a time clock to imprint a timestamp on it. "All right, come with me," she said. She stepped from behind the counter. Robert followed her through the door, propped open with a small plastic doorstop, through the south wall.

The safe deposit box room formed a large U shape with the door in the center of the bottom. Two ranks of safe deposit boxes formed the branches of the U, on the east and west walls of the room and in the center. On the north wall, long filing cabinets squatted on either side of the door. On the south wall, at the end of the row of safe deposit boxes on the left, a heavy door led to the vault. The woman walked three quarters of the way down the right branch and stopped at the east wall. She pushed a small circular stepping stool aside. "Here's your box," she said. "May I have your key?" she said.

"Oh, sure," Robert said. He took the key from his pocket. He'd put the key on its own ring with no obnoxious advertising. He handed it to the young woman. She knelt by the door of box number 1196, the

233

fifth from the south wall on the bottom. Beside it, one closer to the south wall, lie number 1197, wherein Eddie had stored his stolen wealth.

The young woman inserted Robert's key in a lock on the right and inserted a key from her pocket into a lock on the left. She turned both and pulled the door. It didn't move. Robert felt his hairline moisten. "Sometimes the locks stick a little if no one's opened them in a while," she said. She wiggled Robert's key a little until she pulled the door open. "Ah, success!" She withdrew a black box. She presented it to Robert, along with his key, and left the door open. "Here you are. We offer discreet rooms for you just outside. Follow me." She led Robert back out the door. She directed him to the first doorway. Robert stepped into it and closed the door.

The room featured a table affixed to the wall and a chair. Robert set the box on the table and the case on the chair. The door behind him had a lock, so Robert locked it, slowly and quietly to not offend the attendant by throwing his distrust in her face. The walls of the room did not extend all the way to the ceiling; Robert checked the angles to see if anything was peeping in or if he was somehow reflecting out. Neither. No mirrors in the room or holes in the walls that did not have screws in them. Apparently, the bank was offering him privacy. Robert accepted.

He opened the top on the box. It held nothing, no slips of paper or foreign passports in different names. Robert opened the case and slid the papers on top to the side. He took the gloves and put them on. He took the swab out and tore open the foil pack. He unfolded the alcohol wipe and set it on the table; he put the foil pack into his case and lifted the bar out. He took the alcohol swab and polished all faces of the bar, from the 903 Fine to the All Your Base Are Belong to Us, as aggressively as Lady Macbeth, until the alcohol was gone and the pad was dry.

He put the gold bar into the box, base down, and closed the lid. He swabbed the box with the dry monitor wipe until he realized he would be carrying it out of the room without the gloves. He tossed the monitor wipe and gloves into the case and flipped the papers back down atop them. He looked around the room for signs of his presence; he'd left no foil packs or pawnshop tickets. Before closing the case, though, he took inventory again: gloves, wrap, wipe, plywood, stock reports, savings bond. He twisted the door's lock slowly and then the knob. He cradled the safe deposit box in his arms, picked up the handle of the attaché case with his left fingers and the key to his box with the right.

The attendant was back behind the counter. "Do I just put this back?" Robert said.

"We can do that now, certainly," the woman said. "Would you like me to help you with that?"

Robert hugged the box closer. "No, thank you."

The woman smiled and led him into the safe deposit box room. When they got to box 1196, she turned and extended her arms.

"Can I put it in?" Robert said.

"Sure," the woman said, and she moved aside.

Robert crouched until the attaché case touched the floor; when it did, he let go of its handle. He turned the box and slid it into its compartment. He brushed his hands and his arms, hoping the woman would not notice the indentations in his wrists where the box's edge had rested. "Thanks," he said.

"You're welcome," she said. She closed the door and twisted the keys to lock the safe deposit box. She handed Robert his key.

Robert put the key in his pocket and picked up the attaché case. "Thank you very much," he said again.

"You're welcome," she said again. She swept her right hand to let him precede her out of the safe deposit box room.

When they reached the counter, she went behind it and Robert stopped on the business side of it. "Do I need to sign out or anything?" Robert said.

"I've got that." She took the little card he'd filled out and slipped it back into the time stamper machine. She smiled at Robert, professionally but friendly. "Have a nice day."

"You, too," Robert said. He looked at Jeff Sommers, who was helping a couple at his desk and did not meet Robert's gaze, which hopefully meant he hadn't seen Robert. Robert walked calmly and purposefully, not at all like he really wanted to leave quickly, out into the dazzling sunshine.

*   *   *   *

Robert called Michele from his kitchen and offered to drop the key by her apartment in University City, but Michele said she was going to be in and out all afternoon. She did, however, tell him he could drop by in the evening, and she gave him directions. Robert double-checked the map he'd gotten online and looked at the address and directions Michele had recited over the phone. Michele lived in a townhouse just off of Delmar. Robert triple-checked the sheet on the clipboard to make sure he was knocking on the correct door, which wasn't the right door but the left door, and he was because Michele answered it.

She wore a pair of faded jeans and a Washington University sweatshirt. Robert hadn't known what to expect, but he was glad she felt comfortable enough to be herself around him. "Good evening," he said.

"Hi," Michele said. She opened the screen door. "Come on in." She led Robert up the stairs to her living room.

Robert looked over the living room and appraised her computer set-up with a glance. She had two sets of bookshelves. He lingered over the titles, literary sets of John Steinbeck, Ernest Hemingway, and F. Scott Fitzgerald and enough Faulkner, Woolf, and Chopin to have gotten her through college. She also had collections of detective fiction from Muller, O'Donnell, Barnes, and Braun. Robert caught a motion in the corner of his eye; a rabbit bounced across the carpet and sniffed at his shoes before bouncing away.

"What do you have there?" Michele hoped Frodo wouldn't leave any obvious pellets outside his litter box while Robert was standing in her living room.

"There?" Robert realized what she meant and lifted the clipboard. "Oh, I have some notes I took about the bank and a map I drew. I have the key to the safe deposit box right here, too," he said. He reached into his pocket for the key ring, tangled among his keys, and shuffled them around in his pocket futilely. He settled for pulling the whole lot from his pocket; when he did, though, the safe deposit box key freed itself from the bunch and fell to the floor. He jammed his keys back into his pocket and crouched to pick the key up, hoping that the indirect lighting wasn't lingering on his flushing face. "Here you are," he said, dangling the key by its ring and placing it in Michele's hand, careful to avoid contact. He gestured toward the kitchen table. "Shall we?" Robert said.

"Okay," Michele said.

Michele sat before Robert could put the clipboard down and pull her chair out, so he sat on the adjacent side of the table. He considered moving the chair so they were sitting on the same side of the table, but he didn't want to creep her out. So he turned the clipboard sideways to him so Michele could see the map northside up. "Here's where you'll be sitting." Robert pointed to the L shaped counter. "The safe deposit boxes are right here, the fifth one from the wall is ours, the fourth one is Eddie's. You'll put Eddie in one of these rooms when you give him the safe deposit box; these doors are not visible at from the safe deposit box site, so you won't have to worry about him catching you in the act if you listen for the door opening. Do you have any questions?"

"I'll have to see it firsthand to know exactly what I am doing," Michele said. She flipped the map up and looked at the pages beneath. Robert had written out notes about cameras, people, and other items of his interest. His handwriting was energetic printing, pen with no strikeouts. She looked back into Robert's intent eyes. "Do you think it will work?"

"Do you think you can make the switch?" Robert said.

"I guess so," Michele said.

"That's your answer," Robert said. "'Your answer that is,' I mean."

Michele smiled. "It's been pretty simple this far," Michele said. "Especially getting into John Donnelly's house. I would have expected him to have it more secure, wouldn't you?"

"Absolutely," Robert said.

"What would you have done differently?" Michele said. Karen would require greater challenges to getting the tiara, and Michele figured Robert was just the man to help her plot. He obviously had a vivid, although acutely directed, imagination.

*   *   *   *

On Friday afternoon, the telephone rang as Michele, halfway between the bedroom and her purse on the edge of the computer desk, pressed an earring back onto its post. She veered toward the telephone. "Hello?" she expected one of the girls to explain she would be late or to change the venue of happy hour.

"Michele Isbert?" a man's voice said. It sounded familiar, and he pronounced her name right. "This is Alan Bradford at Integral Staffing Solutions. How are you?"

Michele's heart thumped. "Well. You?"

"I am great. We've got a short-term assignment coming up in the banking industry, and we notice you've got some banking experience. Would you be interested in a short, possibly open-ended assignment?" Alan said.

"Short, possibly open-ended?" Michele said. "What does that mean?"

"Well," Alan said, "You'll be filling in for a young woman who's going on jury duty. She'll be on jury service for three days, but she could get dismissed early or she might be selected for a jury that serves for five days."

"When does it start?" Michele said.

"A week from Tuesday," Alan said.

The phone throbbed in her hand. "All right, I'll take it," she said.

"That's great," Alan said. "Can you come by the office next week sometime to fill out the tax papers and show me your employment eligibility documentation?"

"Monday?" Michele said.

"How about ten o'clock?" Alan said.

"Okay," Michele said.

"Great! I'll see you then. Have a nice weekend, okay?" Alan said.

"Okay," Michele said. She hung up and kept her hand on the receiver for a moment before picking it up to call Robert. She'd be a couple minutes late to Happy Hour, but at least she'd have good news on the job front to share with the girls. That was the half of the story she could share.

Michele's Heist

Robert wrote the script for the telephone call and revised it over the week before he planned to call Eddie Bennett. He wanted concision. He wanted clarity. He wanted to introduce that all-important "you" attitude taught by collegiate business writing professors instead of grammar and spelling. Second most importantly, he wanted to convince Eddie to go to the bank tomorrow to check on his gold bar. Most importantly, he didn't want to leave Eddie any clues to Robert's identity.

So Robert found himself a nice pay phone at a gas station in Florissant, a suburb in northern St. Louis County, many miles from his house. He parked his car in the parking lot of a discount department store and walked across its acres of asphalt to the road and across the road to the gas station. The phone booth stood at the edge of the lot, mounted low on the pole so that a driver could reach out and touch it. Robert took the phone off the hook, waited for the tone, and slipped his coins in the slot. He'd written Eddie Bennett's phone number on a nondescript Post-It Note without Eddie's name, and Robert had transposed the last two numbers in the prefix and had reversed the last four digits. He dialed the correct number and crumpled the paper with the phone number. He tucked the phone between his right ear and shoulder.

Robert took the paper with his revised script on it. He'd recopied it several times onto different sheets of paper. Each time he revised it, he recopied it, and tore the new version's predecessor into bits. He didn't want to have to read around crossed-out words and carets when he had Eddie on the phone. It would hardly sound professional. Robert clenched his right fist around the phone number in his windbreaker's pocket.

Eddie's phone clicked off the hook, and Robert sucked in a breath and then let it out slowly to regulate it.

"This is Ed Bennett. Leave me a message including your name, phone number, and the subject of your message, and I'll reply."

Robert sighed. He couldn't have hoped for better luck. "You think you're clever, Bennett, but if you're so smart, how come we have the bar now?" Robert said. He hung up the phone and crumpled the script. He put both hands into his pockets, holding tight the physical evidence. He crossed the street and headed back across the acres of darkly parked sports utility vehicles and cars. He went into the department store and bought himself a bottle of water and tossed all three pieces of physical evidence, the number, the script, and the department store receipt, into a garbage can just outside the store's entrance.

He couldn't have hoped for better luck, really, he thought as he hoped onto Hanley, a north and south arterial road that would carry him back to Overland. He didn't have to actually talk to Eddie since he got the answering machine, and he'd hung up quickly enough to avoid him if he was screening his calls. Unless Eddie was out of town or on vacation, in which case getting the answering machine was very bad, and without talking to Eddie himself, Robert had no way of knowing if Eddie would get the message. Suddenly, his stomach settled heavily.

He could stake out Eddie's house, or he could call back later, but these presented high risk ventures with little to gain. If Eddie got the message, and Eddie reacted, then Eddie might go to the bank tomorrow; if Eddie was out of town, or did not get the message, he would not react, and knowing whether Eddie was home or was going to answer his phone all night was unimportant. *Alea iacta est,* he quoted to himself whenever he felt pretentiously fatalistic. "*Iä! Iä! Alea iacta est,*" Robert said forcefully, so he could hear it over the sound of his car's engine.

* * * *

Michele had spent the week preparing for the assignment. She borrowed a book from the University City library on magic, particularly coin tricks, and tried various types of legerdemain to secret the key in her hands and sleeves. She visited a magic shop in old St. Charles to find what gimmicks it held in the recesses of the artfully antique building and had not liked anything she'd seen, so she rumbled her car back over the cobblestones of Main Street and back home.

In the end, she decided to just put the key in the pocket of her pantsuit. From what Robert said, the other attendant kept the keys in her pocket; Michele hoped she could just switch the keys when getting out the bank's keys. If she couldn't, well, the deal was off, and she knew the guys would respect her discretion. She hoped.

She got to the bank at 8 o'clock, an hour before opening time. She parked in the far corner of the lot and went to door on the parking lot side of the building, about twenty feet to the left of the drive-up window. Michele pushed the button set into the beige brick beside the solid metal door and stepped back so that anyone within could see her clearly through the peephole. Not that they'd recognize her. A man wearing a tie and a collared suit and no jacket and opened the door. "Are you Michele?" he said.

"Yes," Michele said. "Mr. Dennis?"

The bank manager extended a hand. "Come in. I'm glad you accepted such a short-term assignment. Our regular supplemental employee is on jury service the next couple of days, so you'll be filling in for her. She handles our safe deposit room, and her duties are pretty minimal; you should find it an interesting assignment, but not one that will overwhelm you for the duration of the assignment, which might be as little as today. I have one of my best young men to look out for you," he said.

Michele followed the bank manager into the building. He called out to a guy in a Ralph Lauren shirt. Robert had described the bank in cold, clinical detail, so Michele recognized where things were and knew Jeff Sommers, the man standing up from the open desk, was the personal banker with whom Robert had spoken about the safe deposit box. Robert had a keen eye for the logistical details, like the cameras' sweeping vistas capturing her arrival on spinning videocassettes somewhere in a dark closet.

Robert didn't waste time noticing, or at least briefing Michele on, the bank's particular color, the flair that brought it from blueprints to building. The innocuous winter stream print, cut into thirds and framed separately, hanging on the unbroken wall to the right. The potted semitropical trees that flanked the deposit slips counter attested to their life by showing a few brown spots at the edges of their leaves. The three tellers behind the counter fussed with their workspaces, shuffling slips and pens around to suit their needs and arranging their nameplates on their windows for the day.

"Good morning," Jeff Sommers said.

Jeff smiled at Michele, but didn't move his eyes from hers, and Michele appreciated it. "Good morning," Michele said. She extended her hand. "I'm Michele."

"Michele will cover for Jessica," Mr. Dennis said. "Why don't you show her how the safe deposit box system works and get her set up right away."

241

"Yes, sir," Jeff said. "This way." Jeff gestured toward the counter.

"Enjoy your stay with us," Mr. Dennis said. He strode towards the tellers.

"So have you worked in a bank before?" Jeff said.

"Yes," Michele said.

"Good, then you've got some idea of what's going on." Jeff led her to the counter. "This is your station." He stepped around the counter and opened a drawer. "Basically, you have the customers fill out these visit cards when they come to get in their box. If someone wants to rent a box, they get to fill out this form here. The different sizes and prices are right here on the form. They can pay with cash, check, money order, cashier's check, or deduct it from their account balance. When they pay, you take it over to the tellers. Sandy, the one with the red hair that's working the drive up, could deposit it for you. Or you could come get me. Any questions?"

"Not yet," Michele said.

"Don't worry about it, it's a lot, and it sounds complicated, but we've only got a limited number of boxes, and most of them are already rented. Most days, nobody even asks to open or close one. They're like PSLs to the Rams, people just buy them and hold them and then die with them and let their executors sort them out. Where'd you go to school?"

"Washington University," Michele said. She pronounced the whole name.

"Cool. You live in U City?" Jeff said.

"Yes," Michele said.

"Off the Loop?" Jeff said.

"Very," Michele said.

"Cool. Well, all right, I'll let you try the chair out later." He unlocked another desk drawer with a key on a ring from his pocket and took a single key dangling from a bank key chain. "I'll show you the room now. When someone comes in and wants to get into their box, after they've filled out the visit card, you check their signature against the signature cards on file, stamp their visit card with the date and time in this machine, grab this key, and take them into the safe deposit room."

Jeff led her into a room filled with safe deposit boxes. "The people sometimes know where their boxes are, and sometimes don't, so always look at the number they fill in on the card. If they don't know the number, you can get it from the computer; it's not on their key. When you bring them in here, you've got to get their key. If they don't have a key, you can't get in."

Jeff gestured to the left. "Boxes 1001-1099 are on this side. Boxes 1101-1200 are on the right. We don't have boxes 1-1000. I don't know if they used to have more, or if they do like checks and just start numbering at 1001." He stepped to the left and lifted the key to a door. The door had two locks, and Jeff tapped the key on the lock on the left. "The bank's key goes in the left lock, and the customer's key goes on the right. Turn them both, open the door, and give the customer the box." Jeff pantomimed giving Michele a safe deposit box. "Oh, and your key." He placed an imaginary key atop the imaginary safe deposit box in Michele's hands.

"Now, Miss Michele, you can review your box's contents in one of our discreet booths," Jeff said. He led her out the door and to the right. Four doors led into small rooms. "You can close and lock the door. When you're done, I will be right here to help you." Jeff smiled. "Ah, you're finished. Come with me."

Jeff led her back into the safe deposit box room. "Your key? Thanks." He took the invisible key off of the invisible box that Michele wasn't pretending to be holding. She raised her hands when she realized they were still playing. "And let me help you with that." He picked up and slid the box into the safe deposit. "Now, close and lock and here's your key. You don't need to sign out. Thanks, and have a nice day."

"That's it?" Michele said.

"Did it help you to act it out?" Jeff said. "I was at this seminar about training people that said interactive demonstrations help...."

"Sure," Michele said. Although she didn't do any interacting besides holding the box, she didn't want to spend any more time discussing Jeff's training techniques.

Jeff handed her the key. "There you go. I'll be at my desk if you have any questions. Hey, I go to lunch at about one o'clock. If you want, I can show you a little diner here in Maplewood where some of us go."

"Is that what time I go to lunch?" Michele said.

"It's pretty flexible," Jeff said. "You just have to let one of us know, and we can cover for you. Ron and Janice can cover either or both of our positions."

"I'll have to wait and see, then, when I get hungry," Michele said.

"Cool, cool. I'll talk to you later," Jeff said. He went over to the other open desk and spoke to its occupant, a woman in her forties, probably, older than Michele, anyway.

Michele sat down in the chair behind the counter. With a hydraulic huff, the seat sank two inches. Either it did that for everyone, or she'd have to knock off the ice cream at night. Since her pantsuit still fit, a relic of a pre-IT employment era, she figured the chair probably did that for everyone.

Michele tapped the mouse of the computer beneath the counter. The monitor broke out of the screen saver; Michele was looking at an application that let her enter contracts for safe deposit boxes or log visits. She opened the Start menu and looked to see what applications and other things were installed on the machine. No Office or other word processors beyond Notepad. Internet Explorer. Entertainment, including the usual suspects Minesweeper, Freecell, and Solitaire.

She looked in the drawers. The center drawer, angled in the corner of the counter, held pens, pencils, paperclips, rubber bands, a scissors, and a steel, cork-backed ruler. The drawer beneath the counter to her right contained several stacks of visit cards and several contracts for the safe deposit boxes. A separate tray in the drawer contained fourteen completed visit cards, all dated the day before, with times ranging from 9:30 to 4:50. The drawer on the left side contained a bank employee's handbook, a chocolate bar, and a paperback John Grisham novel.

The counter itself was raised above the desk; it had nothing on it. The desk had a couple of pens, which Michele moved up to the counter so customers could easily reach them, a digital clock, and a stapler. Michele opened the stapler and examined the number of staples in it. Full, with a break in the staple bar to indicate someone else was not letting it run out of staples.

The digital clock said 8:54. The bank hadn't even opened yet. This would be a good career, Michele guessed, if you had something else to occupy your time. Like writing, or like conspiracy. Speaking of which, she shifted Robert's safe deposit box key from her left to her right pocket and made sure the bank key was in her left.

The digital clock said 8:55. Michele took out one of the safe deposit box contracts and started to read its terms and conditions as well as the sizes and prices. Maybe then she could browse the Internet or play Solitaire. All of this, and eight dollars and fifty cents an hour.

When the digital clock said 9:36, Michele got her first customer. Elisa Weingartner, box 1032, followed Michele into the safe deposit room. As she led Elisa to the boxes on the left, Michele took Elisa's key and then reached into her right pocket with the same hand to look for the bank key. Elisa didn't comment. Michele touched Robert's safe deposit key with her fingertips as though she was touching base and withdrew the hand from the pocket even as she "found" the key in the other pocket. Perfect.

The digital clock said 9:50 when Elisa opened the door to her private closet. Michele escorted her back to her safe deposit box, locked up her treasures, and bid her good day. By the time Elisa Weingartner was out the front door of the bank, Michele had put her card in the drawer and had fumbled with the computer enough to see that Ms. Weingartner came by every two weeks.

The clock said 10:25 when Michele got up and asked Jeff where she could find cleaning supplies. He showed her a small closet with PurKleen industrial brand all-purpose cleaner and a roll of paper towels. Michele cleaned her desk, her computer, her monitor, and the bottoms of the drawers, particularly the left, where she found what might have been popcorn detritus.

When the second customer arrived at 11:12, Michele had progressed to the filing cabinets in the safe deposit room. The paper towels demonstrated that cleaning crews didn't often reach the tops, sides, or fronts of the long drawers.

Michele shoved the cleaner and towels to the back corner of the cabinet and offered Terrence Oglivy a card. When taking Oglivy to his box, Michele tried her find-the-keys legerdemain again, and Oglivy didn't notice or comment, either. Michele showed him to a closet and went back into the safe deposit room to continue wiping things down. Michele heard the click of the door and met Oglivy as he came out.

Michele found box 1196 and tried the keys on them. The door pulled open smoothly. She practiced opening it, twice, between trips to her desk and to check if anyone needed her attention or was paying her attention. She liked that the door swung so to obscure the door of Eddie's box, 1197. The third time she tried the door, she moved to it quickly and opened it smoothly, using her body to block someone from seeing it was the wrong door. Too quickly and smoothly; she'd have to look as though she was looking for the box, not as though she'd been drilling this maneuver all morning.

The digital clock said 12:42 when Jeff came to her desk. "Hey, lunch time?" he said.

"No, thanks," Michele said.

"You've been busy over here," he said.

"I can't stand just sitting here," Michele said.

"Well, you must be hungry, then," Jeff said.

"I've actually got a little something here," Michele said. "Can I eat it at the desk? It's a nutrition bar."

"Sure," Jeff said. "Are you sure you don't want to come?"

"Yes, thank you," Michele said.

"All right. I'll see you later," Jeff said. He went over to Janice and said something to her and gave Michele a little wave as he walked out the front door.

Michele took out Jessica's Snickers bar and ate it, vowing to replace it tomorrow morning. It was a bank, she thought, I am just taking out a short-term loan.

The digital clock said 2:26 when a man handed his card back to Michele, and her heart clunked when she saw the name, Ed Bennett, and the box number. Michele looked at him, and maybe she could recognize him if she put her mind to it. He'd grown his hair into a rangy mullet and had shaved his face completely. She didn't see any recognition on his part; she was probably just a part of the décor, a piece of bank furniture. "Right this way, Mr. Bennett," she said.

"Your key?" she said when they reached the door to the safe deposit room. Eddie took a plain key from his pocket and handed it to her. "This way," she said. She slipped her right hand into her pocket, letting the key fall from her palm and sliding Robert's key out smoothly, she hoped, before finding the bank key in her other pocket, again. She took a feint step to the left, a last moment improvisation hesitation to slow him and to intimate she didn't quite know where his box was. She knelt before box number 1196, inserted both keys, and opened the door smoothly. She left both keys in the door as she pulled out the heavy box.

She lifted the box up awkwardly. She handed the box to Eddie. He took it without shock, without surprise at its weight. He started to open the lid impatiently. "Let me show you to a private viewing room," Michele said. She led him to one of the closets and let him close the door.

Michele stepped back into the safe deposit room casually, so the bankers would all think she was just going to polish another doorknob. She slipped Eddie's key from her pocket before kneeling by the open door. She took the bank key from the open door and inserted Eddie's key. She turned both keys and pulled, and the door didn't open. She looked at the metal plate, 1197, and pulled again.

"Shit!" she heard, muffled from outside the door. She twisted the keys back counterclockwise and pulled them out. She barely got the bank's key back in the door of Robert's safe deposit box when the door to the closet clicked open.

When Michele rushed out of the safe deposit box room, she met a reddened Eddie Bennett standing in the doorway to the viewing room. "Is something wrong?"

"Nothing you can help me with," Eddie said. He licked his lips and looked around the bank.

"All right," Michele said. "Are you ready?"

"Yes," Eddie said. He followed Michele into the safe deposit box room. "Tell me, do you have a key to my box?" he said.

"No, I don't. I only have the one key; you need both your key and my key to open it."

"Doesn't the bank have a back-up key? In case I lose my key?"

"I don't think so," Michele said. "I think they have to drill the lock out or something. I'm sorry, I'm only a temporary employee, and today's my first day. Is something wrong? Perhaps one of the personal bankers, or a manager could help you."

"No, nothing, thanks," Eddie said.

Michele wondered what his next move would be. Would he investigate her? The bank? She held out her hands for the box. Eddie handed it to her slowly and turned away. Michele closed the door to Robert's safe deposit box and withdrew the keys. She put both sets of keys in her right hand and tucked them into her right pocket to reverse the switch. Her fingers fumbled a bit, but she came out with Eddie's key, and he couldn't see because he was already walking toward the door.

"Sir, your key," she said. She caught up with him at the door and gave him his key back. He took it without a word. His eyes deadened before her eyes, and she could see his dreams bleeding away. "Are you all right?" she said. Maybe she was being too friendly. What Would the Furniture Do?

"The same as ever," he said. He crossed the long room to the front door and stepped out the gloomy doors into the sunshine.

After he was gone, Michele's own body trembled. She went into the safe deposit room to calm down, to vent her shakes without everyone seeing her. She'd come so close, but the door hadn't opened. So Eddie thought someone else had the gold bar, but of course, they didn't. She replayed the scene and scenario in her head a dozen times, much like a drill in reverse, a deconstruction of her memory, until she could get any meaning she wanted from the text in her mind.

The digital clock said 2:39 when she sat back down at the desk.

*　*　*　*

Her own merciful clock said 5:50 when Michele managed to storm her place after a lengthy battle with St. Louis traffic and signals favoring the east-west traffic. Michele changed out of the pantsuit and heels into jeans, sweatshirt, and tennis shoes with great relief. She didn't used to mind dressing for work, but part of the pleasure was in taking the suits, skirts, or dresses off. She petted Frodo a bit, made sure his food and water stash were adequate, and grabbed a cereal bar before heading to Robert's house. She didn't bother with dinner; her criminal gang, besides the occasional felony and attempted felony, ate together a lot.

When she pulled up to the end of Robert's sidewalk, she noted Kevin's car on the opposite side of the street. As she walked up the sidewalk to the porch, she noted Daryl's bike on the porch. Great, she thought, I get to explain my failure to all of them at once. The one task they left to the woman, and I couldn't get it done.

Robert opened the door. He'd shaved, she noticed, even though he didn't work tonight. Either to impress her, or just because he did. Michele didn't know which to believe. "Come in," Robert said. "Daryl and Kevin are already here."

"Hey," Kevin said. He leaned against counter with a bottle of beer in his hand already, even though it wasn't even six o'clock. "Beer? I brought some Pete's Wicked Ale since we're celebrating."

"The champagne of beers," Daryl said from his position at the kitchen table. He wondered how many orphaned beers Robert's refrigerator could take.

"No, thanks," Michele said.

"What happened?" Robert said. Michele hadn't immediately mentioned success, so he feared the worst.

Robert *knew*, Michele thought. "I couldn't open the door to Eddie's safe deposit box," she said.

"What?" Kevin said.

"I turned the keys, and the door didn't open. I got him to go into the viewing room with Robert's safe deposit box, with the fake bar, but I couldn't open the door to his box with his key, and I didn't have much time. He took one look at the bar and was ready to leave," Michele said.

"Shit!" Kevin said.

"So you put the fake bar back in my safe deposit box?" Robert said.

"Yes," Michele said. "It was open, and like I said, he was only in the room a minute or two. The door to his box just didn't open." She looked at Kevin's dismay, Daryl's detachment, and Robert's horror.

Robert felt his face redden and the tingling at his hairline. "Did you jiggle his key?" he said.

"Jiggle his key?" Michele said.

Robert felt his pores burn. "With the older locks, you turn the keys and vibrate them horizontally, along the plane of the key," he said. He must not have mentioned that in the briefing.

"Jiggle the key? Shit!" Kevin said again.

"All right," Daryl said.

"What now?" Kevin said. "What else can we try?"

"We'll have to wait until he takes it out of the box," Daryl said.

"Think outside the box!" Kevin said.

"I can script something that lets us know when he's been to the bank to get the bar out of the box, and then we can make a move," Daryl said. "Did you enter his visit in right away?"

"No," Robert said. Saying it out loud didn't feel liberating, and it didn't calm him down any. He'd thought it would, somehow, that the flutters in his arms and legs that he picked up sometime early this morning would subside.

"No," Michele said. "I just put wrote the date and time on a card and put it in a tray with yesterday's cards."

"They don't even enter the visits into the system every night?" Daryl said.

"I guess not," Michele said.

"I'm done," Robert said.

"What?" Kevin said.

"Look, we've already exposed ourselves too much with this gambit," Robert said. He'd had plenty of time last night to plan this speech; about four of the hours between one o'clock and eight o'clock. "Michele's working in the bank. I have the safe deposit box next to Eddie. So maybe that's a coincidence, if someone comes looking. Whatever comes next, however, we have to expose ourselves, suddenly that's a pattern if someone's looking, and that means we're caught." Maybe with that much time, he could have come up with a better speech, Robert thought. Perhaps he shouldn't have spent two hours of that time watching *Double Indemnity*, or the remainder of the time wondering how they could cast the gold bar into jewelry and get the most for it.

"So you're out?" Kevin said. "The more for the rest of us."

"If Robert's done, I'm done," Daryl said. "If he wants to stop, it's probably too dangerous to proceed."

"You're right," Michele said. Still, the conspiracy had proven educational.

"Shit," Kevin had said. So he didn't have the winning numbers on the lottery ticket after all. He'd have to get another real job. He'd spent the last week cutting tree limbs and carrying wood for some odd job money from his parents and all the leftovers he could carry. He probably had one more weekend of that before his father would begin pressuring him heavily to come back to the shop.

Robert watched Kevin; he knew Kevin had access to a gun, and he didn't think Kevin would become enraged and homicidal with disappointment, but Robert also knew that what you think you know about a person often leads you to forget how much you don't know about that person.

"So what now?" Michele said. "Do we have any clean-up to do?"

"You should go to work tomorrow and finish this assignment at the bank. If possible, you should take another assignment with Integral before you get another job. I'll go to the bank in the next week to retrieve the fake bar. When I get it, I will dispose of it promptly so that no one can trace it to us," Robert said.

"Do you still have the vest and the keys to John Donnelly's house?" Michele said.

"I'll take care of them," Robert said. The others knew about the vest, so he'd have to get rid of it; it would corroborate any stories they might tell to third parties, including the police. He'd get the vest from the closet and the keys from the junk drawer where he'd hidden them among the keys for every padlock, car, or house Robert had ever unlocked.

"Anything I need to do?" Kevin said.

"No," Robert said. Perhaps he should have invented something to keep Kevin busy until the end of the operation. The end, he thought, parsing the words to isolate them and let them sink in.

"Well, kids, it was interesting," Daryl said.

"Interesting? Hey, it was the greatest. Someday we'll sit around over a couple of beers and laugh," Kevin said. "Hey, we could start tonight! Can we still afford pizza?"

Michele was surprised, and not necessarily pleased that no one had upbraided her for failure. They expressed disappointment, yes, but they had not delivered the external disapproval that would have freed her from her own internal recriminations.

She stayed for a slice of pizza and two beers, but she left the boys to Robert's game consoles and to the motley band of beers remaining from other nights that had promised better nights ahead, nights of opulence, nights of wealth at the expense of the thoughtless Chief Executive Officer who had not even considered those he'd wronged. When the thought finally finished making its way through her head, Michele realized she should have applied the food-to-alcohol in an inverse ratio, but at least she'd get to sleep easily that night because she, unlike those she failed, had to work in the morning.

Michele's Second Heist

Michele awakened plenty early for her second day at the bank, ate a healthy breakfast, and spent only ten minutes selecting her day's attire. Mostly, she argued pro and con of skirt, but St. Louis weather could turn cold without warning. So she opted for a pair of slacks and a Chico's top bearing a Native Americanesque design with a jacket that didn't offend the slacks just in case it cooled off.

She rustled through the little wooden box containing her mishmash jewelry collection looking for a matching pair of cubic zirconia. Out of the corner of her eye she spotted the key to Robert's safe deposit box on the edge of her dresser. She'd taken it out of her pocket yesterday so she wouldn't lose it with her wash, but she hadn't thought to put it in her pocket when she went over to Robert's last night. She slipped it into her jacket pocket and figured she could drop it off this afternoon. She had some more questions for him.

She patted Frodo one more time, urged him to guard the house, and went to work.

She survived the hour before the bank's opening. The digital clock, shuffling forward with its elderly digital gait, said 8:12 when Jeff came over and told her about the night he'd spent at the local theatre, watching the amateurs produce something nouveau or avant that they had written or improvised themselves. Jeff had liked it; Michele had not heard of the group before, and probably wouldn't again. The digital clock said 8:54 when Michele finished cleaning the desk and its environs again. The digital clock said 9:00 when Mr. Dennis unlocked the front door.

The digital clock said 9:21 when Michele's first customer of the day appeared. Michele looked up and knotted her hand around the corner of her jacket. Eddie Bennett stood at the counter. "Good morning," Michele said, somehow.

"Morning," Eddie said. He filled his name and box number in the appropriate spaces on the card on the counter and handed it to Michele.

She stood up, brushing her jacket to smooth it and to feel the shape of Robert's key in it. It was there, reassuringly.

"Your key?" Michele said as she led Eddie to the safe deposit room. She noticed he was carrying an olive backpack with him today. Eddie handed his key to Michele. She checked her pockets for her bank keys, which were not in her right jacket pocket, but her fingers found Robert's key there.

This time, Michele didn't need to pretend she was looking for Eddie's box, so she slipped in front of Robert's box smoothly and unlocked the door. She slid the box out and picked it up, lifting with her back like all the occupational safety posters in the back of the department stores said. She handed it to Eddie, who slipped the empty backpack on his shoulder and took the box.

Michele led him to the second viewing room, the one she'd determined had the loudest door. Sometimes the knob froze slightly, meaning the user had to shake it and twist harder until the metal inside slid harshly against metal and the door opened. Eddie pressed the door closed and gave it an extra shove to make the door click shut. Michele heard him twist the lock in the knob.

Michele stepped quickly into the safe deposit box room, drawing Eddie's key like a derringer from a gambler's vest. She kneeled by the doors and took the bank key from the door of number 1196 and inserted it and Eddie's key into number 1197. She turned both keys and pulled the door; nothing, just like yesterday, so she jiggled the keys side to side, on their horizontal axis as Robert had said, and pulled again. The door swung freely, admitting Ali Baba into the cave of the single thief.

Michele slid the box out of Eddie's safe deposit compartment, comparing its weight to the box she'd given Eddie; heavier, she thought. She slid the box along the floor and slid it into 1196, Robert's compartment. She closed the door and withdrew the keys, dropping Robert's key into her jacket pocket and sliding the bank key into the door of Eddie's box. She stood up and brushed the knees of her slacks, briefly considering to drop Robert's key into her shoe so to not accidentally swap them when Eddie came out, but she thought no, that's a little weird, a little too Robert, and she'd just calm down and concentrate. She took a breath. And then another.

The door shook on the closet where she'd put Eddie. Michele stepped out of the safe deposit room to meet Eddie when he finally struggled the door open. "Are you finished, sir?" she said.

"I'm finished," Eddie said.

Michele led him into the safe deposit box room. Eddie handed her the box; Michele judged it was empty by its weight. She shifted it as she put it back into the compartment to see if anything moved. Nothing did. Michele locked the door and took out the keys. "Your key, sir," she said. Eddie took his key.

"Thank you, sir, and have a nice afternoon," Michele said when Eddie reached the counter.

"Not possible," Eddie said without looking at her, his eyes on the door leading to the light.

Michele sat back at the desk and felt her hands trembling. She looked at the card, still on the desk, which had Eddie's signature on it and today's date and time. She slid it on the desk to look at it; if she picked it up, she probably wouldn't be able to read it, she was shaking so much. She could just stick it in her pocket or purse and take it out of here, erasing the only record of Eddie's visit today.

All except one, she thought; Eddie would remember, and if he investigated, he might wonder why it wasn't recorded. Which would lead him to her, and the nTropics connection, and the others. She opened the desk drawer and slipped the card into its box.

The digital clock said 9:39. Michele planned a long, meticulous day of polishing the wheels on her chair and a lunch with Jeff to kill an hour. The lunch proved surprisingly amusing, with Jeff's stories of his wild youth on a farm in a town called Murry, population about fifteen. The wheels proved particularly greasy, probably by design, so Michele left them alone.

The digital clock said 1:38 when Mr. Dennis told Michele that Jessica had been dismissed from service, and that Michele would not be needed tomorrow. He appreciated the extra effort that had been put in by Michele, and that the account representative would be told of her competence. Her own communications skills could be felt bleeding from her by Michele as the man was listened to by her, but he was freeing her, so she thanked him.

When the digital clock said 5:08, Michele made sure she hadn't left any personal effects on or nearby the desk. She felt her jacket pocket for Robert's key for the eighth time that afternoon, gathered her timesheet, and left the bank.

*　*　*　*

When Robert's doorbell sounded, he thought about what weapons he had at hand, which meant a screwdriver, or whether he should get his gun. If it was Eddie, he could call the police or shoot him, neither of which was good, really. If it was the police, he had no dilemma, because that would be all bad. He turned on his television, and it was just Michele, so he felt somewhat foolish for thinking the worst, and then felt somewhat anxious when he started thinking the best, which probably didn't draw Michele to his house on a Wednesday night.

"Hello," he said when he opened the door.

"I've got it," Michele said.

"Got what?" Robert said. Then he knew she meant she had *it*. "Come in," he said, pulling her as much as he could with his manner and body language. She crossed the threshold and Robert closed the door quickly.

"John Donnelly's gold," she said.

Michele had the gold bar after all. Now she was in Robert's living room. Maybe she wanted to cut Kevin and Daryl out of the proceeds and wanted to run off with Robert. Slightly more likely, she was going to kill Robert and Daryl and Kevin and keep it for herself. Robert looked at her purse. Zipped. He'd keep an eye on that.

"Eddie came back to the bank today with a backpack to empty his safe deposit box. When he came in, I managed to jiggle the keys in the locks this time. I had your key because I was going to bring it by after work." She reached into her jacket pocket. She took out his key; Robert tensed visibly when she did, and she didn't know if it was fright or flight. "What?" she said.

"Nothing," Robert said. Of course, the jacket was too even on her shoulders for her to have a gun in only one pocket, unless she were to balance it with something equally heavy, but that would pull the jacket on her shoulders. He took the proffered key.

"So now you've just got to go get it," Michele said. "I've finished my assignment. The regular temp comes back tomorrow. So you can go get it tomorrow."

"All right," Robert said. A week should prove enough of a cooling period.

Michele shifted her weight and saw Robert did the same. "So now we're going to cast it into a bunch of jewelry to sell at pawn shops?" she said.

"That is the plan," Robert said.

"I have a different idea," Michele said.

"What?" Robert said. She hadn't unzipped her purse. Maybe she really did want to run away with him and the loot. He couldn't cut the others out of the deal, but he appreciated the thought.

"You think Daryl's home?" Michele said. "I want to see what he thinks."

Well, Robert appreciated the thought even if Michele didn't have it. "We can call," he said. They did. Daryl was.

* * * *

"Okay, here's my idea," Michele said. Daryl sat in his office chair, leaning back against his computer desk with its pair of monitors. Michele took a deep breath, quietly to avoid being melodramatic. "Let's put it back."

"What?" Robert said.

Daryl emitted his favorite chuckle/guffaw hybrid.

"I'm serious," Michele said. "Listen, there's lots of reasons why we should." Michele had run through the list this afternoon, in great detail, between liquid crystal ticks of the digital clock. "I mean, wouldn't you guys rather be heroes than villains?"

"Heroes?" Daryl said.

"Not quite Robin Hood," Michele said, "But we'd be setting right a wrong done to John Donnelly. Like avengers of a hidden wrong."

"White hat," Daryl said.

"Okay," Robert said.

Michele couldn't believe it. "So you guys agree?" She didn't even have to explain about the historical value of the gold bar or the greater risk with accounting for their ill-gotten gains on their tax records.

"Sure, why not?" Daryl said.

"We have to leave Kevin out," Robert said. "He was in it for the money."

"Yep," Daryl said.

"Okay," Michele said. She'd thought pretty much the same.

"We need to get this done quickly," Robert said. "The evidence is in my possession. I don't want it."

"All right. So we put it back, same as we did when we took the bar the first time," Daryl said. "Let's see when he's going out of town." He spun and tapped his keyboard. His Linux box shrieked to life, its hard drive spinning up to compensate for the slight RAM. He connected to nTropics' Web mail interface. "Bet he hasn't changed his password," he said.

Daryl logged in, and he got to look at John Donnelly's mail. He clicked the calendar icon and looked over it. The rudimentary display of the remainder of the month displayed numerous meetings, but none of the grey dates that indicated he was out of the office. "Uh oh," Daryl said. "Looks like he's staying in house to begin the holiday booking season."

Robert looked at the screen. Donnelly wasn't off until Thanksgiving. "I am not holding onto that bar that long."

"Why not?" Michele said.

"It's a lot of exposure," Robert said. If Eddie did complain to the bank, or dropped a dime, or someone accidentally opened the box, if John Donnelly discovered the bar in his house was a fake.... A series of contingencies, to be sure, Robert thought, but if you were given the choice between ten thousand to one odds of death and no chance at all, which one would you choose?

"All right," Daryl said. "How about here?" He tapped next Tuesday, a luncheon at Agostino's with someone named Hugh Jackson.

"How about tomorrow," Robert said. Thursday, John Donnelly had a lunch meeting that stretched from 11:00 to 1:30 at nTropics.

"Tomorrow? You can't be serious," Daryl said.

"I want to be done with it all, now," Robert said.

"All right then," Daryl said. "Tomorrow it is." He tapped some on his computer. "Can I come in?"

"You'll need to bring down the Web camera," Robert said.

"I can script that," Daryl said, "and set it running on a library PC as a service." He thought about it. It depended upon whether the administrators at the ISP had patched the software. "Or I could bring it down from inside the house."

"You can do that?" Michele said.

"More reliably than I can from outside the house." Daryl said.

"Do you want me to drive again?" Michele said.

"Sure," Robert said. "Assuming we can check the cam from the house?"

"You bet."

"All right, then. We will meet at my house at 11:30," Robert said.

"Will that be long enough?" Michele said.

"We only have to calculate drive time to John Donnelly's house and swap time," Robert said. "It should not take two hours. Besides, it will take me until 11:30 to get the bar and return."

Daryl chuckled again. "It's a lot of trouble for the guy who doesn't even know he laid us off."

"We're not doing this for John Donnelly," Robert said.

* * * *

Robert parked in the grocery store parking lot and walked to the bank again. He carried the attaché case with its plywood bottom again, walked to the bank again—*his* bank, he tried to think himself into character. He went through the doors, nodded to a fellow bank customer, saw his personal banker Jeff standing by one of the tellers behind their counter. Sitting behind the L shaped counter by the safe deposit box room, Robert found the pretty woman who'd been his mark. Well, *their* mark. She looked up, and Robert gripped the moist handle to his attaché. Her name was Jessica, he remembered.

"Good morning," Jessica said.

"Good morning," Robert said. He didn't think she'd recognized him, but she didn't have to; he'd sign a card for her. "May I have a sign-in card and a pen?"

"Sure," she said. She took a card and a pen from the desk behind the counter and gave them to Robert.

Robert took them from her, careful to not come into contact with her hand when he took them, and signed his name illegibly. He handed them back to her and licked his lips. Stop that, he thought, nervous tics in a bank when you're planning to walk out with several million dollars' worth of gold is not the right plan. He felt the tingling of sweat beginning at the edges of his hairline, and that didn't help, either.

Jessica performed the signature comparison and the Robert-to-his-written-description comparison, and she punched his sign-in card. "This way, sir," Jessica said. She stood up from her desk and led him into the safe deposit room. "Your key?" she said when they reached his box.

Robert took the key from his pocket and promptly dropped it on the floor. "Sorry," he said. He crouched to pick it up.

She crouched with him. "No problem," she said. "I'm a bit clumsy too sometimes." She accepted the key from him and put it in the door beside her bank key. She turned them both, opening the door smoothly. She took his box and slid it out slowly, pulling it side to side to get it out. "You must be our best customer," she said.

"I just feel everything's safe with you," Robert said. He realized how that sounded and felt himself blush. "Here, let me get it," he said, picking up the box and lifting with his legs, not his back.

"Thank you." Jessica smiled with what Robert guessed was a professional smile.

"Thank you," Robert said. He blushed harder. "Can I just take any room?"

"Sure," Jessica said. She put Robert's key atop the box and followed him to the safe deposit room door. "Let me know when you're ready."

"Okay," Robert said. He put the box and his case on the table and closed the door softly, waiting for the click and locking it.

He took the gloves out of his case and opened the safe deposit box slowly, almost afraid of what might or might not be in it. He opened the box, and there Robert saw John Donnelly's gold. For real this time, he assumed.

He lifted the bar from the box, carefully not brushing it against the side or making any noise whatsoever with it. He turned it over. The bottom was smooth and unbroken. The real thing. Robert was glad for the gloves; he wouldn't have been able to hold the bar without them.

Robert set the bar on the table slowly. He opened his attaché case and took his own documents out, the United States Savings Bonds and the stock annual reports. He set them to the side, carefully. He felt some sweat prickling his brow, but he didn't touch the gloves to his hairline in case it might leave forensic evidence. He picked up the gold bar and put it into the case. He took the gloves off and put them in the case. He put his documents in his safe deposit box. He closed the box and closed the case. He looked around to make sure he hadn't left anything and opened the door. In the final, winning move, he stacked the key atop the box, picked up the case, and picked up the box.

"Ready?" Jessica said. She appeared at the door the moment Robert stepped out; he wondered if she'd been waiting.

"Yes," Robert said. He followed her into the safe deposit box room.

She led him to the open box. "Your key?" she said, but she took it from the top of his box. She knelt down and put the keys into the door.

"Would you like me to slide the box in?" Robert said.

"If you would like," Jessica responded.

"I would," Robert said. He crouched until the case touched the floor and gladly let go of it. He knelt and slid the box in, wiggling it a bit as though it still weighed a lot. "Thanks," he said.

"Thank you," Jessica said. She closed the door and locked it. She stood up, brushing her skirt smooth, and offered him his key.

Robert picked up the case with his right hand, a tight grip low on the fingers. He took his key with his off hand and put it in his pocket.

"Have a nice day," Jessica said.

"You've already made it nicer," Robert said. He felt the blush again. Good, he thought.

"Bye-bye," Jessica said, dismissing him.

Robert smiled crookedly, the smile that launched a thousand rejections, and walked out of the bank. He'd like to think he'd covered his nervousness with uncomfortable flirtation; he certainly had been uncomfortable, and he'd like to think he'd flirted. By keeping his mind on that, he'd kept it clear of the ramifications of several million dollars in his grip.

On the street, he appraised a pair of young men walking as they approached, met their pleasant eyes as they passed, and glanced obliquely three times to ensure the blue denim-clad shapes continued moving away. He envisioned someone trying to grab the case from him, so he walked on the north side of Manchester, keeping his body between the street and the gold. He pictured someone trying, only to receive the strongest blow Robert could muster with the heavy case. The thought cheered him.

When he got to his car, he skipped the pretense of buying something in the grocery store; he didn't want to leave the bag unattended for a moment. It was 10:49. He started the car and drove very deliberately three miles an hour above the speed limit to his house, completing full stops with looks in all directions as required.

Once More unto the Breach

Robert reached home before Daryl or Michele arrived. He carried the case into the kitchen while he rooted around his junk drawer for John Donnelly's keys. He'd marked each with a drop of clear nail polish, so when he held them up and twisted them, a dot glistened.

He carried the case downstairs while he looked for the scrip of paper with Erika's phone number on it. He'd thrown it out long ago, shredding the paper pretty soon after the first trip into the house. 7426, he thought, but he'd have to ask Michele to make sure. She'd remembered it was John Donnelly's extension. He added a handful of wet napkins, a pen, a pad of Post-It notes, a pair of rulers, and a small tool kit to the case, just in case.

Michele and Daryl arrived at 11:27. When Robert opened the door, he noticed that Daryl's bike wasn't on the porch. Michele must have picked him up. Or, Robert thought, maybe they'd stayed together overnight. The thought daunted him. Both of them were dressed for the chilly downturn in the weather. Daryl actually wore a winter coat, its pockets bulging like a squirrel about to make a deposit in its food bank.

"Hiya," Daryl said. "Is it in the bag?" He gestured to the bag Robert was holding in his right hand while he held the doorknob with his left hand.

"Yes," Robert said.

"Can we see it?" Daryl said.

Robert looked at his watch. "All right," he said. Better here than in the car. He set the attaché on the floor and opened the top. "Quickly."

Daryl looked into the case. Yet another golden brick. "They're all starting to look the same to me," Daryl said. "I guess that's the idea."

"All right," Robert said. "Daryl and I will drop the bar off; Michele, you go to nTropics and make sure Donnelly's there. When

261

you get there, call Daryl on his cell phone. We'll take the computer down and switch the bars. If John Donnelly leaves, or anything else suspicious happens, you call Daryl, all right?"

"New plan?" Daryl said.

"I thought I was driving you guys there," Michele said.

"You remember what kind of car he drives?" Robert said.

"Sure, a green BMW."

"You remember his extension?"

"Why? You're not calling him now, are you?" Michele said.

"It's the code for his alarm system," Daryl said.

"7426," Michele said. "I would have thought you remembered."

"He did," Daryl said. "He just wanted independent confirmation and he's already destroyed the paper where he wrote it down. Right?"

Robert wrote the number on the pad of paper and tore the sheet off and put it into his pocket. He put the pen and paper on his entertainment center. He closed the case and carried it with him when he went to the couch to put on his jacket.

"You could probably trust us with that," Daryl said. He put the pad of Post-It notes into his pocket.

"Habit," Robert said. He patted the pockets to make sure he had the work gloves in them. "Let's go."

* * * *

Michele had kind of wanted to see what the inside of John Donnelly's house was like and to experience the sensual impressions of breaking and entering, but she was also kind of glad she was off the felony hook. She would have to imagine what the inside of a former Nazi's house looked like. Actually, the man who owned the tiara couldn't be a former Nazi; doddering old men don't make very good antagonists. Michele was thinking too hard, too distractedly for her primary mission; she had to brake hard, but not squealingly, to make the turn into nTropics' cul-de-sac.

She didn't need to go far up the drive to see the green Beemer among the crestfallen autumn shrubbery. She checked her mirrors and then executed a Y turn before getting too close to the building. She took the phone from the dashboard and dialed Daryl's cell phone.

"Yes," he answered.

"This is Michele. He's there." Actually, she thought, his car's there, and Robert might not like the assumption. Or maybe she was putting thoughts into Robert's head.

"All right," Daryl said. Michele listened to the softened voice of

Daryl telling Robert and Robert talking back. She couldn't make out Robert's direct words, but Daryl summarized for her. "Park nearby, so you can see if he leaves," Daryl said.

"You guys will call me when you're done," she said.

"You got it."

*   *   *   *

Robert parked his Toyota at the top of the circle. He took the attaché case from the trunk and handed it to Daryl. He put on his gloves and took out John Donnelly's keys and the key code, disguised this time as Missy's phone number. "You did bring gloves, right?"

"Sure," Daryl said. He leaned the case against his leg and took a pair of oversized ski gloves from his coat pockets, deflating the pockets. He put the gloves on and picked up the case.

"You're going to type in those?" Robert said.

"Just you watch."

Robert glanced across the lawn to the street, looking for the bouncy motion of walkers or any other humanity and saw none. He led Daryl up the steps and to the front door. This time, he knew which key to use and where the alarm was. It beeped until he shut it off. Daryl closed the door behind them.

"Hal?" Robert said. He waited for the ticking of approaching toenails on hardwood; instead, he heard frustrated scratching in the kitchen. "The dog's in the basement."

"Good," Daryl said. "We don't have to kill it."

"There's a door in the kitchen," Robert said. He started down the corridor.

"What about this one?" Daryl gestured at the door on the east side of the corridor.

"I've got the key to the other one," Robert said. As long as he followed the same pattern he'd used the first time, he'd feel a lot less nervous. As though he did this every day. Or once a month.

Daryl shrugged and followed him.

Hal scrabbled on the basement door when he heard the intruders. The intruders ignored him this time. Robert used the second key on the door to the computer room, and they went in.

Nothing had changed; nothing had moved. Robert thought it possible that no one else had been in there since he and Kevin had come in, but that was unlikely. He stayed clear of the camera's angle on the fake gold bar they'd left behind. "Put the case on the desk, behind the camera," Robert said. "There's the computer." He felt

263

stupid for stating the obvious.

Daryl sat at the keyboard and tapped the mouse to exit the screensaver. The desktop had the original Windows logo wallpaper and almost no icons. A single terminal window scrolled infrequent messages of network latency status. He looked over the computer setup, the common components, the high quality video camera, the router feeding information to the T1, and the uninterruptible power supply that the computer, monitor, and router's cords all used.

Robert opened the case and laid its contents on the desktop. The bar, the tool kit, the rulers, and the wet napkins. He opened the foil package of a wet napkin and swabbed the real gold bar. He put the foil packet and the used wet napkin into the attaché case and looked at Daryl. Daryl was watching him. He wasn't typing, he wasn't probing, he wasn't hacking. He was just watching. "Are you ready?" Robert said.

"I can give you a minute or two to make the switch. Is that enough?" Daryl said.

Robert bit his lip. He hadn't clocked it, and he hadn't practiced it, but he ought to be able to do it in a minute unless he felt pressured and started dropping things. Thinking he was under pressure didn't help. "I'll have to," he said.

"All right," Daryl said. "Are you ready?"

"Yeah."

"Three," Daryl said. He didn't move, didn't turn to type or click. "Two, one," he counted. At one, he reached behind the computer and unplugged the power cable from the case. The lights on the computer equipment went dark. He plugged it back in and pushed the power button on the front of the box, finding the dimpled button through heavy gloves.

Robert would have gaped, but Robert certainly didn't want to waste time. The minute the monitor went dark and the power fan on the computer began whining down, he clapped the rulers around the fake bar where it lay, lifted the fake bar and put it on the desk, lifted the real bar and nestled it among the rulers, and picked the rulers up. He looked over at the monitor and saw a glimpse of the machine's DMA and IRQ information before the Windows 2000 logo flashed onto the screen. He'd certainly shaved some time off his last swap. If he'd get a couple more practice runs, he'd be an Olympian felon. "Whew," he said.

Daryl applauded lightly. "Now, let's get out of here." He helped Robert put the tools and paraphernalia into the case.

"I can't believe you just unplugged it." Robert said. He looked over the desktop and floor nearby for any signs of their presence. Perhaps they should have worn hair nets or hats to prevent leaving behind hair. Too late to think of that now, but he did look a little more closely. He found nothing, so he closed the case and picked it up.

"The simplest solution is always the most direct," Daryl said. He reached into his pocket, fumbling slightly through the ski gloves. "Shall we?"

"Yes," Robert said.

Daryl glanced at the screen, saw Windows' startup progress bar snailing its way to completion, and patted the gold bar. "Buh bye, sunshine," he said.

Robert locked the door, securing John Donnelly's gold as securely as it was, which was to say, not much.

"Bye, Hal, you attack dog," Daryl said to the basement door.

Robert armed the alarm and locked the door and they were at his car. He put the case and his gloves in the trunk and started the engine. Only when he started to drive toward the street did he feel his body want to quiver. Perhaps it did; perhaps he was shaking madly, and Daryl was too polite to say. He kept his eyes on the driveway, and then on both directions of Litzsinger until they were driving east and away, hopefully for the last time. "Call Michele," Robert said.

Daryl fumbled his gloves from his sweaty hands and snapped open his cell phone and hit the key to return Michele's last call.

* * * *

Michele got to Robert's house ten minutes after Robert and Daryl. Both of them had beers open on the kitchen table. The fake gold bar sat on the table between them like a centerpiece. Well, if they were, she was, so when Robert offered her something to drink, she took a bottle of Fat Tire. "Drinking our lunch?" she said.

"Using the depressant properties of alcohol to regulate our nervous energy," Robert said.

"Spoken like a true alcoholic," Daryl said.

"True," Robert said. He hadn't moved to put away the case or organize its contents. He had all day, really, since he didn't work until tomorrow night. It was a sign of depression, not wanting to do things; he'd have to keep an eye on that. He might begin spiraling downward into listlessness and despair.

"So what's next?" Michele said. "Since we're not going to be rich, what are you guys going to do?"

"We're not going to be rich next week," Daryl said. "But don't

265

rule it out for me."

"I guess I will look for another development job," Robert said. He thought about sitting in a cubicle or office again. He hadn't done much of that these last few weeks and didn't look forward to doing it again. Depression could do that to a man, he thought. Maybe he was manic/depressive, except he wasn't manic.

"I think I might stay with Integral for a while," Michele said, "if they can find a couple more positions for me. I'll focus on my writing a bit; I never really gave that a shot. I don't have any student loans anymore, so I just need enough for the apartment and food." She wouldn't even have to eat Frodo.

"Maybe I will go out to Colorado for a while," Daryl said. "Who knows. Hey, can I keep this?" He tapped the bar.

"Okay," Michele said.

"I was going to destroy it," Robert said. "It's evidence."

"Bah, it's a paperweight," Daryl said. "Or maybe we could sell it on eBay and split the profits."

"The profits," Robert said.

"I'm sure there are lots of people out there who would like to own a piece of history but cannot afford several million dollars. So we sell it as a replica," Daryl said. "Who knows how much we could get."

"I like your paperweight idea better," Robert said.

"Hey, that reminds me, can I borrow your computer?"

"For what?" Robert said.

"I just wanted to make sure that the gold bar Web site came back up. I imagine they have the video feed set up as a service so no one has to log in and run it. But who knows?"

"All right," Robert said. He picked up his bottle and laid the attaché case over the gold bar. Although he didn't think his neighbors could see into his kitchen from theirs, he hadn't been in theirs to check the sight lines and reflections.

Daryl sat at the computer and logged in.

Robert watched Daryl type in the IP address of a proxy server again and felt his stomach drop. Daryl was up to something.

The nTropics Web site loaded, and Daryl clicked the ABOUT US link and navigated to the gold bar's page. Daryl crossed his arms and smirked.

It took a couple of seconds to load, but when it did, Robert could see the difference right away.

Upon the gold bar, a Post-It note, with its glue strip down so that it waved over the top of the gold bar. Positioned so the viewers at home could read its message. "0wn3d by 50uL W33v1Lz." Daryl had even drawn the line through the zero to make it into a mathematical empty set sign, just like the old computers used.

"Oh, my God," Michele said.

"That's not your real hacker name, is it?" Robert said. He felt his face flush and debated the wisdom of a third trip into the house to get that paper before anyone else saw it, but knew it was too late.

"I didn't think you'd let me," Daryl said. He looked at the screen proudly, knowing that maybe now John Donnelly would secure his bar more effectively. They were white hat.